Ruby Slipperjack is an Ojibwa from the Fort Hope Indian Band in Ontario. She has retained much of the traditional religion and heritage of her people, all of which inform her writing. Her first novel, *Honour the Sun,* about a young girl growing up in a tiny Ojibwa community in northern Ontario, earned rave reviews and is widely used in schools.

Ruby spent her formative years on her father's trap-line on Whitewater Lake. Her family later moved to a community along the railway mainline. Ruby went to a residential school for several years and finished high school in Thunder Bay. She earned a B.A. (History) in 1988 and a B.Ed. the following year. She is currently working towards a Master's degree in Education at Lakehead University. She lives in Thunder Bay with her husband and three children.

Silent Words

Ruby Slipperjack

FIFTH
HOUSE
PUBLISHERS

Cover art by Ruby Slipperjack
Cover design by Robert Grey

The publisher gratefully acknowledges the support received from The Canada Council and Heritage Canada.

All characters and events in *Silent Words* are fictional.

Printed and bound in Canada

6 5 4 3

Canadian Cataloguing in Publication Data
Slipperjack, Ruby, 1952–
Silent Words
ISBN 0–920079–93–8
I. Title.

PS8587.L53S54 1992 C813'.54 C92–098064–3
PR9199.3.S55S54 1992

FIFTH HOUSE LTD.

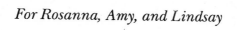

For Rosanna, Amy, and Lindsay

Chapter One

I WIPED THE SWEAT FROM MY FACE AS I walked along the bush path to the corner store and emerged beside the parking lot. There was no one around at all. The street stretched empty in the shimmering heat. I kicked an empty can away from the sidewalk as I approached a stop sign. The store was at the end of the block, and I had a quarter in my pocket. I like bubble gum and that's what I usually buy. I hurried a bit and looked around once more. A group of teenaged boys always beats me up, but I have a pretty good chance if I see them first. They can't catch me if I get a good start.

An old man sat leaning against the wall in the shade between the buildings. A dog lay curled at his feet. It looked like a scene from a scary movie where a huge monster from the swamp ate up all the townspeople. I was halfway to the store already. I hurried a bit more. It was so dry, there were puffs of dust each time I put my foot down. I lifted my head in time to see the boys coming around the corner of the store. Oh, oh, I'm in trouble! They spotted me at the same time. I whirled around and ran back up the street as fast as I could. I heard footsteps fast approaching from behind. I pushed my legs harder, but I knew I would not make it. I was running past the parking lot and onto the sand when I felt a hand grab my hair at the back of my head. The next minute, I was flat on my back on the ground, and one of the boys held my head down as another one spat on my face. I felt a stab of pain in my back as a runningshoe hit me. Then they backed away, jeering and making fun of me lying there. I wish I was huge! I wish I was very big and strong! I would squash their jeering faces! I was just about to sit up when the blond one came running back and showered my face with flying sand as I tried to shield my head with my arms. Then he bent down and I felt the spit land below my right eye. He ran back down the street again, laughing with his buddies.

I sat up and ran my sleeve over my face, trying to wipe the spit and the shame off. I hated the tears that threatened to overflow my eyes! I got up and ran as fast as I could down the road and made a detour through the bushes to the house where we lived. I could never tell Dad about them. Never!

I slowed down as I entered the bush beside the creek. I took a big breath of the damp earth smell as the steam rose off the ground. It was getting hotter by the hour as the sun climbed higher in the sky. I flopped down and leaned back against a small poplar tree and closed my eyes. There was a flutter of wings and the rustle of leaves above my head. I opened my eyes. A little brown bird was there on a branch, twitching to the left and to the right. It had thin yellow rings around its dark beady eyes. Birds move in such jerky movements, like there's no middle speed. They either sit perfectly still or they move very fast. I knew an old lady once who was just like that. In fact, she looked exactly like this little brown bird. She could talk a mile a minute and she ran all the time. I don't remember ever seeing her walk. She did things real fast too, even when she was serving tea. Half the tea would fly out of the cup before it came to a stop in front of Mama, and she had to grab it quick before the cup took off again.

That was last summer. I was happy then. Mama used to wear stretchy slacks all the time with a loose blouse hanging over the waist. Her short, curly black hair was always neatly combed . . . I can't remember what her face looks like! A feeling of panic began to build in my tummy. Why can't I remember her face? I remember now—how her face stretched when she laughed. I felt myself relax again. I closed my eyes. Why do we still see red when we close our eyes in the daytime?

Suddenly the silence was broken by a loud low-pitched

2

rumble that spiralled up into a gurgle and ended in a high-pitched note. I didn't know what on earth the sound was until I felt the echo inside my stomach. I'm very hungry.

I slowly got to my feet and quietly picked my way through the bush until I came to the tall pine trees on the hill. I'll go home and grab something to eat. My friend Tom must have found some rope by now. I don't have any string left of any kind.

I came into the clearing at the back of the house. It was much hotter out here in the open. The air hung dry and dusty in the morning sun. The grass and weeds stood about a foot high in the clearing around the house. The garbage dump was on the left side of the path and the storage shed was on the right. There wasn't a path when we moved here in the spring; I made it myself. It stops when it enters the woods. That way, nobody can follow me.

The old light blue house sat on a hill surrounded by tall pine trees. I stopped at the edge of the clearing and watched the shimmering haze over the dark roof. There was junk everywhere around the house and old boards were sticking out of the tall grass here and there. Small busy flies were dancing above the weeds by the garbage pile. The place was in worse shape when we moved in. Dad and I had tried to pile some things but soon gave up. What's the use when more just came up out of the ground? I moved forward again. The hot July sun beat down on my head as I came around the storage shed.

Dad went to work at the sawmill early this morning, and I don't hang around when he's not home. I have good reason not to, but I am very hungry. Maybe I can just grab something to eat and take off again. I went up the four steps to the kitchen door. The screen on the window is ripped at the corner and the door latch doesn't work. It was quiet inside as I pulled the door open. An awful smell hit me as I slowly walked into the kitchen. There were dirty dishes everywhere and some clothes lay scattered on the floor under the table.

I grabbed a piece of toast off the counter and took a huge bite as I tiptoed into the living room. I heard noises coming from the bedroom. I wonder what Sarah's doing. Slowly I walked down the dark, stained tile floor in the hallway. I

3

glanced into the bedroom that I shared with Sarah's baby. She was asleep in the crib.

There was no door to Sarah and Dad's bedroom, and I came around the corner rather quickly. My mouthful of toast stuck in my throat as my gaze fell upon the dark head and bare back of a man on the bed. Suddenly I burst into a rasping cough as I choked on the lump of bread. Then all heck broke loose! The man whirled around and I saw that he was one of Father's friends. I turned around and ran down the hallway as fast as I could. My throat was aching badly as I burst into another coughing fit. I grabbed a cup of coffee off the table and downed it in one gulp.

I heard footsteps behind me. The cup went flying and my neck jerked back hard as her hand clamped down on the top of my head. Screeching at me, she pulled me around and I went flying into the living room. I hit the floor face down and it knocked the breath out of me. In an instant, I felt her full weight land on top of me. Sharp pain shot through my body as fists landed hard on my back, one after another. Her other hand clamped down on my hair, holding my face against the floor.

I struggled as pain shot down the length of my body and she continued to pound me with her fists. Suddenly she was lifted off me, but she wouldn't let go of my hair. She dragged me up as the man yelled, "Sarah, let go! He's just a little kid!"

I scrambled away to the corner of the living room and jumped to my feet. I heard the kitchen door slam. The man was gone. Then she came around the corner from the kitchen and stood by the door, glaring at me with hatred. I could feel my heart pounding against my ribs and into my head. Her hair was sticking out in all directions; she looked crazy. The baby started screaming and I glanced toward the room when, suddenly, Sarah grabbed me once more by the hair and dragged me down the hallway toward the bedroom.

"Stay in there and shut that baby up!" she yelled, breathing heavily. She pushed hard, and I crashed against the edge of the little cot and rolled to the floor as the door slammed shut. I lay there for a moment as the baby continued to cry. I hurt everywhere as I pushed myself up and gave the crib a kick.

4

"Shut up!" I hissed. The baby, becoming aware that I was in the room, suddenly quieted and lay waiting.

I pulled myself up beside the crib and stood looking down at the baby. She has the same red-coloured hair as her mother. She will probably look like her too. Brown eyes blinked back at me as she lay there waiting to be picked up but oh, she stinks! It's her baby, why should I change the stinky diaper?

I could hear her banging pots around in the kitchen. I'm very afraid of her. Sarah moved in with her baby the same day Dad and I got here. She hits me every chance she gets. But never when Dad is around. She always pretends to be so nice! I told Dad once when she hit me and broke the broomstick over my head. Then she cut my lip when she threw a pot at me, and claimed it was an accident. She told him I was lying when I said she threw it at me, because I was jealous having to share Father with her. She said I tripped off the steps. Dad believed her and yelled at me never to tell stories about her again. That really hurt. Dad picked her side. I hate her! I wish I was with Mama, but I don't know where she is. Dad won't even let me talk about her.

Suddenly it was very quiet, so I carefully opened the door and peered out. I could see her reflection in the mirror that stands in the corner of their bedroom. What is she doing? That's Dad's wallet. She's taking money out! The baby's diaper bag hung over her arm. I got blamed the last time Father lost some money!

Then her eyes were looking into mine in the mirror. I made a dash down the hallway, but I couldn't run, my back hurt so bad. I scrambled into the kitchen and to the door, then I felt her grab my shirt at the back. I was jerked back fast. I crashed against the table, knocking a chair over, then fell to the floor. I felt a sting of pain at the back of my head. I scrambled to get out of the way and curled my body, shrinking, trying to shield my head, expecting something to come down on me. I struggled to shut off the whimper and tears that threatened to escape. I could hear her breathing heavily and giggling softly.

She loves it and just laughs when I cry. She will not make me cry any more! Slowly I pushed myself to my feet and backed up behind the table as she stood there panting with her hands on her hips. I felt something warm and sticky running down my back. I glared at her and her smile faded as she continued to stare at me.

"You'll not tell your father about this morning. If you do, I will tell him you were peeking at me when I was changing. He'll beat you good for that, won't he?" She smiled again. Her face was becoming a blur. My head hurt bad. Her voice brought me back to focus on her. "I found out where your mother is. She's at Colby's Landing. It's on the CN line, just on the other side of Allan Water Bridge. Now, wouldn't it be nice if you went to live with your mama? Your nice, beautiful mama?" Her laughter filled the kitchen as she moved away from the door. The baby was crying again.

I dashed for the door and jumped to the ground. Ouch! My head! I ran as fast as I could, limping along the driveway and onto the road. Mama! Please come and get me! Come and get me! I love you, Mama, come and get me! Around the turn of the road farther down, I finally reached the culvert and scrambled down to the creek. I pulled my shirt off and dunked the whole thing into the flowing water. I bent over the creek and threw the dripping shirt on my head several times. The water ran red off my chin. I felt the sting on the cut each time the cold water hit the mark. When the water ran pink, I wrung out my shirt and draped it over my head and sat there as the cool water dripped down my back.

I heard footsteps coming from the other direction. Short, light steps . . . it was Tom. I wiped the tears off my face. My head still hurt real bad. I heard the steps pause, then showers of sand cascaded down the hill, and the feet landed with a thump across the creek a couple of yards away. I heard his in-drawn breath and still I sat there with the shirt over my head.

Finally he burst out, "Holy smokes! What the heck did she do to you now? Why don't you tell the police or something? There's blood coming through your shirt on the back of your head. It must've poured down your back. There's some on the waist of your pants too! Holy smokes, Danny! Come home with me and my ma will fix you up, okay?"

With a sigh, I yanked the shirt off my head and looked at

the round freckled face across from me. "What the heck do you suppose would happen to me if word got out? They wouldn't punish her, it's me that would get punished. They'd take me away and put me in a home somewhere, and that would be like locking me up! Dad is all I have left! I don't want to go anywhere with a bunch of strangers!"

The next minute, I heard water pouring into the creek. I lifted my head and tried to see through the cotton haze of my shirt.

"What the heck you doing? Are you peeing in the water?" I asked.

I heard him giggle and I smiled as I lifted the shirt off my head. There he was wringing out a handkerchief in the creek.

He jumped across and said, "Let me see that cut." I could feel the numb ache as he mopped up the back of my head. "Not bad, the cut's only about half an inch, at least it stopped bleeding," he said as he turned and rinsed the cloth in the creek again. I watched a brown leaf swirling along the pebbles at the bottom of the creek. It paused a moment, flipped over, and continued past the cloth and disappeared into the dark shadow of the culvert.

"I said I found a string. It's a bit short but I found some other short ones we can tie together," Tom said.

Tom is about eleven years old, same age as me, but bigger. I watched his short stubby fingers wring out the cloth like it was a mop, then he scrubbed his face from side to side.

I smiled and said, "You could get a job at the restaurant, Tom, no problem!"

He looked at me a moment while he tied the blue handkerchief around his neck. "Are you kidding? I've been doing all the cleaning and scrubbing since I was a kid. Ain't going to do that as soon as I'm gone! Dad says I can get a job with him on the CN as soon as I'm old enough." He grinned. I sat there looking at him. I never thought about anything except getting away from here. Far, far away.

Tom's voice came again, "I'll get the string. I dropped it on the road when I saw you sitting there like a stump with a pile of brown squirrel crap on top of it!" I watched him run up the gravel to the road. I smiled, seeing the picture of me with my

7

brown shirt piled on top of my head. I felt a little better now, but I still didn't feel like moving.

"Come on up, we'll put the string across the road at the bend," Tom said as he walked along above me, tying the short pieces of string together.

Dusting off the seat of my jeans, I stretched my muscles to ease the ache in my back. It was still hotter on the road. I dunked my shirt into the water once more and pulled it on, dripping wet. That felt very good.

I walked through the bush parallel to the road until I saw Tom waiting by the curb. "Right here's good. Here, tie this end to that tree there," he said, throwing the string at me.

Pulling it tightly, I tied it good at the base of a pine tree. It was swampy, and the bush was denser on the other side. It might be a better place to wait. I slowly climbed the shoulder to the road. Tom was already on the other side tying the string.

"Lift it up a little higher!" I yelled as I slid down the other side.

The white string came up about two feet high, strung across the hot dusty gravel road. I could see the bushes rustling ahead of me as he tied the other end of the rope. Ducking under the bush, I found him sitting there in the shade. I sat down beside him.

After a moment, he said, "Grandma's coming to get me next week. Nothing ever happens in this town. It's boring. At least I'll have fun at the camp. They have a canoe there, a sand beach, and some kids to play with. Last summer Rob and I paddled to an island. There's a big crow's nest up in a tree—"

"Shut up!" I grumbled, and kicked at a stump.

Tom glanced at me and said, "Why don't you go see your uncle Fred at the reserve?"

I had visions of big fat uncle Fred, cutting off a huge piece of steak and chewing it very slowly while I watched, swallowing the saliva that kept flooding my mouth. I was so hungry all the time there. That was last fall when Dad left me there while he was here looking for a job. I made a face at Tom. Stupid suggestion.

"Don't you have any other relatives you could go to? What about your mother?" he asked.

Suddenly I snapped at him, "No. I don't have any other relatives and I said *shut up!*" I felt so much anger and hate I just wanted to thrash something, anything. I kicked an old branch right out of the ground at my feet.

Tom turned and looked at me. "Why should I shut up? I don't need a stupid Injun telling me to shut up!" he said.

Whirling around, I yelled, "Don't you call me a stupid Indian. Who do you think you are anyway?"

I jumped to my knees, ready to punch him out. We came face to face, glaring at each other for a moment, before I turned and leaned back against the brush again. My back hurt. My head hurt. He sat back down beside me. A deep heavy feeling settled over me as we sat in silence.

I glanced at him and said, "I didn't mean it. I'm just mad. I have nowhere to go . . . "

Tom sighed and laid his head back against a branch. "Sorry I called you a stupid Injun, but don't go picking on me just because you're mad at someone else!"

"I said I was sorry!" I answered, a little louder than I intended.

"You did not! You just said you didn't mean it. That's not saying you're sorry!" He turned to look at me again.

"Just shut your mouth!" I scrambled up again with both fists clenched, but a sharp pain suddenly hit me behind the ear. Tom was facing me with his skinned knuckles from our last scuffle. I started feeling like something was squeezing the lights out of my head. Tom kept staring at me, his fists still up and ready. I sat back down.

Finally he said, "Your head hurts? Maybe your brain got hurt inside your head."

"What the heck you mean by that?" I asked, rather weakly.

"Nothing! Maybe you should go see the doctor. That cut was deep, you know."

I sighed and let my whole body sag against the ground. He looked at me again, then turned away. We continued to sit in silence waiting for a car to come down the road.

Chapter Two

THE WHITE STRING SHIMMERED IN THE heat waves above the gravel road. The sweat ran down my face as we sat huddled beneath the bushes, still waiting. I glanced at Tom beside me. His jeans were very dirty and the knees were full of holes. His faded checkered shirt wasn't in better shape either. He was busy chewing his bottom lip and studying the leaves overhead.

My back was very stiff, as if I had slept in the same position all night in the middle of a rocky bed. Once in a while, the cut on my head felt like someone was poking sharp needles in, but otherwise only a dull ache remained. Darn it! One day when I am big and strong, I will choke her scrawny neck and when her tongue comes out purple, I will rip it out of her! Witch! And those boys, I will do the same to them too!

Tom shifted his weight to a more comfortable spot on the ground. "I'm hungry. I'm going to count to ten, then I'm going. What are you going to do?" he asked.

My eyes came to rest on his worn-out running shoes. I could see his bare toe sticking out. "I'm going to wait some more. Are you counting yet?" I asked.

His blue eyes peeked out from behind his long blond hair that was continually falling over his face. "I've counted up to five already. I figure I'll just add five more when I'm done talking to you." He shoved a stick deep into the ground and pushed his hair back once again.

"Why don't you just cut off that darned hair of yours?" I

asked. He didn't even glance at me. "I guess then you counted to ten already, eh?"

He looked at me and sighed, flinging his head back to look at the clear blue sky above us. Suddenly he jumped up. "It's so danged hot, no bloody fool is going to be driving around in this heat anyway!" I also heard the last part. " . . . and no bloody fool should be talking to you at all right now, either!" He took off at a run, crashing through the bush, and I heard his footsteps fade down the road.

I lowered myself down to a more comfortable position under the shade of the bushes. I couldn't think of a place that would be cooler than this. Besides, I was just too hot to move. My back was stiff, like someone pasted a piece of cardboard on it. I pushed my fingers into my hair to explore the area of the cut. I was careful not to touch the wound. My hair was drying out stiffly in some areas on the side of my head. Must be dried blood. I thought I had rinsed my hair out good. I laid down and closed my eyes.

The slam of a car door jolted me wide awake. I scrambled to my knees and carefully peered out from between the branches. A big man was stomping around the front of his car, pulling at the other end of the rope. "Gawd darn kids! Come out here you little sons of rats!"

Silence met his shouts. I held my breath and bunched up my muscles, ready to run in the opposite direction if he came to this side of the road. Suddenly he jumped into the car and backed up very fast around the bend, out of sight. I could hear the car stop and pull forward and I knew—it was going up our driveway.

Voices broke out and an argument ensued. I ran as fast as I could through the bushes and stopped opposite from the driveway and peered carefully over the branches.

Dad was pushing and swearing at the man, who backed up and quickly got into the car again. I heard another car coming down the road. My heart was beating faster, and I held my breath as the man started the car and immediately shot out of the driveway and onto the road. The other car came zipping around the corner in a swirl of dust, and I flinched at the bang

11

and crash of metal. Glass lay strewn across the road.

When the dust cleared, the angry man's car lay sideways across the road and the other car was in the ditch beside our driveway.

I knelt down for a better view and wondered what would happen next. Sarah came running out of the house, turned around, and ran back inside again. The big angry man came staggering out of the car, holding his neck, and Dad was beside the other car, trying to open the door. The whole back corner of the big man's car was shoved in as if a giant fist had punched it, and the front part of the other car was all wrinkled up, almost up to the front window.

The big man was still walking around in circles in the middle of the road when Sarah came running out again. Dad was helping the other man out of the car in the ditch. Oh oh. I heard another car coming! I held my breath again and got all set to see what was going to happen next. My eyes were riveted on the big man in the middle of the road. The car crept slowly around the curve and came to a stop well away from the accident scene. I let out a sigh of disappointment.

Then my ears perked up once more. I could hear a police car coming! Suddenly a thought occurred to me. What if they ask what the big man was doing there in the first place? The string! I whirled around and scrambled through the bushes until I came to the spot where the string was tied. I quickly pulled out my pocketknife and started cutting the string off the tree branch and rolling it around my hand as fast as I could.

The police car had already stopped by the road around the curve. I glanced around once and listened before I made the dash up the sandy shoulder of the road and scrambled down the other side. My back was aching and my runningshoes were full of hot sand as I ducked beneath the low-hanging branches. I sawed and sawed back and forth on the string about ten times before I noticed that I was holding the darned knife the wrong way. There! I quickly rolled up the string and ran through the bush.

I made a wide detour until I judged I was somewhere behind the house. Wiping the dust off my face and trying to calm my heavy breathing, I approached the clearing. I threw the string inside the junk barrel as I passed the shed. I shoved my hands in my pockets and tried whistling a tune as I came around the corner of the house.

The police car was just pulling out and all I saw was a cloud of dust. Another police car had just arrived and I slipped down the hill to get a better look. My father was standing beside the policeman now, and the two drivers were gone. Then Dad's stern face turned to me with deep dark angry eyes. I stopped. In Ojibwa, he said to me, "Get into the house right now. Stay there and don't you dare come outside until I've talked to you!"

Fear travelled up from my stomach to my throat as I became aware that I was in really big trouble. I turned and made my way back to the house. I remembered the last time I felt the back of his hand across my head. I had ducked a blow from a frying pan that Sarah had swung at me. Her backswing hit the cups hanging on the wall behind her and she dropped the pan and started screaming. Father ran in from the living room. I was by the pot shelf and she started yelling, "He threw the pot at me. He threw the pot and just missed me!" Pieces of the cups were scattered all over the counter behind her. I had nowhere to turn and Dad had descended on me, yelling in his loud booming voice. His huge muscular body blocked all view and his hand came up and sent me sprawling across the kitchen floor.

With slow steps, I approached the ugly, evil house. The boards were peeling and cracked, and the steps had rotted through where the nails once were. I jumped over the first step and landed on the porch with a thump. I pushed the door open. The smell of stale, musty air met my nose again. I kicked aside some junk by the door and entered the kitchen. Flies were buzzing around the piled-up dishes on the table.

Sarah was leaning over the kitchen sink, looking out the window at the men outside. I looked past her shoulder and saw that there were two other cars there now. She turned around with a smile on her bony face.

"What do you think your father will do to you now, dummy?" she asked.

13

I glanced at her. "My name is not dummy, it's Danny!"

She grabbed a wooden ladle off the counter, and I slipped past her into the living room and down the hallway. Her laughter echoed in the kitchen and I heard her yell after me, "I'll tell him I saw you with the rope again, and that you're the one who stole the money I took!" I shut out her voice by slamming the bedroom door.

I looked around the cluttered room that I shared with her baby. The baby was not in her crib right now. Dirty clothes were piled in the corner, and the room reeked of urine from the baby's filthy diapers in a pail beside the crib. I sat on my cot and sank down on the metal springs. The dirty quilt on top was full of holes and I ripped a larger one as I twisted it around my finger. I couldn't think of anything I could say that would make Dad believe me. The string was Tom's and it wasn't my idea in the first place! And the money, I saw Sarah stealing the money this morning . . . Why don't I just take it and get away from here? My heart started to pound as I glanced at the plastic-covered window. I could do it! But I have to go *now* before I chicken out.

I could hear the cars on the road driving away. My window was at the back of the house . . . Suddenly my body sprang into action. I carefully opened the door and made a dash to their bedroom. The house was quiet. I didn't know where Sarah was right now. I entered the room and went straight to her jacket hanging beside the bed. I searched the pockets, nothing! Where? Where could she have put it? Quick! I could hear their voices as Sarah and Dad came through the kitchen door. Then my eyes came to rest on the baby's diaper bag on the floor beside the bed. I grabbed it and, fumbling badly, I searched its many pockets, but nothing. Then my finger slipped beneath the reinforced bottom. I pulled out the money and shoved it into my shirt pocket.

I heard Dad's voice burst into the kitchen as he stomped into the house. "Where's that boy?"

Pressure in my throat threatened to choke me and I couldn't move! Then a honking car and voices yelling for Dad erupted in our driveway. It was his friends coming for their

14

usual party after work. The footsteps retreated and I heard the slamming of the front door. I dashed past the mirror and into my room as the many footsteps and voices spilled into the kitchen. I grabbed my jacket off the floor and pulled the crib close enough to reach the window. I poked and ripped a huge hole in the plastic on the window, stepped on the crib mattress, and threw my leg over the window sill. Pulling myself up, I threw my other leg over, ducked my head under, and jumped down. Boom! Right on top of the overturned washtub! The loud metal boom vibrated beneath me and nearly broke my eardrums as my feet scurried off, leaving a huge dent in the middle of the washtub.

I ran straight for the bushes. I tried to listen to any sound behind me as I ran. Dodging branches, trees, stumps, rocks, sticks, and garbage, I ran blindly until I saw a clearing up ahead. I slowed down. My chest was heaving so hard my side hurt. I veered to the left when I realized I had emerged above the sandpit behind the gas station. Ahead was a large boulder jutting out from the low shrubs. I threw myself down behind it and lay there catching my breath.

It was evening now. The sun had already gone over the treetops. I reached into my pocket and pulled out the money. I had a twenty, two tens, and two fives. This should get me out of here. Where am I going to go? There are too many people at the bus depot. That's the first place Dad will go when he comes looking for me. The train! I wonder what time it is. I have to buy a ticket. I'll get Tom to help me!

I jumped up and ran along the side of the road, ready to hide if I saw a car coming or those teenagers again. Jumping over fences and running across the back yards, I took a short cut to Tom's trailer. I ran around the back of the trailer where, above my head, the clothesline strained under the burden of sheets and towels. I picked up a handful of sand and threw it against Tom's window. Nothing. Darn you, Tom, where are you? I threw another handful of sand, showering the plastic pink flamingo beneath the window where it sat, its wire legs stuck into the ground beside the white plastic duck. Suddenly Tom's head popped up over the window sill, then disappeared.

I waited impatiently for a minute before he came running around the corner. "What happened?" he asked as his eyes grew round. "You look like a wild Injun!"

My jaw clamped shut and I whispered hurriedly, "Oh, shut up! I'm in big trouble. I need you to buy a train ticket for me."

His hands dropped to his sides and his hair fell over one eye. "When are you going? Tonight? Right now? The train's going to be here in no time!" he said.

I grabbed his elbow and pulled him with me as I broke into a run. "Come on, hurry up! I have to get out of here before Dad finds me. For sure he'll beat the heck out of me good this time! It's the witch's fault! She's a witch, you know that?"

"Yep," Tom answered.

Our feet pounded in unison, raising clouds of dust as we raced to the train station.

Chapter Three

Coming up to the station platform, I searched for a place to hide. I spotted a sand bin by the parking lot.

"Go in quick, I'll hide behind the sand bin," I whispered as I shoved the wad of bills into Tom's hand.

"Ticket to where?" he wanted to know.

In exasperation, I said, "Just anywhere, as far as that much money will get me. Wait! Here, before I forget." I pulled out my little silver pocketknife from the back pocket of my jeans and held it out to Tom.

"Danny! Your father gave you that! I don't want to take it. That's all you have!"

Tom stood there facing me. I shoved the knife into his hand. "For gosh sakes, Tom! Don't argue with me now, just go!" I said over my shoulder as I ran to the sand bin. Kneeling down behind the bin, I slipped my jacket on and peered over the box to watch Tom enter the station.

An old Native woman was sitting on a paper box beside the garbage pail by the door of the waiting room. People were milling around by the tracks waiting for the train. A brown dog came up to me, wagging its tail. I kicked at it and hissed, "Get away from here!" It wouldn't go away, it just backed up and stood there, its paws outstretched, ready to pounce. Darned dog! Then it barked, playfully scratching the ground. It barked again. All the heads turned around to look my way, so I pretended to be picking up something. I flung a rock at the dog.

"Go away!" I hissed again.

I glanced over the top of the bin. Holy smokes! There was Tom's father coming around the corner of the station! He had on his white CN section-foreman's hat. Just then the door opened and Tom came out. I could hear his father saying, "What are you doing here? Come on, let's go home." His hand went around Tom's shoulder, and I saw Tom look my way as he deliberately dropped a folded envelope into the garbage can. He glanced my way again as they moved away and walked up the road.

That must be the ticket he threw in the garbage can! The dog was still behind me, with a spark in its eye, its tail wagging, ready for my next move. Gull-darn it! Why did it have to pick on me? I picked up a stick and threw it as hard as I could. The old woman lifted her head and looked at me. Well, the dog had something in its head after all, for it took off after the stick. I jumped up and raced to the dog, which brought me nearer to the garbage can. The dog was standing there waiting for me to throw the stick again. I picked it up and threw it as hard as I could toward the parking lot. When all eyes were busy following the dog, I whirled around and grabbed the blue envelope inside the garbage can and sat down beside the door. I glanced at the envelope and unfolded it, but there was nothing in it! It was just garbage.

The darned one-track-minded dog had just put the stick in front of me again. I threw the stick again and while all eyes followed the dog once more, I glanced inside the garbage can. There were all kinds of papers in there. Which envelope has my ticket? There's one that looks new. My hand shot in quick and I grabbed a folded CN ticket envelope. I sat back down again beside the garbage can.

I could hear the train coming now! The dog was back again, panting, its pink wet tongue hanging out. I wonder if it knows that there's dirt stuck on its tongue. I glanced around the parking lot again and up the road. I was getting very nervous, expecting my father to come running toward me at any minute. I threw the stick again. No eyes followed it this time. Everyone was watching the train coming around the bend. The bell was ringing as the engine approached the platform.

I opened the folded envelope. There it was! I pulled out the ticket. It said Armstrong. Armstrong! That's not far enough. What the heck am I supposed to do there? Then my eyes fell on the money stuck beneath the ticket. That must be the leftover money. I'll have to get another ticket at Armstrong.

The ground rumbled beneath my feet as the engine passed by the station. The windows of the train station rattled above my head. I glanced at the old woman on the other side of the door. She was standing up now and picking up her paper box. Will they let me on the train by myself? I'd better stick myself to the old lady. I fell into step behind her. Her blue, cotton print dress touched the top of her white socks, which clung to her brown stockings underneath. Her tiny feet looked snug in her black runningshoes. I followed her feet to the train.

Maybe I should look like I know her at least. I fell into step beside her when she stopped to wait in line with the other passengers. I smiled up at her. She looked puzzled as her soft brown eyes looked down at me.

"How far are you going?" I asked in English.

She smiled and said, "Armstrong."

"That's where I'm going too. Can I sit with you?"

She glanced around us, then nodded her head at me. Feeling that I should provide an explanation, I said, "I'm going to my mother. Her name is Charlotte Lynx. Do you know her?"

She blinked as she thought a moment before she said, "No."

Suddenly the brown dog that I was playing with set up barking behind us. I glanced behind, but the station was crammed with people. Then, between the back of the old woman's sweater and the huge protruding belly of the man behind us, I saw Dad coming down the road to the station. There was a stick in his hand. That's why the dog was barking. I could see Dad shaking the stick at the dog. My knees had gone very weak. Then the line began to move and I found myself sandwiched between the back of the old lady and the soft pillow of the man's belly touching me occasionally on the back of the head. This must be what a hamburger feels like between lettuce and the bun. The dog was barking farther away now. I dared not look back.

Then it was our turn and I answered the conductor's "Where to?" "To your right!" he bellowed, and I watched each foot disappear under the dress as I followed the old woman up the steps and to the coach on the right.

The coach was full of people milling about, putting jackets and bags on the rack above the seats. I followed the bent form of my companion past the filled seats until she finally found an empty one near the end. She shoved her box under the seat and adjusted her dress as she sat down by the window. I slid into the aisle seat beside her. A man loaded with fishing gear bumped my shoulder as he pushed through the crowded aisle. I glanced nervously through the window at the empty parking lot, wishing the train would go right away. It was getting dark outside now. What if Dad comes into the train to check? Where will I hide? Maybe I should go and sit in the toilet until the train goes. But if I get up he will see me through the window for sure! I will just have to sit and keep my fingers crossed, my toes too.

It was another five minutes before the passengers settled down and I felt the jerk of the coach as it slowly moved forward. I saw the CN tool house and trailers go by faster and faster as the train picked up speed. I let out a big sigh of relief and leaned back into the seat. I felt the eyes of my companion watching me. I glanced at her and smiled. She had pushed her kerchief off her head and it hung loosely around her neck. Her hair was grey only around the sides of her face and was neatly pulled back into a braid that hung down her back. The old wrinkled, weathered face broke into hundreds of deep lines as she smiled back at me. Her eyes didn't seem to fit her face. They were lively and full of spirit . . . they were young. She looked away and gazed out the window at the trees that looked like they were being twirled around a merry-go-round. My eyes came to rest on a bald spot on the back of an old man's head in front of me. I wonder what colour his hair was before it turned white. I just realized that it doesn't matter what colour people's hair is, it always turns white when they get old.

I glanced around the coach. Why do people feel they have to be louder than the clickity-clack of the train when they are only speaking to the person next to them? I'm hungry. I am so hungry, I feel like my stomach has decided to go ahead and eat me up from the inside out. I will turn into a walking stomach. Dad won't recognize me then. Wait, I have money, I forgot. Well, I don't know which coach has the snack counter. I'll go back up to the coach where we came in. I left my seat and walked as straight as a body can walk on a moving floor. Then I met the conductor, collecting tickets. I forgot, I have to pay first. I had better go back and sit down until I finish paying.

"What can I do for you, kid?" The conductor's solid body was blocking the aisle.

My voice came out, "Which way is the pop and candy place?"

The conductor smiled and pointed in the direction I had just come from. I whirled around and retraced my steps back to my seat. The old lady still had her face to the window. I searched my jacket pockets for the ticket and the money. Nothing! My hands flew to my pants pockets. Nothing! I could feel my wide eyes drying up, reminding me to blink. My jaw snapped shut as I swallowed down the fear. What did I do with it? I had the envelope in my hand, the train came . . . My hand flew inside my jacket to my shirt pocket and clamped around the folded envelope. I pulled it out and slowly removed the ticket but left the money in it. Then, as I deliberately put it back into my shirt pocket and sat there patting the envelope, I felt her eyes on me again. With a great big sigh of relief, I smiled at her. She looked like she was on the verge of having a giggling fit.

I turned to the conductor as he stopped beside us. We handed our tickets to the man and our destination cards were slipped above the darkening windows. I sat there for a moment, looking at the numbers and writing on my receipt. The date said "July 11, 1969." I shoved the receipt into the envelope in my pocket. The conductor was gone now. My stomach started a big argument inside me again. I got up and walked past the two seats to the door. I pulled and pulled but I couldn't get it open. Then the door erupted with a loud crash as a man came through. I grabbed the door and slipped through and it banged shut behind me. I was in darkness, and the two connections were sliding back and forth by my feet. I jumped across to the other side. My feet were in constant motion, each moving in opposite directions beneath me as I hurried through the deafening noise to the other door. I pushed the door open into the coach. I passed through the coach and then through another one before I finally reached a corridor and the counter appeared around the corner.

There was a woman in line in front of me. I pulled out five dollars from my envelope. The woman turned around, smiled at me, and gave me a bag of candies. They were white round mints from the many bags of candies hanging in rows on the counter. I smiled at her and took the candies, then it was my turn. The man behind the counter glanced at me.

"One coke and two chips," I said.

"And one bag of candies," he added.

"No, the lady gave them to me."

He shoved his red face at me. "Yeah? I say she didn't. Pay, kid!"

So I paid for the candies again, and he gave me some nickels and dimes back.

Clutching the pop and chips and the candies in my pocket, I made my way back to the door. After what seemed like a long walk, I finally saw the old woman still looking out into the darkness. All I could see was my reflection in the window: a small skinny kid with messy straight black hair hanging just below the ears. My brown shirt under my jacket was open at the neck. I sat down beside my companion and offered her one bag of chips. She smiled and said, "No." Then she moved her head, indicating that I should have them. So I shoved the bag inside my jacket and started filling my mouth with chips as fast as I could, pausing only to open the pop and take occasional sips when, all too soon, the bag and pop were empty.

I had just settled down for a nap when the old woman untied her kerchief and refolded it, then tied it on securely over her head again. The conductor came, yelling "Armstrong!" as he leaned over us and plucked the orange slips from the window. We're here!

I watched the people come to life. There's the man with all the fishing gear pushing his way through to get to the door first. When the train screeched to a halt, we followed the people off the train. We came down the steps last, into the darkness. The lights were bright around the station. There were two policemen standing outside the waiting room. I dodged behind some people and ran to a strip of green grass between the tracks and a road. I thought it was level, but I found myself stumbling into a dip and I fell in a heap at the bottom in some tall grass. What do I do now? I thought, in the back of my mind, that I could just run to the station, buy a ticket to somewhere, and get back on the train again. Now, I couldn't. I scrambled out of the ditch and peered over the tall grass. The policemen were still standing there. I bet Dad got them to look for me. Then the train started moving and soon I could see only the red lights of the caboose. Mama, help me! Mama, I love you. My face was wet and it felt like a big hand was squeezing me around the throat.

The police were gone now. Everyone was gone. The old woman was gone. I didn't even know what her name was. It was not polite to ask. Where shall I go? The black flies and mosquitoes were very bad here. I could feel the stinging ache in several places on my face already. There was a tool shed behind me, but there were lights all around. The police would see me. Well, I couldn't just sit here. Cars were going by on the road. I heard voices from a hotel across the street. Hotel. I wonder if they would let me in. Would I have enough money to pay for a room? But for sure I would not have any left for the train ticket to Mama. Ouch! The mosquitoes were eating me alive.

I jumped up and ran through the dark shadows. There was a clearing, a park of some kind, behind the train station. I ran toward it. Then I heard voices, people were lying down on the ground and some were sitting against the trees. I veered away and ran across the street and ended up at the corner of a store.

"Hudson's Bay" the sign said. Loud voices erupted from the door of the hotel and some men came out and headed my way. I ran along the length of the wall and stopped behind the building. I could just make out piles of junk and stuff all over the ground. There was another road up there on the hill. I scrambled up to it. It was level here, and there were a lot of old buildings.

There was a car coming. I ducked down behind something in the tall grass. The car went by. The mosquitoes were buzzing around my ears, and my face and hands were beginning to turn into one big giant itch. I ran to the road and took off down the street to get away from the mosquitoes. It seemed like I had left the people behind too, for it was very quiet here. Only several houses had lights on.

A dog was barking somewhere behind me, down the other street. I am very tired. I wish I could just find somewhere I could curl up and go to sleep. If only I had a blanket, I could wrap it around me to keep out the mosquitoes. Then my eyes caught a movement between the houses. I stopped. It was just a clothesline. Wait! I walked up to the houses. It was the little house that had the clothesline. The house was dark. I inched slowly toward the walkway, went around beyond the house, and got ready to run if a dog came at me. There on the line were square pieces, like towels and sheets. I slowly climbed up the steps of the platform to reach the clothesline and yanked the first one down. The pins popped and a warm soft blanket fell from my hand to the ground. I can't just take it. I pulled out one bill from my money envelope and pinned it to the clothesline.

I jumped to the ground and ran back to the road, rolling the blanket around and around in my hands. I got to the end of the street. There was a tree at the fork of the road, and bushes beyond. I smelled tar . . . the railway tracks. How did I get back around to the railway tracks? I hit the ground as a car approached, hoping the tall grass would hide me. The car stopped beside one of the houses and a door banged shut. Footsteps crunched on sand, then the sound of a house door opening and then slamming shut.

I scrambled up and ran across the road toward the tree. As

I entered the bushes my face and hands met scratching branches. My feet kept breaking sticks and weeds and crunching rocks. I felt smoother ground as I neared the thick bushes beneath the tree. I marched right to the middle of the thickest bushes I could see and settled down on the ground. The blanket felt like a grey "army blanket," as Dad called them. I wrapped it around me and pulled it over my head and lay down. I wriggled around a bit until I found a spot that didn't have a branch sticking into me. Something was making a loud rustling noise inside my jacket whenever I moved. The chips! The waistband around my jacket had kept them in. My candies were gone. My hand felt along my chest until I located the envelope. Then, with a sigh, I closed my eyes.

Chapter Four

I BECAME AWARE OF VOICES. MEN'S VOICES talking, then a sharp "click, click" of metal striking metal. Then steps on gravel and gradually the voices faded away.

I opened my eyes and saw the grey shade of the blanket over my face. Tiny little squares, millions of them, criss-crossed over my eyes as I lay cross-eyed and very thirsty, trying to remember where I was. Slowly I pushed the blanket down and blinked at the bright sunlight. The leaves were very still, baking in the summer heat. I sat up, but I couldn't see out of the bush anywhere.

I got up to my knees and carefully stood up. My head came up over the bushes. The railroad tracks were to my right, and men in yellow hard-hats were standing around outside the tool shed. Cars were going by on the road behind me, and the voices of children were coming from somewhere toward the train station. I knelt down and folded the grey blanket. I am very thirsty. I wonder where I can get something to drink without being seen. I don't care! I'll just walk down the street to a store, buy something to eat and drink, then . . . what about my blanket? I can't take it with me, they'll catch me for sure. I rolled my chips in the blanket and shoved it underneath the bushes. There were rusted cans and broken bottles all over the place here.

After dusting off my pants, I strolled out into the clearing. I could see a store on the road directly behind the train station. A car went by as I dashed to the road. Dust settled over me as I came up behind the car. I passed by some houses with fences. There was a church there and the green paint on the fence was peeling off, hanging off the rotting wood like shredded skin.

I walked down the road as fast as I could to the store. Some kids were sitting on the benches outside. Three of the five kids stood up as I came to the entrance. They looked like Native kids but I wasn't sure, their hair was very light brown. I glanced at them as I ran up the steps.

The cold air-conditioned air hit my face as I pushed the door open. People were milling around talking and laughing. I headed for the pop section. I grabbed one bottle of pop from the machine, popped open the cap, and strolled down the aisle to the chocolate milk. I took the small one. My mouth was filling with saliva, or what was left of it. I can't wait much longer, I am so thirsty! I passed by the bakery section and grabbed a package of doughnuts as I quickly made my way to the check-out counter. Now, how much money will I need? I pulled out the envelope and saw that all my money was there. What then did I pin on the clothesline last night? My train ticket receipt was missing. I grinned as I took the ten out and shoved the twenty back into the envelope and into my shirt pocket.

There were two people in line in front of me. An old lady with her hair in a tight bun kept staring at me. She didn't look too friendly, and I decided I didn't like her a bit either. Finally it was my turn, and I deposited my armful on the counter and gave the lady the money. My pop, milk, and doughnuts were thrown into a bag and I got four one-dollar bills and some change back, which I stuffed into my jacket pocket.

I was heading for the door when I noticed the kids looking like they were waiting for me to come out. I was so thirsty, I decided to stand around by the door for a minute. I reached into the bag and pulled out the milk. The stupid "open, pull" spout didn't work. Oh, rat snakes! What is this now, kid-proof milk? Finally I got it open and downed the whole thing in one swallow after another. When it was gone, I became aware that people may have noticed, but everyone was still talking and laughing. The old lady with the bun on her head was talking about her kid's baby or something to another old lady. Then she said something about her grandchild's first words or some dumb thing or another.

The kids were still there outside looking at me. Finally, taking a breath, I pushed the door open and went out into the hot summer morning. I ran down the steps and strolled past them, as dignified as I could manage, down the street in my measured stride. About ten steps away, I heard them behind me. I looked back just as the three boys fell into step with me.

The biggest boy, who had a nose full of freckles, spoke first. "Where you going?"

"Oh, down the road," I answered.

The boy on my left asked, "Where you come from?" and the little boy behind me asked, "What did you buy?"

I decided they were friendly enough, so I slowed down and cracked my friendliest-looking face. "Oh, I just came to visit my mother. I bought some doughnuts. Want some?"

We sat on the grass in front of the hotel and I pulled out the doughnuts. Six in the package, two went to the biggest boy, that left me with one more to eat, right after I munched through the first one while the other two were eating theirs. I was feeling much better.

After a moment, the big boy, Fred, said, "Let's go down to the creek. There are some turtles there, maybe we can catch some." So we headed down the hot and dusty street.

The buildings on the right side of the street looked old and run-down. On the left side, along the railroad tracks, it was all bush and weeds. The two younger boys set up a scuffle behind us, wrestling and punching each other. I smiled at Fred beside me. He smiled and shrugged. I took a long swig of the pop before handing it over to Fred, who finished it off in one gulp and a huge belch. I giggled.

Then somewhere up one of the streets we were passing came a sharp whistle. The little boys gave a yelp and, with thundering feet, they took off, scattering between the houses. Fred glanced at me as I started running, trying to keep up with him. I heard footsteps behind us. He whispered quickly, "If you've got any money, hide it somewhere, quick!"

My hand automatically reached for the envelope. All I had

time to do was shove it into my pants under my shorts, and I could feel the envelope slipping down between my legs just when Fred took off between the houses. Then a hand grabbed me by the collar. My feet got tangled up and I fell. The familiar fear and humiliation seized me as I looked up at two young teenagers. They started laughing and tugging at me. Then one held my arms while the other pulled at my pockets. Suddenly a car honked right beside us. Just as quickly, the boys took off and a car door slammed.

A huge man stood over me. "Come on kid. Where you come from anyway? Get in the car!"

I scrambled up and followed the man. He had on jeans and a blue-checkered work shirt. I hesitantly approached the green car, not sure where he would take me. The man's moustache twitched once when his eyes glued on me again.

"Get in!" he ordered.

My legs and body obeyed the command, and I sat perched stiff and uncertain on the front seat. He got in beside me, and the car moved up the street and took a turn at the corner by the hotel, then to the left, up the hill. That was the street I ran through last night! Then he took another turn to the left into a wooded area. I glanced nervously at the man, then his voice became softer.

"Now, tell me where to drop you off. Where you staying anyway? I haven't seen you around before."

I swallowed a lump in my throat. The envelope between my legs was mighty uncomfortable. Just when I was trying to think of something to say I saw some kids playing by a stream. "Right here. You can let me off here," I said.

The car came to a stop and I pulled the door open and slid off the seat. I took a good look at the man and said, "Thanks," and then slammed the door shut.

The car drove away, and I walked to the kids with my hands in my pants while I pulled the envelope out and put it back into my shirt pocket. I searched my jacket pocket for my dollar bills and the change, but my pockets were totally empty! Now I have twenty dollars left. Will that get me to Mama? Oh, Mama, where are you? Shucks, I feel like crying again! Danny, you have to be brave. Mama is waiting for you. Mama is waiting for you. Mama loves you, Danny! The words kept repeating themselves in my head over and over as I took a deep breath and walked forward.

I stopped by the road and watched the kids for a while. There were three boys about the same age as me, and two small girls about seven, I guess. I ran down to the stream. The three boys stood up as I approached and stared at me. I slowed down.

"Hi, I'm Danny. What are you doing?"

They glanced at each other but no one answered. Then the oldest boy said in Ojibwa, "Where did you come from?"

"From Nakina," I answered in English.

The oldest girl asked, "Don't you speak any Indian?"

I stuck out my chest. "Yeah, I just haven't had much practice talking it, but I can understand pretty good!" I looked at the oldest boy again. "Why don't you speak English?" I asked. He glanced at me and shrugged.

"Why?"

I didn't have an answer for that, so I said in Ojibwa, "My name is Danny."

They seemed to relax, and the one called Bobby showed me where the miniature dock area was. The girls were playing with carved wooden canoes, which they drifted down the stream to where the boys were, who then retrieved the canoes' cargoes of dead minnows, caterpillars, and tiny frogs. That looked like fun!

Through the whole afternoon, we retrieved cargoes of many kinds. I especially liked the purple crocus flowers that the girl Barbara sent down in her canoe. We had quite a collection of odds and ends of different kinds of marsh life by the end of the day. The smaller girl, Lisa, sent a big glob of white foam that looked suspiciously like a glob of spit to me, but Bobby unloaded it from the canoe with as much care as he did the tadpoles and the rest. I got a lot of practice speaking Ojibwa, and they laughed with me when I made a mistake.

Suddenly Bobby decided it was time to go home for supper. I immediately became tense. What should I do? No one questioned me, and I came up the road like one of the family. I walked with Bobby, Jerry, and Larry, and the girls, Barbara and Lisa, followed behind, carrying their canoes. I had no idea where we were going, but it felt all right to go with them.

About a block away, we turned off to a path that ran along tall pine trees with bushes only about knee-high. Soon we came upon a cabin set in the clearing. I hesitated and slowed down when I saw an old lady at a fireplace outside the cabin. She was filling bowls with stew, which she handed to the children as they came up. Without question, she handed me a bowl with a smile. How had she known there would be an extra kid? I sat down on a stump with Bobby, who was telling his grandma about the huge frog we saw. I hadn't spoken the Ojibwa language out loud in a long time, so I made a few more mistakes. Then I noticed that they didn't talk very much. Bobby picked up a stick and I saw him glance at Barbara, then she went inside and came out with a knife, which she gave to Bobby. Bobby started carving. I thought that they must be the happiest people in the whole world.

When we all finished eating, we took our bowls inside the cabin. When I entered, I saw a very cluttered room. There didn't seem to be any parents around. The little girls began washing the dishes while Bobby hung up his jacket. He nodded at the girls, then I followed him outside to the woodpile where his grandma was still sitting with a teapot over the fire.

The old lady's head was bent over the fire as she threw another log in and the sparks flew. She tucked the white strands of her hair into her kerchief. There were bright pink and red flowers printed on the kerchief—very pretty. She had on a red sweater and a cotton print dress. Her runningshoes were black over white socks over beige cotton stockings. She looked very comfortable.

Suddenly she turned her head as if she knew I was looking at her. "Whose son are you, boy?"

I immediately became stricken with panic. What should I say? But she smiled. "No matter, every child is my grandchild. What is your name?"

I said in a somewhat squeaky voice, "Danny . . . Maybe you know my mother, her name is Charlotte Lynx."

She thought for a minute, then shook her head. She leaned toward me as if expecting to hear more. I didn't know what else to say. Then she asked, "Is she from around here?"

My heart sank. "No, I think she came from way out west somewhere. I don't know."

My voice shook. She looked at the ground in front of me for a long while, but her full attention was on me. "Well, Danny, you will be all right here in the daytime."

I sat down beside Bobby and watched him carve a spoon for a while. With meticulous care, he held the spoon between his knees and sat hunched over with his tongue sticking out at the corner of his mouth, slowly pushing the knife blade along the neck of the spoon.

Suddenly I said in English, "Why don't you just go and buy a spoon and not have to go through such pain to make one?"

There was a deep silence as if they were waiting to see what Bobby would do. But Bobby just glanced at me, shrugged, and resumed his careful work. I sat until it became dark, then I knew what the old lady meant. For suddenly, just as Bobby was working on the spoon handle, a truck pulled up and out came a huge man who was not very friendly looking to say the least! He had pepper-grey hair sticking out all over his head. He looked scary! He bellowed for all the kids to get in the house, Grandma included. He turned a ferocious glance at me and I took off down the road.

My heart was still pounding when I ran past the graveyard on the left. There was a sandpit there. I slowed to a walk. Well, it must be what? Nine o'clock? I continued down the path until I came across an intersection. Which intersection was it? A car was coming! I ran off the road and ended up in a ditch. Shucks, there was water there, now my feet were wet. The car went by and I struggled back onto the road. The shadows on the sides of the road were getting darker, and the mosquitoes came out of their hiding places again. They must think they're little draculas, out to suck your blood in the nighttime.

What time was it when the train came last night? How do I

find out when the train will come? How am I going to get a ticket to . . . where did she say Mama was? Colby's Landing? How far is that? Do I have enough money? How will I get the ticket? What would happen if I just walked into the station and bought a ticket to Colby's Landing?

I recognized the intersection when I came to it and ran down the street to the left. A dog came up, barking at me, and I slowed down. Soon it got bored with me and decided to leave me alone. I continued down the dark street. Lights shone from windows and I could hear people talking. Some cars pulled up with people laughing and music playing. I finally came to the end of the road and saw the place where I had hidden my blanket. I ran across the road when I saw no cars were coming. Oh, the mosquitoes were bad! They bit me everywhere. I finally got to my hide-out spot and pulled out the blanket. Thankfully my chips were still in it. Funny that a dog hadn't found them. I thought dogs could smell anything. I wish I had something to drink. Where did I see a pop machine? But I can't get any change. I only have the twenty in my shirt.

I just might have to go thirsty again. I wonder what time it is. The light at the grocery store was still on, and people were walking around on the street outside. I put the blanket under my arm. I wish I had a bag to put it in. It was dark now and I couldn't take these mosquitoes any more, so I ran out of the bush and headed back on the street again toward the grocery store. I found an empty plastic bag beside the road. It had a hole in it, but it would have to do. I shoved the blanket inside. I may as well go to the store and buy some pop or milk and some chips. That should give me some change for a ticket. My heart skipped with fear when I thought of walking into the station. What if the police just pick me up and send me home? Maybe I can ask someone outside to go buy me a ticket.

As I neared the store, I noticed some teenagers by the door. I ignored them, keeping my head down, and rushed in to get something to drink just when someone opened the door to come out.

A salesperson glanced at me and said, with some irritation, "We're closing now."

"Can I just get some pop?" I asked, and grabbed one by the aisle.

I paid for the pop as lights were going out in the aisles. I drank it all before I went out and stuffed the wads of change into my pocket. I followed an older couple out the door and stayed close behind them. They were heading for the hotel. Then I noticed the teenaged boys behind me. They looked like the same ones who came after us this morning. I took off at a run toward the railroad tracks through the dark bush, then over several rails. I heard them yelling by the train station, and I continued running as fast as I could to the long line of boxcars that I had noticed during the day. I heard footsteps behind me as I skipped over the tracks at full speed. I ducked and crawled between the wheels under the boxcars and crawled out on the other side. I could still see them, so I crawled under several more cars until I lost them. Geez! the shiny steel wheels were huge! I leaned on one as I swung my feet over the rails again.

Finally, quite a ways east of the train station, I found a boxcar that was open about a foot. I threw my blanket in and hopped up into the dark interior. It smelled dusty and oily. I sat there and tried not to breathe so loudly. I could hear their voices close by again, then they receded. Maybe I'll just stay here until they're gone, but I still have to buy a ticket yet before the train comes.

I could hear a train coming from the west. That's not the train I'm waiting for, it's coming from the wrong direction. I had better get my ticket soon though. What if it comes before I can get a ticket? Does the ticket office close at a certain time before the train comes? I don't think so. The train got closer and closer, and then it rattled by so close to me that I could smell the tar and the engine. I watched the two red caboose lights disappear around the corner. Then I heard a chain reaction of clanging and banging getting closer. Suddenly my boxcar moved with a jolt and my head crashed against the door frame. I was moving! I thought this was the parked row of boxcars. I didn't know this was a freight train on the siding rail. The train picked up speed before I could decide what to do. It was going much too fast by the time the station lights flickered by. Then I was in total darkness. I could now see the skyline above the jagged treetops. The boxcar set up such a deafening banging and crashing, I felt as if I was being rattled to bits. A thought just occurred to me—I had crawled right under the wheels! What if it had moved then?

After what seemed like a long time, I heard the engine whistle somewhere far ahead, over all the noise. I was just now getting over the shock of finding myself here. Maybe I should put my blanket over me. I held the blanket tightly and sat leaning against the wall beside the open door. It was very hard on the butt sitting like that, so I curled up into a ball and padded my head on the jolting floor as best I could. I felt warm tears flowing over my cheeks, but I wiped them away and tried to think about other things. Be brave, Danny! My chest and throat hurt. I wish I was back home! No. Not the house where Dad was. I mean home when Mama, Dad, and I lived at our trapper's shack. Why did they have to move into town? Everything would have been all right if we had just stayed at our cabin. Mama! Please let me find you, please. I love you, Mama . . . I am scared. Mama, where are you?

I wiped my tears away once more, blew my nose on the blanket, and pretended Mama was beside me. She would hold me. I would feel safe. Everything would be all right.

Chapter Five

I BECAME AWARE THAT THE TRAIN WAS slowing down so I scrambled up and peered out the open door. I saw an outline of houses. I must be at another town. Then I heard the train's echo off a rock cliff, and then total darkness for a while before I saw trees again. The train slowed to a crawl before it came to a stop. Should I get off? I don't know when it will stop again if I don't get off now. I rolled my blanket and tucked it under my arm.

There will be people at the place we passed. But how far back was it now? There was an occasional bang and clang and hissing along the length of the train. I heard another train coming. We must be on a siding rail. I could see the light shining on the tracks from the coming train. It shone on solid bush all along the whole length before it passed by in front of me. Soon the train went rattling by with deafening closeness. I watched the taillights as it disappeared around the curve.

Well, if I want to get off, I'd better do it now before the train starts again. I dangled my legs over the opening just as the banging and clanging started from the front, travelling down the whole length of the train. I jumped, twisting my ankle as I landed, but I hobbled away from the moving train as fast as I could and made for the bush on the other side. It was very dark and I couldn't see a thing in the bushes. The boxcars passed by one after the other and finally the caboose, its two red lights slowly receding around the bend, and then it was gone. I stood alone by the tracks in the middle of nowhere. Hugging my blanket, I walked back down the

36

tracks where I saw the houses. Now I am really scared!

I tried not to look at the dark shadows by the tracks. My feet kept hitting and missing the railway ties and fell grating on the gravel in between. I felt an overpowering pressure spreading from my chest to my throat again. Oh, Mama! A whimpering wailing noise started in my throat and I continued walking, crying like a lost baby in the darkness. The noise from my throat was comforting and it began to fall into rhythm with my footsteps. Soon I dried my face on the blanket and concentrated on keeping my feet going. After what seemed like a long, long time I heard another train coming. I have to get off the tracks, but where? I found a sloping rock leading away from the tracks a bit. So I sat down and waited.

Soon the headlight came around the corner, then rows and rows of windows sped by me. I cried bitterly when I realized that it was the passenger train I wanted to get on. Then I was in darkness again. I sat on the rock for a long time. Maybe I even fell asleep. I grew cold, then decided to start walking again. I walked blindly, stumbling in the darkness back onto the railroad tracks. Suddenly I noticed the rock cliff on my left. I also became aware that it was getting light out. I could see the tracks ahead of me. The tears dried on my face as I moved my feet one in front of the other. I became even more terrified as I walked by the rock cliff, looming large and black beside me. Then the rock became lower and lower and finally I could see beyond to the trees. I pulled the blanket over my shoulders as another chill came over me. My eyes felt swollen and stiff from all my crying and hiccups were now plaguing me too.

There's the big tree in the clearing I had seen after the houses went by. I must be getting close to the place. My footsteps hurried a bit, I was feeling reassured that there would be people there. There was absolutely no sound coming from anywhere. The high whistle in my ears sounded very loud in the stillness. I walked with my head down until I noticed a lake on my right. As I came around a clump of bushes, I saw the clear outline of the houses. My feet slowed down and a feeling of utter despair filled me as I stared at the row of broken, fallen-down "houses." Some had caved-in roofs, others were leaning over to the side, and others were just a pile of rubble on the ground.

The sound rose in my throat again, and I sat on a rock beside the tracks and wailed and cried once more. What am I going to do? Mama, help me! Finally, exhausted, I turned around and looked at the lake, so calm and dark. It reminded me of the lake where our trapper's shack was. The sun would be up soon, I could see the red sky over there. I got up on unsteady legs and walked toward the lake. I passed by a huge pile of boards and my footsteps fell on soft spongy ground. What's this? Sawdust? There were piles and piles of it every-where by the shore. I found a clump of bushes by the lake, so I sat down and curled up in my blanket, facing the lake.

I was awakened by something rattling by on the tracks going, "putt-putt." A motor car went by. I didn't feel like moving. I was very hot. The sun was almost right over me. The water looked good. Slowly I stretched my legs. I ached all over. I sat up. My head felt really funny. I think I'll go for a swim. I should wash my clothes, but I don't have any soap. I pulled off my clothes and threw them into the water, one after the other. Naked and sweating, I walked into the lake.

The cool water seemed very slow to register in my head. It covered me all over, right over my head. My body started to drift. I had no muscles. I could feel a cool breeze on the back of my shoulders and head as I came up to the surface. Then my chest demanded air so suddenly that I gasped before I could lift my head. That sent me into a coughing fit, and I realized that I had drifted very far from shore. I started swimming. I was very tired when I finally felt the bottom with my feet. I stood up shaking and slowly waded to shore.

My clothes! My jeans were drifting by the shore. My jacket was farther down. Where was my shirt? It was under my jacket. My socks? My underwear got snagged on some twigs by the shore. After piling my clothes on a rock, I swished them around in the water a bit before I began spreading them on the rocks. My money! With pounding heart, I searched my shirt pocket. Nothing there. I grabbed the soggy jacket, stuck my hand in the pocket, and pulled out a wet ten-dollar bill, a five, and four ones. But the change was gone. I scrambled back into the water and searched among the mud and pebbles. A nickel winked back at me and I quickly retrieved it. I couldn't find any more. I weighed the money down with a rock and finished spreading my clothes out.

I am hungry. I wonder where I dropped my bag of chips, because I don't have them now. I filled up on water by the lake, then curled up in my blanket again. My long sleep was occasionally interrupted by trains going by.

The sun was almost to the treetops when I woke up again. I sat up and surveyed my scattered clothes. My shorts had blown off the rock and I found them on the sawdust. I slipped them on. Next, I pulled my shirt on. But my jeans were still damp underneath so I turned them over. I wonder where my socks went. I decided to put my jeans on anyway and searched along the shore for my socks. Somehow, it was very important to me to find my socks. I must not lose anything. I have to be responsible now. I have to look after myself. But there was no sign of them. Well, I guess I'll have to put my shoes on without the socks now. What humiliation to be wearing shoes without socks. Only beggars have no socks for their feet.

I went down to the lake and lay on my belly and sucked up as much water as my stomach could hold. Lifting my head, I noticed little black bugs zooming around in the water. Had I swallowed some? Will they make me sick? Well, I can't do anything about it now. There was that noise again, "putt-putt," coming back from the direction it went this morning. I ran and ducked behind the bushes as it went by. Now why did I do that? They could have helped me! Now they're gone! I sat down and prepared to bawl my eyes out again when I realized something. Those were sectionmen and they would be going home now. It is evening, after work. So they must not live too far away. Feeling encouraged by the idea, I prepared to walk the direction they went. As I pulled my blanket up to roll it, my socks fell out. I must have forgotten to throw them in the water. I thankfully pulled them on and pushed both feet into my shoes at the same time. Everything was all right again.

With my blanket rolled under my arm, I got back on the

railroad tracks. I had just about reached the rock cliff when I remembered my money. I was in such a big fired-up hurry to chase the motor car that I hadn't remembered to pick up the money! So I turned around and retraced my steps again. When I reached the rock there was my money. Where would it go anyway? Grow legs and run away? I rolled the bills together and stuffed them into my shirt pocket. The nickel was waiting on top of the stone where I had left it.

Off I went again and walked past the rock cliff. Somehow it didn't seem so far now. Then, off on the shoulder of the tracks, I spotted my bag of chips! This must be the place where I had gotten cold and pulled the blanket over me. Why hadn't I heard them fall? Maybe because I was busy bawling my head off. I ripped into the bag with relish and oh, they tasted so heavenly delicious! In no time, the bag was empty. Sadly I rolled it into a tube and stuck it in my pocket. Long shadows were gathering when I came to the double tracks. Then I noticed a path going into the bush on the left, and a tool shed farther down the tracks. I continued walking. There was a clearing on the right, with a section house sitting in the middle. Smoke rose out of the chimney but there was no one around. I hadn't seen this last night! A little farther down, there was another path going off to the right. I heard children there and saw a glistening lake beyond the trees. The sign post said "Jacobs." That must be where the train stops. If I knew the passenger train was behind me last night, I could have got on here. But it didn't stop, did it? You must have to call the dispatcher to put a stop on the train here. I hung around Tom long enough to know that.

I should hide my blanket around here somewhere. I found an old stump and shoved the blanket on the ground beside it. Now, how am I going to get someone to put a stop on the train? Maybe I have to go to the section house I had passed. I would have to explain to the man what I was doing here, though. I walked back to the sign post and stood leaning against it, trying to figure out what to do next when I heard a footstep behind me. Geez! I hadn't even heard him coming.

He was a tall man with a deep sun tan and a yellow hard-hat

on. He stood there squinting against the evening sun, studying me. I didn't move, and didn't know what to say. Well, he must have figured out by now that I am not a martian! I could feel my chin coming up and my shirt tightened across my chest.

Finally he smiled and said, "Okay, you got me! I can't figure out who the heck you are and where the heck you came from!"

I looked down the tracks, but my brain wasn't working at the moment. My head had gone totally empty. He pulled up a straw from the ground and looked down the tracks, following my eyes while he chewed the tip of the grass between his teeth.

His voice came again, "You see, there are only three families here. The foreman and us three sectionmen. I know every one of them, and you don't belong to any of them. On top of that, the train did not stop here last night."

Suddenly I blurted out in English, "Are you Ojibwa? Do you know Charlotte Lynx?"

He thought for a moment, looked at the ground, then shook his head. "Yes, to the first; no, to the second question." Then his head came up. "The freight train! Is that where you got off from?" Still I didn't answer. With a big sigh, he stood there shaking his head. "If I ever meet your father, I swear I'll punch the living daylights out of him!"

Immediately my voice rang out, "You leave my father alone, he never hurt you!"

A smile spread across his face again. "Okay, now I know you have a father somewhere, and this Charlotte Lynx is your mother?" I nodded. "So you ran away, huh? Looking for your mother. You know, it's dangerous for a little kid like you travelling alone. Where the heck did you go since . . . what, midnight last night?"

I watched my foot kicking at the grass and I mumbled, "Down the tracks."

He gave another sigh. "Why the heck didn't you come up to one of the houses. We would have let you in, you know. How old are you anyway? You don't look more than ten years old!"

My voice came out louder this time. "Well, I thought those were houses we passed last night . . . " My voice broke and I stood there blinking. Then he came over and bent forward until he was at eye level with me.

"I'll make you a deal. You come home with me now and I'll pay your way home on the next train, okay?"

"No way! I am not going home. If you send me home, I'll have to start all over again!" I pulled the money out from my shirt. "I have to find Mama. I have some money for a ticket, see? And I am not ten years old, I mean I am older than ten! Would you stop the train for me tonight, please?"

I could feel my lip trembling, so I clamped it tight between my teeth. His arm came around across my shoulders. "Okay, you can go to Savant Lake with that, and some left over. Maybe people there would know your mother. But don't go to Sioux Lookout by yourself. That place is too big."

We were walking side by side up the path leading to the lake as he continued. "The foreman's wife and son are leaving on the train for Savant Lake tonight, so you can go with them. But promise me you'll go to the police when you get there and ask them to let your father know where you are, okay?"

Incredulous, I glanced up at him. "Are you kidding? They'll ship me home immediately! I had to run away from them at Armstrong. They were already there waiting for me. Dad probably called them as soon as I left Nakina."

He laughed. "The police by the station? Oh, they have nothing to do with you. They're always there. They are there on other business. They probably never would have noticed you."

I kicked at a rock and grumbled, "Fine time to tell me!"

"What's your name?" he asked suddenly.

"Danny Lynx," I answered without thinking. He had tricked me again, asking me that right out of the blue, and now he knows where I am from too. Boy, I'm hopeless!

He smiled down at me and said, "My name is Charlie."

I spent a pleasant evening with Charlie and his family. He had two girls aged nine and eleven. His wife was very nice. She was a tall skinny lady with long black hair and eyes that sparkled with laughter all the time. The older girl was very shy, but the younger one, Bella—they called her Billy—was really something else. After a delicious supper, she pulled me to the lake. At a shallow mossy area beside a sloping rock was a huge frog in a can. She described the insides of the frog in every detail, her face stretching in so many ways it was really something to see.

While she was pulling the frog's leg to show me just how long it could stretch, twelve-year-old Andy from next door came at a run toward us, with a younger boy close at his heels. Just then, the frog escaped from Billy's hands, took a flying leap through the air, and landed on the ground, just when Andy's foot came down. We heard a distinct "pop" and the frog lay flat as Andy danced away on one foot. Totally amazed, I watched Billy, without a pause, set up a reporting chatter all around the frog, observing from all angles, only some of which I caught. One breath went something like this, " . . . its whole stomach and stuffing turned inside out and shot out of its mouth and blew out the whole eye part of his head, where the brains gushed inside out and rolled down on top of its stomach parts. It looks like it threw up all its insides out of its huge cracked-open mouth."

Then my attention was caught by the boys still wrestling over something. A slingshot, I could see now. Andy was holding it over his head out of the smaller one's reach. Then he inserted a rock and let a shot go behind him as he twisted around out of reach. The rock just missed Billy's head by an inch and she didn't even notice. A motor started around the point, and a boat shot out from around the bend. It slowed down by the rocks where we were. It was Charlie! I heard him yelling over the sound of the motor, "Danny! Want to come fishing?"

I couldn't believe it! The wind blew into my open mouth before I could get my legs moving. Oh boy! I ran to the rocks and jumped into the boat from the rock farthest out in deep water. I took a seat, and we took off full blast straight toward the middle of the lake. The waves hit the front of the boat with a fast "rat-tat-tat." I took a big deep breath as the wind blew at my hair and flattened it back, combing it slick as a feather.

We stopped by the channel and Charlie, beaming at me, said, "Here, you use this fishing rod." I put a jigger on the leader and set to work. I swung the rod and released the line and just barely missed Charlie's head as the hook banged inside the boat. Charlie laughed as I apologized. I followed his instructions, and after a couple of fumbling casts I finally got the hang of it. We watched a daring loon come really close to the boat.

Suddenly Charlie's rod jerked down and his line started buzzing as it shot in a straight line, first one direction, then another. My rod lay in the boat quite forgotten as I stomped and hooted in joy and Charlie yelled, "It's a big one!"

Grabbing the net, I got ready to scoop the fish in. With much banging and thumping on the aluminum boat, we finally got the huge jackfish in. Oh, it was a beauty! Then Charlie caught two pickerel before it began to get dark.

I threw my line in one more time and was slowly reeling in when it suddenly jerked and I felt the tug and pull of a fish. This was the very first fish I had ever caught all by myself. I was very proud when Charlie scooped out the pickerel for me. It was a good-sized one too! Off we went again across the lake to the cabin. I could smell the railroad from here, the smell of tar in the air. We would hit pockets of cold air, then warm air as we crossed the lake at full speed.

It was quiet when we reached the dock. I stood there with the string of fish as I watched Charlie tie the boat, then I heard myself say, "Charlie, thanks a heap." I stood facing the navy blue lake and the dark shoreline for a while. It would be wonderful to live here. Charlie was ready and we walked up the path, his hand warm on my shoulder. The girls were playing cards when we entered the dimly lit cabin. Charlie's wife was just putting more wood into the stove. She turned with a big smile when she saw the fish. In no time at all she had cleaned them and fried the pickerel, which we ate around the table with the coal oil lamp sitting in the middle.

Billy was babbling on about something again, and I said to the older girl, "Does she always go on like that? If she's not careful someone will call her motor-mouth, or say she's suffering from verbal diarrhoea."

Suddenly, all was quiet. I caught a quick exchange of glances between everyone, but it was Billy who said, "You talk like a smart aleck. If you're not careful, someone will bash you one in the mouth. You are not home now, you know! Who do you think you are, anyway?"

She got up and scrambled to the top bunk in the corner. Her mother smiled and shrugged at me. Well, I guess I have to watch what I say from now on. And I guess she's right, I can't act like I'm at home in someone else's home.

Charlie was talking about the fish I caught and everyone started talking again. It didn't seem very long afterward when Charlie said he'd walk me to the train stop. I watched his flashlight casting my long shadow in front of me as we walked on the dark path. Charlie just smiled when I stopped to retrieve my blanket. The woman and her son were already standing there when we got to the tracks. It was very dark again tonight. I was totally terrified last night and now I was almost sad to leave the place. I didn't know where I would be tomorrow.

I tugged at Charlie's sleeve. "Tell Billy I'm sorry for what I said, okay?"

He reached and ruffled my hair with his hand and whispered, "My grandfather used to tell me to always listen, watch, and learn. Can you remember that?" I grinned up at him. That was a strange thing to say.

We could see the switch light at the curve shining green now, so the train would be here soon. It shone a streak of light on the horizon even before we heard it coming. Finally, with a low rumble, the headlight shone around the curve. Soon the train rolled by and slowed to a stop. Charlie shook my hand as I turned to follow the woman up the steps. My hand came away from Charlie's handshake with a folded paper. I scampered up the steps and into the coach. The train started with a jerk while we were still walking down the aisle and the woman had to quickly grab a seat. I sat down beside them on an empty seat across the aisle. Only then did I open my hand. Charlie had put a twenty-dollar bill in it. Suddenly I wanted to cry. I wanted to go back to Charlie. I didn't know people could be so kind.

I heard a commotion down the aisle and soon the conductor arrived beside me. I gave him a five-dollar bill and I got some change back. Snuggling deeper into the seat, I shoved my blanket under my head and immediately fell asleep.

Chapter Six

I HADN'T BEEN SLEEPING FOR VERY long when the coach started bustling with people preparing to get off. Soon lights from the town came into view, and I noticed big drops of rain running down the window pane. The lights were bright around the train station, and I saw that there were quite a few people standing around waiting to get on the train.

As I stood in the aisle with the woman and her son, she poked me and said, "Charlie gave me money to pay for a room for you too. We're staying at the hotel the rest of the night and leaving again early in the morning. Would you like to share a room with us?"

Quite relieved, I smiled and nodded. Actually I hadn't thought of what I was going to do when I got here.

The people disappeared quickly when the train pulled out, and we made our way to the hotel as fast as we could. It was very dark and raining hard. Soon we were running up the steps and the woman pulled the door open. The light was shining very softly inside, and it smelled like stale cigarette smoke. I stood by the door with the boy while his mother paid for a room. Then we went up the creaky, dimly lit stairs. There were two double beds, a dresser, and a chair. The woman picked the bed by the window and the boy and I shared the other. I was totally exhausted. I took off my jacket and pants and crawled into bed. The boy was still fiddling around with the buttons on his pyjama top. I didn't even hear him get into bed.

I woke up slowly, stretched, and felt the smooth sheet over

me. The bed was soft and comfortable. I heard people talking somewhere down the hallway. A door closed, then all was quiet. Suddenly, fully awake, I lifted my head. They were gone! I wonder when I am supposed to get out. I wish I could sleep some more. I am hungry. I sat up and found the bathroom. I took my time getting ready. I sat on the bed after I got dressed and pulled out all my money from my pockets. I wish I had something to put it in. I could lose it when I just shove it in all my pockets. I still have my folded chip bag too. I think that would make a good bag for my money. I wonder how much breakfast costs in the restaurant. Maybe it would use up all the money. I better not. I'll get doughnuts and milk or something at the grocery store. I'll take out the four ones, that should do it.

Feeling better, I shoved the rest of the money into the chip bag, folded it nice, and shoved it into my shirt pocket. I rolled up my blanket neatly and quietly opened the door, then snuck down the stairway and ran outside.

After walking one direction, I soon realized there was no grocery store there, so I turned around and headed the other way. What miserable weather! There were mudpuddles all over the gravel road. Jumping over them, missing some and landing on others, I neared the hotel again. There were only bushes and trees on the right side of the street by the railway tracks.

Finally I spotted the grocery store. There were people sitting around under the trees. Some were coming out with boxes of groceries. I entered the store and saw all kinds of things in there, more than a person could ever need!

At last I found the milk and cookies. There was an old Native woman in a long dark brown dress ahead of me in the check-out line. She had a cane and looked like she could hardly walk, yet she had quite a few things on the counter. I wonder how she plans to carry all that.

When I came out of the store, I spotted the old lady slowly making her way down the street, trying to balance the bag and her weight with the support of the cane. I sat on a rock beside the road and drank the milk all at once and got to work on the cookies. About eight cookies later, I noticed the old woman still hadn't got past the first stretch of the road. I wonder how far she has to go.

I looked around at the people walking and talking by the trees in front of the train station. Would any of them know Mama? Maybe they didn't even live here. They looked like they just came to town to shop. They had bags and boxes with them. Maybe that old lady would know. I decided to ask her and maybe help her with the bag. I took off at a run after her. I slowed down and walked softly behind her for a while before I fell into step beside her. She just ignored me. She wouldn't even look at me.

Finally, in Ojibwa, I said, "I'll carry your bag for you." She glanced at me angrily and continued her struggle. I tried again, louder this time, thinking that maybe she hadn't heard me. "I just got here last night. I'm looking for my mother. Her name is Charlotte Lynx. Would you know her?"

She continued walking for another long while before she glanced at me again. This time she had no expression. It was as if I wasn't even there. I sighed and slowed down even more.

Then in English, I said, "I have nowhere to go and nothing to do. I just thought I'd help you carry the bag and ask if you had heard if my mother was around here . . . " My voice trailed away. She wasn't even listening. I stopped and started to turn around when her shuffling feet stopped and she looked back at me. She had the darkest black eyes I had ever seen.

Then she said in a crackling voice, "E're," and motioned to the bag with her chin. It looked like her arm was being pulled out of its socket by all that weight. I ran and grabbed the bag and walked beside her. Boy! Her bag sure was heavy. We walked in silence to the corner of the street, then she headed for a path straight to the railroad tracks. I followed behind, watching how her right foot turned on its side when she walked.

Then she said, "I neber 'eard of anyone wit dat name. I wouldn' anyway. Don't talk to people much."

I said nothing. Well, I can believe that. So now what?

We crossed the tracks and walked on to another path heading straight for the bushes. It became very swampy. I could smell damp earth. There was mud on the path and some boards had been thrown across in places. I watched a little blue butterfly bouncing along on top of the pink wildflowers on the side of the road. Then I noticed the back of a cabin.

The path ran along beside the cabin and petered out at the steps in front of it. In the clearing out front was a sawhorse and a couple of short jack-pine trees. There was also a teepee type of structure over a campfire that had wooden racks over it. Then something moved in front of the cabin beneath the window. I had completely missed him at first glance. It was an old man with a very wrinkled face. He turned and looked at me from his padded seat on the ground.

I stopped and stared for a full minute while the old woman cackled and pointed. "Look boy, dat man who 'as lib't more years dan any two of doze people outside da store!"

A dark hole appeared among the wrinkles and a strong voice bellowed, "O is dis you brin' wit you, ol' woman?"

The loud voice startled me even more, and this time the old woman broke into a tinkling giggle. "'E don' 'ear so well, so 'e make sure 'e'll break your eardrums too wile 'e's at it!" Turning to the ancient creature, she said, "Tis a los' boy, a wanderin chile lookin' for 'is mama."

The old man looked in my direction and said, "Ahhh . . . tsk, tsk, tsk." Shaking his head, he resumed his position, legs crossed and hands clasped together between them.

Then the old woman spoke from inside the cabin, "Come in 'ere an put down da bag on da table."

The door was on ground level, no steps. I walked in and saw two single mattresses on the floor in one corner of the room, about three feet apart. In the other corner was a single bed. In the corner to the left of the door was a table with a vinyl tablecloth with a design of red teapots and flowers on it. A cupboard of some sort with drawers underneath stood beside the one window. On my right sat a row of pails and underneath were stacks of wood. Beside the wood was a black iron woodstove with a white oven door. Then my eyes drifted to the walls. The bottom half of the four walls was covered by all kinds of things hanging from pegs all around the room. Above the pegs were bright pictures of all kinds of people in

long gowns and one guy with some kind of light shining
around his head. Stupid Danny! Of course, those were reli-
gious pictures. They completely surrounded the room! Then
I noticed the window, all covered with pink-and-white flow-
ered, ruffled curtains. I decided that the place looked
"homey" enough.

I smiled at the old lady as she moved toward the stove
saying, "Da ol' fool 'as let da stobe go out agin."

I went outside and took a good look at the teepee smoke
rack. I noticed the "ropes" that tied the poles together were
all some type of roots and bark. I kicked some ashes back in
the firepit and looked around the clearing some more. The
sawhorse and handsaw looked as if they had been well used.
This place reminded me of our trapper's shack. Then my eyes
fell on the stacks of split wood piled chest-high in double rows
beside the cabin wall. How do they do that?

Suddenly the old woman spoke behind me, "My son comes
eb'ry once a while to see to tings dat I can't do mysel'. Take
an armful of dose twigs an' birch bark. I 'abe to get da fire
goin' agin. God 'elps doze o 'elps demselbes, I alway say."

Then it hit me! They did not speak Indian. They were
speaking in some kind of strange-sounding English. The flow
of her voice kind of went up mountains and dipped down into
valleys again. It went up and came down in strange places.
They must have come from far away somewhere.

I found the fire starters in a closed wooden box by the
woodpile. I had another surprise as we sat down to eat the
evening meal. The old lady had cooked spareribs and dumplings, which she dished out for all three of us. My mouth was
just watering, and I picked up the spoon and was ready to dig
in when I felt their eyes on me. I stopped and looked at them.
What? They sat there with hands clasped and heads down.
Then the old man's voice boomed over the table in a language
that was absolute gibberish to me. I had no idea what kind of
language that was. Then I heard "Amen!" from the old lady,
so I dutifully said "Amen" too. That pleased the old man very
much, I could tell. I knew for darn sure, though, that whatever
he spoke was no Native language! And it certainly was not

English. I didn't know there was another kind of language. Then they dug in and ate the supper in peace.

After the first mouthful, I looked at the old lady and asked, "What language was that he spoke?"

The old lady cackled again and looked at the old man. He continued eating as if I hadn't said anything. Then she spooned another mouthful before she replied, "Latin."

I raised an eyebrow, then said, "Oh." I had no idea what language that was. Never heard of it. I was very uncomfortable for a while until my hunger got the better of me. That was a delicious meal.

After the meal, the old man went outside to sit by the door again. The old lady clearly didn't want me hanging about either so I picked up an empty pail and asked, "Where do you get the water from?"

She gave me a long look before she said, "Depen's what you want da water for. If you wanna wash clothes, git it from da creek, an' if you wanna drink, git it from da pump. Da pump, it down ober da 'ill a ways."

Well, the direction her arm swung as she spoke would be toward the tree that stood alone in the clearing to the left. I smiled and went out. I totally forgot about the old man beside the door, as I repeated under my breath, "Down ober da 'ill a ways . . . guess I'll find out." I heard a rasping sound behind me and I turned to see the face all wrinkled up like a . . . like a . . . I couldn't imagine anything else quite like it! I smiled and hurried away, swinging the galvanized pail over my head.

Just over the hill past the tree, I saw a yellow pump on a mound of sand, set in a clearing across a road. I ran down a narrow path toward the pump. I had never used one before. I examined the handle and cranked the arm up and down, and all it did was wheeze like the old man when he is supposedly laughing.

After a few more arm cranks a bit of water came out, and soon I had it gushing all over the pail. Quite pleased, I picked up the handle and oh, it was heavy! I swung the pail beside me and it sloshed along with my right leg until I thought my fingers were going to come off. I put it down and picked it up with my left hand and the handle commenced to try separating my knuckles on that side too. My left leg was also drenched by the time I got to the bottom of the hill. How does she climb this hill? I took a breath and struggled with the pail, and by the time I got to the tree, I had lost about half the water. I tried to struggle with a bit more dignity as I neared the cabin. The old man sat there watching but didn't even blink as I passed by him.

I proudly set the pail on the shelf and then the old lady started her cackling laughter as she pointed at my drenched legs, saying, "Don' go swimmin' in it, boy. Da lake ober dere is for swimmin'!" I smiled. Well, so now I know that there is a lake close by. Then she continued, "Dere's a pat runs down from dis way, an dere's no 'ill to clime. Da's da one I use." I shrugged thinking, Now, she tells me. Just for that, in the days to come I made a point of using the hill path, lugging up the water until one day I no longer spilled any.

I slept on the single bed, which I found out was where the son slept when he came to visit. Mr. and Mrs. Old Indian both slept on the mattresses on the floor. Apparently the old man really had no use for a bed. But I never ever heard anyone snore like the old man did! I swear the logs vibrated in there most nights. But I usually went to bed exhausted from running around helping them with the daily work of preparing meals, getting wood, and hauling and throwing out water. I would have slept through a thunderstorm. I never knew there was so much work to just living from day to day. I hung up the clothes just as fast as she washed and rinsed them, I ran for wood as she cooked the meals, and I ran to the store when she ran out of things. Once in a while, they would chuckle and cackle at the way I was doing things. I laughed with them a lot. I never wandered very far from the cabin, I was afraid I would be seen and someone would come to get me, maybe Dad.

As the days wore on, every time I ran into town for something, I asked everyone I saw at the train station if they knew where my mother was. Then one day, I discovered that there was no such place as Colby's Landing! Boy, that made me angry! Now I had nowhere in particular to go, except to find out where "Allan Water Bridge" was. I asked the old lady, and all she said was that it was to the east, not far. Well, if it wasn't that far, I should have enough money to go there and come back here again. I felt safe here and I liked this place. It reminded me of life with Mama and Dad before we moved to town.

I realized then that I liked the old couple and I decided to stay as long as I could. The only thing I had to remember was the prayer before meals and another prayer before bed. The biblical pictures were reminders, as the old lady said, "Gen'le lookin, to rememer da way people ought to be, as God wan'ed all 'uman bein's to be."

That was the reason the pictures were on the wall. The old man never said very much. He would get up in the morning and go and sit outside beside the door. I tried talking to him once but he didn't answer me. Maybe he didn't hear me. There was no clock and no calendar in the entire place. I soon discovered that there was no need to know what time it was or what day it was. But I always made a point of asking the cashier when I went to the store. I had left Nakina on Wednesday. That's all I knew.

Some evenings we went blueberry picking, just the old woman and me. We walked down a bush road, and she knew exactly where to find the large blueberries. She made blueberry jam when we got home and the old man made a point of laughing a lot. All you could see of his mouth was a big black hole, and just for good measure, he'd stick out his navy blue tongue too. I wish there was a mirror so he could see how horrible he looked!

The old man did not move around much. His legs were so bent out of shape he could hardly walk. Most of the time he just sat on his mat, beside the door.

We didn't get many visitors, but occasionally a Native person would come to talk to the old man. The old lady always sent me away on an errand when one showed up.

I found out that it was Sunday morning when a man in a black shirt with a white collar appeared. Now I know a minister when I see one, so I just stepped back and left him to

Mrs. Old Indian with her quick nods, her smile, and a cup of tea. Then she left the old man and the minister outside. I was kind of concerned about the old guy out there with the minister, but the old lady just smiled and let me know that the old man could take care of himself.

During the week, I finally got the courage to buy a ticket to Allan Water Bridge. I boarded the train in the afternoon and after only a few minutes it was time to get off. There were some fishermen getting off there too. I followed along behind them. There was a lake on the other side of the railroad tracks. I saw the large black bridge when the train pulled out. I didn't have to worry about a place to stay since I was going back on the night train anyway. I also had the old lady's bannock sandwich in a small bag slung over my shoulder. I followed the crowd to the other side of the tracks and down a path. The grass and bushes were very tall here, and the path was muddy in places. I could see a house on the right as we approached a clearing. There was also a store beside the river. There were quite a few people inside as we entered. While the fishermen were talking with the owner, I asked the people sitting there if they knew my mother. No one knew anything.

I went out and wandered toward the river. I walked out to the end of a log sticking into the water. The river was very brown and deep. The current sent swirls around and around the middle of the river. I wonder how strong the current is. I bet if you threw something in, it would get sucked to the bottom in no time! Someone yelled, "Hey, kid! Get away from there!" I stepped back along the log and onto the shoreline. What did he think, that I was going to go for a swim? I wandered along the railroad tracks for quite a while.

Then I met an old lady by the train stop. She said she lived by the railroad tracks and, boy, she was loud and sounded cantankerous! But she said she would give me a pop if I walked home with her. I flinched as she yelled at me, handing me a pop and chocolate bar at the same time. She sounded as if she was giving me heck as she invited me to stay at her cabin until the train came in. I watched her doing beadwork by lamplight. She didn't say much, which was a relief. I jumped a foot high every time she did say something. When the train finally came, I watched the light from her window go out as I looked out the window. She had stayed up to keep me company.

A second Sunday passed at Savant Lake, and after the minister had gone, storm clouds began to gather on the horizon. The old man asked the old lady for his tobacco pouch. Facing the clouds, he pulled out a rather long ancient pipe and lit it. The old woman ushered me away, and I left the old man in peace. I spent the time wrapping my change in a chocolate bar cover and folding the dollar bills into my old potato chip bag. I watched house flies bounce and endlessly chase each other around on the ceiling. I caught one and pulled out its legs and let it go. It was so happy, it took off full speed and circled the picture of the man with the golden halo, but it couldn't land. It tried again on the line where the dishtowels hung behind the stove. I lost sight of it. There were too many zigzagging across the room.

About a half-hour later, I went out for an armload of wood. The storm clouds were coming up fast. I could feel the earth shake under my feet as I stepped outside.

The old man was still sitting beside the door, and he spoke as I went by, so I stopped to listen, squatting down beside him. Sometimes it was difficult to understand his accent and I knew by now, by the set of his stubborn jaw, that a lecture was coming. "To honour da Eart, boy, you mus' un'erstan dat it is alibe. Da men wit da machines are like lice dat feed on da libin' scalp o' Mudder Eart."

He paused to draw on his long pipe. The smoke swirled around his head and his squinty eyes seemed to drift into the distance again.

I frowned at the old lady, but she just smiled and disappeared from the window where she had stood watching us. I knew I was going to be here for a long time, I couldn't just leave while he was talking to me.

I shifted around beside him and listened as he drew in a deep breath and continued, "Jesus, da Son of God, knows abou' dese tings. 'e was born outside in da open air wit animals aroun 'im . . . as't should be wit ebry animal born on

Eart. Today, man is bery much use' to da manmade tings dat dey know nuttin else. Dey are born in a manmade place, an dey die in a manmade place. You mus' un'erstan dese tings, boy. We are da chil'en of da Eart. Da Lord was also a chile of da Eart."

I saw his bony leathery cheek sink into his cheekbones as he sucked up more smoke from the pipe. I shifted my weight to my other leg as another rumble of thunder shook the ground beneath me.

I took a breath and asked a question, though I doubted he'd answer this one either, "What's a 'chile of da Eart?'" My question hung in dead air. I poked a black bug out of the ground by the doorstep. I wonder if any climb on top of his sitting pad.

The old man's voice came again, "Da chile of da Eart is someone o 'as learnt dat da ting dat gib em life is da groun' dey walk on. It is da groun' dat gib all life, an all life reach up to da sun. All tings stan' an stretch out to da sun for life. We 'ab da knowledge to talk to an un'erstan da Creator, an we 'ab da knowledge to lead da res' of da worl' to peace an 'eal da sufferin Eart. Dere's a part in da Bible dat talk abou' dat too."

I took a deep breath, then sat down on the ground and leaned back against the wall beside the door. I could tell he was not finished yet. He let out a long stuttering breath before he continued, "Do you feel da Eart shake, my boy? Do you feel da Eart mobe to anser da tunders up in da sky? Don' you feel small, my boy? When da mighty Eart shake an da deafenin tunders roll an lightnin shadders da mighty trees? Who are dey, my boy, da people who do no' hear or see dis? Dey be stone deaf an bline, my boy."

There was silence for a long time as he refilled the pipe and pointed it to the four directions with each puff of smoke.

Suddenly his big voice boomed in answer to the last rumble of thunder and the answering crack of lightning. I jumped about a foot high and sat there pasted against the wall. Geez! That startled the heck out of me! He seemed to have forgotten about me as he shook a fist that looked like the knot of an old tree. "Who are you? Da people who poison

da air! Who are you dat poison da ribers an lakes! You people
who dig deep into da guts of our Mudder an slash an rip into
'er flesh an keep on poisonin' da air she breathes for ebry day
you lib. You lice who feed on da scalp of da libin Eart! You 'ab
los'! You 'ab gibin up da honour dat was gibin to you by da
Creator! It is da people you 'ab spat on an pitied who will stan
up an show you da way. We 'ab not forgodden! 'as da tunder
forgodden to roar? 'as da lightnin mis't a strike? Be sure, you
will feel it when da mighty 'and of our Creator comes upon
you!"

There was something happening! My heart was now thundering deep inside the small enclosure of my rib-bones. I found it
hard to breathe, and I could almost feel the static in my hair.
There was an acrid smell in the air. Suddenly there was a loud
crash and light flashed before my eyes. I saw a puff of smoke on
the other side of the clearing. My back was flat against the wall
when a warm hand touched my shoulder. I jumped and swallowed a huge lump in my throat. My smarting eyes told me I had
forgotten to blink for a long while. There was a bright piece of
exposed wood down the whole length of the pine tree that stood
on the edge of the clearing. It looked like a giant piece of
toothpick had been peeled off the side of it.

The old lady spoke behind me, "Da fire is goin' out an we
all know da stobe isn' goin to walk ou'side an trow some more
wood into itsel'!"

I jumped up and rushed past the old man, then ran around
the side of the cabin and piled the wood in my arms. My
rubbery legs started trembling and I tried to calm down as I
slowly made my way back. The old man was now sipping a
steaming cup of brown tea. He sat deep in thought and didn't
even seem to notice me at all as I came around the corner.
The dark clouds were still rolling and boiling behind me as I
entered the cabin.

I glanced at the old lady and said quietly, "That minister better
not come around too often. The visits seem to be doing some
strange things to his head." I nodded toward the old man.

She glanced at me and laughed. "You mean, 'e 'as been
doin some strange tings to da ol' minister's 'ead! Dey say 'e's

been sayin some strange tings in 'is sermons dese days! Ha, ha! 'e's learnin too fas', I tink! God bless 'is soul! 'e is a wonderful 'uman bein', dat minister!"

The old woman hummed as she made some bannock. Soon the smell of fried bannock and bacon made me forget about the rumbling thunder. I was happy to see the old man enter and have a piece of bannock. He liked to dunk it in bacon grease and flop a wallop of raspberry jam on top of the grease. I grinned and laughed as he smacked his lips in delight and propped himself up on the mattress against the wall.

Several days later, I was coming back from the store with a bag of flour when I overheard someone by the station saying, "Charlotte won't be around any more."

I stopped and pretended to rest, but I didn't hear any more. Then as the woman from the group moved away I followed her and asked if she knew Charlotte Lynx.

She looked at me and said, "Yes, we were just talking about her."

"Where is she now?" I blurted out.

She took her time studying me and seemed to be trying to remember something. Finally she said, "Well, I think she probably went to Collins. She was with . . . Joe, I think."

"Thanks!" I yelled as I took off and ran along the tracks as fast as I could, the flour bag bouncing along under my arm.

I came tearing around the corner of the cabin and stopped at the door to catch my breath. The old man was standing by the table and the old woman was by the stove. Both stood frozen to the spot, staring at me.

Taken aback, I looked at one and then the other. Finally I blurted out, "What? What's wrong? What happened?" They looked at each other then back to me again. I waited, then asked again, "What?"

The old lady sighed, then said in exasperation, "It seem to us chile, dat you are da one wit da news. Wat is't dat we could 'ear your feet comin from down da pat. What? Tell!"

Oh. Looking sheepish, I realized how quickly my search for Mama was forgotten when I thought something was wrong with these two.

"I just found out where Mama is! I'm going to go on the train tonight to Collins."

The old man smiled his toothless void in my direction and said, "Now, Collins isn' goin' to up an move its place for you jus so you can git dere tonigh'. I rememer Collins to be da udder way dan da nigh' train be goin'."

The old lady added softly, "An da train dat goes dere 'as already gone by."

They turned and went back to their usual slow motion. I guess I will have to wait one more day. I brought more wood in and fetched two more pails of water from the pump. I had to keep busy, I was so restless.

Later that evening as I was sitting on the bed barefoot, because Mrs. Old Indian decided to wash my socks, the old one got that distant look in his eyes again. I sat perfectly still as he puffed on his pipe by the stove in the twilight.

His voice seemed to come from far away as he began, "Da 'uman bein' is born into dis worl' like da leaf as't slowly opens into da air an brigh' sunligh'. Da 'uman chile's face is all wrinklt an its 'ands are clench't tight, hol'in on to life. Jus' like da leaf feeds on da sunligh' an spreats ou' flat to take in life, so mus' da 'uman bein' learn to grab an stretch ou' da 'and to lib. At da en' of its summer, da leaf dies flat, after libin its life, 'e goes back to da Eart to feed da grass dat feed da trees dat gib new life. At da en' of da 'uman's life, da 'ands are flat, dey 'ab lib't an now gib up life."

He paused to suck up the smoke again, and I saw his cheeks sink in as the smoke bellowed from his mouth to the ceiling. Then he continued, "Sometime, w'en da spirit leabes da body w'en it wasn't time for it to die, da body try to curl up as't was in da beginnin before it turn't into a leaf, because da spirit is dere no more to tell it dat it was already a leaf . . . pity dat mos' people don' know . . . "

He let the pipe die out, then slowly knocked out the ash from his pipe into the rock bowl beside the stove. I sat and tried to sort out this information in my head. I watched him stretch his bony legs toward the warmth of the stove. I didn't know a baby's face is wrinkled when it's born, and I didn't know about the "curled up" part. And what is a person's spirit? Is it like a ghost?

I heaved a big sigh and noticed the old lady's black eyes on me from the table. I shrugged hopelessly and she smiled and looked away. I just did it! I mean talking not in words but by actions. I remembered my second day here, the old man had looked at the old woman, then at me. The old woman smiled and said, "'e say you talk too much."

I had looked at the old man and said, "What? I didn't hear him say anything."

"No," she said. "Use your eyes an feel inside you wat da udder is feelin. Dat way, dere is no need for words. Your ears are for 'earin all da udder tings 'round you."

I went to bed early that evening. I dreamed some pretty weird dreams off and on all night. At times when I woke up in the night, I saw the moonlight drift through the curtains by the table. I listened to the rip-roaring snore of the old man. Sometimes the old lady got up and gave him some water during the night. Then the room would be quiet for a long time, but eventually he would start again, very gently like a cat purr at first, then louder and louder. Funny how you get used to sleeping through a loud noise like that. I would miss them very much. I would also miss the meals too. I hadn't had two regular meals a day in a very long, long time. Since Mama left.

Chapter Seven

THE MORNING CAME AND I RUSHED about trying to get everything ready that they would need, at least for the week. At lunch we sat by the teepee fireplace where the old lady made a propped bannock in front of the ashes and the old man made tea-porridge. I roasted some sliced bacon with the skin still on it. That was a very delicious meal. No one said a word, but we said a lot. I was learning. I smiled at the old man as he dunked the bannock into his teacup. That was his favourite way of eating bannock.

That was the longest morning in my whole life! I thought about some of the things the old man had said, the bits and pieces that I could remember, and hoped that I would never forget.

Finally the time arrived. I hugged the old lady and the wiry old man one more time before I went out the door with a promise that I would come back to see them some day. The old lady's eyes filled like deep dark pools of water, but the old man's ancient face was like a stone wall, as if I was already gone. I ran down the path and stopped at the edge of the clearing. The cabin stood in the bright sunlight, a few wisps of smoke coming from the stovepipe. It looked so peaceful.

I hurried down the road and ran along the tracks and into the train station. The smell of paper, oil, and cigarette smoke welcomed me in the waiting room where I bought a train ticket to Collins. The ticket agent didn't even glance at me. I still had Charlie's twenty in my pocket, wrapped in a new chip bag. I had spent the rest on potato chips during

61

my stay with the old couple and that trip to Allan Water Bridge. I found that I still had an hour to spend so I stood around talking to everyone who was willing to listen to my chatter. I missed hearing voices.

My clothes were clean but getting pretty worn out I noticed. The old lady had made me sit in the old man's underwear again yesterday morning while she washed my clothes. Without saying a word, the old man kept teasing me about being forced to sit in an old man's underwear. So I jumped up and did a jig for him. His old longjohns flapped around my legs so fast that they probably aged another ten years! That gave the old man endless hours of amusement.

He also developed a taste for liquorice. I had been sucking on a string of liquorice one day when I noticed him looking at me, so I offered him one. He glanced at the old lady, she smiled at him, then he took it. He smelled it, then hesitantly tasted it. Then he stuck it in his mouth and went outside. Later on I came around the corner of the door, and he still had half of it hanging over his chin. Now he really looked funny with the black rope hanging out of his mouth. After that I would give him one every time I came back from the store.

Finally, with bells ringing, the train pulled into the station. There was an air of excitement as a lot of tourists and fishermen bustled off and on the train. I took a seat by the window and watched the houses go by as the train pulled out. I saw Allan Water Bridge and all the little hamlets that I had missed on my night travel to Savant Lake. It was much better travelling during the day. I looked for Charlie when the train went by at Jacobs, but there was no sign of anyone.

I saw the old fallen-down buildings at the place where I had spent that first miserable night. Fee Spur it was once called. It looked beautiful now in the sunlight. There was a big green field with trees in the middle. I just got a glimpse of blue from the lake as we rattled by. That night seemed so long ago.

Sometime in the afternoon, the conductor came and pulled out the slip above my window and said, "Collins next." My heart was beating with excitement as I took the canvas bag the old lady had given me, which held my grey blanket.

Several other people were also getting off. One boy with a very thick head of black hair kept smiling back at me as we stood waiting for the train to stop. His father had a dark green packsack on his back and one of those green caps on his head. I don't know where they came from, maybe Sioux Lookout.

Finally we slowed to a stop, and there were a lot of people standing there, watching the train. I jumped off behind the boy and his father. I searched all the faces there but did not see Mama among them. The train door banged shut, and the train took a deep breath before it roared to life again and disappeared around the bend.

The boy turned around and said, "Where are you going?"

I laughed. "I don't know. I'm looking for my mother."

"Oh, who's your mother?"

"Charlotte Lynx. She's with Joe."

He looked puzzled, then said, "There's no one called Charlotte Lynx here, and the one Joe who was here is in jail somewhere right now."

I must have looked as if I was ready to sit down and cry because he took one look at me then said, "Oh, come home with me. Dad won't mind. My name is Henry. My father's name is Jim."

He pulled my sleeve and we followed his father, who was already walking down the railway tracks. I watched the dark green packsack with its trailing leather strap flapping with each step the man took.

"My name is Danny," I mumbled absently as I took one more quick look around at the people who were now turning away to go back home.

There was a store at the end of the clearing but nothing else that I could see. I fell into step beside Henry. He was taller than me, I noticed.

"Come on, there's just me and Dad. We just came back from visiting my grandpa. You'll like it here. Where you from?" Henry asked. I noticed that his thick black eyebrows touched together when he frowned.

"I came from Nakina, but I've been looking for my mother." I really didn't feel like talking about this right now.

63

We walked in silence, matching our steps to the space on the railway ties. His father turned off a path to the right, very far from the settlement, I thought. Then, into the bush a bit, stood a new log cabin. Gee, it looked real nice! There was a treehouse on one of the huge poplar trees too! And a swing on one branch.

The ground had been cleared recently. There were stumps everywhere. Henry scampered up to the treehouse. I followed him up a ladder that was nailed on the tree. The treehouse had a roof, a real roof with tar paper! And a wooden floor! The sides were made of little saplings to resemble logs, with a window on one side. This was great!

Henry flopped down on a bench long enough to lie on. Obviously proud, he said, "Dad helped me build this after we got the cabin up. We used the leftover roofing paper for my roof. Great, eh?"

I smiled. "It sure is! You're lucky!"

He grinned and said, "We can even sleep in here. See, screens we can pull down on the window and on the door."

"Yeah!" I said as I deposited my bag on the floor. The treehouse was about four-by-six feet, big enough to fit two boys in.

I could see woodsmoke coming out of the stovepipe at the cabin. It looked nice. The cabin looked just like the one Mama, Dad, and I had in the bush.

I could feel tears filling my eyes. The disappointment hit me like a ton of bricks—Mama wasn't here either! Suddenly I felt so ashamed. I quickly tried to blink the tears from my eyes.

Then Henry's father yelled across the clearing. I could see him framed inside the door. "Hey, you lazybones, go get some water!" I glanced around at Henry and answered his hesitant smile.

"Come on, I'll show you where the pump is," he said. I followed him down the ladder and waited while he got the pail.

"Where does your grandpa live?" I asked as we went back down the path.

"Oh, he lives in Sioux Lookout. That's why we went there."

"I didn't go there yet. Maybe that's where Mama is."

He whirled around. "Look, you can go and search every-where you like, but she could be anywhere by now. Ontario is a big place, you know? Or is it Canada? Anyway, if she wanted you she would have found you. It would have been a heck of a lot easier for her to find you than for a kid looking around for a grownup!"

That hurt! I studied his back and felt like hitting him. Who did he think he was anyway?

As if reading my thoughts, he suddenly turned and faced me. "Look, when you're a kid, there's not much you can do except hurt a lot inside, but like Dad says, we have to learn from our mistakes."

I was beginning to wonder what this dad was like. I looked at him and asked, "But what mistake did I make? If it's my fault, what did I do?"

In total exasperation, he threw the pail down and kicked it, yelling, "Gosh darn sakes! How the heck should I know? I only know that it feels good when Dad says it!"

I studied him a moment. What kind of kid was this?

We watched the pail roll back down the hill and into the ditch. I gave the railroad track a big kick, which wasn't a very good idea. I gasped and hopped around as my toe throbbed. Then a bubble of laughter hit me. I glanced at Henry, my foot, then down at the innocent dented water pail in the ditch, then we both started laughing. I didn't know what was so funny, but it was a lot better than crying.

Feeling quite ridiculous, I ran back down the hill and retrieved the water pail. Henry was standing there grinning at me when I stopped beside him again. "I wish I had a brother like you," he said as he took the water pail. We walked in silence until we passed the section house.

"Who lives there?" I asked.

"Terry, the section foreman," he said.

Next we passed by the shim shed. You can always tell what is in there because of all those flat boards with the neat round holes laying around outside.

We continued down the tracks toward the station, which looked more like a storage shed.

"Dad says there used to be a big white station here at one time, two storeys high!" Henry threw his voice at me as if I was a mile away. There were kids playing around in front of the store. "There also used to be a pool hall where those long windows are. And, at one time long ago, they used to push the pool tables aside to show movies in there too," said my tour guide.

"Why did they stop?" I asked.

"How the heck should I know? Would be nice to have a movie place now, though. They just show them once in a while at the school. That's that long green contraption there. Oh, by the way, enjoy the peace and quiet. The generator broke down. They're still fixing it, otherwise all you hear is putt-putt-putt all the time."

I looked at the small grey cement building there across from the station. Then I noticed the pump on top of a mound of sand. It was the same kind that Mrs. Old Indian used. That's what my guide was heading for.

"And this here," he said as he ran up the smooth worn hill, "is the best water you can find around here. Some people from the government were around here this spring telling people they have to boil the water if they get it from the lake. Can you believe it?"

With exaggerated movements, he expertly slipped the pail handle on the handle hook, then he set to revving his elbows with the long arm of the pump. After three spurts of water, he ran around and dumped the water out, just as I was coming up the hill. Of course the water came into collision with my shoes.

"Oh, sorry. It is best to get the pipe water out first, you understand." He grinned. "Okay, here, want to pump the water?" he asked, standing aside.

I got my elbows in motion and soon the water was pouring out so fast it sloshed over the pail long before it was full. Now, who was going to carry the water? Henry made a big show at taking the pail, and I followed him down the mud-slicked mound. I smiled as I plodded along behind him. He was acting like I had never seen a water pail before. Then he veered off the tracks and followed a trail dipping down to an old pump that obviously was no longer in use. The trail ran parallel to the railroad tracks. As we walked across the sand-pit, my guide decided to deposit the pail beside an old stump.

It was my turn to pick up the water pail I guess, since he had gone over the sand hill already. I followed him over a more even path to the cabin. When I entered, I saw that it was nice, warm, and clean. There were two double beds in the opposite back corners, and the table and stove were at the front end of the cabin. I put the pail on the shelf beside the stove.

"Where did you get the fish?" came Henry's question, as his father cut up a lake trout at the table.

His father smiled. "Well, Billy saw us getting off the train and he had caught more fish than he could eat, so he brought one over."

Henry grinned at me. "That's one thing about not having refrigerators, you have to give away what you can't eat before it gets rotten." I couldn't wait to get a taste of that fish.

I watched the slim man quickly slice through the flesh of the fish and throw the guts into the garbage pail. Nails had been hammered into a row on one of the logs behind the door, and his green cap was now hanging beside the row of pots and pans. He grabbed a frying pan and set it on the stove. Jim had a rather narrow face but it was the gentle, light brown eyes that got my attention. One eye now winked at me. I didn't realize I had been staring. I suddenly got busy and walked outside and looked around until I located the woodpile beside the cabin. Gathering an armful of wood I hurried back around the corner.

As I neared the door, I heard Henry saying in Ojibwa, "He has no place to go. It would be nice to have Danny to play with."

The reply came, "All right. But just remember he won't be here for a long time. He belongs somewhere and he'll have to return sometime, and he'll most likely be leaving again pretty soon. You can't hold him here. Someone is probably out looking for him right now."

I stomped on the step before I came inside to make sure they heard me coming, then deposited the wood beside the door.

Jim smiled as he filled a pot with water. "Do you speak

Ojibwa?" I nodded. Then, in Ojibwa, he asked, "Are you hungry, Danny? With the three of us, we should be able to eat the whole fish." I smiled and nodded. I was pretty sure I could eat the whole thing myself!

Henry was sorting through a big paper box full of clothes beside the bed. "Hey, Danny. Here, I am a little bigger than you are so you can wear all the clothes that don't fit me any more," he said as he pushed the box at me.

I couldn't believe it, there were many pairs of jeans, shirts, sweaters, socks, shorts, and even three pairs of runningshoes that looked like they had hardly been worn! I took the box and said, "Thanks! I've been wearing the same clothes for almost a month now." I decided to put on a change of clothes first thing tomorrow morning.

"You can sleep with me on my bed. There's lots of room," continued Henry.

The smell of fish sizzling on the stove made me very hungry. I sat down at the table and decided that this place was very nice. I watched the oil lamp sputter on the table and breathed in the smell of fried fish and coffee brewing on the stove. I could hear a gentle wind stirring the leaves outside the window. I felt my shoulders relax and I smiled at a joke Henry told his father.

"What has a green cap and smells like fish?"

"Ol' Jim?" said Jim.

"Heck no!" laughed Henry. "It's a jar of pickled fish!"

"I thought it was Jim, here," I said.

They looked at each other and burst out laughing. I sagged against the wall. For a moment I thought I had opened my big mouth again when I shouldn't have. But they were laughing with me. Suddenly I realized how much I missed kidding around with other people.

Soon the fried fish was on the table and we all sat down to eat. I sat, waiting, my hands clasped obediently before me, when I sensed the silence again. They were sitting there looking at me.

Then Jim said, "Are you waiting for Grace? Sorry, but she doesn't live here." Henry laughed out loud and Jim grinned at me and said, "Okay, I will say one. Thank you Billy for the fish, and I will remember to give you one also the next time I catch one too many. Amen!"

I almost laughed out loud, and when I lifted my head I saw that Jim and Henry were silently shaking with laughter as they looked at me. I giggled and dug in as they passed the potatoes and canned corn around the table.

After supper, Jim washed the dishes in a dishpan full of very soapy water, and Henry and I wiped them dry. They were stoneware dishes, rather thick with little blue flowers around the edges. The mugs and cups were all different types and colours though. I remembered the four tin plates and cups that the old couple used. I wonder what they are doing tonight. The old man would definitely be sitting beside the door and the old lady was probably making bannock on her treasured stove. Later, Mr. Old Indian probably would go in and fill his face with bannock dipped in bacon grease and jam.

In six minutes flat, the dishes were done. Then we sat down for a game of cards. I had not played cards in a long time. The only game I knew was rummy. Tom had taught me how to play that during the Christmas holidays last winter. But Henry swore he would teach me every game he knew. So we started out with cribbage on a big 29 board that looked like a porcupine with matchsticks. I claimed two black heads, Henry got the red heads, and Jim got the blue heads.

Just as I was struggling to get beyond the skunk line, the door opened and a young man walked in. He was kind of skinny all over, but he had the friendliest face I had ever seen. He turned out to be Billy, the one who gave us the nice supper of fish. He wore a red-and-black checkered work shirt and jeans. I immediately took a liking to Billy. He pulled up a chair, pretending not to be interested, but soon began to inch along beside me, and in no time I caught on that one blink meant good move and rapid blinks meant a disaster. Ha, ha! I even heard my voice squeal when I passed the other pegs and got to the last hole first! I won! I had never won anything in all my life. It felt good.

We had another game, Billy included. So we played double.

Now we could put our heads together, but in the end we lost to Jim and Henry.

Suddenly Billy stood up. "The train will be here soon. I'm going to see who gets off tonight. Old Mary is going on the train to the hospital again. I don't see why they just don't operate on her and get it over with," he said as he moved to the door.

Henry jumped up. "Wait, we'll come with you. Coming Dad?"

But Jim shook his head saying, "No, I'm kind of tired. You go ahead, but come home right after. The bears are probably around again tonight."

My ears picked up. Bears? I had never seen a bear. Suddenly I wasn't so enthusiastic.

Henry noticed my reaction and laughed. "Come on! Bears can hear you coming, and they run faster away from you than you can run away from them!"

Billy poked his head back in the door and added, "You hope!"

I heard Jim's laughter as we rushed out behind Billy.

It was very dark now. I had got so used to not knowing what time it was at the old couple's place that I had no idea what time it was now. We were just crossing the railroad tracks when a light shone around the curve. The train! We ran the rest of the way from the shim shed to the station. The engine roared by us as we came to a stop beside the people already lined up to watch. With a loud hissing and screeching wheels, the train came to a stop right in front of the station building.

A young girl and a woman got off the train. The girl glanced at me with curiosity as she passed by. Then an old woman, moving very slowly, boarded the train. The conductor pulled up the little stool and up he went, the door clanged shut, and that was it. The train pulled away and soon disappeared into the darkness. Everyone moved away and dispersed into the night. Billy yelled "Goodnight!" as he walked away and everyone there answered in a chorus, "Goodnight Billy!" Henry and I broke out laughing and made our way back down the railroad tracks.

"Don't you have a flashlight, Henry?" I asked.

"Sure we do, but with the sudden rush for the train and the talk of bears, I forgot it!" he said.

We walked rather hastily in the intense darkness, hanging on to each other's sleeves, when finally, the path took a dip into the bush. After a few minutes, I saw the light from Jim's window. We slowed down and tried to look casual as we walked into the cabin. Jim was on his bed looking at the ceiling. Henry babbled on about all the things we had seen, half of which I didn't remember at all.

Finally we were all in bed. The smell of woodsmoke and lamp wick hung in the room. Only the occasional crackle of the fire broke the stillness. There were no loud snores filling the room tonight. I listened to the soft breathing until I finally drifted off to sleep.

Chapter Eight

THE NEXT MORNING, JIM DECIDED TO take us fishing. I was so excited I ate my porridge and bannock too fast and had to find other things to do while I waited for Henry. They were talking about the meaning of a fish's life. I decided to get some water.

I had on my new used clothes, which fit perfectly. I even had a pair of runningshoes on that didn't feel like they were intent on shrinking my toes. I chucked out my old runners and decided to throw out my old jeans as well. They were much too short and the brown shirt now had holes in the elbows.

There was no one around as I walked down the railroad tracks. I heard dogs barking down the path somewhere. An old black-and-white dog was curled up fast asleep beside the shim shed. I plodded down the tracks, trying not to think about Mama or Dad. In the back of my mind I was always wondering where to go next. I just put my stuff together again this morning. My blanket was rolled up and back in the sack, just in case I had to run away in a hurry . . . if Dad shows up, I have to be ready to run. Maybe it would be best to just concentrate on where I am and the people I am staying with right now. I like Henry and Jim. Maybe if I make myself useful and stay out of trouble, they will let me stay. I wonder where the girl who got off the train last night lives.

I was tempted to leave the pail there and go see the lake. I could see the water glimmering in the morning sun. Better not. I'll see it soon enough. Henry probably figured out by now why fish are meant to live. I didn't see what the big deal was. What's alive is alive. Why try to figure out why?

As I stood there pumping out the stale pipe water first, I saw men in yellow hard-hats sitting around on the little putt-putt motor car parked on a platform, off the railroad tracks. I waved and some waved back. The little motor car was now a familiar sight to me. I think Henry said Billy was a trapper. He didn't work for the CN anyway. But Jim, on the other hand, was a sectionman and was on holidays until the end of the month. I wonder if he knows Charlie. The section-men all seemed to know each other. Would Tom's father know these guys? Maybe not. Dad could ask Tom's father to check if anyone had seen me . . . That meant I should avoid all sectionmen. That's impossible! Jim said everyone in these small places works on the CN. There are no other jobs.

I took a big breath of fresh air as I slowly made my way back down the railroad tracks. When I entered the cabin, there was a box on the table with three fishing rods, a tackle box, and a teapot. Henry was still dashing around pulling towels out of a box from under the bed, and Jim was already going out the door. I put the water pail down and grabbed the teapot and tackle box. Jim was heading down the path with the food box and fishing rods. Henry had towels and a blanket, and he grabbed a jar of jam as he pulled the door shut behind him. I laughed as we hurried to catch up with Jim. We could see the motor car putt-putting down the tracks, going the other way. Jim was already on his way down a hill through some tall pine trees. I noticed that Henry's chubby chin doubled up when he glanced back. I giggled and fell into step beside him. We must look funny. One chubby kid and one skinny one. Jim had said something about putting meat on the stringbean last night when he offered me another helping of fried fish and potatoes.

We ran to catch up with Jim. Gee, he walks fast! He took a detour to a cabin by the lake where Billy emerged, hair still tousled from sleep. We left Jim and Billy to talk as we made our way down to the lake where the canoe was turned over by Billy's landing. We flipped the canvas canoe right side up. I remembered Charlie's big boat. This definitely did not come with a motor. It was a paddling canoe. The canoe Mama, Dad, and I had was a square-back canoe with a three-horse-power motor on it. That was what we used to get to the road to town.

We gently lowered the canoe into the water under Henry's direction and loaded the stuff in it. Finally Jim came down to the lake. Then, for the first time, I took a good look at the lake. It was very large with many islands in the middle. The water was very calm right now. I felt like crying for some reason. Maybe because I was almost happy. I saw a canoe behind the small island on the left.

Henry yelled and waved his arms, "Charlotte! Yeooh!" Suddenly Jim whistled a sharp high-pitched note. Henry was immediately quiet but smiling as he brought his shoulders up. "Sorry," he said under his breath.

Jim pretended to scoff and look down his nose at Henry and said, "What a lady can do! Turn an otherwise level-headed man into a snivelling snot in one second!" We laughed as we cautiously stepped into the canoe. Henry up front, me in the middle, and Jim at the back, the last to get in.

I glanced at the canoe again. There were two people in it. Henry spoke softly this time, "Charlotte was the one laughing when they got off the train last night." He continued, "She lives in the second cabin by the lake, right across from the island. She is in the same grade as I am. What grade are you going to be in this winter?" he asked.

I thought a moment. "Six."

Our canoe suddenly rocked to one side as Henry whirled around, saying, "Hey, we'll be in the same grade! I go over to Charlotte's sometimes to help her with math."

Then Jim's voice came in, "To help *you* with math."

I smiled and Henry giggled as the canoe moved away from the shore. We had only two paddles, one for Henry and one for Jim. I leaned back on the crossbar and watched the shoreline drift by.

"I'll paddle back. It will be your turn to sit in the middle," I offered to Henry.

Jim laughed. "Henry, paddle? He just sort of lets the paddle float by the canoe, lifts it up, and watches it float by again." Henry smiled.

We came to a bay with bobbing yellow and white flowers and lily pads. Some crows were having an argument up on the hill somewhere. Pine trees stood tall and gawky-looking, their needles missing from halfway down. They seemed to be standing guard over the pond. Or maybe they were trying to hold back the swamp. Anyway, they must be taking a beating, they didn't look too healthy. The canoe drifted past the mouth of the bay and continued along the shoreline. There were long sloping rocks that looked like they had gushed out from between the trees. Seagulls were having a convention of some sort on the island ahead of us in the middle of the lake. I breathed in the fresh air. I had never experienced anything like this before, not that I could remember anyway. I guess I was too small to remember the rides with Mama and Dad— what they felt like, or what the places looked like.

I took everything in. I wanted to remember this. No one spoke and I watched Henry's stubby fingers curl tightly around the paddle with each swing. After about half an hour, we rounded a point of land and came upon high rock cliffs standing straight out of the water! They looked very . . . mighty. Henry steered to the left and we drifted along below the cliffs. The fishing rods came out and the hooks were attached. I sat and let my line down into the water. I didn't dare throw it, remembering that episode with Charlie when my hook landed in the boat. Henry's line sang out as the hook sailed into an arc overhead and entered the water with a "chomp." It was very quiet. I was content to let my line drag the bottom.

Jim spoke behind me, "Reel in the line a bit, Danny." I turned the little handle until Jim said, "Okay. That will do it."

The sun was now well up in the sky and the temperature continued to rise. A fly came zooming around our heads several times before it took off in another direction. There was a big sloping rock across from us on the other shore with chunks of rocks scattered about by the shoreline. It looked like a good place for a swim.

Henry must have been thinking the same thing for now he turned and said, "Good swimming spot, deep enough. We usually make a fire there to cook lunch. I go swimming after tea and Jim comes and fishes here."

I moved my numbing butt and crossed my legs in front of me. I bet Mr. and Mrs. Old Indian would just love it here. Too bad they did not live by the shore. The lake seemed so alive, reflecting the sun, shifting, shimmering, always moving. I knew it could also become very dangerous when it grew large waves to hit you with.

I reeled in my hook as Jim was doing. The canoe thumped as he picked up his paddle and steered toward the sloping rock. Henry held his paddle out as if he was going to poke a hole in the rock. The canoe stopped and he got out carefully. He swung the canoe to the side by the shore and held it while I straightened out my aching legs. I looked like an old man as I stood up and stepped out of the canoe. Henry was still giggling as we unloaded the paper box and the teapot. We pushed Jim back out into the water. He paddled away back to the spot.

Henry ran around gathering wood and I followed, copying what he did. When he had neatly stacked a pile of twigs, he pulled matches out of the box and soon smoke billowed and flames flickered out like hungry red tongues between the sticks. I took the teapot and headed down to the lake. Jim and the green canoe sat out there below the rock cliffs in perfectly calm water. The smell of the woodsmoke hit my nose and I fanned it away.

Henry was opening two large cans of beef stew when I arrived. I set the pot on the rock beside him. He pointed to the fire. "Put it on to boil." I took the pot and put it down on top of the fire. The sticks shifted suddenly and the teapot fell over and there was a big billow of steam, smoke, and ash! I heard Henry yell, "Why the heck did you do that for?" Henry grabbed the pot, now covered with ashes, and set it to the side and began poking around at the drenched ashes. He glanced at me, then smiled and started to laugh. He was still laughing as he said, "Come on, no big deal! Get some more water and I'll just make another fire, that's all!" He handed me the pot and I walked to the lake.

I could hear Henry crashing around in the bush, and I heard Jim chuckling. He was watching us from the canoe. He waved an arm and I waved back. I rinsed out the pot and filled it up again. Henry had a new fire going in a different spot by the time I put the pot down beside him. "Here, try again. You have to kind of shift it around until it's sitting on solid wood. See these two big ones? Try to put the pot down on top of them so they'll hold up each side of the pot," he said.

I picked up the pot again and set it down gingerly, making sure it would not tip over, before I released the handle. There! I smiled. That made me feel better.

Henry threw a pair of shorts at me—swimming trunks! We shed our clothes on the rocks and pulled on the trunks, and I raced Henry into the water. After thrashing around a bit, Henry got out to throw some more wood into the fire and some tea into the teapot. The canned stew stood on ashes beside the fire. A little later, Jim paddled back to the campfire and rummaged around in the box while Henry and I were still diving for shiny white open shells in the muddy bottom. The water felt great, but I was also very hungry. I got out and sat beside Jim in the shade of a huge pine tree. He had a cup of tea in his hands.

"What day is it?" I asked.

"Today is Saturday, and I go to work on Monday, July 30th," he said.

"I have a friend in Nakina," I said. "His name is Tom. He always goes to his grandma's summer camp. This must be what it is like because he talks about canoes and birds' nests . . . "

Henry's head shot out of the water, blowing water like an elephant before he went back down again.

Jim said softly, "We lived by the water before we built the cabin on the other side of the tracks. I think Henry misses the water the most. Though it's no big thing to just walk down to the lake." It sounded like he was thinking out loud.

I got up and put a few twigs into the fire. The opened cans of beef stew were steaming and the teapot sat beside the fire. I picked up the other two cups and filled them with tea. They should cool off by the time Henry comes out of the water.

Then he climbed up the rock, hair slicked back and water still dripping down his back.

We had a nice lunch of bannock, beef stew, and tea. Afterwards, Henry and I lay around on the blanket in the shade and Jim took the canoe back out to the rock cliff.

"Jim said you used to live by the lake. Where was that?"

Henry closed his eyes. "It was on the left-hand side of the bay that we passed, after the rock cliff beside Billy's."

Yes, I remember that place. But there was no sign of a cabin there. At least I hadn't seen anything. "Is the cabin still there?" I asked.

Henry opened his eyes and looked at me. "No."

Oh. I lay on my back looking at the clouds. There was one that looked like a big bumpy, ugly face with sagging eyes, drooping mouth and one long pointy, dragging ear.

Henry asked, "How long are you going to stay with us?"

I shrugged. "I don't know. I have to find Mama."

There was silence for some time before Henry asked, "Where's your dad?"

I paused for a moment. Shall I tell him? Well, he already knows where I come from. "Nakina," I answered.

Suddenly Jim gave a loud hoot, and we could see a big fish splashing water as he hauled it in.

Henry yelled, "What is it?"

Jim called back, "Trout!" Oh, boy! I remembered how good that tasted last night.

We started joking and fooling around again and Henry did a dance on the rock before we decided to go for another swim. The sun was almost over the treetops when we heard Jim give another hoot. Another trout! That seemed to satisfy Jim. He paddled back and we poured the leftover tea on the campfire ashes and loaded the paper box into the canoe. When we were getting in the canoe, Henry insisted he was going to paddle again. Only this time, I figured out that he just liked being out in front.

I settled down very comfortably in the canoe this time. I took the rolled-up blanket and spread it where I was going to sit. Now I was ready to ride back like a king! Jim giggled but didn't say anything. It was absolutely quiet out on the open water. I couldn't believe it. We could even hear the dogs barking from the community. There was also the endless squawking from the seagulls, of course.

When we arrived, Billy was there to pull in our canoe. He was very happy to see the fish, and they planned the menu immediately, even before we were all out of the canoe. Billy had homemade beans bubbling on the stove, and he would bring them when he figured Jim had had time to clean the fish. Then he would come and eat with us. Henry was already up the path with the teapot and fishing rods. I followed behind with the light paper box. The only things in there were milk, sugar, the package of tea, three cups, and the two empty beef stew cans.

I looked at Billy's cabin sitting sideways beside the shore. It was a small cabin with a window on each side. It stood about three blocks from the railroad tracks. I smiled, remembering when I had told Henry that it was quite a ways to go for water, a good three blocks. He had looked at me, rather puzzled, and said, "Blocks? What kind of blocks?"

I hurried to catch up to Henry, and he slowed down when he heard me coming. "What can we have for dessert?" he asked. How should I know? Then he said, "I know! We'll make a chocolate cake!"

I thought about that a moment. There was no oven on the woodstove they have.

"How are you going to bake it?" I asked.

Henry laughed. "Dad made one on the stove once. We still have a package of cake mix somewhere. Let's try it!"

We hurried along the path and broke into a run toward the railroad tracks. The cabin stood dark and quiet in the middle of the clearing. We ran inside and threw the things down. Henry got the fire going in the stove. I had already got the water, so I sat down at the table and Henry plopped down on the bench beside me, holding a box of chocolate cake mix. The cake picture looked delicious, but I was rather dubious as to how he was going to cook it. I went outside to bring in some more wood. When I came in, Henry had the manual egg-beater going pretty fast at first, then it sort of laboured slowly. The door opened and Jim came in with the cleaned fish. He picked up a big metal washbowl and deposited the fish in it. Jim stopped and looked at Henry's hair just flying as he cranked away like crazy on the egg-beater again. The mixture looked like thick black mud.

Henry glanced up at me and wiped the sweat off his lip with his sleeve and said, "Here, grease this just enough to make flour stick to it when you sprinkle it." I scooped some lard with my finger and began greasing up the square pan.

A big puff of smoke came up when Jim flipped the lid open, and tongues of fire lapped at the opening before Jim flopped the frying pan over it. A large wallop of lard hit the pan and immediately began to spread. I had finished greasing and flouring the pan, and now Henry poured his mudlike mixture into it. It was almost overflowing when he stopped. Jim looked at the pan and shook his head as Henry gingerly tiptoed across to the stove, trying not to spill the mixture. The cake went on the left side of the stove, the pot to boil potatoes went on the right, and the trout was now sizzling in the frying pan.

I surveyed the mess we had made on the table and set to work quickly, trying to clear it before Billy showed up with his pot of beans. The heat had now reached the cake and it began to move.

Jim turned from the stove, a smile tugging at the corners of his mouth. "Now listen boys, you look after your cake."

Henry and I examined the cake. It was higher on the heated side so we turned the pan around to heat up the other side. Jim began cutting up the potatoes into the pot. When Billy came through the door, the smell of baked brown beans reached me and my mouth watered.

Suddenly Henry started to dance by the stove, yelling, "Danny, a rag, a pan, a plate, something! It's overflowing!"

I grabbed a cup and rushed over to the stove in time to see the brown stuff swell and overflow in long rivers of goo down the side of the stove and lay in gobs on the floor.

Henry cried, "Bring a spoon!"

I rushed and grabbed a spoon, and Henry began scooping

the overflowing mixture into the cup. The cup was almost full when the cake finally stopped rising. It was very hot by the stove and Henry's face was shining with sweat. We turned from the stove to see Jim and Billy, shaking with laughter.

Finally the fish and potatoes were cooked, and Jim put more wood into the stove and closed the lid. The pan of cake went on top, and he dropped the metal dishpan over it. The coffee pot was set to brew beside the stovepipe. We had a big feast in the lamplight. I never laughed so hard, at the jokes Billy was telling and at the way Jim described our little incident over the stove. My tummy was full and this was just so nice.

After the meal, we decided to play cards again. By this time, the smell of chocolate cake was filling the room. Henry decided to turn it over, just to make sure it was cooking evenly. He covered it over with the pan again. My guts were rumbling and filling up rather quickly. The beans! I think I ate too many beans.

After about an hour, Henry stuck a sliver of wood into the cake and it came out clean. In triumph, he put what looked like some kind of brown bannock on the table. Now we had to put the icing on. Billy and the cards moved well away from our corner of the table. Each gob of icing on the cake began to melt and run down onto the plate. I guess we were supposed to wait until the cake was cold! We kept scooping the melted icing back on the cake.

We played one more game, but we couldn't wait any longer. Henry tried to lift the cake, but the icing had glued it to the plate. He scraped the icing off the plate and tried to paste it on the top and sides, but it kept falling out in clumps like a mudslide. Jim and Billy were having a great time laughing at us. Now, the taste test. It looked terrible, but it was good! There wasn't a crumb left when we were finished. Billy looked like he had huge holes in his teeth where pieces of chocolate cake lay plastered against them. He looked so funny!

The next morning, Billy showed up with a packsack on his back, which he dropped by the door. "Come on, hurry up.

Little Foot killed a moose down the tracks and everyone is going to get some meat. Gee, Shims has made two trips already!"

They laughed and I wondered who they were talking about. We had finished our breakfast and the dishes were done. We were just about to get some water, now we grabbed our jackets instead. Jim was packing canvas bags, bread bags, a thermos, a knife, a file, and a small axe into a packsack, which he threw on his back. In five minutes, we were going out the door with Billy.

It was very windy as we headed east down the railroad tracks. The view was beautiful. The bay was glistening with white-capped waves in the morning sunlight. The wind slapped and puffed out our jackets, so we took them off. It felt so good. We matched our steps together as we walked behind Billy and Jim. We walked past the rock cliff and then beyond that, they suddenly veered into the bush. Henry and I left the tracks and also entered the bush. We could hardly see the path, the bush was so thick. We caught up with an old man with a packsack on his back and an axe in his hand. He stood aside to let us by. I smiled and ducked my head to get around branches. As I stepped around him, I noticed his red-soled rubber boots cut off at the ankles.

"Who's that?" I asked when we were well out of hearing distance.

"Oh, people just call him Shomis. He's one of the old guys here. I think we only have four old guys and two old ladies. I mean, great grandmas, and great grandpas kind of old people," said Henry.

Billy and Jim were walking very fast, Henry was already puffing, and I was breathing hard when Henry suddenly slowed down, then stopped. He stood looking around, so I asked, "What's the matter?"

Henry turned around. "There's something weird here. See? I don't see any tracks. The tall grass over the path should be bent if anybody had passed by." Suddenly he whirled around again, saying over his shoulder, "Come on!"

He was chuckling as I ran to catch up with him. We went

quite a ways until we came across a log beside the path. Henry stopped and sat down, a grin on his face. I sat beside him. I was tuckered out too but we shouldn't be sitting here, getting left behind! I was just about to say something when I heard low voices coming down the path where we came from. Then Billy and Jim emerged.

Henry stretched and said, "Boy, you guys are slow. We had to sit and wait for you to catch up!" They chuckled and walked by us again, and we fell back into line behind them.

I nudged Henry. "Where had they gone?"

Henry giggled and said, "They hid on us. We walked by, and they probably wanted to see if we would know they were no longer in front of us. But we outsmarted them, didn't we?"

We heard laughter and men's voices as we came around a curve on the path. People were already there. There was a swamp ahead, and there looked to be a pond or a small lake somewhere to the right. But Billy and Jim turned to the left, and we walked through a swamp of rotten logs and moss until we came across the group. There were nine men and four women working in a circle. A huge skinless thing lay in the centre. It showed pink-and-white stretched layers and blotches. Then I noticed a longhaired furry thing piled on top of some branches. The smell of blood was everywhere. I heard a man's voice saying, "What's the matter with him? A city Indian?"

Suddenly I became aware that they were laughing and looking at me. I smiled and followed Henry to the other side. I nudged him. "How did they get here if we were the first ones to come down the path?"

Jim answered from behind me, "There's a path coming in from the other side of the lake. That one runs from the graveyard road. Then there's another way you can get here, that's through the portage by the lake. So everyone got here by whichever was the shortest distance from their homes. If it had not been so windy, we could have paddled to the portage and walked across the tracks to here."

Billy came up. "Okay, boys. Spread out the bags and put the meat in as we throw it to you."

They joined the group who were now hacking away at the

moose carcass. We could hear the axes crunching and grating against flesh and bone. The women set up a giggling fit at whatever the men were saying. They worked, laughing and talking in the musty swamp.

I got up to find the lake. Henry yelled, "Take Billy's pail if you're going to the lake!"

I saw the old man. He was busy shoving a long bloody chunk of meat into his sack. His cut-off rubber boots were covered with mud and smeared with blood right up to his grey woolen work socks. I smiled again as I stepped around him.

I wandered down into some bush and swamp, skipping over puddles, and jumping to clumps of dry grass. Finally I came out of the bushes. There were boulders dotting this side of the lake, but they were too far to reach. I found a spot where I could fill the little pail. The water looked clear enough. I lugged it back out, laying branches and rotten logs over some spots since I couldn't jump around with a pail of water in my hand. I made it back to the group with a full pot of water. I gave it to the first lady I saw.

"Oh, water! He got us some water. We were getting very thirsty. Best not to build a fire, so none of us brought water. Jim already passed his thermos around." She paused as she took a couple of good swallows before she handed the pail to the next person.

I felt very proud as I watched the pail being passed from one person to the next. Each person glanced at me when he or she took the pail. Suddenly a chunk of meat landed at my feet.

Billy smiled and said, "Go put it in the bag and come get some more."

I hesitated, then closed my eyes and grabbed the gooey mess. It wasn't too bad! It felt like whole uncooked chicken from the store. I flung the meat at Henry when I got to the clearing where the bags were. He turned in time and caught it. He seemed surprised when the chunk of meat landed in his hands. I laughed and ran back to the butchering. I picked up several more pieces and flung them at Henry again. I picked up a sheet of flat things—ribs! I held it out away from me as I walked to the clearing.

Henry's lowered voice came, like the storyteller from a scary movie, "In the village of the dead, out came the murdering zombie of the Collins swamp, holding out the poor bones of . . . Danny Lynx!"

I burst out laughing and tried to swing the meat out to throw at him, when suddenly, Henry's face changed. He put his head down and I turned to see Shomis. He stood there glaring at us, then turned around. I slowly put the meat down and asked Henry, "What's with him?"

Henry shook his head. "I should not have done that. We should not be playing with the meat." Oh.

When we had packed all the bags, Jim and Billy stopped to talk to a skinny, little wiry man who cracked a toothless smile at us as we stood there waiting.

"Who was that?" I asked Henry as we began to move away.

"Oh, that's Little Foot, Billy's father," he said over his shoulder.

Billy's father! Why didn't they say so? When I turned to get another look at him my foot hit a root and I crashed into the bushes. Someone from the group had seen me, and Henry's laughter joined everyone else's. I got up rather embarrassed and began walking, a bit too fast.

When we got to the railroad tracks, it felt like the meat flopping against my back was pushing the shoulder strap right through my arms. It was so heavy. Henry was squirming with his load too. So we sat down and pretended to adjust our straps. Then we scrambled to catch up. The wind had died down a bit, but we could still hear the waves crashing along the shoreline.

I watched Billy and Jim in front of us. They looked like brothers. I wonder how long Henry and Jim have been alone. I wonder what happened to Henry's mother. I glanced at Henry beside me. He was watching me. We smiled.

Then I asked, "Henry, what happened to your mother?" He slowed down a bit and concentrated on his footsteps. I quickly said, "Never mind."

But Henry didn't seem to hear me. His eyebrows knitted together, then he said, "Mother froze to death two

Christmases ago. We used to live by that place I told you about by the lake. There was a party one night and she left to go look for Dad. He came home the next morning, shaking me awake, and he wanted to know where she was . . . They found her on the ice . . . She must have been on her way home. Something happened to Dad. He burned our house down and then he decided to stop drinking. We stayed with my grandpa in Sioux Lookout until Dad built this cabin the next spring."

"Sorry," I said.

Henry glanced at me, then asked, "Why did your mother leave?"

I kicked a rock off the rail. I guess it won't hurt to tell him. "We used to live in the bush at our trapper's shack when I was small. Then we moved to our reserve just outside of town. I knew Mama was going to have a baby, but then she found out that Dad had a girlfriend in town, and she was going to have a baby, I mean the girlfriend. Mama got mad, they had a big fight, then Mama was taken to the hospital. When she came home, there was no baby. They had another big fight about who was going to keep me. I guess Dad won because Mama just packed her stuff and left. Then Dad moved us to town, and he moved that woman and her baby into the house with us. She hates me and beats me up all the time. So I ran away to find Mama . . . and I still can't find her!"

We walked in silence for a few steps, then Henry said, "At least your mother is still alive somewhere."

I nodded my head, but it didn't make me feel any better.

We walked in silence a bit more, then we saw Billy hit his foot on the rail and just about trip. We burst out laughing at how he looked when he suddenly lurched forward—his arms shooting out, his knees buckling before his feet could catch up with his upper body! They stopped, and we all laughed together before we continued toward the station.

"Where does Little Foot live?" I asked.

Henry pointed with his thumb over his shoulder. "Over there, third cabin along the shoreline. We'll go see him sometime. He lives there by himself."

He didn't look anything like Billy. I never would have

figured out that he was Billy's father. "Why is he called Little Foot?" I asked.

Henry glanced at me, smiling. "Maybe he has one foot smaller than the other. I don't know! I never stopped to measure his feet!"

Billy and Jim stopped to wait for us by the station. They had decided to roast some moose meat for supper by the open firepit at Billy's place. It was too windy and bushy to have a fire outside at our place tonight.

We turned off from the station, past the store, and down the sandy road to Billy's. Jim reached out and pulled a twig out of my hair and said, "You pretending to be Caesar, with twigs in your hair?" I laughed as he ruffled my hair. Everything was all right.

Chapter Nine

Several weeks later, late in the evening, there was a particularly mean poker game going on at a house near the lake. Billy did not want to leave the game, so he asked me to run to his cabin and throw some logs into the stove to keep the fire going.

It was raining, pouring in buckets outside as I dashed across the clearing and down the path to the cabin. I entered and saw only a few embers in the woodstove. I threw a couple of whole logs in and nothing happened. Then I noticed a coal oil can beside the stove, so I poured some inside on top of the log because that's what Henry and I always did to get the fire going. But the oil ran down the underside of the can and spilled on the floor. So I grabbed a rag and wiped the oil off the floor and the oil can and dropped the rag on the metal sheet in front of the stove. Suddenly the billowing smoke burst into a "whooff!" and flames exploded in the stove. I watched the fire roar for a moment as the lid lifted several times in a rapid "rat-tat-tat" emitting puffs of oil-laced smoke. When the fire settled down to a regular roar, I shut the door and raced back across the clearing again.

About fifteen minutes later, I was just about falling asleep waiting for Henry and his father to go home when a neighbour stuck his head in the door and yelled, "Your cabin is on fire!" I didn't know who he was talking to, but the whole place emptied of the card players in no time. I felt numb, and my heart was pumping a lot of pressure up my throat. It was a familiar feeling by now. I felt exactly like I did that time when

I was cornered in that room back home. Suddenly I shot out of there so fast I didn't even know where I was going. I raced up the hill across the railroad tracks, straight for Henry's cabin. I caused the fire! I started the fire in the stove! Now all of Billy's things will be burnt up and he won't have a home any more, and it's all my fault! The accusations pounded in my brain with each footstep as I ran even faster. They will send me back to my father! They won't want me around any more. I flung open the cabin door and stood there turning in circles for a minute. Henry and Jim won't be back for a while yet. They were probably still with the rest of the people watching Billy's cabin burn down.

I have to run away before they call the police, before they turn me in! I have to get away before my father comes for me! I grabbed my sack and stuffed my blanket and my jacket inside and took off as fast as I could down the path again and up along the tracks. I ran and ran, heading east along the railroad tracks. I ran the first mile then became too exhausted. It was very dark, but the rain had stopped.

Where am I going to sleep? I continued walking. The clouds parted somewhere about the second mile. Feeling quite miserable, scared, and angry with myself, I could feel tears trying to break their way through my eyes again. No, I will not cry. I wish there was somewhere to lie down and sleep. But the ground was all soggy and mosquitoes were driving me to walk faster and faster. I ran for a while to leave them behind, but I'd only meet new ones again. Big puffy black clouds covered the sky, but a bit of lighter sky was showing between the clouds.

I came to a rock cliff and could barely make out a shelf with an overhanging rock on top. Maybe it was dry there. I scrambled up the rocky hill, slipping on wet moss and bush. The moon was trying to peek through the clouds, and I could just make out shapes. One of the shapes looked like it could move any minute! Do bears walk around at night? I stood very still, but my breathing was so loud in my ears I was quite sure anyone across the tracks could hear me. Anyway, that black thing had not moved. It must be a rock. I walked closer and discovered it was a little pine tree with thick bush around it. I found the rock cliff and it was dry enough. My feet and legs were soaking wet as I lowered myself down on the rock. I pulled out my blanket and wound it tight around me and used the sack and my jacket for a pillow. I learned that mosquitoes have needles that will push right through the blanket and shirt to get at you. I had to sit up again to put my jacket on, then I wrapped the blanket around me once more. This time I felt no more stings. I snuggled deeper into the blanket, pulling it over my head, and thought of happier times.

Daylight forced my eyes open and I realized that I was once again in the middle of nowhere. I lay still and listened. It was very quiet. Maybe it was all just a nightmare and when I woke up I would be in bed beside Henry again. But, no. Here I was, stiff from lying on rock all night. I realized now that I had panicked last night. I was half asleep or maybe I was still asleep when the man came in yelling about the fire. Now it was too late to go back. They will think I am such a coward. I couldn't face Billy, Jim, or Henry. For sure, they would have called my father by now. I had better keep going.

A warm mist hung over the railroad tracks. I sat up and stretched. I could feel the heat of the sun where it was shining against the rock cliff on the other side. It felt like steam from a hot shower. I stuffed my blanket in the sack and scrambled down the cliff. Maybe I should go back anyway and hope they are on my side. I am very hungry. But what if Billy comes after me and what if Henry and Jim won't let me in? They must be very angry with me. Besides, I didn't belong there anyway. I always felt out of place, like I had no business being there, at times when Henry would hug his dad, or when Jim would put his arm around Henry's shoulder and pull him and kiss him on the head. I always pretended I didn't notice, but I wished I could disappear at those times. No. I'd better keep on going.

I could hear a train coming. Trains and nightmares, water and mosquitoes, I had had an awful night! I walked with my head down to keep from tripping on the ties until I got my steps paced right. As I was nearing the third-mile post, I smelled campfire smoke. I stopped and listened. The mist had evaporated by the railroad tracks, but the bush was still damp. I caught a whiff again as a breeze stirred the air. I walked a bit farther, all senses alert. Then I noticed a path coming from one side of the tracks and up the other side. I turned off the tracks and followed the trail. I could see a lake between the trees, and sure enough there was the campfire I had smelled. There was a clearing over a flat rock, and off to the side, I saw an old man with his back to me, tying up what looked like a tent he had already folded. He had on old, dirty dark green pants and a green-and-red checkered cotton shirt. He wore a pair of black rubber boots with pink undersoles. He seemed to be carrying on a one-sided conversation just under his breath. I stood and watched as he pressed the roll of canvas with his knee while he tied it up.

Then he said in Ojibwa, "Sit down and have some tea. There is some bannock there in the wooden box beside the fire."

How did he know I was there? I didn't think he saw me. I walked to the fire and picked up a tin cup and poured tea from a blackened teapot. I didn't see any cream or sugar. I sipped the hot liquid and relaxed as I sat leaning against a tree in front of the fire. The old man was still fiddling around with the canvas roll. Finally he stood up and nodded to me, and a grin appeared on his bewhiskered face. His hair, eyebrows, and whiskers were a mixture of black and white hair all sticking up in every direction. I smiled back. He really did look funny! He kept glancing up the path as if he was waiting for someone. Finally he came and knelt over the box, took out some bannock, and pulled off a chunk. He pulled a hunting knife from his belt and sliced the bannock in half. Then he took out some lard and deposited a clump on the bannock with his knife. My mouth watered as I watched his every move. Then his hand extended to give me the bannock. I grabbed it and had to force myself to eat slowly as he went about clearing his camp. He said nothing more as I sat there chewing.

His solitary conversation started again as he turned over a shiny, dark green canvas canoe from the bushes and lowered it into the water. He loaded it with his tent roll, axe, a large green packsack, the one-by-two-foot wooden box, and a canvas sack tied crisscross with a rope. Then he came to the fire and picked up the teapot. He glanced up the path one more time as he filled the tin cup I had emptied with another cup of tea. He offered the cup to me, but I found the tea a bit acidy without the cream or sugar so I shook my head. He downed the tea in one gulp and poured the rest into the fire. The fire hissed in a billow of smoke and ash. He filled the pot with water by the lake and poured it over the fire.

He looked at the sky for a minute. It was clear blue and the sun had already finished steaming everything dry again. He picked up the tin cup, dropped it into the pot, and deposited it into the canoe. I had not moved from under the tree, and I decided that I would sit there and watch him paddle away. I had nothing else to do but walk farther east along the tracks. I didn't feel like going anywhere at the moment, it was just too humid. The railroad must be searing hot by now.

After about fifteen minutes of walking around, checking the area, and reshifting his load in the canoe, he finally came up and squatted down beside me. "Are you alone then, son?"

I looked at my black runningshoes and nodded my head. "Well, now . . . " He thought for a moment, then continued, "I have been waiting for my grandson all weekend, but I guess he decided not to come. He did tell me he was not coming with me this summer, but still I had hoped he would. He is much older than you, you see. Well, now . . . " I made no comment as the information sank in and my mind began to conjure up some possibilities. You could tell his mind was also working by the way he kept squinting and nodding his head. Then he said, more slowly, "I'm going to Whiteclay Lake," and waited for me to respond.

I didn't know what to say. I had never heard of the place. I didn't even know how to explain what I was doing here right now. I didn't know where I was going or what to do next. So I decided to ask the question: "Can I come with you? I have nowhere else to go." I held my breath and waited for an answer.

He studied on that and took a long look at me before he said, "If there won't be any people following us, if a policeman doesn't come looking for me, if your guardians don't send me to jail, if you are not sick, and if you will do your share on this journey. I want you to think about that while I turn the canoe around. If you won't bring me any of those problems, then you may get in front of the canoe and start paddling."

I was getting discouraged by all the "ifs," and I wasn't sure about the police either. Would Billy or Jim send a policeman after me? I didn't understand about the "guardian" part . . . I watched him push the canoe out and gingerly lower himself on the back seat, then push the canoe away from shore. His green-and-red checkered shirt stood out very sharply over the dark green reflection of the canoe in the water. The canoe drifted lightly on top of the water, and he turned it to face me. Well? What do I do? I can't go back, so I have to go on ahead. I got up and dusted the seat of my pants, grabbed my blanket sack, and approached the canoe. The old man had turned the canoe sideways for me to get in. I had never got in a canoe all by myself. Jim or Henry always held it, and I never got to paddle once! The canoe also looked very small, and the paddle was stuck at an angle in front.

He must have noticed my hesitation, then I heard him start his rasping chuckle. "Well, well. I see you have much to learn." I glanced at him and smiled as I brought my shoulders up in a shrug. "Take the paddle, poke it on the bottom of the lake on the other side of the canoe to hold it in place as you slowly step in. Don't lose your balance."

I threw my blanket sack into the canoe, pulled the paddle out, and stuck the end into the bottom of the lake on the other side of the bow like he said. But I ended up facing him, toward the back, and I was leaning over the canoe now as the paddle pulled and threatened to topple me into the canoe.

Between his chuckles, he caught his breath long enough to say, "Turn around and step in the canoe with the leg that is touching it."

I quickly turned and got my balance first before I lifted my right leg. Immediately the canoe hit the inside of my left leg and nearly knocked me off my feet. He could have warned me! I stepped in and transferred my weight to the right leg, which was now slipping left and right. It was like trying to balance on top of a rubber ball in water. I slowly lowered myself down on the seat and swung my left leg in. Suddenly the bottom of my paddle slipped underneath the canoe and almost plucked me off the seat, and the handle nearly yanked my arm out of its socket as it disappeared under the canoe. The rasping chuckle had now rolled into a belly laugh that shook the canoe. Then the handle of the paddle popped back up above the water. The old man steered for it and I leaned over carefully to grab the handle.

"It's stuck in the mud!" I gasped as I pulled and pulled. Finally, with a long sucking sound, it came free in a swirl of mud. I held up the paddle and grinned back at the old man.

The canoe sped forward, and I tried to match the monotonous dip and swirl sound of the water from his paddle. I glanced back and saw the steep sand cliff of the railway tracks running along a bay on the other side of the point. Then a motor car went by in its little orange "putt-putt" box. From habit, I waved and watched it disappear behind the trees.

The old man kept making noises back there. Then, in a low voice, I heard him say, "You remember this part, don't you?"

I answered in a low voice, "I have never been here!"

The conversation continued before I finished speaking and I realized he was talking to himself again. I felt kind of silly for answering him when he wasn't even talking to me.

The sky was clear blue and the wind blew gently on the lake. There was a constant swirling sound at the front of the canoe as it sliced through the water.

A seagull came circling around above us. It sounded like it was chuckling, almost like the old man. I turned around and asked, "What's your name, Grandfather? My name is Danny Lynx."

I noticed that he was sitting with a green string wrapped around his leg. The string pulled tight into the water. What was he trailing behind? His arms continually churned in an unbroken pattern as he paddled. He spat out brown liquid into the water and shifted a wad of tobacco into the other cheek.

It was quite a while before he answered, "Keep paddling,

son. Build muscles before we have to paddle against the wind and high waves. Your hands will start to hurt, but it is better to have blisters because it allows for a second layer of skin to grow underneath. We will hit a portage shortly. We will cross that and keep paddling until we hit another portage with a creek running beside the path. We will cross that and move on to another lake. It will be about noon by then, and we will stop whenever we have something to cook for lunch."

Just how far is this place we are going to? Is it a town or a tourist camp, or maybe an Indian summer camp? What does he mean by "when we have something to cook for lunch"?

His voice came again, "Jim. They call me Ol' Jim. There is a young man back there who is called Jim. That is why I am Ol' Jim."

Ol' Jim. That fits! What other name could he possibly have had? So how would Henry's father, Jim, explain this particular name? Because, if memory serves me, he had said that "the human being is shaped by the name he is given because personality and appearance is attached to a given name and that is how he or she will be treated and expected to behave."

My thoughts were interrupted by Ol' Jim's loud spurt of tobacco spit hitting the water behind me before he said, "Danny Lynx. Where on earth are you from, son?"

I thought a minute and decided that there was no harm in telling him where I came from. Once I got going, though, I told him my life's history from the time I was born. I found myself telling him that I remembered how gentle and happy my father was when we were in the bush. Then when we moved to the reserve, he was never home. When he did come home, he was always irritable and angry, and then, when Mama left, he started hitting me. Then we moved to town. Things got worse. Most times I dodged the blows, but there were times when I got it good, from both him and the witch! After a while, I didn't think it was my own father any more. The father I knew was gone.

We drifted along the shoreline for quite a while. I was getting thirsty. Boy, it felt so good to tell a grandfather my problems.

"You know, that was a stupid thing to do!" came the voice behind me.

Which one? the running away, the ride on the freight train, leaving Charlie, leaving the old couple, leaving Henry and Jim in the middle of the night, or burning the cabin down, or coming with him or . . . ?

We were coming through high weeds as we entered a muddy bay. I trailed my hand in the water again to wet my lips, and I gasped when I was pelted on the back with water from his paddle. His voice came again, "Danny, I just told you that that was a stupid thing to do. Huge jackfish live here and they don't check first to see if that is a human hand. They will grab anything that hits the water. Now, no more of that! Dip your paddle sideways, tip it up and let the water run down into your mouth. If you want to wipe your face, let the water run from the paddle into your hand or dip your socks into the water to wipe your face, but keep your hands away. You can also wash your socks at the same time that way and hang them up on the crossbeam in front of you. Your safety depends on how careful you are. There are no doctors or hospitals out here."

We came to a portage at the end of the bay where Ol' Jim had steered us. There were two logs sinking into the water where we pulled up the canoe. I didn't even get a chance to breathe and look around because we seemed to have been ambushed and surrounded by an army of warlike huge mosquitoes that had set out to suck all the blood out of us. After numerous bumps and scratches we hastily unloaded the canoe and ran across the swampy path to the other end several times to get all the stuff across, then loaded up the canoe at the other end of the portage and got out of there as quickly as we could. We breathed a sigh of relief when we got out once again to the open water. Ol' Jim didn't seem to carry any mosquito repellant.

A bit of wind was fanning the water as we paddled across a narrow lake. I wonder what Henry and Jim are having for supper tonight. Maybe it's best I am not there any more. I might do something worse next time.

In a voice louder than his usual mumbling, Ol' Jim said,

"Duck your head one more time." I quickly lowered my head and looked around to see why I was to do that, when his voice continued, "I could have killed you right where you stood that time, Moose. We were hungry then."

I could feel my eyebrows brush the hair on my forehead. I don't know about this.

The sun was high over our heads as we paddled across the lake. The slight breeze felt good on my sun-beaten back. We came across high rocks, and Ol' Jim steered us up against a high cliff while he rummaged around in his packsack. I knew by now not to ask stupid questions because he just pretended he didn't hear me anyway. Finally he pulled out an old-looking tobacco pouch. He took a pinch of tobacco and mumbled to himself, then reached out and put it on a rock ledge. The canoe rocked to the side, and I figured he must feel it was important enough to send both of us into the water.

Then a thought occurred to me. "Ol' Jim, is there someone there? Why would you leave tobacco if no one was there to take it?"

"You are right, son. There is someone there. There are a lot of beings here. The Memegwesiwag live there. They see us go by. Long ago they were able to communicate with us when there were people who could see and understand them. Now we have lost our communication, so all we can do is know that they are there. It is our fault that we have lost the level of thought and knowledge to be able to see and talk with them. Now all we have left is to acknowledge their existence by leaving 'ahsamah.'"

I looked up at the high rock cliff. It looked like a giant wedge of cheese cut straight down. There were bits of sticks poking out from the cracks against the rock, like whiskers on a brown, wrinkled face.

"Ol' Jim, what are they like? What do they look like?"

I heard another splat of spit landing in the water behind me before he answered, "Well, they looked like us, they spoke the same language as us, but they lived inside the rocks. The ancient people used to tell us that the Memegwesiwag knew what you were thinking. At one time when the people knew them, they had the power to give you all you would need, and in return you had to give them what they wanted and had no way of getting. They had supernatural powers." Another spit landed on the water, and we drifted along the rock face before his voice came again, "So we must remember to leave something when we travel past the homes of these people because they are our relatives." Ol' Jim paddled sideways and steered the canoe up against the side of the last piece of rock cliff.

I was so intent on watching him put the tobacco on the rock shelf that it caught me off guard when the canoe lurched to the side as he settled himself back down. I grabbed the sides of the canoe and dropped my paddle in the water. Ol' Jim heaved a big sigh and swung the canoe sideways so I could reach the paddle. I grabbed it and started to paddle away without a word. Ol' Jim said nothing and another splat of spit hit the water behind me. I paddled the canoe away from the rocks with extra energy.

Chapter Ten

I THOUGHT ABOUT THE MEMEGWESIWAG and imagined what it would look like inside the rock. We were coming around a point when Ol' Jim said, "See that point there? The canoe headed straight out to the lake from that point."

I looked and squinted but I saw no canoe, so I said, "Where? Where's the canoe?"

Ol' Jim just continued, "I put the largest louse in there."

I sat straight up. "Louse? You mean the kind that grow on heads?"

"I put two paddles in there with that louse."

"In this canoe? What paddles? You mean you put a louse in this canoe?"

Ol' Jim just continued talking. "I made sure that he was the leader so that all the rest of the lice that ever crawled on me would take off across the water after that old sucker of a louse and I never had an itch again! That little three-inch birchbark canoe I made for him was the best craftsmanship he ever saw, and those little paddles were the most smooth and perfect miniatures you ever saw. Yes sir. That little canoe took to the waves like a pro!"

At this point, I figured out that he had the inside of my head all twisted around and tied in knots because that sounded to me like a perfectly logical thing to do. I figured I would just try that if I ever grew lice on my head.

In no time at all, we had travelled across a small lake and came to a channel with a creek running off it. I could tell because there was sand beach and I could hear the roar of the current through some rapids. We pulled the canoe up on the beach and prepared to unload as quickly as possible. The sun was almost overhead now.

I was about to ask him if we could have a lunch break when he announced, "We will stop for tea and whatever else at the next portage. It is only a short distance."

I picked up the large packsack and pulled the leather straps around my shoulders, then threw my blanket sack on top. The bottom of the packsack was hanging very low on the back of my legs. I picked up the axe and followed the path to the other lake as fast as possible, taking tiny steps because the packsack kept hitting my legs every time I tried to take bigger steps. I ran along the noisy river rapids until I reached the other end.

Steam hung in the humid air and flies danced over the mud. I deposited my load and ran back once more. I wrestled with the "grub box," as he called the wooden box. It had no head or shoulder straps, so I had to carry it by the rope handles at each end. I threw the tent roll on top of the box. By now he had balanced the canoe over his head and carried the paddles as cushions on each of his shoulders. I watched him stagger on ahead of me. I decided to ask him to put straps on this box or something so that I could put them over my shoulders or head. This looked like a well-used portage. Why isn't he stopping here? I'm starving to death. I watched his black rubber boots sloshing and sliding over some muddy spots. I put the box down to rest my arms and ran back for the canvas sack and the teapot. The sack was even heavier. I carried it beside me, bumping a leg with each step I took, cutting my fingers through with the rope, while clutching the teapot in the other hand. I switched to the left hand, then to the right, before I reached the wooden box again. I left the canvas sack and picked up the wooden box with the tent roll on top and walked as fast as I could, trying to balance the weight.

The tip of the canoe was touching the ground, and Ol' Jim was just pulling the paddles off his shoulders when I dropped the box beside the packsack and ran to fetch the canvas sack again. I reached it with a sigh. I hate this sack! I hefted it up and held it with both arms against my chest and held the handle of the teapot through a loop on the string then walked as fast as I could to the other pile. The canoe was now in the water, and Ol' Jim had just finished wiping the sweat off his face when I dropped the canvas sack beside the others and joined him.

Ol' Jim turned and smiled at me and nodded at the pile already there. I grinned. He reached and ruffled my hair. "Let's load up and get out of here. The mosquitoes are buzzing around my ears and it takes some mighty hungry ones to find them," he said as he lodged the canoe between some rocks. He was off mumbling and talking to himself again. I was a bit disappointed after working like crazy so I could get something to eat! I gave a big sigh and started lugging the stuff to the canoe where he stood and loaded it all in.

"They came through here like a pack of wild animals," he said as we started paddling again. I was learning to distinguish between his "talking-to-himself" voice and his "talking-to-me" voice. I smiled. What was going on inside his head now? He seemed to be remembering all these things as he saw each point, bay, and portage.

"Lunch!" he yelled behind me, and I glanced back in time to see him reeling in the green string he had been trailing behind him all morning. Suddenly, with a huge spray of water, he pulled in a very long, big, toothy fish.

"A huge jackfish! You will have to eat lots, my boy! I knew this was where I was going to catch him!" With a thud, the end of his paddle hit the fish behind the head. It quivered, then lay still. The old man removed the hook and rolled it up on a long stick. The fish was sliming the bottom of the canoe, right beside my blanket sack.

"Ol' Jim, throw my sack out of the way."

He seemed to see it at the same time and threw it on top of the packsack behind me. Now I knew I would be eating something when we reached the portage. I was so hungry I could have eaten the whole fish myself! I paddled on with more energy than ever.

We entered a narrow channel and I could hear the sound

of rushing water, a rapids. I hoped he wouldn't decide to go down the river. I wouldn't know what to do to steer the canoe. I could see the opening in the bush where the path came spilling out into the open muddy, marshy, and rocky shore.

Ol' Jim steered the canoe to a muddy space along the shore, and when I jumped out my foot squished into the mud, ankle deep. I engaged in a tug of war with the mud, trying to get my shoe back while Ol' Jim was busy firing the bags and sacks into a clump of tall grass. It was very hot and damp here. The bush and trees cast a shadow by the shore where flies of all kinds played their chase-around games.

I managed to pull my foot out of the sucking mud and tugged the canoe up a little farther. Ol' Jim had cleared a section in the canoe for him to walk along to the front, then he gingerly stepped on a flat rock. I grinned as he made a bewhiskered face at me.

I grabbed the packsack and headed up the trail. I figured I may as well try to get all the stuff to the other side right now. I picked up my pace as I followed the meandering path along the river. I had gone quite a distance when suddenly I heard a "whoof!" from directly around the bend ahead of me. A bear? My heart jumped into my throat and my feet froze to the ground! Still closer, another "whoof!" Then I heard a noise, footsteps . . . I whirled around and my packsack flopped around behind my legs like a rag as I tore back down the path and sailed out of the bushes and into the clearing, then crashed right smack into Ol' Jim!

Fish guts went flying and Ol' Jim did some fancy footwork while I yelled, "Bear! Bear! I heard him go whoof, I heard him go whoof!" Ol' Jim was just getting his feet under control when I came to a stop by the canoe. He stood there listening for a minute, then walked to his fire and sat down.

"Aren't we jumping in the canoe? A bear is coming!" I yelled.

Ol' Jim yelled back at me over the roar of the rapids, "Get over here and get me some water!"

Reluctantly, I left the safety of the canoe and walked to Ol' Jim, glancing up the path occasionally. I filled the teapot by the river and quickly got back to the roaring fire. Ol' Jim already had the fish sizzling in a pan over the fire, so I crouched down beside him.

Suddenly he turned his head to listen, then yelled in English, "Come eat fish! Tea good hot!"

I looked toward the path and out came a scrawny, bent, white-haired old man with a paddle in each hand. Behind him, an aluminum canoe emerged and a pair of large legs carried it to the shore where it was lowered gently at the edge of the water. The huge man straightened. He had a packsack on his back and his red hair shone like fire in the sun. As the old man tottered over the mud and rocks toward us, he coughed from deep in his chest, "whoof!" and once again, "whoof!" Then I knew—this old fellow was my bear!

A wheezing noise began beside me. Ol' Jim had tears in his eyes before his mouth opened and out came the most horrible sound I ever heard! I stared at him to make sure he was laughing, but when he jumped up and started hopping around and slapping his knees, I knew for sure that he was near to killing himself laughing.

I could feel my ears burning and close to singeing my hair while Ol' Jim danced around the fire. The bent old man stood grinning a toothless smile, framed between his two paddles. The big man deposited his packsack into their canoe and stood calmly watching Ol' Jim, then came forward and bent to stir the smoking fish while Ol' Jim slowly burnt out to a frizzle. He stood there wiping his eyes with the end of his checkered shirt, and the bent old man waited to hear what was so funny. I decided to get some wood.

I ran a ways off and pulled out some dry wood from the bush and hauled it to the fire. They were now seated around the fire eating. My mouth watered as Ol' Jim handed me a double section of fried fish on a sheet of birchbark. I sat down and listened to the talk about the best place to fish where these men had come through, ahead of us. I listened to Ol' Jim's strange kind of English. He sure didn't waste any breath with words like "it, as, at, of" and just got right down to saying what he wanted to say.

He turned to the old man and offered him another piece of fish. "Ol' man, eat more. Keep strong. Scare strong young man there, he see for hisself, real ugly he be your age." That was the longest string of English words I had heard come out of Ol' Jim yet!

I watched the big man gulp down the rest of the leftover fish, then stand up and stretch once more. My mouth hung open when he poured a cup of hot tea and drank it right down. Then he grabbed our big packsack, slung it over his shoulder, threw the tent roll on top, grabbed the canvas sack and my blanket sack, and with long strides, he disappeared back up the path. All that was left were the wooden food box beside the fire, the teapot, and the axe! Quite pleased, I sat with a big grin on my face. Ol' Jim had the food box all packed up again, and this time he was tying a rope around the box to make it easier for me to carry.

In no time at all, the big man emerged again with a large packsack, a tent roll, an axe, a fishing rod, and a teapot. I sat on a boulder by the shore and watched him deposit his load into their canoe, then kneel down by the shore and splash water over his face, head, and shoulders. He walked to the old men and gulped down another cup of tea, then went back to our canoe. In one pull, he had it all the way onto the ground, lifted it, and tucked the paddles inside, positioning them on his shoulders. Then the canoe came down on his shoulders and the tip slowly lifted off the ground and levelled off, and now the canoe with its two new legs marched across the clearing and disappeared up the path.

I ran to the fire and grabbed the wooden box. It was the most awkward thing! "Wait!" yelled Ol' Jim. He came and wrapped an old towel around the long rope handle, lifted it, and slipped it across my chest and over my shoulders. Hey, now this is a lot better. I took off at a trot up the path, hoping to catch up with the big man. I smiled when I passed the section of the road where I had turned to make my mad dash back to the canoe. The old man said he thought it was the funniest thing when Ol' Jim finally stopped laughing long enough to tell him.

I was ready to start running a bit when I saw the clearing up ahead. I didn't catch up to the big man after all. There he was with the canoe down by the water already. He grinned as he wiped his head. "It's hot!" he said in a loud booming voice. I just realized that he had not said anything until now. The old man did all the talking.

I was trying to figure out how I was going to get the rope off my chest—I couldn't lift the box up to slip it off, it was too heavy to swing to the side so I could slip it over my head, it probably would scrape all the skin off my legs if I tried to let it slide down . . . Then I heard his booming laugh and in a strange accent he said, "Sit down, kid! Easy now, just lower yourself until you feel the box touch the ground. I could help you, but you got to do it again anyway at the next portage."

By this time, my knees suddenly bent too fast and I crashed against the box as it landed with a thump on the ground. I grumbled, "Boy, this has got to be the most miserable thing I've ever carried in my whole life!"

The booming laugh echoed louder than the roaring river. "I think it is I who have carried the most miserable thing in my life! There is a portage ahead that is more than a mile long and I had to carry that miserable bag of bones back there, and he kept kicking me on the backside with his long feet and poking me with his bony elbows and knees, yelling, 'Go, Caesar! Go, you ol' mule!' I would threaten to make him walk if he didn't stop, then he'd get madder and jab me something worse."

I was hearing so much love in his voice when he talked about the skinny bent old man that I hesitantly asked, "Is he your grandfather?"

"No, he is my father. He would not get on an aeroplane again to take him back home to town. So I decided I would take him on a last canoe trip home. He is getting too old for this," he sighed.

He picked up a rock and sent it sailing in an arc across the sky. It hit the water with a clean "chomp!" and a small ripple appeared. That was pretty good throwing! Quite impressed, I followed the big man up the path again. There was nothing left to take across the portage.

Then he turned. "Hey, what's your name, kid?"

I quickly replied, "Danny Lynx, and what's yours?"

"Angus Solligan. Remember that and look for me if you ever get to Longlac. Okay?"

I grinned, for I knew that I would never remember a name like that unless I made it into a sentence like, "hang us all again." I giggled. My footsteps covered three for every one of his as I scrambled behind to keep up.

When we got to the clearing, there was the skinny old man perched inside the front of the canoe, but the canoe was still sitting on dry land. I started laughing. Now that looked funny! Angus grinned as he walked up to the canoe and lifted the front with the old man and all and pushed the canoe into the water. I glanced around for Ol' Jim, but there was no sign of him. The fire was out, and there wasn't a thing left on the shore.

The old man waved and yelled, "The old weasel went along the river to catch a few bites!"

With a wave, Angus pushed the canoe out with his foot as he got in and settled himself at the back. The canoe sped forward with each powerful stroke from Angus's paddle.

I turned and ran along the roaring river until I could jump from rock to rock, but it was getting difficult. I jumped at a huge boulder on all fours to be safe, but the moss started peeling off in chunks under my hands and feet. I thought I was going to land in the river for sure. With a big kick away from the peeling rock, I landed on a smaller one at the bottom. Boy, this is like trying to jump off the side of Henry's cake. That black scale stuff on the rocks is like the lumpy chocolate mess Henry made for icing and . . . Gee, I miss Henry. I wish he was here with me right now.

That cedar tree leaning over the river, I remember it from the curve on the path above. I made quite a noise as I scrambled up and over the bank and pulled myself up by the roots and branches of cedar and pine trees. I could hear the sand and rocks cascading down the bank behind me and hitting the river in a spray of water.

Finally I crawled up on soft moss and little purple flowers.

There was a huge ant hill in front of me. I pulled a rotting log aside and watched the ants come to life. They had white rice, long-grained rice, that they were scrambling to gather. They disappeared down into the many holes that went deeper down. I watched one ant grab a particularly large grain of rice. He couldn't turn it around between two blades of grass. He put it down, scrambled over it, and grabbed it again from the other side, then sped down into a hole. I lifted a fist-sized rock and saw more ants scurrying about. I threw the rock a ways behind me. Suddenly a yell pierced the constant roar of the water. Bushes crashed and I scrambled up, trying to figure out which way to dodge. Then I saw Ol' Jim between two trees, shuffling away as fast as he could with his pants down around his ankles and his shirt tail flopping about between his legs.

I stopped, then yelled, "Ol' Jim! It's me!" I glanced behind me to make sure he was not running away from something I didn't see. I saw him stop, then with his back still to me, he bent over and slowly pulled up his pants. I started giggling. I took a big breath and burst out laughing harder than I had ever laughed in my whole life. Through my tears, I saw Ol' Jim walking briskly toward me, buttoning up his pants and rubbing the back of his head. There wasn't a thing I could do. I roared like a wild creature and did a weird dance around the moss and ants, gasping for air, leaning over and slapping my legs. I collapsed beside the ants and lay flat on my back. I opened one eye and saw Ol' Jim crank his shoulders back, tilt his chin, and march back into the bush to the path. I let out one more bubble of laughter and got to my feet. I went down the path, whistling like nothing in the whole world ever happened around here.

There he was by the canoe, sitting on his haunches, chewing on a blade of grass. My tummy was full and I really did not want to travel any farther. I wish he would let us stay here for the night.

I took a deep breath and walked down to the lake and sat beside him. "That river would sound really nice during the night," I said.

He turned his head away so all I saw were his brown

cabbage ears lifting, but I could tell he was smiling when he said, "That huge bear back there would come around for sure during the night. I was tracking him down when you crashed that rock on my head."

When he turned and locked on to my eyes there was no way I could keep my face from stretching. First I tackled the left side, then the right side of my mouth, but both escaped and I cracked into a big smile and giggled, "If that yell didn't scare him away, I'm sure the sight of your behind did!"

I saw his hand come up just as I rolled away. He landed on top of me and down came his arm with a handful of soft mud, which he sloshed and squished around my nose, mouth, and eyes.

Suddenly he stopped. "Listen!" I listened but did not hear anything. He scrambled up and grumbled in his talking-to-himself voice, "I should never have let the kid distract me." All the rest I couldn't hear, because he was dashing left and right, loading the canoe.

I breathed a sigh of disappointment and started helping him. I had stopped to throw some water on my face to wash the mud off my eyes when I heard it. A sharp crack of wood! Like splitting wood or ripping old rotting wood off the ground. Ol' Jim was over at the other end of the clearing, and I saw him stand still to listen too. I suddenly sprang into action, and we were in the canoe and paddling away in less than half a minute! There actually *was* a bear!

Ol' Jim spoke behind me, "I saw two bear tracks and baby cubs. I thought it was the same bear, but you know, I think it was two females with their cubs, or one had two or three and the other had one or two . . . anyway, there was a good chance of a fight if we happened to wander anywhere in between."

We cleared the channel and came out onto a large open lake. "This is Smoothrock Lake," said Ol' Jim behind me.

I paused occasionally to pull the caked mud off my hair and eyebrows. It was now the middle of the afternoon, and I could tell Ol' Jim meant business when he got into the rhythm of his long-distance paddle strokes. I resigned myself and let my arms lift and fall.

We went to the left, past several islands and some high rock cliffs. Once more, he left some tobacco to the Memegwesiwag.

We moved on again, past some beautiful sand beaches and the water became calm. The "tat-tat-tat-tat-tat" in front of the canoe had turned into a "tsh, tsh, tsh," then it became a slow gurgle as we slowed down along a sandy shore with tall pine trees. From here, it looked like the ground was very even, like a park, except for the short bushes. Then, between the shadows of the tall pines, he steered the canoe to a clearing and we came to a stop on a bed of soft moss. I stepped out to what looked like a ready-made camping area.

Ol' Jim mumbled to himself again as he walked up and looked around picking out where we should put up the tent. I concentrated on pulling out all the stuff from the canoe and hauling it up on the sand to the camp area that Ol' Jim had already picked out. He began chopping off some pine branches, making a bed of long pine needles beside some logs he had already thrown down for the fire. I smiled and ran back to the canoe. With a tug I managed to get it out of the water far enough so it would not drift away.

When I got back to the campsite, Ol' Jim seemed lost in thought as he looked at the sun now way past the treetops somewhere. There was no sunshine here, but I could still see it shining across the lake on the islands. Suddenly Ol' Jim turned and pulled apart the canvas bag, unfolding it into a tent. Then he walked to a tree where some tent poles were leaning.

"How did you know they were there?" I asked in surprise.

Ol' Jim laughed. "I put them there, that's how I know! Now come here and hold these two together while I tie the top ends."

I held the poles together while he tied them. Then I held the other pair while he tied them. Next I had to hold the back pair while he put the centre pole in between. Then he walked to the front pair and put the other end of the centre pole in between, and slipped the tent through the middle, from one hole at the front to the other hole at the end. Then he secured the tent to the poles. Now all we had to do was stretch the sides tight by tying another pole along the ground from which we tied the tent tight along the sides. It seemed like a lot of work just to sleep overnight.

I was just about to go in when Ol' Jim said, "Now, you will have to run and find a bunch of large pine branches to put on the floor so that we don't get sand on our blankets and things."

I saw him walk into the bush and disappear. I stood and listened for a long while before I dashed around breaking branches. I knew I would get spooked if I did not get busy right away. Soon I was too tired to care. I heard Ol' Jim somewhere in the bush once in a while, but I wasn't very concerned. I was more intent on making sure I had enough branches to cover the floor before he came back.

I had the branches scattered over the floor and was satisfied with the effect by the time he came around the corner of the tent. He peeked in and went "Humph!" with a big smile on his face, but did not say anything. I shrugged and took that as a good sign and followed him to the lake again.

He hauled out the heavy canvas bag that I had lugged around all day and loaded it into the canoe. Then he pulled out a rock about the size of a brick from the shore and loaded it in also. The evening was quite calm now and, almost whispering in the stillness, we paddled away to a channel between the islands. The canoe floated on as Ol' Jim untied the sack and out tumbled a silky navy fishnet. He pulled out the lead rope and steered the canoe to one end of the island and tied it to an overhanging tree. Then I watched him unravel the net.

"Try to steer right to the end of the other island over there," he said. I set my sights on the little spurt of grass at the end of a rock and paddled and paddled until he yelled, "Woowh! Too fast. Slow down! I didn't say race, you know!"

I glanced back to see him let the fishnet down into the water in spirals from the canvas sack. Occasionally the sinkers would twist and one flick of his wrist would swing the sinker back around and the fishnet would spread like an invisible fan into the dark water. Behind us, in a straight row, floated the pink, green, grey, white, and black floats. He said he had scrounged around a couple of years to accumulate enough plastic floats for a fishnet. Finally the net was all in the water and now he tied the rock to the end rope and dropped it overboard. I watched it sink deep into the water behind us.

I was very hungry by the time we paddled back to camp. I didn't know what he had in the food box, but I was sure looking forward to it. I watched him impatiently as he started the fire in front of the tent, and out came his teapot. He gave me the pot to fill at the lake. I ran down as fast as I could and quickly filled it. Back at the camp I gently put the pot on the fire. He was busy pulling blankets and a sleeping bag from the big green packsack.

"Throw a handful of tea in the pot," Ol' Jim called. "It is in the green can in the box."

I approached the food box very slowly. I had not looked in it before and did not know what was in there. I didn't know if I could keep myself from eating everything in sight--that's how hungry I was! I opened the lid, but what was this? There was nothing in there! No food!

There was a bag of flour, oats, the can of tea, sugar, lard, and something called baking powder. Where was the food? I was getting quite concerned as I reached for the tea. What if we starved to death out here! I carefully opened the lid and took a handful of rough, dry tea leaves and dropped them into the pot as Ol' Jim had done at the portage. I replaced the cover and decided to explore. For sure, he would see that I did not like the idea of starving to death. I just realized that it scared me very much to be hungry.

I ran down by the lake and jogged along the sand beach until I came to a point. The shoreline curved into a bay. That looked like an interesting place, I'll check it out tomorrow. I turned around and retraced my footsteps. It was very calm and the water was like a huge glass mirror. Seagulls were screeching somewhere on the left side of the lake. Occasionally, a fish of some sort jumped up, disturbing the surface of the water. I breathed in the fresh air, smelling of rich earth, water, and sometimes the plants from nearby bushes. I found

111

a can by the shore. I didn't remember ever seeing one like this in the stores anywhere. It must come from tourists from somewhere else. I must hang it up on a branch. If I found one of their coats, I also would pick it up and hang it on a branch. It is theirs. Maybe one day they will come back and pick it up. I hung the can where they could easily see it.

As I neared the camp, something smelled absolutely delicious! I ran up the path and saw Ol' Jim frying bannock. He handed me a porridge made from the tea. He dropped a bit of sugar into it, stirred it, and handed me a cup with a spoon and a chunk of fried bannock. I sat down on a log and smiled. He knew how to make Mr. Old Indian's favourite porridge! The image of the old man popped into my head. I remembered how his face turned into a zillion wrinkles when he put the porridge-dipped bannock into his mouth. I grinned and said in English, "Ol' Jim, you're the greatest!"

By the time we finished our meal, I had developed a king-sized itchy pain on all exposed flesh. I decided to duck into the closed tent and dive into the sleeping bag. Those weren't ordinary mosquitoes out there, they were ancient blood-sucking birds of the worst kind! My blanket sack made a great pillow. I could smell some kind of burnt moss in here.

Soon Ol' Jim came in, stumbling over the scattered pine branches as he deposited the food box inside the tent. I heard him grunt and sigh as he settled into his blankets. I lifted my head to see him gently blowing on a bowl of embers. So that was the sweet smell that seemed to repel the mosquitoes.

I smiled to myself and listened to the gentle crackling of the wood in the fire, the seagulls having a big argument, the laughing mallard ducks having a party at the bay, and the occasional fish taking a breath of air above the water.

Chapter Eleven

Early the next morning, i awoke
and heard the crackling of the flames from the campfire. I
couldn't hear Ol' Jim out there, but that smoke sure smelled
good. I lay still and listened to the many sounds. A fly came
zooming by outside the tent in full speed like a miniature
aeroplane, a mosquito was bouncing along the tent wall
sounding like a little drill, and a bird was singing like there was
no tomorrow. Suddenly I heard a stick breaking, then Ol'
Jim's footsteps approaching. Something fell with a thud and
the flames exploded into a popping spree. I got up and pulled
my shoes on, then poked my head out of the tent. Ol' Jim was
gone again.

The sky was clear blue and the sun was just about to come
out from behind the trees on the horizon. I stretched and
walked to the lake. The water was still, and there was a red
path on it going to the sun. I knelt and splashed water all over
my head, neck, arms, and face. The back of my neck really
hurt. I wiped my face with my sleeve and walked back to the
fire. The teapot was smoking and there was Ol' Jim pulling the
fur off a rabbit. I watched him skewer it on a stick over the
fire. I poured some hot tea and sat down to watch him work.
He pulled off the feet and paws. Then he turned the fur inside
out and began stuffing it with moss.

"Why are you saving the moss? Are you going to carry it in
there?" I asked him.

Ol' Jim cackled and answered, "No. I'm stretching the
skin to dry. When it dries, I will pull out the moss and use

113

the skin for something. But watch this."

He worked the skin back around the ankle bone of the rabbit paw and pulled it inside out. The bone popped out, leaving a soft paw packed with fur! That was neat. He threw it at me and I sat there examining it, then stuck it into my pocket. He hung the stuffed rabbit skin over the top of the tent pole, then he disappeared into the bush with the guts. I sat watching the birds twittering and hopping around in the bushes behind me.

Soon the rabbit was cooked, and we had some of the leftover bannock from last night dipped in hot tea. It was still good! Ol' Jim seemed content to sit back and watch the sun come up, but my neck was getting all itchy and it started to feel quite stiff. I reached and gave it a good scratch and my fingers came away bloody. I decided to go for a run along the beach, so I headed for the bay on the other side of the point.

Running past the point, I slowed down and quietly walked along the sandy beach. About halfway around the bay, I came across a little creek running into the lake. I thought I heard something that sounded like a puppy. Must be a raven. That's the only thing that can sound like anything and not sound like something at all. I jumped the creek and clambered along the shore, where bushes and boulders now blocked my way. I turned and saw something small by the creek, then it disappeared. I wonder what that was. A fox? It was black though. I ran faster to the creek, trying to see what it was before it disappeared. I looked through the bushes but saw nothing. I jumped across and started to walk along the shore. I picked up a stick and tried to fish a huge, speckled, brown blood sucker out of the water, but it kept slipping off. Then I heard it again, that same whining sound. I turned and a shock went through me, clear to my toes! There stood a black thing about twenty feet away! A dog. No. A wolf! A movement caught my eye, and I saw a smaller head poke through the bushes and disappear again. A wolf pup. I still couldn't move my body. The wolf stood there facing me. It had not moved either. Then the neck stretched forward and lowered a bit more and the dark eyes looked at me through shaded eyelids. The paws were planted firmly in the sand and still it did not move. Suddenly my lungs filled with air. I quite involuntarily took a big breath, but it got me moving. I dragged my feet away, slowly walking backward. Then the wolf's ears twitched and the head turned to the side. It stepped away and now it stood sideways. The head turned my way again and the eyes looked into mine once more, then it was gone, back into the bush. I whirled around and ran as fast as I could, feet pounding along the hard-packed sand of the water's edge.

As I came around the point, I saw Ol' Jim drifting along in the canoe where we had set the net. I was safe now, within sight of the camp and Ol' Jim there, watching me. I stopped and knelt down by the water and splashed my face and head. My legs felt like rubber and, shaking at the knees, I threw more water over my neck. It stung. I lifted my head again and saw that Ol' Jim had turned the canoe around to come back to the camp. I brushed back my hair and ran along the water's edge, then came tearing down the beach at full speed.

I could feel the wind pulling my hair back as my feet pounded on the sand. I saw Ol' Jim paddling faster, and suddenly it became a race to see who was going to reach the campsite first. I ran very fast, but all Ol' Jim had to do was swing his arms back and forth and the canoe sped forward. He came first by two steps.

Giggling and breathing hard, I pulled the canoe up and held it as he stepped out. I saw one pickerel and one sucker and the pile of wet fishnet. He lugged the fishnet to a clearing along the beach. Then he took the lead rope and strung it between two young poplar trees and looped the fishnet over the rope on every other sinker. He left it swaying in the light breeze as he picked up the fish from the canoe. He picked up the sucker first and slit the sides off in chunks and threw the rest into the lake as far as he could. In less than two minutes some seagulls circled, then dived for the bones. Two more arrived and the next thing I knew there was a big squawking fight out there! Ol' Jim chuckled and picked up the pickerel, then walked back to the tent. I had had such a strange experience with the wolf, I couldn't figure out how to explain it to Ol' Jim.

I ran and got another teapot of water, which he set to simmer on the ashes. I settled down against an old grey stump and watched him dismantle the tent and the tent poles in such an organized manner that it never occurred to me to try to be helpful somehow. The pickerel lay in the shade and flies were already buzzing around it. I knew that was lunch, so I picked up a long stick, flicked some of those loose pine branches that served as our bed last night, and covered the fish with them. Ol' Jim seemed pleased with my idea. Then, suddenly, he went off into the bushes again.

Well, since he had taken the tent down, we must be going again. So I rolled all the blankets and packed them into the packsack. I still rolled my blanket into its own sack. When I had finished, I laid it beside the big one. Then I ran around with the canvas tent, matching corner to corner, fold to fold, until I thought it was just right. Then I tried to roll it, but it was too huge, rough, and bulky. It was a much bigger roll than when Ol' Jim rolled it, but it would have to do.

Suddenly sticks crashed into the fire behind me. Ol' Jim stood there looking at me, his grey whiskered face twitching. My glance told him that if he said anything I wouldn't be rolling that tent up again for the entire trip!

"By the way, how long is this trip?" I said in English. He pretended not to hear me, so I switched to Ojibwa. "When are we going to get to where we're going?"

Ol' Jim sat down and started scraping tree bark into a little dipper. That was the pan he made his tea-porridge in last night. I had used the little tin cup. He glanced at me a moment before he dug into his pouch and put a handful of tobacco into the scraped-off shells of bark and put them in the fire. Then he poured a little water in the dipper with his bark scrapings and set them to boil in the hot ashes. By this time, his tea was ready and he made himself a cup while he picked up his rabbit-skewer stick and scraped all the brown stuff off the wood until it was white again, then he skewered the pickerel on, whole, with the guts still in it and anchored it in the ashes.

116

The back of my neck was hurting bad, and it was itching worse by the minute and getting stiffer and hotter. I ran down to the shore again and splashed more water on my neck and let the wind dry it. It felt much better for a while. I ran to check the net. The nylon squares were dry but the cotton string was still wet. I walked to the canoe and started loading the axe, the tent, my blanket sack, the big green packsack, and my jacket. All we had left were the fishnet, the food box, and the teapot. I found it hard keeping track of all these things.

His little dipper was cooling off beside the fire when I came up the path. He motioned for me to sit beside him on a pile of pine branches he had scraped together. Quite puzzled, I sat down beside him.

"No," he motioned, "on your knees in front of me, head down."

I flipped around and put my head down. I felt his hands scoop my hair aside at the back of my neck, then begin to move across my scalp.

His voice came quietly, his talking-to-himself voice, "I knew of a dog once. He was always beaten so bad by his master. The last time I saw the dog, it had a red film over half of one eye, half the head was swollen real bad, it had cuts and scars all over its head and snout. He limped. That was just before they shot him for killing his master." He was off in his memory world again.

I remembered the wolf. "I saw a black wolf this morning. There's a creek there in the bay. There was also a smaller wolf." The hands stopped, waiting for more. I continued. "I felt like I turned to ice, I couldn't move. Would it have attacked me if I ran?"

"No," he answered.

I could see his hand dip into the little dipper and bring up a wad of his bark scrapings. He washed them over the mosquito-bite sores on my neck. That felt absolutely wonderful!

"Why did the wolf just stand there and stare at me? What was it waiting for?"

He didn't answer me for such a long time that I was beginning to think he hadn't heard me. Then he said, "He probably knows you from somewhere and waited to see if you knew. You obviously did not."

A shiver ran down my back as another stream of warm liquid washed over the sores on my neck. "What do you mean? Like I had seen it before? That was the very first time I had seen that ugly thing, and I don't wish to see it ever again!"

Ol' Jim's hands dropped from my head and he turned to tend to the fish. He said no more about it and I stood up and put the rest of the stuff into the canoe. He was very quiet. I wondered if I had offended him or something. I decided to keep my mouth shut and make myself useful. The pickerel wasn't even cooked yet when I put the food box into the canoe. I folded the fishnet neatly into the canvas sack and put it in the canoe.

When the fish was cooked, Ol' Jim just pulled it off the ground, covered it in pine branches, threw it into the canoe, then stepped in behind me. I turned and gave him my biggest smile. He grinned and splashed me with his paddle as we headed out full speed into the open water of Smoothrock Lake, heading toward Loon Narrows. Halfway there, he pointed to an island where he said the strange people had buried their dead in the "scaffolds" fashion long ago. Since then the island had been avoided, even though people no longer remembered why.

Ol' Jim pointed out the "Magic Rock" when we stopped to eat the pickerel. It was at the mouth of a narrow channel. There was nothing special about the rock at all. Just a round rock about three feet high, sitting beside the water.

"Why is it called Magic Rock?" I could tell Ol' Jim knew that question was coming because he was already into explaining before I finished saying it.

"Well, Native people have travelled through here for many, many generations back, and that rock has always watched people go by from the other side of the shore over there. You see, the rock had always been near the water, but it was sitting on the main shore. Then one spring, as soon as travel allowed after the ice melted, the first Native family that came through noticed that it was now on the opposite shore, where you see it now. They told everyone about it and of course everyone came and looked, and sure enough, the rock was not where it had always been. That was indeed magic, so they called it Magic Rock."

While we were there, we stopped at a point across from the rock. I was totally surprised by the constant whir of wings. Partridges and their babies were flying off in different directions as I followed Ol' Jim into the bushes. I wished that I had a slingshot to kill a partridge. But Ol' Jim still had some tricks up his sleeve. He was a perfect shot at throwing rocks. One sharp rock from the shore at each, and two partridges toppled over! I knew I was going to sleep with a tummy full of food tonight.

I grabbed as many rocks as I could hold from the shore and chased a partridge up a tree. I let a rock go that whizzed by its head, hit a branch, and just missed Ol' Jim's head! He whirled around and waved a rock at me. I got the message. I giggled and took off after another partridge.

After a whole afternoon of romping through the bush chasing partridge, we were back on the open water again. Ol' Jim decided to enter Smoothrock Lake again and go down the length of it to Loon Narrows.

When we reached Loon Narrows, it was such a closed, desolate-looking place, I kept thinking Ol' Jim must have got lost somewhere. I looked down to see long green weeds, like hair, flowing and waving under the water. Long green hair, shifting and rolling off the huge humpback of the Big Green Troll who lived in the murky waters . . . Suddenly, Ol' Jim stopped paddling. We were drifting toward an opening along the shoreline. This must be where he wanted to camp. It was at the edge of a swamp. I got out and held the canoe for him. After pulling the canoe up, we walked into the clearing. I looked around but didn't see anything. Then Ol' Jim pointed out a fallen-down, once-upon-a-time log cabin off to the side. I would never have seen it if Ol' Jim hadn't stood over it and pointed to the old mossed-over logs. Anyway, I was in no mood for exploring, I just wanted to get the canoe up and turned over, the tent up, and a partridge in my belly.

I watched him dry the sucker meat over the fire and roast the partridge at the same time as I went through the process of finding pine branches to spread around the inside of the tent again. When we finally sat down to eat, I devoured a whole roasted partridge by myself. Ol' Jim had his eaten before I got through the two legs on mine.

I giggled as his eyes squinted through the smoke across from the fire. The smoke seemed to have taken a liking to him this evening. I was ready to crawl into bed when I saw him take out the little pot again and drop in another wad of treebark. I sat up and waited.

When he was ready, he pushed my hair back, then stopped for a minute. I could feel his hands moving again over the back of my head before he said, "Danny, I can see at least five scars on your head. Surely your father did not do this to you?"

I was silent for a while trying to think how to answer. Can I say that Father did that to me if he didn't actually do it with his hands? But he did put me in that house. Finally I said, "One scar was a cut I got when I pulled a string that was hanging down from the roof of the storage shed. I didn't know it was tied to an old axe and it fell on my head when I pulled it off the roof." Ol' Jim shook against me as he laughed under his breath. I continued. "Scar two was when my friend Tom and I were wrestling. He tripped me and I fell back and banged my head on a sharp rock. Scar three came from some town boys who decided to check if my blood was red like theirs. Scar four came from Sarah when she hit me over the head with a cutting board, and scar five when she threw me on the floor and my head banged on the table leg."

He made no comment, and the liquid washed over my aching sores. When he finished washing my neck, he dabbed some dark powdery stuff over it. Then I went in the tent, rolled into the sleeping bag, and immediately fell asleep.

Some time during the night I heard a thud, thud, and the ground shook under my head. I reached over and tried to find Ol' Jim in the dark when his hand closed over mine. "Sh, sh, sh," he said. My heart was pounding. I didn't know what was out there, but I could tell it was HUGE! Then suddenly a "splash, suck, splash, suck" sound came from the water's muddy edge. Ol' Jim whispered, "A moose." I could hear him getting up and crawling to the door. Then I saw his dark shape against the canvas door flap. I scrambled up and crawled behind, following his feet out the door and onto the damp grass and sand on the clearing. The splashing was now coming from farther down and was interrupted occasionally by a swooshing of water.

"He's dipping his head into the water to eat the weeds," Ol' Jim whispered back to me.

Suddenly there was a constant swishing sound. It was running. I ducked down, then Ol' Jim suddenly jumped to his feet and tripped right over me! I heard him landing with a thud in the bushes and saw him scramble up again. I clamped a hand over my mouth to keep from laughing and hustled to follow him to the water's edge, and there we saw the moose, its antlers like a drifting log with the trunk roots lifting above water. We stood and watched him swim across the swampy bay to a small island of trees and tall bushes. We heard the pouring of water when the huge animal walked to shore. We couldn't see him from here. It was still very early in the morning, and the sky was only a shade lighter where the sun would come up.

Mosquitoes found us by the millions, and Ol' Jim was scratching his arms and belly. I covered my head with my shirt to protect my neck, but in doing so exposed my back. I turned and ran back to the tent and dove into my sleeping bag. I could hear Ol' Jim hitting leaves in the bush down there. Soon he scrambled into the tent and closed the flaps tight, but I could hear many mosquitoes inside already. I heard Ol' Jim strike a match, and I popped my head out to see what he was doing. He was lighting the wad of mossy stuff he used to get rid of the mosquitoes. The fragrant smell filled the tent and I burrowed deeper into the bag.

I awoke to the sound of Ol' Jim breaking branches and of flames crackling over birchbark and twigs. I could hear him rummaging around in the food box. The teapot rattled and his footsteps faded to the water. The moose! I jumped out of bed, slipped my shoes on, and ran outside. The sun was already up and was about to be covered by a thick layer of black clouds. I ran around the clearing and sure enough, there they were! Big moose tracks! I followed them down to the lake. Boy, he had walked by real close to the tent. No wonder I had felt the ground shake. Ol' Jim was still standing there with his teapot in hand.

"We have to go as soon as we finish eating. The rain is going to come, and I think if we go past the two portages we could make it to Whitewater Lake this morning. Then we can pitch the tent where we will find all we need to eat. We can stay there until the weather clears. Do you mind paddling in the rain?"

I grinned and shook my head. "No, I don't mind!"

I walked up ahead on the path to the camp, and Ol' Jim said behind me, "Your neck looks good. Don't touch it, and next time don't scratch your bites."

My hand automatically went up to explore my neck but his slapped it away. "I said, don't touch!" I ran laughing up to the tent and began hauling out the sleeping bags and rolling them up. Ol' Jim put the teapot on the fire and headed off into the bush. He was gone for quite a while, so I went about loading all the things into the canoe, leaving only the tent standing, the food box, and the teapot. I was proud of myself. That was the first time I turned the canoe up all by myself. The moose had passed right by it. I wonder what he thought it was. Maybe he never even saw it.

I ran up the path again and flipped the boxlid open. There was only a bag of flour, oats, sugar, baking powder, tea, and a can of lard. I still couldn't get over it! I took a small handful of the loose tea and threw it into the pot of boiling water.

Ol' Jim came back from the bush, rolling up a piece of snare wire. "No rabbits. Strange, very strange. This used to be a very popular camping spot. Everyone that travelled through would stop at this spot and sleep overnight and have rabbits for breakfast. What winds are blowing . . . " I tuned out because he was now in his talking-to-himself voice.

I went in the bush and looked around. It was all mossy

ground on one side. There were some old, rotted brown clumps of moss stuck between the branches of trees and bushes. Up on one tree, quite high, I saw a leather thong tied around, with a thick dried-out leather bag of some sort hanging down. I wonder what that is.

Ol' Jim spoke behind me. "Tell me what you see, Danny Lynx? Look around you." His arm swept the area.

"I see the clearing out there where our tent is. I see some old tent poles leaning against the tree. I just realized I never saw you cut any down!" Ol' Jim rolled his eyes in exasperation, so I continued, "There is strange moss on the branches, and there are tree stumps, and that thing hanging up there." I waited and he waited. "Well," I continued, "I think people lived in this place before." I shrugged and looked at him out of the corner of my eye.

Ol' Jim sighed and walked down a ways with me, then turned me around. "Look, one clearing for one family, another clearing for another family, and over there is where the cabin stood. The moss up in those branches was used for babies' diapers in the cradle boards." He said nothing about the dried-out leather bag. I followed close at his heels back to camp.

Just then I saw a squirrel take off with Ol' Jim's last piece of bannock. Ol' Jim saw it at the same time as we came into the clearing. He pulled off his rubber boot and fired it at the squirrel, who was sitting pretty as you please on top of the food box with his arms stretched tight around the bannock. Well, that boot went flying and bounced off the box and fell into the fire! Ol' Jim danced and hopped around the fire, trying to find a stick that wasn't burning. Finally he just kicked it out of the fire with his other booted foot and the boot flew out of the fire in a ball of smoke and landed on top of his coat. He hopped to that now in full speed and shook the embers off the coat before he stomped the hot ashes from the boot. I was now doubling over, I was laughing so hard. He just glanced at me as he examined his boot. Oh, he looked so funny!

Soon he had the tea-porridge ready, and then he filled up my tin cup and handed it to me. Later, I filled the cup with tea to wash down the tea-porridge. That was good! The wind was picking up pretty fast now, and it was getting a bit chilly and damp.

Ol' Jim took the tent down quickly and I put out the fire. He was folding the tent when I ran down to the canoe with the food box and the teapot and axe. Soon he came down with the canvas tent roll and off we went, paddling swiftly through the channel and, before long, reached another portage.

The rapids were quite loud, but I never got to see them. The path ran through the bush directly to the other side. We crossed a small lake over to another portage. This portage was on a steep hill and was very long. Ol' Jim had to rest halfway with the canoe, and I made many more trips bringing the things a little ways at a time. I was always counting the bags to make sure I did not forget anything.

Ol' Jim stood with the canoe swaying from side to side, and I wondered what he was doing now. I came up behind him and he said, "I just chased a bear cub off the road. Stay close behind me. I don't see the mother, but you can bet she is not too far away."

Oh, no! Not again! My heart was pounding as I walked under the canoe behind Ol' Jim, occasionally scraping the back of his heel with my toe.

"Not that close, you'll trip me!" I heard him say as loud as he could. "Keep talking, talk as loud as you can. Make sure she knows where we are." I walked along in silence behind him. "I said talk! Talk as loud as you can," he said, and I watched his baggy pants flip to the left and right with each step.

"I don't know what to say. What do you want me to talk about? You're the one that's always talking. You even talk to yourself, and now you are not talking and telling me to talk instead . . . " I rambled on.

He grunted in disgust and said, "Okay, be quiet. Help me put the canoe down."

We had entered the clearing and now faced another small lake. He helped me get the rest of the stuff, and after quickly firing the things into the canoe, we were on our way again as the drizzle began to lay heavy on our backs.

Chapter Twelve

THE RAIN STARTED FALLING GENTLY ON the rippling water as we paddled across the lake to the next portage. It looked like millions of little bugs disturbing the surface. I paddled harder. The skin on my thickening palms was hurting as I adjusted my hold on the paddle again. My hair was getting wet, and I could feel the dampness settling over my shoulders. I glanced back at Ol' Jim. His head was tucked in tight between his shoulders, and he was trailing that green string again, which I knew now to be the hook to catch our next meal.

Finally he steered the canoe to a dismal, muddy clearing along the shore by some tall pine trees. I jumped out of the canoe and pulled it up as far as I could until it hit bottom right where Ol' Jim was sitting, still busy pulling in his fishing line. All of a sudden he jumped up in the canoe, tipping it to one side. Everything slid over and then I saw him slowly lean over the side. One leg got out and chomped into the water, and the other leg slowly slipped out of the tipped canoe. Ol' Jim was now kneeling in the water. I came to life and rushed to pull the canoe up a bit more. I pulled it in far enough to reach the stuff and pulled it away from the edge of the canoe. By this time, he was winding the string up like crazy and soon the back of a fish appeared! He had caught a jackfish off the shore! He came sloshing up out of the water and threw the fish on the ground. It was a big one, enough to feed both of us for two meals. He watched the fish flopping about for a second before he looked down at his legs. He was covered with mud right up to his thighs. I made sure I was well out of

125

the way before I started to laugh, in case he decided to come after me. His shoulders started to shake and soon a bellow of laughter escaped his throat. He turned to pull up the canoe to dry land. Still grinning from ear to ear, I started unloading the bags and box out of the canoe, while he took the hook off the fish and rummaged around in the packsack for his extra set of dry clothes. He disappeared into the bush and before I could figure out where to put the fish, I heard him crashing back, so I turned my attention to other things.

We were working pretty fast, and I ran up the path with the huge packsack and my blanket sack as soon as I could. I didn't worry about bears too much. I figured nobody else would be crazy enough to be out and about on a miserable day like this. Even a bear had better sense than us as far as I was concerned. I was surprised when I emerged into a clearing that looked like the end of a bay. I deposited the packsack and bag under a tree where it was a little drier, then ran back for the rest. I met the canoe with Ol' Jim's legs about halfway down, and I stepped aside as he went sloshing by in the mud. I ran full speed, grabbed the food box, and noticed that the fish was still on the ground, so I fired the fish into the food box, grabbed the teapot, and hurried back. I dropped the box about halfway and turned back for the fishnet and axe, which I dropped with my other pile. Then I ran back once more. I struggled with the awkward tent roll and threw it on top of the other things as soon as I reached my pile.

As I sat there, out of breath, I noticed a rumble from somewhere. Thunder! I have never been out in a thunderstorm. Remembering the violent thunderstorm at Mr. and Mrs. Old Indian's place sent a shiver down my back. I grabbed the food box and threw the axe and teapot on top. I went banging and clanging down the path and met Ol' Jim halfway there. He smiled as he stepped aside and I continued at a faster pace. The sacks were already in the canoe when I reached the landing. I deposited the food box inside and loaded the axe and teapot. I could see big clouds coming over the horizon. I heard Ol' Jim behind me with the rest of the things, which he deposited in the canoe. I knew he was going to set the net somewhere again as I watched him load a narrow rock into the canoe by his feet. I got in and felt Ol' Jim get in behind. He pushed the canoe off and we went down the narrow opening path among the reeds.

The green reeds and cattails swished in the breeze along the shoreline. I could see some ducks swimming along the open water among the reeds under the steel grey sky. Some yellow and white flowers bobbed in the wake of the waves from our canoe as we passed by.

Soon we entered a wider body of water and the canoe headed straight toward a channel. When we came around the corner, Whitewater Lake spread out ahead of us. Ol' Jim started rummaging around in the canoe. I turned around and watched him unpack the fishnet, then I steered the canoe to the left shore of the channel. We approached an overhanging tree, and he pulled the canoe in so he could tie one end of the fishnet lead rope to the branch. I could smell mint or something from the bushes beside me. I grabbed a handful and took a deep breath of it.

"Steer straight to the other side," he said. I got the canoe lined up toward another tree and started paddling slowly. He seemed to be having trouble with the net, and stopped occasionally to untangle it. Finally he grumbled, "I was beginning to think I must have put this away in my sleep until I remembered that little pup had put it away himself out there on the beach. He was in such a big hurry to leave." I felt my face stretch into a big grin and pretended to examine the shoreline ahead of me.

Finally he called a halt just as we reached the shore. I turned and watched him loop the end rope of the fishnet around the narrow rock, tie it securely, and drop it overboard. I watched the rock sink with the fishnet rope. A chill ran up my back as a gust of wind blew cold rain against my face. We paddled faster against the wind.

We passed the channel and headed to a small campsite on the righthand side. I could see sand beaches everywhere! Thunder was now rolling closer and closer as we quickly pulled the canoe in. I ran with the rest of the stuff into the clearing where Ol' Jim was already unrolling the tent and pulling the tent poles through it. I was tugging at the canoe when I heard him coming through the bush from the campsite. "Run and find some dry kindling before you get cold."

I ran through the bush, and mosquitoes pasted themselves to my wet face as they tried to stick their needles into me. I found some dry twigs under trees and dead dry branches underneath healthy ones. I turned over an old birch log and pulled off some bark. I kicked an old stump over and retrieved some splintered dry wood. I had quite an armful when I met Ol' Jim with his axe, and he quickly pushed and chopped down a dry barkless poplar. I ran back to camp and saw that he had everything inside the tent already. I kept the kindling under my arms and stood inside the tent with the door flap open, waiting for Ol' Jim. Several minutes later, he emerged with three-foot logs, which he threw on the ground beside the door. He took half my kindling and put it inside the tent, then he deposited the rest between the big logs while he chopped more wood. A minute later he had a good fire going and from his big packsack inside the tent, he pulled out a large piece of white plastic tarp. This he stretched over the door of the tent and the fire. He tied the corner strings to some nearby bushes.

We sat down beside the fire and listened to the loud splashing of water on the plastic overhead. The wind picked up and we were deafened further by the slap and crack of the plastic over our heads, but at least it was dry and warm.

I grinned at Ol' Jim. He turned and looked at me. "Where's the jackfish I caught at the portage?" he asked.

I smiled and said, "I didn't want it rubbing against my leg. There was nothing to wrap it in, so I threw it into the food box."

He thought about that a minute, then said, "We are going to have a very fishy food box. The flour will taste fishy, the sugar will taste fishy, the oats will taste fishy, the wood will smell fishy, my clothes will smell fishy, but we will have fish for supper."

I started giggling again. "You put your clothes in the food box?"

"Where else was I going to put them since you had already

disappeared with the packsack. By the way, I guess I didn't tell you not to pull the canoe up on top of a rock. That's what made the canoe tip over, you know? I didn't think I needed to tell you that. You rush too much, you know that? I have never been in such a big hurry before in my whole life. This is the first time I have made this trip in one big mad dash! I don't even remember seeing what changes there may have been in the last two lakes we passed. You should take time to look around and remember how things are, son. Would you remember how we got here if you had to do the trip all over again without me?"

I put my head down and examined my shoes, then said, "I would remember the first two days . . . But since Loon Narrows, I don't know if I would remember where the portage was."

He kicked a log into the fire and said, "Now, don't go thinking I blame you entirely for being in such a dang hurry. After all, it was raining and getting miserable. I enjoy a look around when I'm paddling, but there ain't any sense in drowning to death in the rain while I'm at it. Give me the fish. May as well stake her in the ground here."

I watched him reach back and hack off a long slender bush with the knife and trim the branches away. I entered the tent and opened the food box and, sure enough, there was fish slime all over everything. I picked up the fish by the eyes and carried it out to the fire. Ol' Jim picked it up and pushed the stick through the eye and down the length to the tail and stuck it into the ground over the fire. I watched the fish smoke and drip and the fire pop.

"Take off your shoes and hang your socks to dry," he said as he picked up his axe again. I saw him reach inside the food box and drag out his muddy, fish-slimy clothes and fling them over the branch of a pine tree beside the tent. I giggled as he disappeared into the bushes.

I was very comfortable by the fire and I pulled off my shoes. They were covered with mud. My socks were also black with mud. I took Ol' Jim's knife and rounded off the ends of two of the branches he had hacked off the roasting stick. I planned to toast-dry my socks by hanging them over the ends of the sticks. This way I could just shake off the mud when it dried. I stuck the ends into the ground and hung each sock over the fire. I propped up my shoes before the fire, well away from the flames, and watched the steam rise from them. I leaned back against the food box and closed my eyes. The rain was coming down steady now, the thunder rolling and cracking somewhere on the north side of the lake. That storm just missed us. I watched my socks swaying back and forth as they were pelted by little red rockets and fireballs from the fire. Some missed and flew to the wet ground, others were direct hits, "kaboom!" I saw many black flecks of ash accumulating on top of the mud. Maybe I have them hanging too close.

Suddenly Ol' Jim walked by with a whole messy tree, its branches scraping everywhere. He dropped it beside the fire and the branches flipped around, spraying water and mud all over the place and knocking both my toast-dried socks off their sticks and into the fire. All I had time to do was pop my mouth open before my socks burst into flames. The branch flipped around once more and I dived for my shoes and grabbed them before they got swept into the fire too. Ol' Jim continued his battle with the tree of many arms, chopping each one in turn, until he was left with a log. Then he scraped the branches together and broke them into smaller pieces and threw them into the fire. I watched the sparks fly, and the ashes that had once been my socks disappeared. Then he proceeded to chop the log into pieces, and I watched the fish start to sizzle and drip beside my two empty sticks.

With a sigh, Ol' Jim shook off the water from his grey, spiked hair and took off his jacket, shaking it so that he sprayed me with water all over again. His grinning face was shining wet and glowing in the firelight as he sat down beside me. He stretched his feet out to the fire, and I noticed him studying my two empty sticks.

Finally he said, "Was there anything on those two sticks, or are you roasting invisible bannock rolls?"

I hadn't quite figured out what I was supposed to wear on my feet now. I didn't like the idea of not wearing socks inside my shoes. I was suddenly reminded of my first night in the middle of nowhere. I shrugged and said, "I had a sock at the end of each of those sticks but that branch knocked them both into the fire. Bannock rolls sound good, how do I make them?"

I heard a wheezing noise and his shoulders shook as he turned away to throw another log into the fire. I heard him rummage around in the box behind me, then he put the pan down, dumped some flour in, dumped a bit of baking powder in, stirred it, poured some water from the teapot, stirred it again and made a flour mud pie until it was quite thick and hard to move around. When it was a hard ball, he took another roasting stick and wound the dough around and around on the tip of the stick and handed it to me. This was great! I took the stick with the spiral roll of bannock and held it over the hot ashes. I watched it slowly puff up and turn light brown, but it started to sag, so I had to continually turn it around and around to keep the light brown spreading evenly all around. Ol' Jim tends to daydream, and his roll got some burnt spots on it. He grinned each time his bannock started to smoke.

Ol' Jim turned the fish around once more and the drops sizzled into the fire. The rain had slowed a bit, but the sky was still a solid grey. Our bannock was cooked perfectly before the fish was, so we ate the bannock and had some tea while we waited for the fish. My shoes were almost dry, but I propped them up some more.

I heard Ol' Jim digging around in his packsack inside, and when he came out, he handed me a pair of his grey work socks. "Here, put these on. I always carry an extra, extra pair in case a branch decides to take some socks with it into the flames," he said. I pulled the warm socks on and wiggled my toes in them.

Slowly, carefully, he took the fish off the stick and settled it on a piece of birchbark. He cut it in half through the back and slid the flesh of one side off the bones and then slid the flesh off the other side. All that was left on the stick were the bones, still intact and holding whatever else was inside the bone cavity. We settled back and enjoyed the fresh-roasted fish under the tarp beside the fire.

Suddenly Ol' Jim stopped, put his fish down, and bent over

to rummage around in the box behind me, saying, "I can't believe it! You know, I forgot we had a bit of salt in here. Salt is very good on fish. Not very complementary on other things like rabbit or partridge, but it sure is good on fish. Here, try some!"

I had almost resigned myself to eating without salt, as long as I had something to eat. It was indeed a luxury to sprinkle out a dash of salt on fire-smoked and roasted fish. Yum, delicious! I smiled as I examined his salt container. It was marked "penicillin." I had noticed it stuck in a corner with the matches. I thought it was his medicine.

I decided to go and take a nap, so I put my dry shoes on and entered the tent. The ground was wet inside and I hesitated to put the sleeping bags on the ground, so I just curled up on top of the empty fishnet canvas bag and shoved my blanket sack under my head. I pulled my army blanket over me and listened to the clink, clink of Ol' Jim's axe on branches. He was the one who complained about travelling too fast, yet he never sat still himself. It was close to evening now. The raindrops from the branches above continued to splatter on top of the plastic whenever the wind picked up. I could hear the swish, swish of waves lapping against the rocks along the shoreline.

The sound of chopping wood woke me. I must have dozed off. It was getting dark now, and I noticed a strong smell of pine before I saw the two big mounds of pine branches inside the tent. Ol' Jim came in and handed me a cup of steaming hot tea. Very grateful, I got up and sat on the packsack and watched him settle down on his knees with his back to me as he began to stick each branch into the ground. Slowly sipping the hot tea, I watched him expertly handle the branches. Side by side, he marched the pine branches across the front and backed up to push another layer into the ground.

"The ground is growing pine feathers," I said. I suddenly remembered the branches that I had scattered on the ground the night before.

I could barely see his hands at the corner when he finally pushed the last branch in. Our tent now had a thick green, carpeted floor and smelled wonderful. The branches were damp, but it kept us off the wet ground as we rolled out the sleeping bags. The light from the fire cast huge shadows of our bodies as we sat outside and ate our evening meal of hot tea-porridge. A burst of rain sent me into the tent, and Ol' Jim threw a stack of wood inside and we settled down to sleep. Occasional chills shook my body before I generated enough warmth through my damp clothes. I listened to the rustling plastic and crackling fire for a long time before my eyelids became heavy. I fell asleep to the sound of Ol' Jim's monotonous wheezing.

Early the next morning, I woke to find Ol' Jim gone. I yawned and crawled out of my blanket. I couldn't smell or hear the campfire. That was strange. I went outside and stood there listening. Birds were chirping and the wind was blowing through the trees. The tree branches showered water on the leaf-covered ground when the wind blew. I kicked aside some of the yellowed bush leaves on the ground. Most still had some green in them. The wind must have blown so hard it blew the drying leaves off the bushes. The sky was overcast yet, and the waves crashed one after another along the shoreline. They must be very high. We might not be able to go anywhere today. I saw that the fire was ready to be lit. The teapot was filled with water. I walked down to the lake and saw high waves with white peaks marching down through the big channel that opens out into the lake. The canoe was gone and there was no sign of Ol' Jim. I could see the point across the channel where we had set the net, so I started hopping and running along the shoreline. I came to a place where the rocks stopped and I could not go any farther. From here, I could see the exact spot across the channel where Ol' Jim had tied the fishnet. I should be able to see the multicoloured floats in the water, but there were none in sight. Where could he have gone? I turned around and headed back to camp. I walked up the path and into the clearing. The axe was there leaning against the tree. Everything was still here, only the canoe was gone. The canvas fishnet wrap! I ran into the tent and, sure enough, it was gone, too. That meant he went and pulled up the fishnet. But where did he go then?

I found the matches in the food box. It sure did smell fishy in there. I got the fire going and set the teapot on it. After a coughing fit caused by the smoke from the fire, I picked up more wood from the tent. I got the fire going good and hot and stood around waiting for the tea to boil. We will need more wood. I picked up the axe and headed out into the bush where Ol' Jim had gone, and I saw where he had chopped down a tree. I looked around until I saw a dry birch tree. I started hacking away at it. The axe seemed to just bounce off. I kept swinging away and finally the axe bit into the soft wood. When there was about an inch more to go I stopped and pushed and pushed until I heard a crack, and the small tree went down. I was very proud of myself. I walked down the length of the tree, whacking and breaking off the branches, and then cut the tree into three-foot lengths. I was working up quite a sweat when I finally got the tree into three pieces. I took one piece and the axe and struggled, staggering, back into the clearing at the campsite. Still no one around. I went back for the other two pieces. My shoes were soaking wet when I got back.

There it was again, the thought I had been trying to block from my mind—what if something had happened to Ol' Jim? What if the canoe had tipped over and he had drowned out there? What was I to do?

I took the teapot off the fire and put the two logs on. Then I heard his voice and the thumping of the canoe. I ran to the lake and saw Ol' Jim coming, rolling back and forth, the canoe sliding side to side, riding on the edge of the waves. At times, he looked like he was sitting on top of the water, then the canoe would disappear altogether, with just his head sticking out. Still, he came on, talking a blue streak in a very angry voice.

I stood rooted to the spot, wondering what was wrong. As soon as he saw me, I heard him yell, "That darned moose! The stinking darned moose . . . " I waited for more, but I couldn't hear him over the water crashing on the rocks. Finally the canoe came near enough, riding on a wave that lifted it and deposited it on the sand.

"Watch the rocks, watch the rocks! Don't let it go sideways!" he yelled as I grabbed the front of the canoe before it was lifted by the waves again. He scrambled to the front, and we hauled the canoe in over the rocks and onto dry land. He stood there panting and dripping wet. His green cotton jacket looked black. He looked like he had gone for a swim with his clothes on. I saw two pickerel in the canoe. He ran his hand over his face and scratched his head.

"Where did you go?" I asked.

He didn't even seem to hear me as he took the fish and walked up the path, saying over his shoulder, "That dumb moose had to swim right across my fishnet! I finally found it tangled in the bush right into the trees and up the hill. I found the end rope way, way—dumb stinking moose! The net is all ripped to shreds . . . stupid moose!"

He stomped to the fire, his baggy pants hurrying to keep up with his legs. A giggling fit doubled me over, then he turned on me, "Where's the tea, sleepy head?" I hurried to take the pot off the fire. I had forgotten to put the tea in! I grabbed a small handful of tea from the box and dropped it into the pot and settled it over the hot ashes again.

"That's the first time in all my years I had to pick up fish from between leaves and trees, deep in the bush!" he said as he shoved the roasting sticks into the mouths of the pickerel and staked them into the ground over the fire.

I was so relieved to see him back, I really didn't care about the fishnet. I smiled and said, "You should have put up a warning sign for the moose."

He sprayed water on me as he took off his jacket, wrung it out, and hung it over the fire. His shirt was soaking wet too. I noticed a dry spot under his arms. He stood close to the fire and steam rose off him. He looked like a huge smoking brown cigar. He was so irritated.

Then I finally hit on an idea. "Can you show me how to set a rabbit snare?" I said as I sat leaning against a tree beside the fire. Without comment, he knelt beside me and took out a roll of snare wire from his pocket. He gave me a piece of wire and I followed his hands as he shaped and twisted the snare. I did the same with my snare wire. Then he explained how to set the snare, where the most likely place to find a rabbit-run was, and how far off the ground it must be. The tea was ready, and we had some tea-porridge while we waited for the fish.

When the fish were cooked, we shared one pickerel with salt added. We saved the other fish for lunch. The sky had cleared and now spotlights of sunshine filtered through the trees. The wind continued to blow, and the constant crash of the waves left the campsite a very noisy place to be.

Ol' Jim grabbed his jacket and we headed into the bush to look for a rabbit trail. It was not as wet in here as it was in the swamp where I went this morning for the firewood. There was a lot of moss on the ground, and soon the noise by the shore faded and the sounds of birds and squirrels could be heard. Then the sound of quacking, cackling ducks told me that there was a pond to our left. I followed the old man over mossy mounds of rocks, crawled over fallen trees and stumps, and jumped over puddles when finally he stopped and looked around. He was pointing to some little piles of light brown peas. We went farther into a swampy section and the light brown peas became greener. I noticed many funny-looking pink packsacks turned upside down. He told me the Ojibwa name for them. I think the school teacher had called them Lady Slippers. I saw Ol' Jim standing there surveying the area between two small pine trees in a dip between two high rocks. It was there he set his snare, slowly and carefully, and I watched every move. Then he waited for me to decide where I was going to put mine. I picked a little trail that looked well used. He watched silently.

When I was finished and did everything he had done with his snare, I stood back. He said, "That is kind of a hard decision to ask a rabbit to make."

"What do you mean?" I asked, puzzled.

"To stretch or duck under. I think I would decide to duck under if I was a rabbit," he said as he walked away.

Stretch or duck under? Why doesn't he just say that it's too high? I pushed the snare stick lower and the snare came down about an inch. That should do it. I turned and ran after Ol' Jim, who was now going up a hill.

When we came down the other side, the view took my breath away! The sky had cleared and the sun shone bright and hot. There was a long sand beach that curved around like a shimmering golden highway. There was an island right across and beach all around. I couldn't help myself as my feet took off at full speed, through the soft sandy ground and onto the beach. I ran along just out of lick of the waves as they charged and crashed with all their might on the beach. I ran until I noticed tracks on the sand. Deep pointed tracks. Moose? Must be. I stopped and turned around and there was Ol' Jim lying on the sand, all spread out. I laughed and raced back, hooting and hollering. This was just great! I was about to jump over his body when his leg and hands came up and I was pulled over. We rolled, with sand spraying into my face, and I was sent flying about three feet away onto the softest sand I had ever felt.

We spent the whole afternoon by the beach. Ol' Jim decided to go for a swim and wash all his clothes at the same time. "You just finished drying off and now you want to go back in the water?" I giggled.

"Well, I was wet when I didn't want to be and, besides, I don't particularly like the smoke-dried smell," he said as he sloshed into the water with all his clothes on. I chased after him and he sideswiped me with his soaking-wet jacket right on the back of the head.

I was the one who went swimming though. All he did was sit in the water and let the waves and sand do all the work. Later, sand scrubbed, sprayed, and hosed down by the waves, we lay stretched out on the sand with just our shorts on and our pants and shirts hanging on the branches of the tall pine trees. Seagulls flashed in the sun as they screeched and swerved in the windy sky, and the high waves continually crashed against the beach, one after another, all along the shoreline, washing away all my footprints. I wished then that we could stay there forever and forget where we came from and where we were going. I wanted this place and time to never end.

Sometime in the late afternoon, I heard Ol' Jim's stomach rumble and he sat up and started pulling on his shirt and pants. I did the same and it became a race. I pulled on my shirt and pants first and ran into the bushes with Ol' Jim close behind me.

We emerged in the clearing behind the tent. I dashed for the woodpile and put the branches, twigs, and birchbark on the ashes and was rewarded with a puff of smoke from our dying fire. Ol' Jim had gone down to the lake with his muddy clothes from the day before. I raced behind him and attempted to fill the teapot between the waves. He laughed each time I made a run for the calm water between the rocks before the second wave came up. I finally filled up the teapot as he threw his muddy clothes into the water. The waves grabbed the clothes, swished and twirled them between the rocks, then each new wave pounded them against the rocks so hard that the pants stuck to the rock before another wave pulled them back into the water. We stood around and watched the waves at work. Ol' Jim had a stick that he used to fish the shirt back with every time it tried to escape. Soon he said the clothes were clean, so he set about fishing them out with the stick between each wave.

I rushed back to the campsite and put the teapot on the fire. I threw in some more wood and watched the flames eat up one piece of wood after another until Ol' Jim finally came up and threw his clothes over the branches of the pine trees beside the fire. I threw in another handful of tea from our dwindling supply of food. In a few minutes, I saw him emerge from the tent with the other pickerel from this morning, which he set by the fire to heat. He mixed up another batch of the roast-over-the-fire stick bannock, which we each propped up over the fire as the fish warmed up. I settled back with a big smile as I watched our supper sizzle.

The wind died down a bit by the time we sat down to eat. Later we set out to cut some more wood and piled up quite a bit inside the tent before we went to bed.

I listened to the gentle waves lapping at the rocks on the shoreline, the whistling sound of wings as ducks flew over the tent along the shoreline, and Ol' Jim's soft breathing before I went to sleep.

Chapter Thirteen

T HE NEXT MORNING, I AWOKE TO BIRDS singing about what a beautiful day it was going to be. Ol' Jim had taught me by now to listen to the birds. If the white-throated sparrow finished its song, it was going to be a beautiful day. If it was going to rain, though, it would stop in mid-song like it was choking on the words, then start over, but it would choke on the words again and never get to finish its song. That meant bad weather for sure.

I smelled the campfire smoke and I could hear Ol' Jim rummaging around in the food box. He must be getting some tea. Sure enough, I heard the teapot lid being flipped open and closed again. I sat up and pulled my socks and shoes on. I flipped the tent flap open and stood there blinking at the bright, clear blue sky and the promise of the sun coming up big and hot. The dew lay dark on the ground, releasing the rich smell of earth, leaves, and moss. I smiled at Ol' Jim as he went about making his prop-in-front-of-the-fire baked bannock. I liked that second best. Ashes always got stuck to it. Now my favourite bannock was the kind roasted on a stick.

I ran down to the lake and stopped for a moment to look at a loon as it popped up by the channel. It went down again without a sound. I splashed some water on my face, neck, and arms. The mosquitoes had found me already! I had no towel, so I wiped my face with my sleeve. Ol' Jim's medicine worked pretty good, the mosquito sores on my neck were healing very quickly. I looked out at the calm water and examined the shoreline around the lake. The rocks across the lake looked pure white as the sun shone on them. They looked like the sides of white-painted houses. The beaches were like strips of light-gold satin ribbon bordering a royal blue lake, trimmed with ruffled green velvet. It was so beautiful. For some reason, it made me sad. I looked at every single detail, trying to memorize every inch of it.

I had seen something like that once, a huge pillow, a room . . . a bedroom? I can't remember, but it was in a movie I went to once, with Tom. A movie with horses and swords . . . Tom. Somehow I couldn't see Tom in a beautiful place like this. He belongs in a town. I thought about Dad. He belongs in a town now too. If he was by himself, though, maybe he'd like it out here. But then he'd miss all the things he can do in town. Isn't that why he moved to town? So he could get a job and live with the witch? Besides, the father I knew when I was small is gone now. I don't know him any more! A pressure was starting to build in my chest, pinching the base of my throat, making my eyes water. Mama . . . no! I must not think about Mama. I took another swipe at my eyes with my sleeve. I sure could imagine Henry here though. We'd probably stay here the whole summer if we could. I wish he could see this! I took a deep breath and watched a bloodsucker come waving by under the water. I turned at a noise behind me and saw Ol' Jim's hunched back slowly disappear between the bushes, back to camp. Why didn't he say anything?

We were still in shadow here, and I couldn't wait to get out to the beach on the other side again. I know! I'll just check the snares and go for another run on the beach before we get on our way. I knew he would want to leave soon because the lake was very calm. I could see the perfect reflection of the seagulls circling above. I bet that's why they were doing it, too, to see themselves soaring in the breeze. I could just hear them saying, "Here, here, here I am! Such a beauty, such a beauty, ha, ha, ha!" I smiled and flung a rock at one that passed daringly close to my head. It swerved to avoid the rock and screeched at me. I ran back to the clearing, and there was Ol' Jim roasting a rabbit over the fire.

"You checked the snares! Why didn't you wait for me?" I asked as I sat down beside the fire.

"I just checked my snare while I was down there. Yours is a bit too far. You can check that one yourself. I put my snares close to my morning path," he said as he went about turning the bannock around on the pan and banking the ashes a little bit higher.

I ran into the bushes and retraced our steps, skipping and hopping over the rocks and logs until I came to the spot where my snare was. It had not moved. No rabbit had gone near it. I pulled the snare off the stick and ran through the bushes and over the hill, through the tall jack-pine trees toward the beach.

The sun was shining over the horizon onto the sand, not yet drying the overnight dampness from the surface. I could tell because my feet made a track on the top of the damp sand, exposing the powder-dry sand of yesterday. I ran again, as fast as I could, to the rock-pile divider on the beach. It continued on the other side of the divider for another mile or so. I turned and retraced my steps, slowly, relishing this new feeling of being alive, well, and happy.

I took a big breath of the clean fresh air and watched a few fancy, bright blue, tiny dragonflies hovering over some weeds by the water. A squirrel kicked up quite a chatter over my head, near the shore. What's ticked him off this morning? I noticed some ancient-looking, black, one-inch-round spider shells attached to some boulders by the shore. When I picked one up, one leg broke off. It was very dry and clung tightly to the rock. The creature had left a neat round hole where it had crawled out of the back of the ugly spider shell, the white threads remained blowing in the wind, like lacing undone. I put it back down on the rock beside the other one. I must remember to ask Ol' Jim what kind of thing came out of there. Then I noticed others behind the rock, in fact, all the rocks were covered with them! If I was some other kind of animal, what would I smell? What would I notice? I hunched down and pretended I was a wolf. I sniffed the damp warm air as I trotted to the edge of the water. I kicked up some small, spiral-shaped, empty pink shells on the sand. Hm, what kind

141

of creature lived in them? Among the weeds by the water, I noticed bundles of thin sticks about one inch long. They were moving! I picked one up and turned it over and saw thin hairy legs sticking out. I dropped it back into the water. Why does it look like a bundle of sticks? If it is a worm, why doesn't it just be a worm and look like a worm instead of hiding inside and pretending to be a bundle of sticks? Wolf forgotten, I stood up and looked across the lake.

I could see every tree, shade, and hollow of the gold-ribbon-bordered island across from me. The beach stretched all around the island as far as I could see. It would be nice if we could sleep there, at least overnight. Ol' Jim said the Native people call the island Ochichakominising. Ha! I remembered! Ol' Jim said I'd probably forget it the minute he told me. I turned and ran back to the bushes, heading for camp. That rabbit must be cooked by now.

I paused to watch a squirrel peel off a pine cone as I walked through the swampy edge of the woods. He looked like he was shucking corn or something. Then he popped it into his mouth, and I watched his little cheeks quiver before he whirled around and scurried down the tree. I passed by the Pink-Packsack Lady Slippers as I called them now. I walked around them so as not to disturb their early-morning meal of dew and flies. I pulled out some high soft moss to clean the pots with. It was great for absorbing grease from a pan, not that we ever had much grease left in the pan. Ol' Jim called this moss Baby-diapers and said it has some kind of medicine in it that keeps babies from getting rashes when they are diapered with it.

I heard his voice before I entered the clearing. Ol' Jim, sipping tea with his feet stretched out to the fire, was deep in conversation with himself again. I dropped the snare wire with the moss on his lap and picked up the other half of the rabbit on the birchbark. I always pretended I couldn't eat any more, so I left him a leg from my half while I filled up with some of his delicious bannock.

"Ol' Jim, what came out of those big black spider things? There are a lot of them on the rocks over there on the beach.

Each one has an opening on the back and something untied it, came out, and left the white strings hanging there," I said between bites.

He glanced at me, then said, "There are many of them on the rocks down by the lake here too. You are getting better at noticing things, but let your eyes tell you all of what they see."

I waited for more, but he seemed to have forgotten my question, so I repeated, "What used to live in the black spiders?"

His stubborn chin went up. Then suddenly he said, "Right there!" and pointed to the sky. I saw nothing. He was still pointing, and then I noticed that his finger was following a big green dragonfly. He said, "You have to be patient! I was waiting for it so that you can see what it looks like. In the spring, it crawls up on the rocks from the water. There it sits, anchoring its claws on the rock. Then it begins to unlace the seam on its back. Its head and upper body come out first, then its long skinny bottom begins to uncurl as it comes out of the shell. It is all bright green at this point. Even the wings are like new leaves, all wrinkled and curled up. They begin to uncurl and spread out to the summer sun. When the wings have all dried up, it flies off. My, that must be such a wonderful feeling."

Things uncurling to the sun. That reminded me of something Mr. Old Indian had said, if I remembered correctly. I decided to see if it made any sense to Ol' Jim. I looked at the old man beside me, his dreamy eyes to the sky, probably still thinking about the dragonfly. I said, "An old man at Savant Lake said that wrinkled babies are like leaves uncurling." Ol' Jim turned and smiled at me. I continued. "Then he said something about dead leaves and flat hands."

Ol' Jim now sat with his head down, then he picked up one of the brown leaves from the ground. He sat there turning it around and around, but said nothing. I got up and poured another cup of tea and set it down beside him. I waited some more. Then he said softly, "The words of the Old . . . " He turned to me. "It is important to remember exactly what is said so that you in turn, when you are an old man, can tell it

to a little person like you. But you did good. I understand."
That's it? He sipped his tea.

He seemed to be taking his time getting the stuff together,
so I didn't rush him. After the scrumptious breakfast and a
cup of hot tea, I checked out the swamp to the right of us and
discovered a partridge. It flapped its wings and dove into thick
brush. I waited and threw a stick to chase it out of there. It
took flight to a tree. It sat there, turning its head to the left
and right. I could even see its eyes blink from this distance. I
stepped into a waterpuddle and swore in Ojibwa as I hopped
to drier ground.

Ol' Jim spoke behind me, "Where are your rocks? Go get
some!"

While he was in there keeping an eye on the partridge, I ran
to the shoreline to grab as many half-fist-sized rocks as I could
find and hurried back to the bush with a shirtful. We ended
up on a very fine partridge chase, with an occasional "Don't
hit me!" coming from Ol' Jim as I ran dashing around in
circles, trying to get a good shot at the partridge. Ol' Jim
finally managed to clip it on the head with a sharp stone.

"Get em! Get em! It's on the ground now! Right there! Get
em!" he screeched as I scrambled over some fallen-over logs,
puddles, and bushes. Finally I landed on the partridge, its
wings flailing at my face as I scrambled to keep my knees and
feet out of water. I got it!

We were panting and laughing so hard when we came to
our camp that it took a moment to register that something
wasn't right. The food box was upside down, the teapot had
rolled into the bushes by the path, and the tent poles were
knocked aside. It was a good thing the tent was already rolled
up tight and inside the canoe with the rest of the things. The
canoe! We both rushed down the path and found it unmo-
lested. The bear tracks were unmistakably clear on the sand
around the campsite. He had spilled a bit of flour but seemed
to have found the lard more to his liking because that was all
he took. Now we had no more lard. Oh well, we didn't use it
that much anyway. Ol' Jim only used a bit on top of the
tea-porridge and not much of it on anything else. The oats and

the rest of the bannock were still under the box too. Maybe we scared it away before it got to the rest of the things, which meant it was probably still close by. Suddenly I was in a big hurry to get under way again. I loaded the canoe before Ol' Jim even had time to finish plucking the partridge, so he just threw it into the canoe.

He mumbled as we got in, "Bears are very hungry this year. They're not getting enough to eat out there. They must think we're tourists or something!"

That must be why they are coming around when they hear us. They are probably looking for food. I would feel safer sleeping on an island. Are there bears on islands too?

Off we went into the open waters of Whitewater Lake. We were nearing Best Island when, on the spur of the moment, I turned and said, "Ol' Jim, couldn't we stay here one night? It is so beautiful, I don't know if I will ever see such a wonderful place again."

The paddling stopped and we drifted for a few seconds before the canoe suddenly swerved to the left toward the island. I glanced back with a big smile on my face. "All right! You're great, Ol' Jim!" I heard him chuckle as we neared the clearing by the beach in front of some tall jack-pine trees.

I jumped out and pulled the canoe in. Ol' Jim pulled it up the rest of the way while I ran through the clearing. There was an old campground here. I could tell because of the familiar tent poles leaning against the trees. There was an old makeshift table wedged between two trees and rocks arranged in a circle, holding in a pile of ashes. This was just wonderful! I ran a bit farther and saw that there were campsites all along the beach that you couldn't see from the water. I emerged by a pile of boulders and made my way to the water. Seagulls were circling overhead and the water lay still and calm in the bay. I ran along the water's edge back to the campsite. I could see Ol' Jim tying up the poles for the tent. I stopped and pulled an old dead branch down and threw it on the firepit. I ran down to the canoe and finished unloading the rest of the stuff and quickly piled it up beside the wooden table. I ran and filled the teapot with water and hurried back to the campfire.

I was just sweating hot. We were in full sunlight, with no wind or shade. Heat waves shimmered over the white sand.

Ol' Jim smiled and said, "Let's go for a paddle between the islands and set some hooks."

I grinned and threw some twigs and bark into the firepit while I waited for him to finish checking over a long rope with a pile of three-inch hooks attached that he had pulled out of his sack.

When he was ready, we slowly made our way to the shore. He threw an oblong-shaped rock into the canoe, and we paddled out to the channel in the calm hot afternoon. I knew he used a rock like that for the fishnet, but he didn't have a fishnet now, only the hooks on the rope, so what does he need the rock for? I decided not to ask and started paddling. We slowly made our way around the island. When we came around the point, I got the full view of the lake. It was huge! I looked down both sides of the shoreline and decided that it was a good thing the waves weren't high today. Ol' Jim trailed his green line around the point and soon he gave a yelp and hauled in a huge jackfish from the swampy bay we were passing. That made me very happy for I knew that we would have fish to eat again for supper.

We hugged the shoreline where the trees provided shade. I could smell mint from the trail of little round leaves sprouting from the bed of moss that was draped over the rocks. I watched the four-legged spiders that ran around on the surface of the water. Ol' Jim said they are called Loon Lice. Suddenly he stopped paddling and whispered, "Rabbit." I looked along the shoreline and a movement caught my eye. Right by the water, under a leaning cedar bush, sat a brown rabbit, ears twitching. Then one hop and it was gone. The paddling started again behind me.

Then his voice began, "She stood there on that rock at the point. She had the baby . . . she had the little one . . . "

I closed my ears and looked across the lake. I just get confused when I listen to him. I could spend the next half-hour trying to figure out what he was talking about. Hey! The lake doesn't end here. I could see another long stretch to the left. How big is this lake anyway? I had another drink from my paddle. Dip, tilt, and drink.

The flies were dancing above the mud patches by the swampy bay before the rocks took over the shoreline. The rocks looked as if they had been poured in layers and had then flowed out into the water. A giant hand poured grey cement mixed with white and black paint that wasn't shook-up enough, poured it in stripes and blotches to the water's edge. Suddenly we scraped on something. I could feel it under my left foot. At the same time Ol' Jim swore and rocked the canoe to the right and we were free. I could see the huge golden shimmer of a rock just under the water as we passed by it.

I was feeling quite ashamed. I should have been watching for rocks. I kept my head high and my back straight and the silence was loud behind me. I diligently searched ahead for any more rocks and was quite aware of every movement behind me. I saw another rock coming so I steered the canoe to the right and we glided by safely. I was very attentive for the next half-hour before the constant gentle gurgle at the front of the canoe began to lull me into another lazy, dreamy state. My eyelids were half-closed to shut out the glare of the sun dancing on top of the water, and my arms slowed to one dip for every two of Ol' Jim's. Dip, tilt, and I let water pour down on top of my head. Another dip and tilt to wash my face, another dip and tilt to wet my chest, then suddenly a big splash of water landed squarely across my shoulders! I gasped, laughed, and glanced back, then choked as a sheet of water landed full on my face. I wiped my eyelashes free and gave the paddle a big slap on the water at what I hoped was the right angle. I was rewarded by the sound of water hitting its target. I glanced back to see Ol' Jim wiping his face. We chuckled as we paddled on again.

When Ol' Jim steered the canoe toward a beach by a rock cliff, I decided to go for a swim. Ol' Jim sat there baiting the hook on his trailing line with the cut-out cheek of the jackfish. I pulled off my shirt and, careful not to tip the canoe, yanked off my pants and threw myself overboard. I splashed in headfirst and I heard the gurgle of water against my ears as I pushed my body to the bottom of the lake. I touched the soft sand at the bottom and felt the quick sting of the water in my eyes as I looked around. The long blades of grass swayed in flowing wavy motions as I swam by. Then the tall weeds brushed my hands. They were very straight and tight, as if the ground under the water held them tightly, while at the same time they were pulled hard to the surface of the water by the sun. That must be a very difficult place to grow. They were pulled from both directions at the same time.

It was very bright under there, and I could feel the water becoming warmer as I popped my head up. I was almost to the shore. I let out a spray of water and took a big breath. Ol' Jim was still sitting inside the canoe, cleaning the fish against the flat side of his paddle. I heard him chuckle as I dove once more into the deeper, cooler water.

When I popped up out of the water again, Ol' Jim was in the shade at the base of the rock cliff, talking to himself. He was pointing to the east and west. I came up closer to the canoe and caught a whiff of pipe smoke.

"Aren't you going to get out?" I yelled.

He turned and looked at me but did not answer. Then I caught a movement by the base of a tree and there sat the strangest-looking person I had ever seen in my whole life! I came forward to get a closer look. The creature sat so still that he blended right into the forest. Maybe he was one of *them!*

"Ol' Jim," I whispered as I reached the canoe, wiping the water away from my eyes. "Is he one of the Memegwesiwag?"

Ol' Jim started shaking with laughter, and the other old man's eyes twinkled but he said nothing. He looked like a movie Indian! His white hair was very long and he had a red rolled-up cloth tied around his head. He had on an old dark green shirt and work pants. Then I noticed that his hair was not all white but had a lighter brown mixed in it . . . an old whiteman! What was he doing here? Then I realized they were speaking English, or Ol' Jim's form of English anyway. They were talking about the weather and mosquitoes.

I looked very carefully along the shoreline, trying to figure out where the old man had come from. I saw no trace of a cabin, path, canoe, or anything. Maybe he was lost and we were finding him. But he didn't look lost, and he had not moved from where he sat leaning against the tree. Then Ol' Jim made a motion for me to get in the canoe, which he balanced as I scrambled in. I waited to see what the old man was going to do as he slowly unfolded his body and stood up. He had stooped shoulders and was rather skinny, but his step was sure and firm as he approached the canoe and reached to take the fish that Ol' Jim held out to him. Our supper! I watched the old man wave and slowly disappear into the forest. I was just bursting to ask questions when the canoe finally started out into the lake.

"Who is he? Where did he come from? What is he doing here? Is he lost? Did someone leave him here? He wasn't a Memegwesi, was he? Does he live here?" There was only silence behind me as the canoe sped forward once more. By now, we were around the channel between the island and the mainland. We paddled into the shadow of the high rocks and tall trees.

The paddling stopped and Ol' Jim said, "The man lives on the island. There are cabins in the woods that you can't see from the water. He makes sure that he doesn't disturb the natural surroundings. I wish there were more people like him."

"But where did he come from?" I asked.

"Oh, he's been here for years." He said no more, and I tried to figure out why anyone would want to live here in the bush all by himself. I was getting hungry. I pulled on my shirt and pants.

It was evening now and the sun had disappeared behind the trees. We paddled between two islands, and here Ol' Jim decided to tie one end of the rope with the three-inch hooks attached every foot or so to an overhanging tree and let the rope out into the water. The hooks were baited with the fish guts from the jackfish he had given away. When we got to the end of the rope, Ol' Jim tied on the rock that he had put into the canoe and let it down into the water.

I thought of the partridge back at camp, and I paddled faster as the canoe turned toward the long finger of golden sand where our camp was. A loon was whooping and laughing like a maniac by the bay. I cupped my hand and blew a whistle the way Henry had taught me and, immediately, water pelted me across the back. I gasped and glanced back. Ol' Jim looked stern. He shook his head, but said nothing. I did something wrong. I hunched my shoulders and vowed to remember not to whistle like that again. A loon popped her head up right ahead of us! She answered the cry from the bay. Oh, she was beautiful. She spread her wings and flapped them over the surface of the water. Suddenly she went under again. I watched the water all around, waiting for her to pop up. I waited a long time before, finally, I caught sight of her way over by the bay. That was a long way to go under water.

Soon we were back at the campsite. I was very tired and hungry. I held the canoe as Ol' Jim straightened his cramped legs. While he set the partridge to roast, I ran to gather more firewood. I walked all along the beach and soon I found a trail much like the rabbit trail at our other campsite. Just then I saw Ol' Jim by the canoe, so I yelled to him, and he came and examined the path.

"That's a duck path," he said.

I wondered out loud, "If that's a duck path, so much like a rabbit path, couldn't you put a snare for a duck like you did for the rabbit?"

Now that was a challenge for Ol' Jim if I ever heard one, and he went for it! "Well, of course!" he said.

His chest puffed out and he pulled out the snare wire from his pocket and set about creating a fence along the open sand with little pieces of sticks. When he was satisfied that all access points had been blocked off to the inland pond, he set his snare on the main path. Time was going by and my stomach grumbled again.

Finally I asked, "Won't the partridge be burning?"

"No," he said.

So I sat back and watched, absorbed with the detail and care that he put into the job. Then we backtracked and he swished the sand around with a pine branch until it looked as though no one had been there at all.

It was late in the evening by this time, and we headed back

to camp. The fire was almost out, but the teapot sat slowly steaming by the ashes. I could smell the partridge cooking in it. I watched as Ol' Jim poured some oats into the teapot and stirred them. Since we only had one pot, I wondered how we were going to have any tea.

Soon the teapot lid was lifting and boiling over into the fire, so Ol' Jim moved it away a little farther and settled down to watch the fire crackle and pop. I was too hungry to sit still, so I ran down to the beach again, to the west. At the end of the beach I noticed a path. It went straight into some tall poplar trees. I followed it and emerged on the other side of the point. There were the islands where we had set the hook line.

I walked on the sand pebbles and stopped to examine a few. Some were polished pink and white, others were caramel gold and looked like candies. Candies, sweet and delicious—the thought made my mouth water. I want candies, I am dying for candies! For chocolates! Chips! Pop! Cold, sizzling pop. I sat on a boulder and watched the shadows darken. Flies of all kinds were buzzing around my head or tearing around like little black helicopters. Blackflies, horseflies, houseflies, and every other kind of fly I could think of. Even a big yellow bumblebee paused to sniff at my knee before it took off in another burst of buzzing. Frogs from the swamp croaked, one after the other, back and forth.

That partridge must be cooked by now. I felt like I could eat the whole thing myself. I hoped the old man at the other end of the island was enjoying the fish. I grabbed one caramel-coloured rock and one shiny white one and shoved them into my pocket as I took off down the path again. Ol' Jim had birchbark plates all ready when I arrived at camp.

"Did you see or hear anything?" he asked as he dished out the steaming partridge pieces onto the bark and gave me the "penicillin" container of salt.

"No. I figured out, though, that frogs keep afloat on the lily pads by passing gas."

I salted the partridge and gave it back to him. I could see him turning this over in his head before he smiled and began to giggle. I grinned between mouthfuls and watched his shoulders shake once in a while. We leaned back against the trees, enjoying every mouthful. I watched him break the bones with his knife and suck out the marrow. I decided to try it and cracked my drumstick bone just like he did and sucked out the marrow. Hey, that was good! Then Ol' Jim poured the partridge-porridge into the dipper and handed it to me, along with a spoon. It was the most delicious meal I had tasted yet. I finished it in no time, and Ol' Jim filled it up again as he too went for seconds. I was very full so I just watched as he finished his third cupful. We washed the food down with water from the lake and cleaned the dishes at the same time.

It was very quiet that night. My stomach was jam-packed full and I was toasty warm. The fire crackled and, occasionally, the wood fell into the flames and the light became brighter for a while, before it settled down to a constant flicker against the tent wall again. I wonder if any of the ducks have gone to the entrance with the snare yet. Ol' Jim said that there were other paths to the pond at the opposite end of the swamp. Of course, they could also fly in and land on the pond. So there might not be a duck in the snare. Unless one happened to be walking by the beach and decided to visit the pond. Well, there was a path and whoever made it would go there again, wouldn't they? What if it was a seagull path? What would we do with a seagull? No, Ol' Jim said it was a duck path. What is the difference between a seagull path and a duck path? Maybe seagulls don't make paths. Maybe they have different footprints. What does a duck footprint look like? I had seen the prints that seagulls made, but I hadn't examined duck footprints. I must remember to do that tomorrow and ask Ol' Jim which duck made which track. I yawned. There was no sound of wind or waves. Ol' Jim breathed quietly and evenly.

Chapter Fourteen

I WOKE UP EARLY THE NEXT MORNING. OL' Jim was still sleeping, which was a surprise. I had to go to the bush. I must have had too much water to drink last night. I sat up and pulled my socks and runningshoes on and quickly ducked outside. There was a heavy mist all around us. It must have been raining. I heard the mallards already quacking by the pond. They sure get up early, if they even go to sleep at all.

I walked down the path to the lake and did my business quickly in the bushes. I came back to the path and listened. I could hear splashing of some kind in the water, across the lake. I wondered what it was. If Ol' Jim was here with me, he would tell me.

The snare. Had any of those all-night-partying mallards walked into it? I raced down the path and along the shore, then slowed down, carefully approaching the area. There was some commotion there, and as I approached a duck set up a desperate, panic-stricken flapping of wings. I knew he was in trouble. I ran forward and saw that he was caught in the snare!

I tried to pounce on him, but my hands kept slipping to the left and to the right, amidst flying feathers, slaps to the face, and scratches to the hands. I finally got a hold of him and we rolled around in the sand and thrashed in the bush, then he slipped away from me again. That was the most slippery, agile critter in the world! I landed on him again and, finally, my hand came around a leg and I hung on, and then my other hand found the neck. I laid down on it and twisted the neck around like Ol' Jim had when he showed me how to kill a

153

rabbit. Suddenly all was still. My heart was thumping so loudly in my ears I could hardly hear anything. I felt like laughing for joy. I did it! I killed it! Breakfast! I will have breakfast cooked for Ol' Jim before he wakes up!

Just as I was getting off the duck, the wings suddenly flapped and showered my face with sand. My eye! I got sand in my eye! In agony, I held onto the duck's neck as I raced to the water. I went down on my hands and knees and shoved my whole face in. I could feel a kick once in a while from the duck. I had anchored him to the bottom with my fist. I rolled my eyeball around in the water and after the initial sting, I felt instant relief.

I scrambled up and pinned the duck's neck under my foot while I took my jacket off and wiped my face with it. The only part that was dry was at the back. I shoved the jacket under my arm and ran with the duck to the campsite, the snare and anchor stick flopping along on the beach behind me.

When I arrived, there was no sign of anything having changed. How does one go about getting a duck ready to cook? I have to take the feathers off. I grabbed the teapot and ran down to the lake again. Look at that! There was a silver lake floating above the treetops with a row of trees around it. It wasn't there yesterday. I must ask Ol' Jim about that. I dropped the duck and filled the teapot with sand and scoured it as well as I could, then rinsed it once more before I filled it with water and set it on the shore.

Suddenly the duck started thrashing around again! I pounced on it and tried to wring its neck a second time. It was like trying to twist a piece of rubber hose. I finally got the idea to put it against the rock, and I stomped on the neck with my shoes, but the duck kept sliding off. So I got another rock and pounded the neck until I made darn sure it was no longer alive. I examined the duck. There wasn't much left of the neck. I had almost severed it in two. The skin hung in shreds. I turned it over. It was all wet and covered with sand. I shook it, then I started pulling the feathers off the tummy. The wet feathers stuck to my hands and chest, and the dry inside ones went flying all over the place. No, that won't do.

I walked to the bushes and sat down, then carefully started pulling out the feathers and shoving them into the ground. There, that was better. I plucked and plucked until the duck was all bare-skinned. I ran back to the shore and grabbed the teapot. Hey, the lake above the treetops had disappeared. I ran back to the camp. Just as I approached the campfire, Ol' Jim came out of the tent. He looked at the duck, at me, and at the teapot, then burst out laughing. I looked down at myself and noticed that I was wet and covered with feathers, on my clothes, my hair, I even had some on my face and eyelashes. I stood there grinning back at him.

I lit the fire and soon Ol' Jim came back and put the duck on a roasting stick after he had cleaned out the insides, cut off the wings, and burnt the rest of the feather-down off the head and body. While the duck was roasting, Ol' Jim set some bannock to cook over the fire. My mouth was watering.

"There was a lake with trees all around it, and it was floating above the treetops across there. Why did it look like that?" I asked.

Ol' Jim shrugged and said, "It's called a mirage. With the mist in the air and the sun coming up on the horizon, it creates a reflection. When the mist starts to dry up, the picture begins to fade."

Oh, that made sense. I smiled and glanced at the tent and Ol' Jim nodded. That told me I should get busy taking the stuff down to the lake. We had to be on our way again. While I ran to get more wood, Ol' Jim quickly took down the tent, and I folded and tied it up into a bundle. Slowly the stuff accumulated inside the canoe, and all too soon the duck was ready, the bannock was golden brown, and the tea was brewing in the pot.

We sat in front of the fire and took our time eating. The sun had rapidly dried up the mist, and it looked like another very hot day. The water was calm here in the bay. If we were going to paddle along the big long lake, I hoped the wind wasn't going to blow too hard.

When we had finished cleaning up the campsite and loading up our stuff, we slowly paddled to where Ol' Jim had dropped his line of hooks. I watched him carefully winding up the rope and tugging at it as he placed the hooks in a row inside the canoe. Suddenly his arm was pulled sharply into the water. He heaved and pulled and the canoe rocked to the side. I grabbed on tightly as Ol' Jim groaned, and soon a huge strange-looking fish emerged. It was long, dark, and slick. It had no scales, only some flat circles of bone along its back and sides. The nose was pointed and rubbery with a huge sucker mouth underneath the head and thick white whiskers. I watched Ol' Jim giggling excitedly as he hit the four-foot-long fish over the head with the blunt side of the axe. The fish trembled and Ol' Jim hauled it into the canoe. When he pulled the rest of the rope up I was very thankful to see there weren't any more of those monsters to share the canoe with us.

"Sturgeon!" said Ol' Jim. "What a delicious treat we will have. That is the best-tasting fish you will ever eat!"

I was not too sure as I glanced at the peculiar creature lying at the bottom of the canoe. Well, we would have enough for lunch and supper anyway. The fog in the low bushes of the swamps to our right was disappearing quickly now as the sun shone its way through the haze. Seagulls were already squawking and creating a big racket somewhere to the north of us. We paddled by the sharp point of Best Island, and I looked along the beach I had gone tearing down the evening before. There were no words to describe the beauty of this place.

I breathed in the fresh air and listened to the swishing of the water against the canoe, the birds chirping along the shore, the ducks quacking in the bay, the croaking frogs, the buzzing flies from the bushes, the seagulls squawking up above, the occasional splash of fish on the water . . . the place seemed to thrive in a certain natural rhythm. It reminded me of the time I had listened to Henry's stomach.

We paddled along the shoreline. Ol' Jim said, under his breath, "He was laid to rest there, the Medicine Man." We were passing by some majestic sand cliffs. There were trees standing upright by their roots, the trunks about five feet off the sandy ground. Strange. Ol' Jim's voice came again, "The mass burial ground over there is all but forgotten now."

I turned, but didn't catch where he had indicated it was. We paddled on for about a half-hour when I noticed a pile of round rocks jutting out in a pyramid in the middle of the lake.

Ol' Jim must have seen that I had noticed the rocks because before I could think of a question, I heard him say, "Don't point at the rocks. They are not to be pointed at."

"Why?" I asked.

"A big wind will come and swamp us. We will drown here in the middle of the lake," he said.

"But how did they get there? Can we paddle there to see?" I craned my neck to get a better look.

"No. They are sacred rocks. We would stop to offer tobacco if we had to pass by them. But right now we have no business going there."

I watched the pile of rocks as we glided farther and farther away. There were long stretches of sand beaches everywhere.

After a couple of hours of following the shoreline Ol' Jim steered to a small island at the mouth of a river. We stopped and he built a fire by the shore. He cut up the tail part of the sturgeon and threw it into the teapot, which he had filled with water. This, he set to simmer while he arranged the rope with the three-inch-long hooks again. Next, he used the fish guts to bait the hooks and placed them in order inside the canoe. The teapot began to boil and he added some of the salvaged clean flour to it, and we ended up with a tasty sturgeon dumpling stew!

Ol' Jim slit the rest of the sturgeon into a flat piece with crisscross cuts. The fish was held flat by the roasting stick, which was slit down the middle, and was sandwiched in between and held flat by two smaller crossed sticks. This he propped over the hot ashes. I watched the flesh turn pink, then brown. I ran to explore the area and soon found another of the old leather ropes tied around a tree, quite high up. People must have lived here too, long ago.

I scrambled around between huge boulders and munched on some dry blueberries before I made my way to the shoreline again. I saw minnows flashing in the shallow water by the bay. Then I heard Ol' Jim chanting and singing. It sounded eerie, and I could feel the hair on the back of my neck stand up. I sat on a boulder in the shade and listened for a long time until all was quiet. Then I decided to head back.

When I was close to the campfire site, I heard Ol' Jim talking to himself again. He was by the lake, rummaging around in his packsack. I threw some sticks into the fire and sat down. We ate the roasted sturgeon in silence.

We spent a lot of time on the island, and it was already evening when we approached the mouth of the river. I could hear the roar of the rapids. Here, Ol' Jim carefully strung the big hooks on the rope right across the channel. I watched the rope sink to the bottom. He sank both of his lead-end ropes, tied around rocks, to the bottom of the lake. He did, however, make sure that he could reach the end rope by the shore with his paddle.

We pitched the tent by the canoe-landing clearing at the portage. I didn't like it here very much. As far as I was concerned, the river was far too noisy to hear anything. A bear could walk up and sniff my behind before I even heard it! This was also the first time Ol' Jim had to cut the poles for the tent himself. That told me that people don't normally sleep on this portage, so why were we? I didn't voice my concerns however. He seemed to know what he was doing, and who was I to question why he did things?

We built a fire and made a pot of tea. We ate a bit more of the roasted sturgeon. There was so much noise, I didn't bother trying to talk. When it came time to go to bed I just curled up in my sleeping bag and went to sleep.

Sometime during the dark hours, a loud hooting echoed in my eardrums and shot up my spine, sending shivers through me. It took a while before I recognized the sound—an owl. I must say that was the loudest and closest-sounding owl I had ever heard. I listened to the obnoxious creature as it forced every other creature within hearing distance to stay awake and listen to it. A few minutes later, I realized that I was not listening to one owl but two—one to the east of us and the other answering from the west. Ol' Jim and I were cornered. What did he care, anyway? He snored softly through the whole owl conversation without a pause. I listened until I discovered that I could actually force my ears to shut out Mr. and Mrs. Owl by concentrating on the continual, uninterrupted sound of the rapids—the water rushing and pouring, swirling around rocks. I had to go to the bathroom, but no way was I going to go out there all by myself in the dark!

Early the next morning, Ol' Jim shook me awake. "Come on, get your shoes on and let's go check the hooks."

I jumped up and pulled on my socks and shoes while Ol' Jim got a good fire going. I hated to leave the comforting smell of fire smoke and the warmth as we headed out into the cool early morning mist. As soon as the sound of the rapids faded, the quiet returned and my ears got a well-deserved rest. I turned and smiled at my quiet companion.

I could hear a loon calling, sad and lonesome all by himself somewhere out on the lake. Suddenly another loon answered and soon they were carrying on like two old friends catching up on news.

I looked at Ol' Jim and asked seriously, "Why do people say 'the lonely call of a loon,' or 'the eerie hoot of an owl' when I have never heard these things by themselves. There are always two or a whole bunch of them!"

Ol' Jim chuckled and said, "Well, when you don't understand the language, all the voices sound the same, don't they?"

Along the shoreline, I noticed a long awkward stick move at the top and realized that it was the head of a very long-legged bird. One leg bent at the knee and poised there for a minute before he moved the other leg.

"Blue heron," said Ol' Jim behind me, as we paddled past the creature amidst the reeds.

Soon we reached the spot where the rope was, and Ol' Jim fished in the lead rope with his paddle while I made an effort to have the canoe stay facing one direction. Ol' Jim was pulling us along the length of the canoe when something caused the whole front end to swerve left and right.

Then, suddenly, another huge sturgeon came into view. I dodged to the side quickly and immediately Ol' Jim's voice rang out, "Take it easy now, it's a very big one!"

With plenty of water swishing and splashing, Ol' Jim finally managed to bonk it on the head with an axe and haul it into the canoe. I saw the dark moustaches on the fish. The one yesterday had white moustaches. I could see a huge sucker mouth on the underside of his head. Again, I was relieved when Ol' Jim threw in the rest of his hooks and there were no more monsters of this kind attached to them.

When we returned to camp, Ol' Jim had to make two roasting sticks. The flattened top part of the fish was on one stick and the flattened tail part was on the other. That was a lot of fish to eat! The supporting crossed sticks were pushed over the flesh to keep it flat while it was propped to smoke and slowly cook over the hot ashes. If Ol' Jim can keep it from getting rotten, we will be eating it for about three days.

While he was busy cooking the sturgeon, I hauled the rest of the things over the portage. The path wasn't too long and it was rather pleasant, except for the noise of the rapids. After the third trip of taking my time, I sat beside Ol' Jim and waited. Finally he took the roasting stick aside and cut off a piece onto a sheet of birchbark for me. I decided I liked sturgeon roasted better than boiled. It had just enough fat, the flesh was firm, and no bones! Then we sat around with our cups of tea. I didn't feel the need to be in such a big hurry any more. I was jam-packed full.

Ol' Jim said his son was just on the next lake. We should get there by evening. Somehow, I didn't want this trip to end so soon. I wanted to travel with Ol' Jim like this forever.

I asked, "How long do you usually stay there? Are you coming back by canoe again?"

Ol' Jim squinted against the campfire smoke and said, "Well now, I usually stay there until freeze-up, then I fly on the aeroplane with my son back to Collins. The aeroplane comes to the camp every week to bring supplies and things. Now, that's not saying you have to stay there with me all that time. There's school, don't forget. You will have to go home to go to school. You can get on whenever the plane lands. It goes back to Armstrong. You can take the train from there. If you don't have any money, I will give you some. So don't worry

160

about anything. Enjoy what you see around you right now. Things will work out."

Finally Ol' Jim wrapped the rest of the sturgeon in birchbark and put it inside the food box. He picked up the paddles and arranged them over his shoulders as he lifted the canoe. I busied myself with the food box and teapot and hurried along in front of him. On the other side, I watched the swirl of water as it flowed from the rapids into a pool with clumps of white foam floating around in it. The foam washed ashore by the portage as I waited for Ol' Jim to put the canoe down. I could tell it was going to be a very hot day again.

After we loaded the canoe, we took our time paddling along with the current onto another portage. Everything was very quiet and peaceful here. I had a holding-your-breath-waiting-for-something-to-happen feeling. I liked this portage though. It had flat rocks and quiet-looking openings in the bush that I wished I had time to play in. We touched shore on a quiet bay with a gently sloping rock padded with soft mud. The flies weren't bad and it seemed like a very friendly place. I walked across the portage three times, deliberately carrying only a few things at a time.

As we sat eating a couple pieces of sturgeon and bannock at the other end of the portage, I smelled a skunk. The ground was all sandy and it had low pine trees everywhere. Ol' Jim indicated that it was a good habitat for skunks and such. Well, I wasn't about to wait for a skunk to come and invite himself for lunch, so I was in a bit of a hurry again to get under way. We paddled slowly and softly along some long and lonely beaches, high sandcliffs, and rocky shores.

I noticed a cloud of flies above the water as we paddled across the bay. I pointed at them and Ol' Jim nodded and stopped paddling. The canoe drifted forward. I stopped paddling too and watched the cloud of flies hovering above the surface of the water come closer and closer. Suddenly, with a swoosh, a huge black furry thing rose up above the water!

A shock went through me, and I was about to jump out of the canoe when I heard Ol' Jim's calm voice. "Steady, boy. It's a moose coming up above the water. He dunks his whole body into the water sometimes when the flies are driving him crazy."

The moose came up about five yards away from our canoe. The canoe floated over the waves from the moose, then we just drifted slowly past him. He didn't seem to notice us at all because he just dunked his head back in again.

We saw some ducks and their babies. The young ones were almost the same size as their parents now, but they weren't as colourful. Baby seagulls were also flying around in their dirty grey feathers, pretending that they were just as pretty as their snow white parents. Then, right in front of the canoe, we had a couple of playful otters put on a display for us. Showing off and taking advantage of having an audience, they did some tricks and backflips and tried to outdo each other.

Toward afternoon, we came across some very high rock cliffs. We paused again in the now-familiar routine of leaving some tobacco on a shelf in the cliff. Here, Ol' Jim said, is where he would have put his fishnet in if it wasn't in pieces back there at the channel in Whitewater Lake. I smiled.

I turned to see him looking up at the towering rock, and he said, "There are drawings on the ones at the other end of the lake."

"Drawings? What kind of drawings?" I asked.

Suddenly he indicated that I should be quiet and look. I turned to see four large black animals by the water. Moose! Then I noticed another one between the cedar trees. He had his head stretched out toward the branches. The other four moose by the water saw us at that moment and, without a sound, they melted away into the bushes.

"Strange, very strange," said Ol' Jim behind me as he put his paddle into the water. We shot forward so fast the water gurgled at the front of the canoe. I swung my arms with new energy, trying to match the paddle dips behind me.

It was late when we came around a point, and Ol' Jim steered the canoe close to the shoreline all the way around the bay. Then I saw the smoke coming from a cabin by the lake in front of a small sand beach.

In the quiet evening, it looked so calm and inviting. I set my paddle across my lap and breathed a big sigh. We were here. I noticed the dock and several gas cans lined up along the shoreline. A boat and an unfinished cabin sat farther along the beach. We paddled along in silence.

As we neared the boat landing, there were no children yelling and no dogs barking. I waited for the birds to say it was okay territory. I heard none.

We approached and the canoe gently nudged the shore. I jumped out and pulled it in, then waited for Ol' Jim to get out. He was acting as if he had aged a hundred years as he took his time getting out. He stood there for a minute before he decided to go in search of his son. There didn't seem to be anyone around.

I pulled the canoe up beside the dock, unloaded all our stuff, and waited for Ol' Jim to come back. I saw him disappear around the bush and down the path toward the unfinished cabin. I sat on the dock and waited until, finally, he came down the path with a younger version of himself, except the other man was much, much bigger. I mean the biggest man I ever saw! Every ounce of him jiggled and bounced as he came down the path. The man's cheeks sagged below his cheekbones and lay in folds around his neck, giving the impression that he was frowning.

There were no introductions, and I decided then and there that Ol' Jim's son was the most miserable man I had ever met in my life. Right from the moment he laid eyes on me, he made up his mind that he didn't like me. It was about the same time as I decided I didn't like him either. He reminded me too much of my uncle Fred, so cheap and stingy, he nearly starved me to death! I watched the big man pull his sagging pants up over his hips as he talked. Maybe he was disappointed that I had come with Ol' Jim. He must have seen us coming. Maybe he had thought I was his son when he saw me in the canoe.

He totally ignored me and concentrated on updating his father on the happenings there and about over the spring and summer. I sat and listened to his soft voice. That surprised me. I thought he would have a loud voice. He apparently worked with someone else who was in town right now, getting supplies. His boss would be arriving in a couple of days to see how the ice shed they were building was coming along. There were wood chips, sawdust, and piles of cleared brush everywhere. This seemed to be the beginnings of a summer tourist camp.

I decided to stay out of the way as much as possible. For the rest of the evening, the man pretended that I wasn't even there, so I spent the time checking out the area. I followed the shoreline until I came to the place where they were putting up an ice shed for the winter. The logs on the shed were not even peeled.

I was starving by the time Ol' Jim yelled that supper was ready. I walked back to the cabin. There were no pets here. I didn't even know why it should be important to have a pet here, miles away from anyone, but you got to have a dog, or a cat at least!

I entered the dark cabin and found clothes hanging all around the thin plywood walls. The floor was made of the four-by-eight plywood as well, and they sagged at each step the big man took as he crossed the floor and sat down on a stump by the table. Ol' Jim sat beside the only window. I perched on the edge of a bunk and waited to see what was going to happen next. I could see a big pot of stew in the middle of the table. As I watched hungrily, the man dished out one huge ladle after another of a macaroni and meat concoction until I thought there would be none left for Ol' Jim or me. Ol' Jim dished out a plate and handed it to me. The man frowned and I noticed that Ol' Jim sure didn't get very much. I slowly ate my share in the silence and wondered if Ol' Jim was going to have enough sense to pitch our tent outside. But, no such thing. As soon as they finished eating, they left the cabin and wandered off again, talking in a very low outdoor voice. When I finished, I checked the pot. It was scraped clean. I decided that the man was indeed a hog! He hadn't even saved enough for a second helping for his father.

I put another log into the stove and filled the pot with water to heat for the dishes. After that I stood around outside for a while. The lake was very calm and the sky was clear. I could hear loons out there somewhere, but I was not happy. I do not like this place! I could hear Hog, as I called him, and Ol' Jim out there by the bay, beside the unfinished ice shed.

I picked up more wood and brought it inside. The water was now warm enough for the dishes. There was no detergent anywhere, so I just dumped the dishes into the pot and rinsed them out. I didn't see any dishtowels either. I propped the clean dishes on the table and spilled the water outside, just as the man was coming around the corner of the cabin. I got him right on the top of his belly, and the rest landed on his feet. He looked as if he was ready to kill me. I retreated into the cabin and sat on the bunk, waiting to see what would happen next.

Nothing happened. Again, Hog just pretended I wasn't even there, and that made me mad! Who does he think he is anyway? They made a pot of tea before bed. The only problem was that Ol' Jim had passed me his cup, and the big man filled a big pitcher for himself. Ol' Jim barely got enough to fill a bowl. I felt so miserable. I pulled out my blanket and curled up on the floor beside the door to make sure Ol' Jim got to sleep on the bunk bed at least.

I would have to take some drastic action tomorrow. Maybe I could convince Ol' Jim to let me pitch the tent somewhere. Hopefully he would continue to do a little fishing for us. What am I going to do here? How long will I have to stay? Maybe I should take Ol' Jim's canoe and go back myself. I think I could find my way to the portage, but how would I get the canoe across the portage? The aeroplane. The big man had said his boss was arriving in a couple of days, and the other worker would be coming back with supplies. I still have the twenty dollars in my sack. How much will it cost? How much will I need from Ol' Jim? Something just ran across my blanket. Another ran across my hair. Something small—mice! I could hear them scurrying under the table. What does he keep under there? I can try to trap them tomorrow. It will give me something to do. I listened to the mouse convention under the table until I fell asleep.

Chapter Fifteen

THE NEXT MORNING, I GOT UP QUICKLY and got a fresh pail of water and brought in more wood. Then I walked around a bit outside until I decided it must be time for breakfast. But when I went back to the cabin no one was there. They had tea all right, but there was no sign of breakfast. I was hungry! I could hear the sound of a handsaw going back and forth and the steady banging of a hammer echoing through the woods. I shrugged and looked around. Well, I guess I could clean up the cabin. Besides the fully loaded nails on the walls, there were also shelves all along one wall, and every shelf was jam-packed full of stuff—boxes and containers of food. I picked up an old broom from the dark corner beside the garbage pail and swept the dust and sand off the dirty wooden floor. The floor looked as if it had not been washed in a whole year. No way was I washing it. After sweeping the sand into the corner, I threw the broom after it. I washed the cups again and hung up the wet cloth that was used to dry the dishes. It looked like the back part of a shirt. I looked inside our food box and found a piece of sturgeon left in the birchbark and some bannock. I took them out and stuck them into my sack along with my blanket and walked out.

I followed a path to the right, along the shoreline where we had come from. I detoured around a swampy section and discovered that there was a creek flowing through there, but it was just too far to jump across. How was I going to get across? I needed to get to the other side to join the mainland again. I put my sack down and explored the area. I would need some logs to put across. Maybe I could tie them together and make a sort of bridge. I walked around looking up at the thick, tall, healthy trees. What am I thinking? I don't even have an axe.

I went back to the rock and sat down with my packsack on my lap. If I was a muskrat or a lynx, I could swim across. My name is Lynx and I can swim across! I pulled off my shirt and pants and stuck them into the sack with my socks and shoes. The flies had found me by then and the sun had disappeared. It was cold. Well, I can't stand here all day. I put my feet in the water. Oh, that is cold. It must be water from a spring or something. I jumped in and the water came right up past my waist. Gasping from the shock, I held the sack high up over my head with both hands. The muddy bottom squished between my toes as I pushed my feet forward. I walked a few more steps when, suddenly, the ground was gone and I plunged in over my head. My arms thrashed around trying to bring my head above water. At last, my head popped out and I gasped and lunged for my sack, which was floating in front of me. I pushed my arm through the string loop and dog-paddled as quickly as I could to the other side. I kept sliding off the rocks and couldn't get my footing until, finally, I flung the sack between the rocks. It got wedged in between and I pulled myself up. I stood there shivering, wondering what to do now. After I stopped shaking a bit, I decided to head for the rock pile around the bay. I could dry my clothes there where no one could see me. I hopped from rock to rock along the shoreline until my feet began to ache. I came around a point just as the sun broke through the clouds. I was now facing the open water. I pulled my sack open and dumped out my wet clothes. I wrung my pants out and hung them up and threw my shirt over the branches. I used my socks to dry my shoes as best I could before I hung them up in the branches. My runningshoes were in pretty bad shape. I pulled a soggy grey thing out of my jacket pocket. The rabbit paw. Then I wrung out my socks. I smiled when I remembered that these were Ol' Jim's work socks. I draped them over the rocks. Next, I examined my fish. It was soggy, but edible. I put it on the rock. The bannock, on the other hand, was a sorry mess. I left it on the rock. Occasionally a horsefly came zooming by, but seeing as he wasn't expecting a naked human being around these parts, he didn't stop to investigate. So I spent a relatively quiet afternoon, basking in the sun and enjoying the warm breeze. I ate the sturgeon when I thought it was around lunch time.

Later in the afternoon, I put on my dry clothes and shoes and continued down the shoreline until I came upon a large area of flat rock. Hey! I like this place. There are no sand beaches here, just slabs of flat smooth rocks. I started gathering some square flat ones and began building a fort. Later I decided that it would be an excellent fireplace. It was evening when I finished building that.

I was wrestling with a slab of rock for a table when I heard Ol' Jim say behind me, "That looks nice." He was sitting there in the canoe, drifting quietly in the calm evening waters. I hadn't even heard him coming.

I smiled. "Can I stay here? Would you let me put the tent up here?"

Ol' Jim didn't answer that, but he said, "Get in. We will go and set the fishnet. He gave me his net, he never uses it anyway."

We spent a nice quiet evening. But, no, he would not live in a tent when his son was in a cabin nearby, and I could not stay here by myself either. So I had to stay in the cabin with Ol' Jim and Hog. I slept curled up by the door again.

In the morning, I noticed a small brown rabbit by the edge of the clearing, so I pulled out some dandelion leaves by the beach and set them down on the path. After patient coaxing, it finally came out in the open where I could watch it. I called him Browny Rabbit. On the third morning, I had run to the outhouse when I heard a gunshot. I knew what it was even before I came flying out of the outhouse. Sure enough, there was Hog reaching down to pick up Browny Rabbit's limp body. I took off into the bush and refused to go back until it was dark. Even then, I kept smelling cooked rabbit. I was so hungry, I decided to pull off a piece of bannock without permission. Hog just glared at me. I hate this place! The aeroplane had not arrived yet. I already asked Ol' Jim if they would let me on when the plane lands. I want to get out of here!

That night before I went to sleep, I found an old mousetrap under the table. I set it on the floor beside the table leg. The next morning, the mousetrap caught Hog's toe as he sat down to eat. I had forgotten about it. Ol' Jim decided to take me on an overnight trip to the rapids to catch some sturgeon. In the morning we caught two of them. We tied a rope through the sucker mouth of one, like a leash, and tied the other end to a tree. It swam around by the shore while we cooked the first one. We were just pulling the sturgeon in from the water to take it home fresh, when we heard it. The aeroplane. There was no way we could get back in time. We heard it land and take off again. I was disappointed, knowing I would have to go back to the cabin, but at the same time I was relieved that I didn't have to go right now. When we got back we found out that it was the boss who had flown in to inspect the construction.

The next day I was by the dock when I saw the snake. It was a black snake with a white stripe on each side. I thought only skunks had white stripes like that. The snake stopped behind a rock. Maybe it was hungry. What do snakes eat? I bet he'd like to eat some of those mice under Hog's bed. I approached softly and stepped on its tail. It whipped around and flipped about so quickly, it was like trying to grab a rope that had come to life. I finally got a hold of it. It was about as thick as Hog's thumb and about two feet long. I held the rope of muscle with both hands. It struggled and tried to twist, so I whispered, "Sh, it's okay. I am going to put you where you can have all the mice you can eat and you will never be hungry again." It felt like moving velvet, and the little black tongue continued to flick out, moving left and right. I carried it up to the cabin and released it under Hog's bed. There was no sound, and it disappeared under there somewhere. I found something else to do. I made a very nice slingshot from the Y of a sturdy branch and cut half an inch off the top of an old rubber boot I found under Hog's bed.

It rained in the morning, Hog threw a fit when he found his boots. Now the clouds were just rolling by, in a big hurry to get somewhere. I was over by the point beside the dock when

169

I heard a yell from the cabin. It sounded like Hog. I heard a lot of banging on the floor, then the stove lid clanged. A little while later, Ol' Jim came down the path and informed me that we were going on an overnight trip again.

I followed Ol' Jim to the canoe and threw my slingshot in. As we paddled away, I heard Ol' Jim say, "I think that snake borrowed two legs from somewhere." I stopped. That's what that yell was about. I said nothing and started paddling again.

We spent the night by the rock cliff to set the fishnet. Then we stayed another night to smoke and cook all the fish we had caught. That was where we were when we heard the aeroplane land the second time. We just glanced at each other, but didn't say anything about it. There wasn't a thing we could do anyway. And besides, it will come back again.

When we got back, we heard Hog pounding in nails at the construction site. The boxes of nails had arrived, but still no co-worker. The two small boxes were stacked on a stump beside the dock. I picked up several three-inch nails and examined them. Hog had apparently just taken a handful from each box and left them open. I decided to see what kind of nails were in the box on the bottom, but as I was trying to lift the top box, they began to topple over. I had a handful of nails sticking in one hand and the other hand was just not strong enough to hold the heavy boxes back. They came crashing to the ground, upside-down. Just then, I saw Hog coming down the trail. I grabbed the top upside-down box, but it came up empty, scattering the nails everywhere in the process. Ol' Jim appeared from somewhere and hurried to intercept the very angry man, but I high-tailed it out of there quick.

I was way over by the bay when Ol' Jim came by in the canoe, saying, "Get in. Let's go cut a big piece of cedar for use at the construction site. We'll stay overnight." I smiled and got in. We paddled to the other end of the lake, and I saw the most impressive sandbanks I had ever seen. We set up camp at a point close by where small poplar trees shaded the sandy ground. It was just beautiful there! After a supper of fried fish and bannock, we set out to find a large piece of cedar.

After breakfast the next day, I left Ol' Jim hacking away

with the axe, taking the stringy brown bark off the block of cedar we had found. I stuck my slingshot in my pocket and sat on an old log by the lake. There was a loon close by the shore. I watched him cleaning himself. He was poking at the feathers on his back, and then he lifted one wing. He poked around under his arm, then he lifted up his foot while he poked away on his belly. Gee, he looked funny. He started going in a slow circle because he only had one foot peddling in the water, the other one was still up in the air. He was lying on his side in the water. I could see his red eyes very clearly when he turned sideways.

I watched the loon for another minute, then ran down the beach and clambered along the steep sandbanks that had intrigued me from the canoe yesterday. There were holes in the sand about as big as both of my fists, or the size of Ol' Jim's mouth if he were to crank it open as wide as he could. Anyway, the holes were way too big to be the home of snakes or squirrels or anything else I had seen. I scrambled around the bottom of the cliff by the shore, looking for a stick to poke into the holes. I couldn't find one, so I scrambled to the top and pulled myself up by a root of a dead cedar. Then, from beneath my foot, I dislodged a stick right beside the largest hole. I grabbed it and examined the smooth, round hole. I thought it might be a fox hole. Or maybe a big bird of some kind. I should have asked Ol' Jim when I saw these yesterday. I started to chip away at the opening and poked the stick in as far as I could, but I was scared to stick my hand in too far. The stick I had was only about a foot and a half long, and the knob at one end fit neatly in my hand as I chipped away at more of the sand. The sun was now shining right against me on the sandcliff. When I turned to wipe my forehead, I saw Ol' Jim waving his arms at me.

I slid down the sandbank to the bottom and threw the stick into the water. I picked up some strange flat pieces of rock and skipped them along the surface of the lake. I grabbed another and I skimmed this one pretty good with nine, ten, eleven skips! I ran back to the campsite.

Ol' Jim had some roasted fish ready to eat. I gulped mine

down hungrily. Then he said, "The sandcliff. Ghosts of ancient people live there."

I felt fear creeping into my chest. "What do you mean ghosts?"

He didn't answer me for so long that I was beginning to think he hadn't heard me at all. Then he said, "That is an old burial site. A spirit might enter your soul and try to live again through your body."

I could feel my eyes stretch wide. "What do you mean? Ghosts inside my body?" I asked.

Ol' Jim looked down the shoreline and said, "Some souls who loved life so much may have refused to leave their bones to go to the other world. Now they just wander around the area where their old bones are. Don't go near areas like that and don't pick up anything from the ground!"

Suddenly a thought occurred to me. "That stick I used to dig the holes, it could have been a bone. What if it was one of their bones? What if one already jumped inside me?"

Ol' Jim turned, and his black squinty eyes peered into mine as he said real certain-like, "Oh, souls like that would not want to be anywhere near me. You see, once they know I know they are around, they get scared that I may send them away from the place. They know I can do that so they stay away. I would know if they came near you or me. They will not come near us." He sipped from his teacup and continued, "But just to be nice and to let them know that we know they are there, we will leave them some tobacco when we go. They will not follow us if they have some tobacco all to themselves. They have no time value, one second of their time can mean years to us." I knew by the tone of his voice that he was now into his talk-to-himself time.

I dashed to get our stuff into the canoe. I just wanted to get out of there fast. When he finished eating, we cleaned the dishes and packed up the food box. Soon everything was in the canoe and we got in.

We still had one more very important thing to do as far as I was concerned. We paddled to the spot where the holes were. He got out and disappeared behind some bushes. I sat there and waited for Ol' Jim and his powerful tobacco to keep the wandering souls where they belonged, or at least as far away from me as possible. I heard his talking-to-himself voice as his footsteps sent sand cascading to the bottom of the sandbank. Then all was silent. I held my breath until I heard him coming through the bush again. Okay, let's go! We returned to the cabin.

Early in the morning, I awoke to flies buzzing around my ears. The sun wasn't up yet but the birds were, and they were whistling at each other and having a riot outside the cabin. I smiled and rolled out of the blanket, glancing at the bunk. The big fat man had his mouth open as he slept. There was a trail of spit running from the corner of his puffed lip to his pillow. I turned away and slowly opened the door. The fresh air hit me like a breath of life.

As I stepped outside I could feel something in the air. What was it? I went to the dock and lay down on my belly, sticking my arms into the cool water. I began to feel an urge to dunk my body in as I held my arms in the cleansing waters. I pulled off my clothes and ran, totally exhilarated, into the cool water. I felt like letting out a yell, but I dared not. I might wake them up. I dipped and dived as deep and far as I could. I flipped and floated to my heart's content until I heard the frantic squawking of the seagulls overhead. What was going on? I slowly waded to shore listening and looking around. I couldn't hear or see anything unusual. Where had all the birds gone? Wait! Then I saw them. They looked like huge mountains looming over the treetops. Clouds! I walked ashore naked and tugged my clothes over my wet body. After that battle, I walked to our canoe and dragged it out of the water and into the bushes beside the trees. By now it sat about forty feet off the shore in the bushes beside the cabin. The way I figured it, if they were the same kind of clouds I saw at Mr. and Mrs. Old Indian's place, we were in for a mighty big storm.

I hid our tent and paddles under the canoe and made sure that if for some reason we had to leave in a big hurry, we'd have all the things we'd need. Of course the food box was inside the cabin and so was my blanket and Ol' Jim's sleeping bags.

I entered the dark cabin to find that they were still asleep.

I went back out and brought another armload of wood inside the cabin and pushed some birchbark into the holes inside the woodstove. I piled on some twigs and wood on top and lit a match through the pie-shaped opening, and the bark and wood roared to life. I ran down to the lake and filled the teapot. By this time the sky had gone very dark and angry. It looked like it was ready for a big fight.

I hurried back and put the pot on the stove and hoped that Ol' Jim would be up by now. He wasn't on the top bunk when I returned. He came in a few minutes later, grinning. "Good thinking, boy! You learn fast."

Then the big sleeping mound rolled over and sat up. "What you babbling on about ol' man! Get the kid away from the door, I can't see a thing in here, so dark . . . "

He heaved a big grunt as he sat up, and I shrank as small as I could beside the door.

Suddenly a big clap of thunder rolled across the sky. I sprang to my feet and, looking for something to do, grabbed some teabags from the jar where the big man kept them. I threw them into the simmering pot. Another roll of thunder shook the cabin as the huge man stepped outside. Then the rain came down. It poured like water from a big giant hose in the sky!

A few minutes later, Hog staggered in, spitting and coughing as winds whipped up around the door, slamming it backwards against the outside wall. He reached out and his arm was pulled so hard he was slammed against the cabin, but when the mighty wind took another breath, he pulled the door shut. The wind shook the windows and the smoke in the stove reversed, showering us with hot ashes. There was some loud banging and crashing, then came the crunch and crash of huge heavy trees grinding against one another. Things were crashing against the window and I heard a "pang!" as the cracks in the window formed a road map on the glass. More things crashed across the window but the glass stayed together. By now the cabin was full of smoke and we were coughing as ashes continued to billow out of the stove opening. I could hear the water pouring inside the stovepipe, and soon there was not a whisper of smoke left in the stove. I could almost feel the branches twisting and wrenching as trees were uprooted all around us. The roar intensified outside and I could hardly breathe. I kept close to the floor, hugging my grey army blanket. It seemed like an eternity, but it was actually only a few minutes before the calm settled in again.

The big man was the first to go outside. There were round white balls everywhere, about the size of robins' eggs. The sky and the lake were a dark steel grey. Hog stood by the door for a moment, then stepped outside. A few pieces of chopped-up, golden leaves were filtering from the birch and poplar trees, and some landed on his head as he whirled around and stomped back inside the cabin. Ol' Jim hovered by the fire for a minute before he pulled out some cups for tea.

I poked my head out the door and saw that our little canoe was safe and that the big man's boat was almost sinking, with two feet of water inside.

We sat and slowly sipped the tea while Ol' Jim whipped around making porridge and bannock over the now-roaring fire. I could see some trees across the lake exposing new flesh-coloured undersides. Many trees had blown over and there was something else lying beside the woodpile by the lake that wasn't there before. It looked like dark green tar paper— the roofing! I ran out and, sure enough, there was a big section missing from around the stovepipe. The birds! There wasn't even a peep anywhere! Maybe the balls of ice had hit them on the head and knocked them all out or killed them.

All was quiet outside. We seemed noisy, out of place, as our footsteps broke the silence. Hog and the old man seemed to be waiting for something. Suddenly the wind whipped up again and the roofing paper disappeared down into the bay somewhere. The rain came again, this time blowing showers of fine mist to the ground. Then the sun came out. All was quiet. No birds. No noise. All at once the wind started again, and I held my breath as I watched the trees across the lake sway and bend like grass on a lawn. Then it was all over. The trees shook themselves and water pelted onto the rooftop. I looked across the lake and saw the most beautiful rainbow.

The sun cast an orange-gold light as a giant hand slowly pushed the dark clouds off the sky and left them hanging uncertainly over the horizon. We ate some tea-porridge and bannock and the big man went about his business, putting on his overalls and thick gloves, then heading toward the new ice shed.

Ol' Jim followed his son, and I busied myself with bringing some more wood inside. I could hear the hammer banging on the logs. I lay down and thought about the events of the morning. I couldn't believe that hailstones could be that big! I must have dozed for a while because when I woke, I could tell it was well into the afternoon. I made a pot of tea. When it was done, I took it to Hog and Ol' Jim. They were busy making notches on logs for another cabin. I set the pot down along with the sugar. Hog just sat there waiting for me to go away. When I got back to the cabin, I went down to the lake and noticed that the water had really gone up.

The big man's boat was over half-full of water. I took the water can that was floating around inside the boat and began bailing it out. I untied the ropes and pushed the back end toward me so I could bail out the rest of the water a little easier. Hog hadn't used the boat and motor since we arrived. I pulled the boat alongside the dock, and just as I was about to tie the front end to the dock again, I stopped to examine the motor more closely. The handle had "Start" written on it. I noticed the notch and decided that you must have to turn the handle to "Start" and pull the rubber T-handle on top with the string on it to get the boat going. I bet I could do it all by myself!

I lay down on my belly on the edge of the dock and with one hand I reached for the handle and turned it to "Start," then I reached for the rubber handle on top and pulled as hard as I could. Nothing happened, so I gave it another big pull. It started with a loud roar. I almost rolled off the other end of the dock to get away. It scared the daylights out of me! The nose of the boat was on the gravel shore and water was now churning white as sand boiled away behind the boat. How do I shut it off? I quickly reached for the motor again and turned the handle to "Off." Suddenly the noise grew even louder, and the motor turned and hit my arm very hard. I watched as the boat took off straight for shore. I had turned it the wrong way! The boat was now grinding away, trying to bore a hole in the rocks. Suddenly there was a loud clang and the props stopped turning. Before I could think of what to do, the big man had arrived and jumped into the boat to shut off the motor.

He whirled around, and there was no doubt in my mind that he was going to kill me! My feet carried me in a streak up to the cabin. As I grabbed my sack and blanket, Ol' Jim stood at the door, panting, with his back to me, blocking the doorway and yelling, "No, no! Leave him alone. He'll run away! He'll run away into the bush! Leave him alone!" Without a word he was thrust aside and the door slammed shut. I was alone. I heard the door latch click on the outside.

Looking over my shoulder at the door, I rolled my blanket up and stuffed it into the sack, then sat down on the bunk. He had locked me in! If I could run away, where would I go? It's all bush. I began thinking about the rivers and lakes we had paddled, the many nights we had slept to get here.

I could feel my shoulders slump. I looked at the door again, then my shoulders came up. I walked to the door and flicked the latch down, locking it.

The way I figured it, he was in worse shape than I was. I was all nice and comfortable in here, while he was outside. Of course, I'd let Ol' Jim in. I sat at the edge of the bunk swinging my feet for a long time. Then I heard it—an aeroplane! It must be the supplies that Hog was waiting for. He had ordered some groceries the last time it came, and he also was still waiting for the co-worker.

The noise echoed in the cabin as the aeroplane roared overhead, took on a higher pitch, then slowly faded into a "chug, chug." It had landed and was now coasting to the dock.

I waited. Soon I could hear them talking. After some banging of cans and the thud of boxes, the talking voices became louder, then the other voices thought there was something very funny, but I didn't recognize anyone's laughter. Finally I heard Ol'

Jim's shuffling footsteps. "Danny!" he said, "the pilot is taking you back to town."

I didn't need to hear any more. I flicked the lock back and opened the door at about the same time I heard him flick the latch back. He giggled and pointed at the door. "You locked it! You locked the door!" When I stepped out, he handed me a five-dollar bill, saying, "Go back to Collins. Call your father from there."

I took the money, but couldn't think of anything to say. He was still chuckling as I followed him down to the lake. There were piles of boxes on the dock beside a swaying man. He looked very sick. That must be the co-worker. He gave a big grin when I approached. The pilot glanced at me and started laughing as well. I climbed inside the aeroplane and sat on the wooden crates behind the pilot. He motioned for me to take the front seat beside him. I scrambled to the seat and made myself comfortable. The pilot got in and I waved to Ol' Jim as the aeroplane floated away from the dock. The engine started with a chug, chug as it made its way out to the middle of the lake. The chug became a roar as the plane gathered speed. Oh boy! It was just like Charlie's boat, except I was inside and higher.

The waves began to slap against the pontoons real fast, then silence. The lake grew smaller. We were up in the air! Soon we were over the treetops! The aeroplane turned and circled, and I had my face pasted to the window beside me. I could see the bay, the dock, and there was Ol' Jim standing there waving. I waved back with both hands to make sure he saw me, then we flew over the hill and past more trees. I saw a river and decided that must be where we camped the night Ol' Jim caught the sturgeon. It felt strange to see the lakes from up high after you've seen only the shoreline from below. I leaned back and settled down to the business of getting back to town.

I saw blue lakes, winding rivers, and ponds that looked like rotten mouldy milk left in the cup for a whole month. The trees looked like a bed of flowers in a rock garden. Yellow, orange, and red puffy flowers framed in dark green leaves. The rocky hills and cliffs, the lakes and . . . what's that? I

178

pointed to the thing that looked like a black bug crawling out of the grass to a puddle. The pilot yelled "moose," just as we went over it.

The muscles on my face began to ache. I hadn't realized that I had such a huge grin. I glanced at the pilot again and he smiled back. This was great!

It didn't seem long at all until we started circling. I could see other aeroplanes in the water down below, and some rooftops and a large dock. I was so excited, my legs were shaking as the pontoons touched the water. The "rat, tat, tat" gradually turned into a "shhhhhh" noise, and the engine started its "chug, chug" to shore.

Several men were at the large dock as we got nearer. The aeroplane engine stopped, and they grabbed the wing and pulled us alongside the dock. They pulled the door open and I jumped out. My legs felt funny all of a sudden as I clutched my sack and made my way to land.

I stood and watched the men loading the aeroplane with boxes. I wonder how far it is to town. Well, I can't stand here all day. I started walking up the road, which I thought must be the road to town.

It was very hot here. The road was sandy gravel and hard to walk on. It took a sharp turn farther on. I'd been walking a long time when I heard a loud noise coming up behind me. It sounded like a hundred gas drums rolling down the hill. I ran to an even stretch of road to make sure the driver saw me. A blue truck with two men in it came around the corner and rolled to a stop beside me.

The driver yelled out, "Get in back if you want a ride to town." He did no more than glance at me and continued talking to the guy beside him. I scrambled on.

There must have been a dozen very large empty gas cans in there. I had no sooner flopped down between two gas cans when the truck started again. We had not gone very far when I realized I was in for another set of problems. Besides bursting my eardrums with the noise, the gas cans were standing upright, and every time we hit a particularly rough section of road they came to life and marched around all over the place. I was getting squeezed from both sides when we went downhill. Then I noticed a space between the cans. I scrambled to my hands and knees and quickly crawled to the opening, dragging my sack behind me. Then a banging jolt nearly pushed my kneecaps up my legs, so I sat down quickly. I could feel the truck going up another hill and, sure enough, the cans were lining up to attack from the rear! This time, I took a stand. I wedged myself at the rear corner and cushioned my back with my sack. I stretched out my legs and braced myself. In no time, the killer gas cans were rubbing against the soles of my feet, but I managed to hold them off. When we went downhill again they withdrew to regroup for the next battle plan. But the driver foiled it, for suddenly we were driving into town.

The truck stopped in front of the restaurant, and I grabbed my bag and jumped out. "Thanks, good-bye!" I yelled, but the men just glanced at me. They probably had forgotten I was back there.

I reached into my jacket pocket and took out the old folded-up potato chip bag. It turned out to be a very good wallet. I took out Charlie's twenty-dollar bill. I hate to spend it, but I am very hungry. I looked toward the train station. I had the five dollars from Ol' Jim to get a ticket. The door opened at the store and people came out. I couldn't believe it—there was Henry and his father, Jim, behind him! Henry looked very pleased to see me as he came running.

His questions came fast, "How did you get here? Where did you come from?"

Henry's father laughed as he walked up, looking me up and down. "Woow, hold on! Let him breathe first. How about supper at the restaurant, boys?"

I shoved the chip bag back into my pocket. That sounded real good to me! I gave them the general rundown of my adventures. I'd fill in the details later.

Then, just to say something else, I asked, "When did you get here?"

Henry answered, "We went to Nakina first and then to Longlac, then back down around Port Arthur, then we got up here to Armstrong this morning. We've been gone a whole week!"

Oh. They went to Nakina! I wonder if Jim had looked for Dad. Better not ask.

"By the way, did Billy find another . . . place to live?" I asked.

Henry laughed as we entered the restaurant. After we sat down at a table, he leaned over and said, "Billy wanted to thank you for saving his home." My chin dropped to my chest in surprise. Henry continued. "They said a burning ember had dropped from the airvent and fell on a cloth or something that caught on fire and spread to the floor by the woodpile. Then the woodpile behind the stove started burning. Well, the men were able to put it out in time. It was because he lived so close to the water, and there were so many people at the card game next door. Billy said he always puts his coal oil can behind the stove and that, for sure, would have been the end of his cabin. Anyway, he found the oil can beside the woodpile outside the cabin. That's why he wanted to thank you!"

I smiled, very relieved and quite pleased with myself. "Well, it was a habit I picked up from the old couple I lived with at Savant Lake. The coal oil can was always kept outside beside the fire-starter box."

Henry looked at me as if I was some kind of hero. We ordered our lunch and that was the best hamburger and chips I had ever tasted.

Jim turned to me as we walked back down the street. "So, Danny. What have you learned from all this?"

Quite puzzled, I asked, "What?"

He continued, "What I mean is, you should not run away when something happens. Figure out what to do about it. Things never get better when you run away. If you had hung around, you'd have found out that Billy only had to patch the burnt floor and touch up the wall a bit."

I bit my lip and said, "Yeah, but I was the one who threw the rag there after I wiped up the spilled oil off the floor. And besides, if I hadn't run away I would never have met Ol' Jim."

We walked in silence a few more steps before he asked,

"Do you know where you are going to go to school? It's the second of September already, you know. School starts next week."

Suddenly the familiar chilling fear was back. I could feel panic rising up to choke me. They will send me back home! I stopped and turned over a piece of glass on the road with my foot. I will not go back there again! Jim stood there looking at me, and Henry decided to get busy collecting garbage on the grass.

Jim said in a lighter voice, "Hey, don't look so stricken, we'll figure things out. Come home with us to Collins. Billy will be glad to see you!"

I felt relieved and hopeful once more. Okay. Jim winked at me and smiled. I couldn't believe it was September second, already! I asked, "What day is it today?"

Henry smiled and said, "Boy, a real bushman you turned out to be! It's Saturday today." We all laughed as we headed for the train station.

"Oh, I guess you don't know, the train changed schedule, now we can go home on the afternoon train." Henry smiled back at me.

"You mean we are going home right now?" I asked in surprise.

"Yeah, and I'll even buy a ticket for you," said Jim as he disappeared into the train station.

I looked at Henry and said, "You have the best father in the whole world!"

He had a rather sad smile as he said, "Yes, I know."

The smell of tar and diesel from the railway tracks and train station was strong. It reminded me of fear and excitement. There weren't that many people around the station. I pointed to the tree with the bush underneath and said to Henry, "See there? That's where I slept that first night when I ran away."

Henry's mouth flew open. "Wow, you *are* brave!"

I smiled but said nothing as Jim came out. I pulled out the five-dollar bill and held it out to him. "Here, I forgot. Ol' Jim gave me that for my ticket to Collins."

Jim shook his head and chuckled. He said, "Go buy yourself

some chips and candies. Don't be gone too long. The train will be here soon."

Henry and I took off to the store where I had bought the milk, pop, and doughnuts what felt like many years ago. We went in and I bought the things I had been craving for. Gum! Chocolate! Pop! And, most of all, potato chips! Henry grinned, but all he'd accept was a package of gum. I stuffed my face with the goodies as we walked back to the station. We spent a few more minutes alone with Jim before people began arriving, and soon the train pulled in.

Henry and I sat together on one seat and his father took the seat beside us. We had no sooner sat down when a small lady with long black hair came and sat beside Jim. They were laughing and talking and totally forgot about us.

I nudged Henry. "Who's the lady?"

Henry made a face and said, "A lady we met at Sioux Lookout." He seemed quite annoyed and spent the next twenty minutes that it took to get to Collins looking out the window.

When we jumped off the train with Jim behind us, Henry was back to being himself again. The place looked peaceful and quiet, and the evening air carried the smell of woodsmoke from the cabins along the railway tracks.

The next day we spent the whole time cleaning up the cabin, cutting wood, and piling it in the wood shelter that Jim had built beside the cabin. It was good to be back. I felt I was welcome and needed.

The day after that was cold and rainy. In the evening as we sat around the table, Billy walked in. Jim was watching us and right away I knew something was up. Billy reached into his coat and pulled out a brown puppy and handed it to Henry. I lunged across the table to pet the pup when Billy nudged me, and there was a black one with a white-tipped tail draped over the palm of his hand. Mine? Yes, it was for me!

We pulled out an empty box and lined it with some rags. Ever wonder why puppies brace their hind legs so far back when they drink milk? Henry said it stretches their tummies a little longer. I think it keeps them from tumbling over. Soon we had them bedded down and Henry and I crawled into the single bed we shared in the corner. I snuggled beneath the covers and my whole body relaxed.

The rain was falling steadily on the roof, very gently, without the sound of roaring wind. We listened to Billy and Jim playing cards by the lamplight on the table. Jim had just lost another game. I watched Billy's face crease into many lines across his cheeks as he chuckled over something Jim said. Jim's hair was always falling over his eyes. I noticed his hands as he pushed his hair back again. His hands were thin and long compared to Billy's short thick fingers. Billy chuckled again.

One of the puppies made a whimpering noise and there was some scratching on the side of the box, then it was quiet again. It was Jim's deal and I listened to him shuffling the cards: one, two, three; one, two, three . . .

Chapter Sixteen

THERE WERE BUSHES EVERYWHERE IN the clearing, bursting with yellow, orange, and brown colours. The setting sun cast long shadows into the clearing, and laughter came from the cabin. Henry and Jim were making supper tonight. I smiled, remembering the rock-hard bannock I made yesterday. It was good to dunk in the tea, though.

I like coming up here to the treehouse when I have something to think about. The puppy's cold little wet nose brushed my neck as it turned to find a more comfortable position against my chest. I petted the round little head.

Jim had sat me down at the table when Henry went to get some water yesterday. He told me he had gone to see my father at Nakina that time. I thought so. It's strange, but I don't even think of him as "Dad" any more. I just say "my father" now. I used to love Dad, but "Dad" disappeared when Mama left. Anyway, Jim said that my father would not talk to him about letting me stay here. He wanted Jim to send me home immediately if I ever showed up here again. Jim just put his head down when I asked if my father had been drinking. I guess that was a yes. Yesterday I had noticed that Jim was very angry about something when he came back from the store. Later he told me that he had called my father and asked him again to let me stay here. He had also told him that I didn't want to go back to Nakina. He said my father just yelled at him and said he was going to come and get me whether I wanted to go or not. Jim seemed very angry with him, that means Jim must have been on my side.

The evening train went by just as we finished supper. I tensed up again and kept glancing down the path. I kept my bag packed every day, just in case my father showed up. I caught sight of Jim looking at me. He shook his head and winked. I shrugged and smiled. It was Jim's turn to wash dishes, so Henry and I decided to bring some more wood in. As I bent to pick up a piece of wood, a figure appeared on the path from the train station. My heart skipped a beat, but it was not my father. It was a small figure, a woman.

She came hesitantly up the path and we stopped to watch her. Henry stood bent over in the act of picking up a piece of wood. He seemed frozen there. I waited to see what would happen next. I heard the cabin door open, then the lady's face lit up and she smiled as she hurried forward. There was Jim by the door with a big smile on his face. Henry looked like he was ready to battle it out with her right there in the clearing. Then, to make things worse, she stepped on Henry's puppy's tail, rolling it like a rubber sausage as she disappeared into the cabin. She didn't even notice when the pup yelped in pain. That did it! Henry moved angrily toward the door. I grabbed the back of his jacket and pulled him back just as the door closed in his face.

"Here," I said, shoving his puppy at him.

With puppies under our arms, we climbed up to the treehouse to plan a course of action. Henry slumped by the door, and I leaned against the wall by the small window.

"Look, first of all, your father likes her so we've got to be nice." Henry just glared at me. I continued. "I mean, she seems okay. And guys have to have wives, I guess."

Suddenly he shot to his feet and looked ready to slug me. "That is not true! My dad doesn't need a wife!" he said through clenched teeth.

I was backing into a corner in the small space. What is he getting so mad at me for? "Wa . . . wait! You want him to ask you first if he should see this or that lady?"

"My dad does not need a lady, he's got me!"

"I guess you are not enough then," I said. Oh, oh! I have pushed him too far! I saw a blur in front of my face, pain registered on my cheek, and I crashed against the side of the window. The little house rocked to the side, and I quickly grabbed his pup off the floor and held it like a shield in front of me. "Henry, Henry! Stop it!" I yelled.

Henry stood there breathing hard, looking at me, then he flopped down to the floor and sat there with his head down. I rubbed my cheek. Ouch, that hurt! It was sore but he hadn't hit me all that hard. I looked at him again and put the puppy on his lap.

"At least she isn't bringing a baby with her! And your father won't hit you. And besides, she looks small enough for you to beat her up if she decides to clobber you!"

I sat down on the floor beside him. He still had not said anything. I edged along the floor and braced my back against the tree trunk.

Henry's voice now sounded defeated and helpless. "What do you know anyway?" He glanced at me and picked up the puppy again.

I put my pup on my lap and murmured, "You're not remembering the reason why I ran away from home in the first place."

Now I felt like crying too. The whole situation had changed. What am I going to do now? I had been looking forward to staying here. Jim would have protected me from my father. I cannot stay here. All of this reminded me too much of the witch! Then I remembered Billy. I can stay with Billy until Ol' Jim comes back for the winter. I had found out that Ol' Jim lives by himself beside the lake. That's what I'll do.

Henry squared his shoulders, but said nothing more.

Later, in the quiet darkness, we heard Jim and the lady's murmuring voices laughing and talking softly inside the cabin. Then we heard the door open and Jim's voice rang out, "Hey you guys! Get in here before you freeze to death!"

Suddenly I stopped breathing, then whispered, "I have to leave. I can't stay here now. I'll go to Billy's."

Henry's voice came, "You can't leave, school starts in a couple of days. My dad spoke to the teacher already, remember? You have to go to school here."

"Yeah, I can stay in Collins, but I can't live here with you guys. I don't belong here now. Do you think Billy would let me stay with him?" I asked.

Henry sighed, "Yeah, maybe that's a good idea. Then if I can't stand it, I can come and stay with you guys."

We scrambled down from the treehouse and ran into the cabin. The lady was sitting at the table with a cup of tea in her hand. Jim introduced her as "Norma." I nodded and pulled out my packsack. I stuffed the puppy into it then headed for the door. Jim grabbed my arm and turned my cheek for a closer look. I smiled, then without a word he walked me outside.

"Where the heck do you think you're going?" he whispered in my ear.

I looked up at his face. "Henry doesn't like this too much. I just thought it would be better if I went to Billy's for a while until you guys sort out . . . " I nodded my head at the cabin. With a smile, I added, "Maybe I'll come back when the fight is over. I already got decked once, I don't want to be around when the battle starts!"

He expelled his breath with a "humph," smiled, and said, "You're a good kid." He rumpled my hair with his gentle hand and went back into the cabin.

Rain tapped me on the head and dampness spread across my shoulders as I walked down the path. I scrambled up the sandy shoulder and ran to the railway tracks. It was getting dark now and the misty rain had begun to freeze.

Lights flickered in the window at foreman Terry's house. They must have the television on again. The generator was creating a deafening noise as it echoed through the tall stand of pine trees. I ran down the path to the lake. The lights were on in Billy's cabin and smoke was coming from the stovepipe. I heard the radio playing as I pushed the door open. Billy looked up with a smile from the pile of papers he had on the table.

"What are you doing?" I asked as I deposited my sack on the floor and pulled Snotty out.

"My schoolwork," he said. "I've got to go back to school too you know. Well, it's a paycheque, and it helps since I don't have the trapline any more. Wasn't much left to trap out there anyway. Froze my butt off for a few pelts a month. Couldn't even pay all my grocery bill with that. Now I'm just pushing pencil and shufflin' papers for a paycheque. So, moving in with me, are you? Put your pack there. You'll have to sleep on the floor for tonight but I'll rig up a bunk for you tomorrow." He smiled and continued. "Saw the new Mrs. Jim getting off the train this evening. Pretty lady."

He threw his pencil down and gathered up his papers, then shoved aside some dirty dishes on the table and filled a bowl with stew from the pot. He pushed it toward me. I could do with some food. Mmm, delicious!

Suddenly Snotty gagged behind us and Billy said, "It looks like rabbit fur, where did he get it from?"

I jumped and pulled soggy fur out of his mouth. I giggled, saying, "Ol' Jim gave me a rabbit paw. I forgot I had it in my pocket!"

Billy laughed as he put a bowl of stew in front of the pup. The little pig dug right into it as if he had no stomach.

We played a couple of games of cribbage before I started yawning. After bringing in another armful of wood, Billy threw a couple of logs into the stove and closed the airvents and blew out the light. I lay cozy warm in a sleeping bag beside the stove. Snotty kept licking my ears. I pushed him farther down inside the sleeping bag. I lay still and tried to sleep. For some strange reason I felt like crying. I was back on the outside again. I didn't have a home any more. Maybe I could make it feel like home here. It could be a lot more fun beside the lake! Just then Snotty sneezed and sprayed wet stuff on my face. Yuck!

I could hear the springs squeak from Billy's corner every time he moved. I think I will ask him to put my bed over at the other corner. It was too hot here.

About two weeks later, right after I got home from school, Billy came home from his adult education class acting weird. Finally he sat down beside me on my bed and said, "Danny, I just talked to your father on the phone. He called me at school. He is in Armstrong, and he says he'll be here this evening but will leave again on the midnight train. He says he has to talk to you."

That was only a couple of hours away! I jumped up and ran out the door and followed the path along the shoreline. I had no intention of seeing or talking to my father. Next thing I knew I was at Charlotte's cabin. The door was open, so I walked in. Sarah, Charlotte's mother, was dishing out spare-ribs and dumplings, and she gave me a plateful. She didn't even seem surprised to see me. I sat down by the table with Charlotte's father. He was a very skinny, quiet man who never said much. Charlotte said he was sick. He only came home from the hospital once in a while.

Charlotte was talking about our new teacher, and her little sister was playing with the rib bones from the plates. I burst out laughing when she turned around from the table and grinned at us with four bones sticking out of her mouth, like long white teeth. After supper Sarah sat me down on the bench, threw a sheet over my shoulders, and proceeded to cut my hair. She didn't even ask me if she could, but I thought it was nice of her to give me a haircut. Suddenly her hand stopped and her fingers began to part my hair all over the place. Then the old man came over and no one said a word.

I knew they were looking at the scars on my head, so I shrugged and said, "That's why I left home."

Still without a word, she began to clip my hair, and the old man sat back on the bed. Afterward my head felt light, and the mirror told me that she did a good job. Then she and Charlotte began to get dressed to go outside.

Charlotte explained: "We're going to Savant Lake to get some things from Grandma. Mom says we will only be there a couple of hours and then we'll catch the other train back."

That would be just about the amount of time I'd need! I have some money at Billy's. I could run and get it. But how would I get on the train at the same time as my father got off? People get off first before other people get on the train.

I watched Charlotte come out of the back room with a nice skirt on. A skirt . . . I grabbed Charlotte and pulled her outside.

"What? It's cold out here!" she objected.

"Sh, listen! I have to sneak on the train. Father is coming to get me and I don't want to go with him. What if I borrowed

one of your skirts and a scarf to go over my head? I could
sneak by behind your mother and jump on the train?"

Charlotte's face screwed up into a grin. She nodded her head
and ran inside. I took off back down the path to our cabin.

Billy wasn't there when I ran inside. He was probably out
looking for me, or maybe he went to see Jim to find out what
to do about my father. I grabbed my sack and rummaged
around until I found a ten-dollar bill. This will do! I ran back
to Charlotte's place again. It was getting dark. The train would
be here any minute. Charlotte and Sarah already had their
coats on, and Sarah took her purse as she walked to the door.
Charlotte shoved one of her skirts into a paper bag and
draped a scarf over my shoulder. I heard the old man chuckle
as I followed them out the door. I decided to put the skirt on
at the station just when the train pulled in. That way everyone
would have their eyes on the train.

We could hear the train in the distance as we hurried down
the path. We had just arrived at the station when the train
came around the corner. There were some people around,
but I didn't see Billy or Jim.

"Charlotte, block me!" I whispered as I pulled her into the
open door of an empty room at the station.

I took the long skirt out of the bag, pulled it up over my
jeans, and tied the scarf over my head. One minute later, I
stood right against Sarah's back with Charlotte close behind
me. I kept my head down as my heart pounded like a huge
ticking clock. People were brushing right against us as they
got off the train.

I saw his big boots and felt his hand brush my arm as he
went by. My father! Then we were moving toward the steps of
the train. Other people were milling around behind us.
Everyone was talking and laughing, calling out to people who
were getting off. I went up the steps close on Sarah's heels and
hurried behind her down the aisle. She found a seat on the
other side, and I slipped ahead to the window seat. Charlotte
sat down beside me. I kept my head down behind the back-
rest while I worked the skirt off my legs. Finally we were
moving. I got the skirt off and then yanked off the scarf.

191

Charlotte laughed at me. My hair was sticking up all over the place. Sarah sat perched on the opposite seat. I shoved the rolled-up skirt between us and pulled out my ten dollars as the conductor approached, but he didn't even look at us. Sarah paid for everyone.

It didn't seem long before we pulled in at Savant Lake. The store was open. Sarah was buying supplies and Charlotte was everywhere, looking at everything, going from aisle to aisle, top to bottom. She was going nuts! I laughed and got some liquorice and a chocolate bar for myself. I gave my leftover money to Sarah. She smiled and took it, but didn't say anything. We followed her out of the store, each carrying a paper box, and headed back to the station. We left the boxes behind the counter at the ticket office and followed Sarah across the railroad tracks and along another street until she turned onto a section of road where a little house stood. I saw someone looking out the window. I was trying to remember where this was when I noticed the clearing between the streetlights. There sat the yellow water pump on the mound!

I tugged at Sarah's sleeve and said, "Can I run and visit someone? Just up the hill there. I'll meet you back at the station, okay?" She paused for a moment before she nodded her head.

I waved at Charlotte and took off full speed along the path and up the hill where I had struggled so pitifully with the water pail. I giggled. I ran past the tree and there was the cabin, light shining from the windows! They were usually asleep by now. I slowed down as I approached, then stopped by the door. There was absolute silence. I pushed the door open, and there they were—Mr. and Mrs. Old Indian.

They had not changed at all. The old woman was the first to move. Her chin came to my forehead as she put her arms around me. She smelled of woodsmoke and berries. She felt soft against me as my arms went around her body.

I said, "You shrunk a little. You're shorter now."

The old man put a shaking hand on my shoulder as the old woman stood back. I remembered something. I pulled out a string of liquorice and held it out to Old Indian. His face cracked into a zillion wrinkles before we heard his rasping chuckle. Then I saw a man sitting by the table. I hadn't even noticed him when I came in. He sat there smiling. He was a big-boned man with thick grey hair.

The old woman spoke. "'E be my son. 'E come to take us away fer da win'er. We be back agin in springtime."

The man spoke now. "So I guess you're the Danny I've been hearing so much about. My name is Jonas."

I nodded to Jonas and asked, "When are you taking them?"

Jonas laughed suddenly and said, "I've been trying to get them to leave all week! But, no. One thing or another has to get done first. We go through this every year, you know."

He smiled at the old couple who were now sitting on their mattresses on the floor. I detected so much love and warmth from the big man as he looked at them. For some strange reason, I felt tears spring into my eyes. The old woman poured me some tea, which I sipped as I sat there absorbing the silent words, the little things I had almost forgotten. I saw the old woman's eyes flicker to the old man and she started to giggle. He was sitting there with the long string of black liquorice hanging out of his mouth. I giggled until my face began to ache.

Jonas said, "Are you staying for the night? You can sleep on the bed. I'm getting on the train tonight. Now they're sending me to Armstrong to see someone for them."

"Oh, I forgot! I have to get back on the train too. I came with a woman and her daughter, and they're waiting for me at the station." Suddenly, on impulse, I knelt down between the old couple and whispered, "I dressed like a girl and snuck on the train. I have to put the skirt on again when we get there and slip off the train without being seen."

The old woman rolled her eyes to the side and made a face, and the old man burst into his rasping chuckle again. His liquorice slid off his mouth and lay pasted against his shirt.

Jonas stood up and said, "I'll walk with you to the station." He picked up his coat and lit a candle beside the old lady. Then he blew out the lamp by the table. I left the old couple laughing as we went out into the darkness.

I followed Jonas down the swamp path to the railroad tracks. Sarah and Charlotte must be at the station already. We were walking along the railroad tracks in the dark when I asked, "Where do you take them in the wintertime?"

"I take them home with me to Minaki. I have an apartment downstairs in my house where they stay. But they like the outdoors so much."

"Can your father sit outside someplace in the winter?"

"That's one of the things I can't do anything about. I have no place to take him to sit. I have a bench beside the door, but he doesn't like that very much. I will tell you something, the old guy is my uncle. When my father died many years ago, my mother moved here to Savant Lake to look after her brother. She has not left him since. She will not leave him or let someone else look after him, and they will not get rid of that cabin!" I heard him chuckle in exasperation.

I could see the lights from the station now. "When will you be bringing them back here?" I asked.

"About the first of May they start pestering me to bring them back. How about I call and leave a message for you when I have them settled back here again. You are at Collins?"

"Yeah, that will be good."

He stepped inside the station and went to the window to buy a ticket. Charlotte was sitting there on the bench, and Sarah just came out of the ladies' room. There was an extra box there on the floor. Charlotte said it was a fishnet. It reminded me of Ol' Jim's fishnet, the one the moose got tangled up in, so I told them the story. They were still laughing when people began coming in and Jonas sat down beside us. Then I told them what had happened to me when I thought I was hiding inside an empty boxcar at Armstrong.

Sarah shook her head and murmured, "Oh my. Oh my." I thought it was a funny story, but she just looked like she was very sorry for me. Soon we heard the train roll into the station.

About five minutes from Collins, at a place called Shultz's Trail or something, I had to wriggle back into the skirt again. Jonas had taken a seat way at the other end, so I didn't have to worry about him seeing me. Sure enough, a minute after I had buttoned the waist, the conductor came, grinning at Sarah. I swear that if we had become three or four kids instead of two, he still wouldn't have noticed us. Then Charlotte saw some young women she knew coming up the aisle as the train came to a stop at Collins. I leaned over, pretending to tie my shoelaces when they passed by us. I slipped the scarf back on and pasted myself behind Sarah again as we made our way to the door. Down the steps we went, one, two, three, four. I slipped into the darkness to the left as soon as my feet hit the gravel, then took off down the tracks and into the field. No one seemed to have noticed me as the train pulled away. I stopped at the school outhouse and pulled off the skirt and waited. After a minute, I heard Charlotte and Sarah. I ran out and fell into step beside Charlotte, grabbing one of the boxes from her hand. We walked through the bush right behind Sarah. I put the box down beside the others when we arrived.

"Oh, there's some tea on the stove. Thanks for carrying the box. Do you like your haircut?" she asked as I stood there.

I grinned, then threw the skirt and scarf at Charlotte saying, "If you tell anybody, I'll steal all your clothes!"

That got a smile out of Sarah, and Charlotte broke into a squeal of laughter. I turned and ran out.

Billy was on his bed looking at the ceiling when I came in. I noticed a box on the floor beside him. He looked at me a moment, then said, "That's for you. And where did you get that haircut? I've been looking for someone to give me a good haircut like that for years!"

I sat down on my bed and took off my jacket. "Sarah cut my hair." I walked to the box and shoved it with my foot. "What is it?"

He got up on one elbow. "A record player."

I knew who had put it there. "I don't want it!" I said as I kicked off my shoes.

"Put it away then. Shove it under the bed."

When I grabbed the box and fired it under the bed a painful howl erupted from underneath and I heard little claws frantically scratching to get out. I had hit Snotty! Billy burst out laughing as I scrambled to my knees and pulled out poor Snotty.

"Why didn't you tell me it was your birthday today?" he

asked as I sat down beside him to examine the pup. He seemed to be okay because now he wanted to play.

"I forgot," I answered.

He poked my ribs with his big toe. "You'd never convince anyone you are twelve years old, you look more like ten," he said with a grin on his face.

I went to my bed, pulled the covers back, and shoved Snotty beside the pillow. Billy continued to study the ceiling as he said, "Boy, that was a big meeting you missed, you know—your father, Jim, and I. For a while there, I thought I would have to go for a piggy-back ride on Jim's back, but they decided to be civilized. Then I got involved in the discussion, and at the end I had two hundred dollars sitting on the table. Then it was time to go to the station, and, you know, while everyone was busy gawking at the lovely young ladies getting off the train, I saw the strangest little woman slip out from behind Sarah's skirt. But she disappeared into the night." He put a hand over his heart and sighed, "Oh, I have been smitten by love! I have been thinking about the sweet little thing ever since."

I grabbed my pillow and threw it at him, hard, saying, "Don't you say anything to anybody, hear? You promise now!"

He rolled away laughing, then threw the pillow back at me, saying, "Okay, okay!"

I put a log into the stove and closed the airvent, then blew out the lamp. After I had settled in bed, Billy said, "Do me a favour, Danny. Next time, tell me where you are going. I won't chase you or try to stop you, but just tell me where you are going, okay? Maybe I'd even help you."

Well, I guess I could write him a note or something. Notes don't yell back at you.

His voice came again, "Now, about the money he left for you, do you want to keep it, give it to Jim or me to keep for you, go shopping at Sioux Lookout, or what?"

I pulled my blanket over my shoulders and said, "I don't want it!"

Billy said nothing. Snotty made little barking sounds in his sleep and started to kick with his feet. I petted him and he lay still again.

Chapter Seventeen

ABOUT A MONTH LATER, I WAS IN BED with a very bad cold. Billy had gone to the store for some medicine. I hoped he wouldn't bring that awful white liquid for coughs. Yuck! Snotty and I had made ourselves at home here. Henry had given me enough clothes to last a whole year, so I was all set for the winter. I learned that Billy had about six of the red-and-black checkered shirts and four pairs of the same kind of jeans. That way he never had to think about what to wear, he said.

My mind was just wandering, half-awake and half-asleep, thinking about things. There had been evening meetings between Jim and Billy, until Billy seemed more comfortable with our living arrangements. I knew my father was sending money for my keep. I didn't get into fights in school here, everyone just sort of minded their own business. I just plodded to school every morning and waited to get out at lunch and breathe some fresh air, then went back in again until after school. The days came and went without any complications as to which adult was caring for me. Jim had stopped talking to my father and last week Billy had come storming in, cursing him. He didn't tell me why, and I didn't ask. I didn't want to know anything about my father!

There were now patches of snow on the frozen ground. The lake looked very dark and cold and had started to freeze along the shoreline. Funny how the fall colours smear together before the white snow comes in. Then the white gets smeared with it before the spring colours come in again. I

197

remember painting once, at school. I had red, green, yellow, and blue. But when I mixed them together, they turned into a dirty brown, just like before the snow comes. If I could separate the colours again, I would get spring.

The crash of the stove lid brought me fully awake. "Sorry Chips, I dropped the lid." Billy threw some more wood into the stove and a puff of smoke spread into the room. Then I noticed the smoke curl around as it was sucked back into the stove at the bottom airvent. "Here, I got you some aspirin and some stuff called lemon something."

He mixed the whole thing into a cup and stirred it with a fork. He pulled the fork out and brought the steaming cup to me. Yuck, it was the awful stuff all right! I held my breath and drank it all down.

"I'll get you for this!" I croaked as I put my head back down.

He chuckled and threw a bag of potato chips beside me. It had become a joke after a while with the chips. Every time he went to the store he'd ask if I wanted chips or popcorn. I always said chips, so now he just called me "Chips."

I watched Billy sit at the table with his books again. No, those are my books. What is he doing with my books? Probably doing my homework again. He got half of them wrong the last time! I suddenly broke into another coughing fit before I could get my tummy muscles ready. Ouch, that one caught me off guard. It was a school day today and everyone must be in school now. Nothing to do around here anyway. Henry and I just generally snoop around and visit Little Foot or Ol' Jim. There was never any mention of Jim's new wife, Norma. She was still there. I saw her at the store sometimes. She didn't go anywhere. I never saw her visit anyone.

The aeroplane had landed last week and Ol' Jim and Hog got off. The green canvas canoe was tied to one of the pontoons. Henry and I sat on the dock and watched them unload the thing. Hog did not even look at me. I was glad to see him get on the train that afternoon. We spent the whole day with Ol' Jim, getting him settled in his old cabin beside the lake. Boy, the place was filthy! We hauled about four pails of water for him. Whenever Henry and I went there, Ol' Jim put us to work right away, but we didn't mind.

Now and then Charlotte came with us, but she always ended up in an argument with Henry. Henry had developed a nasty streak and Charlotte did not like it at all! Charlotte would say something, and then Henry would make a remark and Charlotte's fists would come up. It was always the same. One time I stepped in between them and got a punch on my chest and a push from behind. Next time I'll stand aside and let them fight it out. Now that would be interesting.

Jim walked in with Snotty at his heels. He looked serious as he nodded in my direction and looked at Billy, then Billy grabbed his coat and they went out. I could hear their footsteps fade down the road. Probably another enraged phone call from my father. Snotty jumped on the bed and flipped my hand up on top of his head and waited to be petted. His fur was cold and wet.

Several days after I had recovered from my cold, Henry and I were walking along the tracks back to Henry's cabin with our dogs. The dogs were fooling around and wrestling ahead of us. The cold wind was blowing hard, straight from the north. My ears were starting to ache so I put my hands over them. Beside me, Henry was doing the same. I wished I had a toque. I glanced back at Henry to say so, when suddenly, I saw a train headlight emerge from the rock cut around the bend. I hadn't even heard the train coming! I pointed to it at the same time I felt Henry tense beside me. Our dogs were way ahead of us, still wrestling and rolling around in the middle of the tracks. Henry suddenly took off toward the dogs. The train whistle blasted loudly several times as I chased after Henry, yelling, "Henry! Get off the tracks!" I ran as hard as I could and, finally, I grabbed for the back of his jacket but missed. Then I got a handful and pulled him off the tracks with me. One glance and I saw the stupid dogs still rolling around in the middle of the tracks! We stumbled down the shoulder and in that instant I saw something shoot out from the train like a kicked football. It rolled down the hill, spraying blood, as the thundering train roared beside us. The blood was bright against the white snow. A sick feeling mounted in my stomach as I looked at the severed head of Henry's dog where it lay in front of us. I started pushing Henry farther downhill but he wouldn't go. I finally pulled him along by the sleeve, then my stomach turned and I threw up as the train rattled by, deafening me. I saw the caboose pass in a gust of wind as I straightened up.

Henry was standing there looking at the dog's head. Then he turned away and quickly disappeared down the path to his cabin. I stood there in silence for what seemed like a long, long time when suddenly Snotty emerged from the other side of the tracks and slowly came toward me, sniffling and whimpering. I had never seen such a wonderful sight! He seemed okay and I knelt down to pet him. He was shivering a lot harder than I was. On wobbly legs, we followed Henry home.

I came into the clearing in time to see Henry's feet disappear into his treehouse. Jim came rushing from the bush with an axe in his hand, which he flung by the door as he yelled, "What happened? I heard the train whistle when I was cutting wood."

I nodded at the treehouse. "Henry's dog got hit. The head came flying toward us."

Jim swore as he ran to the treehouse and scrambled up the steps. His feet disappeared through the small door. I decided to go home. Snotty and I took the path by the sandpit.

Weeks went by and Henry refused to speak of the dog, and he wouldn't even acknowledge Snotty. In fact, he hardly talked to me at all since the dog got killed. I saw him coming from Ol' Jim's cabin one morning, and he didn't look at me, so I thought I'd go see the old man to find out what Henry was up to. I walked along the swampy path to the little cabin beside the lake. Ol' Jim now had all kinds of things lying around outside all over the place. There were square wooden frames that he used to stretch the pelts he sold. There were tubs, pails, and an incredible number of odds and ends. I pulled the wooden handle. I stood by the door a moment until my eyes adjusted to the dark inside the cabin. I saw him sitting beside the woodstove. I came forward and sat down on a bench beside a brown-tinged window. You could hardly see outside through it. We didn't speak for the longest time.

Finally I asked, "Is Henry okay? He won't talk to me."

He glanced at me and thought for a minute before he answered, "Be patient. He knows where to find you."

I waited, but he said no more. He seemed deep in thought about something. I shrugged and left him sitting there. I closed the door softly behind me.

I walked back down by the water and strolled along the shoreline. There was a rim of ice around the lake. It was white where it touched the shore and gradually became thin and see-through by the open water. In the middle, the lake was very dark, like a tub of grape drink. The rocks jutting out of the water stood out clear and bright above the darkness of the lake.

I reached Charlotte's cabin. There were two dogs on the porch, and they lifted their heads as I walked across. I pushed the door open but there was no one inside. Strange. I went back out and then I noticed Sarah down near the lake, by the woodpile. I walked down to see what she was doing. She looked up and smiled. I sat down and watched her take the guts out of four large trout. Their backs were very black. Water was still dripping off the canoe where it lay turned over by the shore. She must have just come back from the lake. I haven't been out there in a long time. There was always that yearning to go somewhere when I saw Jim's canoe turned over by Billy's landing area. I wonder what Ol' Jim would say if I asked him if we could go on another trip in the summer, but not to Whiteclay Lake again! I found out that Henry didn't like to do those things.

Sarah gathered up the paper bag and fish guts and I got up and held open the lid on her huge gas-drum trash burner. She shoved the garbage in there. She picked up two fish to wash off by the lake, and I picked up the other two. She giggled as I played with one, trying to make it swim. I realized we had not said a word. I followed her back into the cabin where we put the fish inside a washpan. As I turned to leave, she said, "Take one." I smiled and picked the smaller one out of the pan. I left and walked home as fast as I could with the fish flapping beside my leg. I had my fingers wedged under the gills, and it was beginning to cut into my hand. Boy, it was heavy! Charlotte must have been in somebody's cabin, otherwise I would have heard her laughing somewhere. You usually could. I took the path by the shoreline and emerged near the dock.

It was a cold, crisp day. The ground was frozen solid now and it had snowed several times, but it didn't stay very long. We had a lot of frozen rain, but not much snow yet. Billy's face broke into a big grin when I came in with the fish. We had a nice supper of boiled trout and potatoes. Snotty made a face and wouldn't touch any. He satisfied himself with a piece of bannock and some dried-out bologna. This dog does not eat fish.

As the weeks went into November and the snow began to pile higher and deeper along the paths and doorways, there were definitely some strange things going on with Henry. Yesterday I was on my way to the pump to get some water when I heard voices over the brain-rattling noise of the CN generator. I stopped and carefully peered over the snow embankment by the tracks. I couldn't believe it! I saw Henry take a swing at Norma. She blocked the punch and they went down, thrashing in the snow. I was ready to run and help my friend when I saw that Norma was doing her best to grab his hands, and soon she had him pinned under her. She was talking to him all the time. Then she got up and pulled Henry up, and they stood there hugging each other. I could tell Henry was crying so I decided to disappear and get the water. For some reason, I felt such a pain in my chest that I cried all the way home.

Billy and I had worked out a kind of system where we just stayed out of each other's way, and if something went wrong, it was always Snotty's fault. For one thing, Snotty had developed a knack for picking things off the table without being seen. I saw his head come up over the table once at Linda's place, and he took a big piece of meat off her plate while she had her arm out pointing at something as she babbled on to Billy with her mouth full. You should have seen her face when she looked down to cut another piece and it was gone. She looked around on the floor, but Snotty had already quietly slipped out the open door. She rolled her tongue around in her mouth for a minute. You could tell that she was trying to figure out why she didn't remember eating the whole piece of meat. Billy saw it all and he glared at me but didn't say anything. We had a serious man-to-kid-to-dog talk when we got home. There was no denying that we had a thieving dog in the house. Billy just kind of laid the law down, but he said as long as things didn't disappear off our table, Snotty was still welcome in the cabin.

There was hardly any smoke coming out of the stovepipe as I got to our cabin. I stopped to fill my arms with wood and kicked the door open. Billy was not home. I put some more logs in the stove and fed Snotty some dried-up bannock from the table. I went about making a pot of tea, then I heard footsteps crunching in the snow and coming around the corner. The door opened and Billy came in with a bag of groceries. He saw Snotty with a mouthful of bannock and said, "I had visions of leftover bannock soaking in hot tea while I made supper tonight!" Snotty gulped the last piece down and stood waiting to be let out into the cold air. I chuckled and opened the door.

"I had another crazy conversation with your father," Billy sighed as he grabbed a frying pan off the nail behind the stove. I decided to go get a pail of water, but as I pulled my coat on Billy said, "You have to talk to him sometime, you know? He wants to come here to see you."

I whirled around. "No! No! I don't want him to come here, I don't want to see him!"

Billy slapped the pork chops in the frying pan. "I told him that, so then he said I should bring you home myself at Christmas. I told him I had no wish to go visit him."

I pulled off my coat again. "Then tell him we don't want to see him and that he can't come here. And tell him that Jim doesn't want to see him either."

Billy threw the frying pan on the roaring stove and turned to me. "What would you do if he just got off the train and came here to get you?"

I sat down on the bed and felt my shoulders slump. "I guess I would just take off and run as fast as I could and make sure he never caught me."

Billy stirred the pork chops like soup in a pot and said, "Well, if he ever comes I will just have to make sure I remember to lock him in the cabin until you are long gone to a place I know you're going to before I let him out again. Okay, Chips, set the table."

I felt a lot better. I set the table for the two of us. I had to elbow everything aside to find enough room though. There were the playing cards, a cribbage board, books, papers, pencils, ashtrays, matches, a candle, a lamp, the kitchen utensil glass jar that sits beside the coal oil lamp, and some dishtowels at the corner, and jam and butter at the other corner. All this on the one and only table. I like it this way. It is like Billy.

I think I will go skating tomorrow. The kids usually appear on the ice before the parents can think up work for them to do. Ol' Jim said we've had too much snow and not enough cold and that the ice was not thick enough to walk on where the current was. We just laughed. That's old people's talk. Ol' Jim always sits beside the door at the store. I think the rest of the people think he's just another piece of store furniture.

One day the store got cleaned out of all the pop and only had tomato juice left. It was the first time Ol' Jim had ever drank tomato juice, and it was no more than five minutes when he felt the first effects. He said he had heartburn, then began spitting up red stuff. All the ladies went into hysterics, thinking it was blood! The storekeeper gave him a dose of antacid stuff and that fixed him up. I think I like him better the way he was in the bush. He tries to run the whole store these days. He was even giving Charlotte a lecture yesterday on why she should buy oranges instead of apples or something like that. And he is always after me about where I get my money from, every time I go and buy a bag of chips. I gave him back the five dollars, too, so it isn't like I am using his money! He's just getting on everyone's nerves.

The sun shining on my face woke me up, or was it Snotty

rubbing his cold nose on me? I rolled over and slipped off my bunk. Billy had not kept the fire going all night again and it was cold. His head was sticking out of his sleeping bag. I hadn't even heard him come in last night. He was at a party at foreman Terry's place. I dragged my blanket with me to let Snotty out and opened the airvent on the stove. Nothing happened. Totally black. There wasn't even an ember.

"Hey! It's cold in here, see?" I went "huh, huh" blowing clouds of mist into the cold air.

All I heard was a grumble from the blankets saying, "Oh, shut up." So I went about the business of getting the fire started and sat huddled, basking in the warm heat of a roaring fire, when I heard Snotty scratching to come in.

I decided to visit Henry after I made a pot of very lumpy porridge. Billy will probably sleep all morning again. I scooped out the soft part on top before the rest turned to solid rubber at the bottom. I gobbled it up quickly and put on my warmest clothes and pulled Snotty along behind me. He wasn't too fussy about eating the porridge, but he did eat some of Billy's burnt bannock from yesterday. Billy was so busy getting beat by me on the cribbage board that his bannock burnt on the stove.

I walked briskly up the path, hearing the crunch, crunch of the snow under my new ski-doo boots, up along the railway tracks and then down the path to Henry's cabin. I saw smoke coming out from the stovepipe on his treehouse. I yelled, "Hey, Henry! Are you up there?" It was a long while before he finally poked his head of out the little door.

"Come in, come in and make yourself at home," he called.

I scampered up the steps and crawled in the door. Gee! There was a little woodstove about two feet high and a foot wide, sitting in the corner. It took up half the space in the little room.

"Where did you get that?" I asked. Henry, sitting on a stool, motioned for me to take the other stool. That was all this place had room for.

"Why build a fire if you have screen windows?" I asked.

Henry smiled. "Well, when I covered the windows it got all

full of smoke in here. I got the stove from Dad's tool shed. He used to use it in the trapper's shack when he went trapping. But he doesn't use it any more so I decided to take it. I can't make big fires though, gets too hot in here. Norma and Dad are out getting wood. Let's go play cards."

He closed the airvent on the stove, and we climbed down to the ground. When we entered, I could see the cabin had changed. It looked very homey, with ruffled curtains at the windows and beds made nice and neat.

"Doesn't look the same any more, does it?" I said.

Henry smiled. "No. But I kind of got used to it."

We were playing a poker game with matchsticks, and I had almost cleaned Henry out of a whole box when we heard laughter coming from the path behind the cabin. I shuffled the deck again.

After a lunch of macaroni and spaghetti sauce, Henry and I went out to visit Ol' Jim. We saw him shaking out the sleigh as we approached.

"There you are. I knew you were coming today, so I got ready to show you where my woodpile is. You can pull some wood home for me today," he said with a wide grin.

Henry and I smiled at each other as we took the rope of the sleigh and followed him up the trail. He was ready to put us to work again as usual. We always come prepared with warm mitts. He still had quite a big pile of wood when we got there. He heaved first one log and then another off the pile, and we loaded them on the sleigh. Five in all. It was going to be a heavy load to pull. When we finished tying them onto the sleigh, I noticed Ol' Jim standing there all out of breath with his hand clenching the left side of his chest.

Concerned, I asked, "Are you okay, Ol' Jim?"

"Oh, I'm fine. Just fine. Got a heartburn again is all. Too much bannock," he laughed.

He followed behind as we pulled the heavy load back. We quickly stacked the logs by the sawhorse and entered the cabin behind Ol' Jim. He threw some wood into the stove and put the teapot on.

I could smell the stretched animal skins he always had

drying on the ceiling rafters. Ol' Jim told us he would be leaving soon to go to the trapline for the winter.

After tea, we slowly walked back to Henry's cabin. He gave a big sigh. "Norma and Dad were planning for us to go to Saskatchewan to visit Norma's parents. I don't feel like going. How can I get them to let me stay with you guys?"

I thought a moment and said, "How about we go and stay with Ol' Jim at his trapline over the Christmas holidays? We could get Billy to take us there when school is out, eh? That way, I wouldn't have to worry about my father showing up there."

Henry's face broke into a big grin. "Yeah! But can you get Billy to ask my dad? He could tell him you need a buddy to help you get wood and things for Ol' Jim."

I nodded and we hurried toward the cabin. Halfway there, we spotted a very nice little pine tree. I pointed to it and Henry shook his head with a grin. We ran the rest of the way to his cabin and grabbed the axe from the woodpile. Back we went to the tree. Henry trudged through two feet of snow to reach it and began hacking away. Finally it was down. It would make a wonderful Christmas tree. I carried the axe and Henry dragged the tree behind me. The trees were casting long shadows over the narrow path as our feet crunched over the snow.

Jim was lying on the bed with his hands behind his head, and Norma was cleaning fish for supper when we pushed the tree through the door. Henry leaned the tree in the corner of the room so carefully you'd think it was going to fall apart.

Norma started laughing, then shook her head. "We don't have any decorations to put on that thing."

Henry laughed. "We'll make them ourselves!"

Jim spoke from the bed, "Not right now, you can do it tomorrow. Trees. Do you know how sad it looks in the towns and cities the day after Christmas?" We all waited. We knew another lecture was coming. He continued, "After Christmas when you are finished with the tree, take off all the branches and put them by the doorstep for people to wipe their feet on, then saw the thing into stove-lengths to be used for firewood.

Don't waste any part of the tree. It looks so sick—the tree skeletons that people throw on the sides of the road, waiting for garbage collection. It is not garbage, it is a tree! It was a living thing! It ought to be treated with more respect."

Henry smiled and winked at me. We had a game of cards again, and he won all his matchsticks back before Norma cleared us off the table. I stayed for supper and enjoyed fried fish, canned peas, and boiled potatoes.

I walked back to Billy's with a smile on my face. Henry and I decided to go skating this evening. He will meet me at Charlotte's cabin by the lake. I wonder if Billy would mind having a Christmas tree. Just a small one on top of the table or something. I'll ask him.

Chapter Eighteen

I OPENED THE DOOR AND SNOTTY RAN inside ahead of me, just as a rubber boot came flying. It hit Snotty right on the side of the head. He whirled around and knocked me aside as he ducked back out. What's going on? What on earth is that stink? Billy was sitting on the bench by the table, holding the other rubber boot between his knees.

"What are you doing?" I asked as I bent over to see.

Billy heaved a big sigh. "I hung my boots over the stove and went to the outhouse. While I was gone, one boot fell on top of the stove and burnt a big hole in the toe, see? I know they don't have them in my size at the store, so I figured I'd cut a piece from the top of the other boot and patch this one. But the darn things will not stick together!" He threw the boot into the corner with the other one. "Did you eat yet? There's some rabbit stew on the stove."

I sat beside him as he poured us each a cup of tea. "Yeah, I had supper at Henry's. Can I borrow your skates again this evening? Henry is going to meet me at Charlotte's."

Billy shrugged. "Yeah, sure. But you know, you really should have a pair of your own. How about we go to Savant Lake or Sioux Lookout this weekend and get you a pair of skates and some other things, eh?"

My face stretched into a big smile. "Yeah! I'd like that!"

Billy clinked away, stirring his tea. "I talked to your father this afternoon. He is sending you money to buy some Christmas presents for yourself. He also said that he wants you home after Christmas. You come home or he will come and get you."

I could feel the familiar pressure in my chest threatening to choke me. I took a deep breath and said, "No! I don't want him to come and get me! I am not going back there! I'll run away again if he takes me back there! No! I said, No!"

Billy looked at me for a minute. "Are you saying that you would stay with your father if he took you home somewhere else?"

I hadn't thought about that. In fact, my brain had refused to think about Father, or that place, or what I was supposed to do. I hadn't thought about anything.

I swallowed my fear and said through clenched teeth, "I will not stay wherever that witch is. I will not go back to that evil, ugly house."

Billy reached for the skates and started untying the laces. "Okay, Chips, I will tell him that when I talk to him again. In the meantime, you won't take off and leave me all alone, will you? Got so used to having you around, I certainly would miss you a whole bunch. Now, put another pair of socks on top of those."

"I already got two pairs of work socks on my feet," I said as I kicked off my boots.

Billy laughed. "Even if you had six pairs of socks, these skates would still be too big. Anyway, we'll get you a pair of skates, exactly your size."

I laced the skates up tightly and wrapped the laces around right up my legs. "Hey, Billy, can we go get a Christmas tree tomorrow?"

Billy looked up from the table. "What are you going to decorate it with, your stinky socks? Or maybe your stupid dog's ears? He stole a chocolate bar right out of a child's hand at the store today, you know? Do something with that dog and I'll see if we have enough money to buy some decorations when we go shopping. Okay?"

"Yep!" I said, and wobbled across the floor. That brought a chuckle from Billy as he lay on the bed studying his math book, faking interest was more like it. I smiled and slid out the door.

I walked and skidded across the path to the lake until I reached the shovelled-off skater's trail that ran all along the shoreline. The sun was shining on the tall trees and rock cliffs on the opposite shore. I spotted some kids down by the lake near Charlotte's cabin. Sure enough, I could hear Charlotte laughing. She is such a character that one! I saw her shoot the cap right off Ol' Jim's head with her slingshot once, and he was quite a distance away too! I never heard anyone apologize so elaborately and for so long in my whole life! Ol' Jim was so flattered she could have hit him again if she wanted.

The ice was very rough in sections, like someone had stirred it one last time before it froze solid. My body is going to get jiggled numb before I get there! Charlotte was pushing her sister around in an old metal tub as I approached. She was dressed in a big thick overcoat and a skirt, with pants sticking out above her skates. She pushed her long hair away from her face as she straightened up. Her huge black eyes twinkled and she broke into a smile as she looked at my long skates. Just then, Henry came skating around the bend by the beach and stopped in a shower of snow, much to the little girl's delight. He seemed taller and more self-confident as he stood there looking at Charlotte. Then he bent forward and, skating hard, he pushed the tub around in a circle. The little girl giggled as she came around once more. I watched Henry come to a stop in front of us, smiling and breathing hard.

Charlotte was looking at my feet again and she laughed. "I wonder if you can actually skate faster with those long skates?"

I didn't know if she was teasing or if she was actually wondering, but somehow, it hurt.

"Want to race to the dock?" Henry grinned at me, then skated away like a pro.

He didn't even wait to see if I was coming. I glanced at Charlotte, but I couldn't think of anything to say, so I took off after Henry, heading straight for the dock. I skated as fast as I could, but my skates kept wanting to go off in other directions. I was only halfway there when I saw Henry skating past the dock toward a couple of dogs wrestling and rolling around on the ice by the cliff. I yelled for him to wait, but he just waved and continued on. I slowed down, then turned around and headed back to Charlotte. When I got there the

211

little girl who had been in the washtub was crying, and blood was running down her chin.

Charlotte giggled and wiped one mitt over the child's chin. "The tub tipped over and she banged her mouth on the edge," she said as she pulled her sister up.

I put my hand out to the little girl, but when she pulled I went flying, feet up in the air. Charlotte went into another fit of laughter while I struggled to get up with as much dignity as possible. The little girl was by the door already as I followed Charlotte to the cabin.

Hot air rushed at us in a cloud of mist when we pulled the door open. It was very hot in there. Charlotte's mother was by the stove pulling and stretching a piece of white moosehide. Sweat was pouring off her face. She smiled and said, "There's some tea on the table. Bring me a cup too. I have to keep pulling this until it dries, then it will be nice and soft."

I wobbled on unsteady feet over the wooden floor to the table and sat down for a cup of tea. After two sips I was starting to sweat buckets. The little girl was crying about something again, so I downed the rest of my tea and decided to go find Henry. Maybe he went to see Billy. Charlotte's mother giggled as I wobbled across the floor. I could feel my face turning red. I'll be glad when I have my own skates.

I skated slowly along the shoreline to the dock. About halfway there, I noticed people running back and forth and yelling. My hair was beginning to stand on end at the back of my neck as the sound of panicky voices reached me. I skated faster to see what was wrong. More people arrived as I neared the dock. I pushed through groups of people making their way toward the rock cliff. The blood in my ears was pounding louder as I began to hear bits and pieces of conversation. The voices were saying something about someone falling through the ice! As I came around the corner, I saw some people around the mouth of the creek. Then I saw black open water with blocks of ice floating around in it. There was Billy running toward me. He grabbed my arm and quickly turned me around.

I started yelling, "What's going on? What's happened?"

Without answering my questions, he yelled, "Go home, right now! I will meet you there!" I watched him disappear into the bushes and up the path.

I was skating slower than I have ever skated in my whole life! I willed my legs to go faster and faster but I felt like I was moving in slow motion. Finally I slip-shuffled my long-bladed feet up the path and slid into the cabin just as Billy came up behind me. He pushed me down on the bench and immediately began pulling off my skates before I noticed the tears streaming down his face. I became totally still. I knew the worst was coming.

At last my skates were off. Billy reached for me and hugged the breath out of me before he said, "It was Henry who fell through the ice, Chips. He's kicked so far from the hole they can't find him!"

I started struggling, trying to run. Billy wouldn't let go. I felt myself falling on the bed. Billy was holding me tight until I felt the dam break inside me. An agonized cry burst from my mouth, but Billy was there, holding onto me when I thought I was going to shake to pieces.

Someone came in and started talking to Billy, then they left. Snotty was there licking my hands. I rubbed his cold wet nose. He flipped my hand up over his head. He wanted to be petted. I was back on the bench. Snotty was all wet and steam was rising off his fur. Why was he wet? He looked like he had gone for a swim . . . The door opened and Billy came back in. "Are you okay? I'll go there with you if you feel up to it. They have already called the police and the doctor," he said as he went to wash his face.

We left Snotty in the cabin, closing the door firmly behind us. There were men in a canoe hacking away at the ice when we got there. Charlotte came running toward me, and Billy was clinging to Henry's father to keep him from diving into the water. Everyone was there. As night descended, the men worked quickly to widen the hole. Still there was no sign of Henry.

Sarah came and put a hand over my shoulder, but she said nothing. Charlotte stayed beside me. Then I noticed Billy leading Jim away to our place. I ran after them, following close behind as they slowly made their way up the path. We entered the cabin and Billy went about making another pot of coffee. Billy's friend Ned also came inside to warm up.

Jim hadn't said anything since we came in. He looked so different, I would not have recognized him if I had not known that that was Jim sitting there! I kept my eyes on the floor, it was too painful to look at him. I had only taken two sips of the coffee when we heard a yell from Norma as she came running from the lake. Billy and Jim were already out the door before I could grab my coat.

I couldn't see over the backs of the people as they pulled the body out about twenty-five feet from the spot where he fell in. Everyone moved with the group as they carried the body up the hill and down the path to the waiting room at the store.

I started to move with the group, but Billy pulled me back. "I want to stay with Henry," I said.

Billy got down to eye level with me and I heard his voice, "Listen, Chips, he's not there. Henry is gone. Little Foot used to tell me that those who die wait for us on the other side. We will see Henry again when it is our turn to go."

I could feel my bottom lip stretching again and I bit down hard. Then I followed Billy and the rest of the guys to foreman Terry's house to wait for the train that would bring the doctor.

Listening to the conversations around me, I found out that one of the skaters had noticed Snotty barking like crazy and frantically circling a hole in the ice. For some reason, Henry had decided to skate to the bay where the creek was. We all knew that it was dangerous there. We all knew that the area was never frozen solid because of the strong current there. Why did Henry go there? Unless . . . he was chasing something. Snotty was all wet. Maybe Snotty tried to save Henry . . . or maybe it was Snotty who fell in first! Knowing Henry, he had probably tried to save the dog and fell in himself.

Suddenly a hand came across my shoulder and Billy whispered in my ear, "Sh, sh. Don't think about things you cannot change." I sagged against his warm, hard comforting body. His arm tightened as the humming sound became louder. The train! Everyone trooped out of the house and down to the station. The doctor arrived on a freight train, and they put the body inside. I watched Jim and Norma get on the train too. I never saw Henry again. They buried the body beside his mother's grave at Sioux Lookout. Billy and I didn't go to the funeral.

A week later, we went on the train to Savant Lake to get some Christmas things. We left in the afternoon and planned to take the night train back. We went right to the store and bought all the stuff we needed, and then we hauled the boxes to the train station and left them behind the counter. Just like Sarah, Charlotte, and I had done. We were going out to find something to eat when Billy said he had to go to the washroom and told me to wait for him. I stood there looking down at the railroad tracks when I heard footsteps behind me. I turned and there was my father!

A shock went through me, clear to my toes. I could see the smirk on the side of his face that he got when he had been drinking. He was by himself. I was getting very tense, ready to run, trying to find a way out. He reached up and tilted back his baseball cap. I refused to look into his eyes. I saw the hand, scratched at the knuckles, and I backed away.

"Well, Danny, aren't you going to say hello? Boy, you are big! Come here!" The hands reached for me and, suddenly, I was able to move. I tried to duck under his arm, but he got hold of me. "Danny! Why do you always make me get mad at you? Do you know what you are doing to me? You are my son!" He paused for breath, and I stopped struggling for a second. He thinks it's all *my* fault!

Between clenched teeth I said, "Leave me alone!"

He let go for a second as his hand went to his face, and I ran out of the station as fast as I could. I could hear him calling me as I ran faster, around the corner to the path where the old woman used to go, but there was no path! It was a dead-end road now. I stopped and looked on both sides of the road. There were houses and driveways, wait, there was a road on the other side. I ran up a trail between two houses and came upon a street on a hill. I ran down the hill and crossed the railroad tracks, then ran onto another road going up the hill. I was looking for the clearing with the fire hydrant. Then I remembered. The old couple wouldn't be there.

I slowed to a walk. The snowdrifts were very thick and high on the hill. I slowly walked back to the train station. I saw no one. I waited by an old building until I saw Billy and Father coming out of the hotel. A taxi pulled up and Father got in. Billy looked like an old man as he made his way to the train station. I watched the car disappear down the road.

I ran to the station, and there was Billy with his head in his hands, sitting on the bench. I closed the door softly behind me.

"You tricked me," I said.

Billy sat up and took a big breath. "I'm sorry, Chips, but I had to do it. He had to see for himself. He wouldn't believe me. He thought I was trying to keep you for myself. Come here." I sat down beside him and he threw an arm across my shoulder. "Darned Lynx, if you had a tail, I'd cut it off and hang it on my cap! The train will be here in about an hour. Let's go find something to eat, I'm hungry!"

That was our one trip out of Collins together. Most times, Billy and Jim go shopping together. I won't go anywhere with either of them any more. You just never know!

We got a small Christmas tree for our little cabin. Billy made a big production about how to take care of Christmas trees. He must have learned a lesson from Jim's lectures. It looked very nice. But every time I looked at it, it reminded me of Henry. Billy and I put foil wrappers from the Christmas candies on the tree, and I scrounged around for the foil paper from cigarette packages. Billy showed me how to wrap the foil around a pencil and push it, all wrinkled up, into a three-inch tube. Then I bent it and hung it on the tree. They looked like little silver wreathes. Billy also bought a dozen shiny balls, but they were too big and heavy for our little tree. I laughed when it sort of sagged as he tried to hang them all. We only put six on.

One evening, shortly after school was out for the holidays, Billy said we would go to Ol' Jim's trapper's tent at Smoothrock Lake. Then, today, he said we were going tonight. Some guys came in after supper, and Billy left with them. There was a party going on or something at foreman Terry's place. I was disappointed, but prepared to wait. I packed my sleeping bag and a pair of socks and got dressed in several layers of clothing. I even put on three pairs of work socks. We had two gifts for Ol' Jim, and I slipped them inside my sleeping bag. Then I waited. I lit the lamp and turned it down low, then I banked up the fire and turned down the stove. The moonlight shone through the window and the stars twinkled big and bright in the cold crispy night. I stretched out on the bed and listened for the sound of footsteps.

A snowmobile roared by close to the cabin and came to a stop outside the door. The door burst open and Billy and Ned came in. "You ready to go, Chips? Good!"

Ned was dressed to the eyebrows. I glanced at the clock. It was almost midnight! Billy went to tie Snotty by the doorstep so he wouldn't follow us. I grabbed my bag and ran out the door. There was a sleigh tied to the back of the snowmobile, with some boxes and bags tied under the canvas. Ned got on the machine behind Billy, and I settled down on top of the sleigh.

"You ready kid?"

"Yeah!" I yelled. "Bye, Snotty!"

I could only see Snotty's mouth opening as the machine started and away we went. No, away they went. I landed on my behind right in the middle of the road!

The machine stopped and Billy yelled back at me, "Get on top of the box and hang onto the ropes!"

I ran for the sleigh and hopped on again, just like in the Westerns. I hopped on the back of my horse and grabbed the reins.

"Yahoo!" I yelled.

Off we went this time, along the railroad tracks to the crossing, and what a rough crossing that was, then down the shoulder and onto the quiet eerie bush road. We zipped through the endless black stripes on the road cast by the shadows of trees, then up rocky hills and rough bumps and humps. I was getting pretty good at swaying to the left or to the right to balance the sleigh at each turn when, suddenly, we came out into a clearing. I could see white space ahead of us. We stopped, and Ned took over the driving. Off we went again. As we zipped across the lake, snow began to cake on my hood and around my face. We went around the bend and along another bush road, then came out onto a lake once more, and the machine stopped again.

Billy walked back to where I sat. "Are you okay? Cold?"

I shook my head. I had long forgotten about my horse, but I wasn't desperate yet, so I said, "I'm okay!"

Billy went back to the machine, and Ned got on behind him, and we were off. We roared along the shoreline and up another bush road. I was getting pretty cold.

The rides on the lake were especially cold. Snow was continually blowing around my face and forming white frost on my eyelashes. My hands were numb and felt like they were frozen solid around the ropes. Clouds were beginning to roll across the sky, sometimes covering the moon for a long time. This bush road was unusually long, and my legs were aching from bracing myself.

We emerged into another bay and followed a channel. Hey! I remember this place! Ol' Jim and I had paddled by here. This was the portage where we had heard the bear! It looks so different in the winter. Then we came out into a big clearing and the machine came to a halt once more. There it was, the whole wide Smoothrock Lake in the moonlight.

The north wind was blowing strongly and white ghosts drifted across the lake. Billy and Ned stood there talking, then they came toward me.

Over the noise of the running engine Billy said, "We think we should roll you inside the canvas on the sleigh. The wind is going to get pretty bad out there in the middle. Here."

He pulled off his fur cap and jammed a toque on his head, pulling his parka hood up around his face. Then he pushed the fur cap over my toque. It went over my ears and almost down over my eyes. He tied it on real good. Ned was rearranging the boxes, moving them right behind the machine. He held the canvas open for me. Well, I was ready, so I lay down with my head to the back end of the sleigh and my feet over the boxes right behind the machine.

218

"Okay?" Billy asked as he folded the canvas up and around my head.

Then they wrapped me up and tied me like a baby in a cradleboard with the canvas and rope. It felt very warm and secure in here now.

I giggled and yelled, "Okay! It's cozy in here!"

Billy's face poked into view and he said, "Have a nice ride! See you at Ol' Jim's!"

The machine roared again and the sleigh started to move. It felt strange! I smiled and enjoyed the new sensation, but it was no more than five minutes before I began to get apprehensive. Snow was whipping around my face so badly I couldn't see anything, and the snowdrifts had piled so high on the road that the runners on the sleigh would slide to one side, hit the edge, and whip back to the other side. Soon the sleigh was fishtailing from one side of the road to the other. It bounced along so hard over the snowdrifts, I was sure my teeth were rattling loose in my head.

With all the banging and crashing, my security bag began loosening up! But the ropes still tied my arms to my sides and I couldn't move. My hands couldn't reach anything to hang onto. I was slipping out! A new fear engulfed me and, suddenly, the folded flap of canvas at my head opened up and I felt the edge of the sleigh under my head. I could hear the runner right under my ear. The sleigh sailed over a huge snowdrift and came down with a crash, and I felt the rope give. The next thing I knew I was being dragged behind the sleigh. Snow was rushing into my coat near my waist. I couldn't control my arms, they were flapping around up over my head somewhere! My right foot was stuck in the canvas, and I felt a stab of pain as the sleigh crashed to the side again. I struggled and kicked with all my might until I freed myself. I saw a blur of stars and black shapes, and then all was quiet. The noise of the machine disappeared as another gust of wind whipped around me.

I lay stunned for a minute before I thought to move. I let my senses check out my arms and legs first. I couldn't move my left arm! Then I realized I was lying on top of it. I slowly rolled over and my arm came out. I moved it. It was okay. My legs were all right. I sat up. The wind whipped more snow around me. The clouds covered up the moon, and it was very dark again. I got to my feet. Ouch! My ankle hurt! I was a bit dizzy but I found the road. I looked down at my feet and realized that I didn't have a boot on my right foot. I still had my socks on though. I started walking in the direction where I thought the machine had disappeared. I was shaking and my teeth were chattering badly as I limped along. Now what do I do?

There was a small island ahead to my right. Am I going in the right direction? Did we pass this already? I didn't know because I couldn't see anything when I was in the canvas. All I had seen was the sky. Should I go to the island and break off branches to sit on, to get me off the snow until they come back? Or would the wind wipe out my tracks? I might fall asleep and freeze. I don't have any matches. No, I think I will stay on the road. I don't know if I am going back or if I'm going ahead.

My foot! I couldn't feel my toes very well. If my foot freezes, they will have to cut if off. I have to do something now! I pulled off my parka hood and yanked off Billy's fur cap. I pulled my toque back on my head and tied my parka hood on tightly. I sat down on the snow and pulled off my snow-clogged sock, then pulled off the second sock. I left the one next to my skin on. My hands were so cold, I couldn't tell if that sock was wet or not. I shoved my foot into the fur cap and closed it tightly, then pulled on the second layer of sock right over the fur cap to keep it in place. I held the snow-covered sock for a minute, but I didn't know what to do with it, so I just threw it on the road. I just realized my mitts were gone too, and I couldn't feel my fingers any more! I pulled out my sweater sleeves from the wristcuffs of my parka and pushed my fingers into the opposite sleeves, working my hands up my arms until my fingers began to tingle with feeling. I stumbled along against the ice-cold wind trying not to lose the path.

Snowdrifts were forming so fast over the snowmobile trail that I sometimes veered off to the side until my foot hit the edge of the road. Another gust of wind took my breath away, and I heard a whimpering moan coming from my throat. Just like that time last summer on the railroad tracks when I found myself all alone in the middle of nowhere. Well, here I am all alone in the middle of nowhere again. No! This time I know Billy will come back for me. I just have to keep going until he comes back . . .

Wait! What is that? I would know that noise anywhere! Wolves were howling somewhere on my right! I started to run as fast as I could. They will catch me! They will kill me! I ran and ran, then began to stumble, and soon could only shuffle along, dragging my huge right foot as it accumulated snow like a snowball. The clouds slid off the moon, then, there they were! Four large dark shadows emerged from the other side of the island. Three seemed to be sitting down but the big one, off to the side a bit, lifted his head and his howl drifted up into the heavens. My hair stood up straight on the back of my neck. The others now joined the first one, and their voices merged and separated as the sounds echoed back and forth through the hills. My heart was threatening to choke me and I could hardly breathe, but I managed to calm down again. As long as I keep going, I will be okay. My face felt stiff. I yanked my hands out of my sleeves and cupped my face. My tears were freezing on my cheeks!

The wolves did not come any closer. They would run ahead, sit down, howl again, and watch me some more before they ran ahead and howled again. What are they trying to do? Scare me to death first so they don't have to kill me before they eat me? Or are they waiting for me to fall down so they can come and eat me alive? Suddenly I stumbled and fell flat on my face. I listened and was sure a wolf was going to pounce on me and sniff at the back of my neck any minute. Nothing happened. Then the howl came again, right beside me! I whirled around and saw that they were the same distance away, just keeping pace with me. You ugly mean creatures! You blood-thirsty animals! "Go away!" I screamed at them. I scrambled to my feet and continued walking again, one foot in front of the other. Then I heard it! The hum of the snowmobile! Billy is coming back to get me! There they are.

The light came around the corner of another island and raced toward me. It bobbed and faded against the blowing snow, but soon Billy jumped out and I was crushed against one person, then another. Someone even gave me a wet kiss on the forehead. I was so relieved I just wanted to cry. Then I remembered the wolves. I whirled around to point, but they were gone. The cowards! Bloody cowards!

Ned turned the machine and sleigh around. This time I sat in front of Billy and Ned got on the sleigh. We still had a long way to go across the lake, but as we neared the shoreline I finally spotted a lamplight among the trees. We came to a stop in front of the doorway of the tent, and Billy helped me up and ushered me inside. There was a fire blazing, and Ol' Jim shoved a cup of hot tea into my hands as they stripped my feet and got my coat and stuff off. Soon I was rolled like a baby into a sleeping bag by the fire.

I was just drifting off to sleep when I heard Ned say, "Sure is a smart kid that one, lots of spunk. I still can't get over those wolves!"

My ears perked up when Billy added, "When we realized he was gone, I was afraid we would pass him or run him over if he was lying on the road, because in some places that snow was whipped up so thick we couldn't see very far in front of us. So I shut off the engine to yell, then we heard the wolves! They watched over him and let us know exactly where he was. When I saw the wolves, we slowed down and started looking for him. He was covered with white from head to foot. I only saw him because of his shadow when the moon came out!"

My eyes stared off into the blackness of the blanket for a moment as the information sunk in. The wolves had watched over me? I thought they were waiting to eat me!

Then Ned's voice came again, "That kid has some pretty strong protectors!"

Hmm, I like that idea. As I drifted to sleep, the image of the big wolf stayed with me—the tilt of his head and the glistening fur on the ridge of his nose in the moonlight, the ears laid back and the strong open jaws as its strength flowed out into the night . . .

Chapter Nineteen

I HEARD THE ROAR OF THE MACHINE quickly fading away. They were leaving me in the middle of the ice! Wait! Wait! Suddenly, Ol' Jim was at my side shaking me. "Danny! Wake up, it's okay. You're just dreaming. You're all right, my boy. You are safe. It's only a nightmare. Sh, sh. Your father will be here soon. You'll be safe with your father soon. Sh, sh . . . " I heard the door close and I opened my eyes. Where am I? The tent above was bright and it had the same blotch design as . . . last summer. Ol' Jim's tent! I know where I am now. But where are Billy and Ned? There is nobody inside but me. I noticed that the tent was draped over the top of a plywood floor. The walls were four feet high and there was a small wooden door attached to a frame. Then I heard Ol' Jim coughing outside. What had he said about my father? Did he say my father was coming here? No. I must have been dreaming.

The door opened and Ol' Jim came in with an armload of wood. I went to swing my feet down and banged my heels hard. I was on the floor.

"Well, how you feeling?" he asked as he threw a few logs in the stove.

"Fine, where's Billy and Ned?" I asked, stretching my aching body. Gee, it feels like someone has stomped on me. I examined my feet. My right ankle hurt a bit, it was blue and swollen on the side.

"Oh, they left some time ago. They waited for you to get up but decided you seemed okay. Besides, they wanted to get out before you beat the heck out of them for dragging you and dumping you in the middle of the ice last night." He chuckled and added, "They have to get back before dark. It's afternoon now, you know."

I smiled and checked my hands. They seemed okay. I pulled on the pair of socks Ol' Jim had dried over the stove for me, then got up and staggered outside to look around. Ol' Jim's tent was in a bay. I don't remember seeing this last summer. I don't even know which side of the lake we're on right now. I followed a path and stepped off to do my business, then slowly made my way back again. One thing that struck me was that he didn't have very much wood stored up. I shrugged.

I entered the tent again. Ol' Jim had just heated up a big pot of beaver. I'd never had beaver before. Ol' Jim dished some out for me. I hesitantly took a small nibble at a bone with chunks of meat stuck on it. He saw my hesitation and said, "Eat all the meat, and I'll tell you what to do with the bone when you finish." His eyes twinkled.

I took him up on the challenge and started pulling off chunks of meat, one bite at a time. Hey, it wasn't bad. An odd-looking bone appeared. It was donut-shaped and had a handle on it! I held it up to Ol' Jim.

His belly jiggled as he said, "It is the beaver hip-bone. The ancient people used to say this every time they killed the beaver. Now, stick your pointing finger out way over your shoulder and hold the bone out like a slingshot with your left. Try to point your finger and see if you can make it go right through the hole. Here are the words, 'I will emerge, right by the beaver dam, and if I hit the mark I will find more beaver there!'"

I giggled and slowly advanced my finger. Then Ol' Jim laughed. "Faster! You're cheating by correcting your aim!"

I laughed and pulled my finger back again and shot it straight for the hole, and through it went! Ol' Jim sighed and shook his head. "You never said what I asked you to say. Now try again, do it right!"

I pulled my arm back, with some practice I'm sure to hit the mark again. I said the line again rather quickly, and my finger hit the bone and slipped off to the right. Rather disappointed, I put the bone down on the table and Ol' Jim sent a cloud of pipesmoke toward it.

I heard him instruct again, "Try once more, and this time say, 'When I come home, I will come straight into this hole to find you,' and aim your finger through the hole right in the middle!"

For some reason, I remembered Jim and Henry. They used to laugh like this. I was always watching them, laughing with them. I liked how they made each other happy. I blinked back an overwhelming pressure of tears and concentrated on chewing.

Then I held up the bone again and pulled back my right arm. I stuck out my pointing finger and grinned at Ol' Jim, saying, "Hear me, hear me, when I come home, I will come straight into this hole to find me."

Ol' Jim broke out sputtering and choking on his tea before he caught his breath and said, "No, no! You are supposed to say, to find *you!*"

I looked at him and said, "But who will I find? I can only find me!"

In a rasping voice he said, "Boy, when you come home, you don't just find yourself, you already got yourself! What you find are all the people who love you!"

I looked at him a moment. What is he talking about? He's a lonely man all by himself! Where are all his people who love him? I looked down at my feet. I am a "people" who love him. He didn't say how many people there had to be. I looked up and gave him a big grin as he puffed and puffed on his pipe. Since when did he start smoking a pipe? I had never seen him with one before. He was trying to light it with a stick he had set on fire, but he was holding it way off to the side.

"Here, let me do that for you." I took the burning ember and stuck it into his pipe as he puffed away, and soon smoke came out. I worried again about the wood. It was getting to be late afternoon. "Do you have a pile of wood stashed away in the bush somewhere? I'll go get some if you'll tell me where."

He puffed several more times before he said, "No, not right

now. We are waiting for the aeroplane that will bring your father."

I looked at Ol' Jim in disbelief. No, no! I don't want to see my father here! I jumped up and rushed outside. How dare he come here! This place is good, it's peaceful, and he is going to bring all the ugliness to it. I glanced at the sky. Thick grey clouds were coming up over the treetops. I went back inside.

"There's a storm about to hit us and it looks like a big one. Where's your woodpile?" I said as I grabbed my parka off the nail by the stove.

He seemed surprised, and thought about that for a minute before he said, "Well, if that's the case, you go get the marten traps along the river. Hate to leave the traps out there. I will take care of the wood. I have wood back there along the path by the east shore."

The wind was coming up hard and fast. We could hear it whipping around the top of the stovepipe, making a howling noise. I hope Billy and Ned make it home okay before the storm reaches them. I pulled on a pair of thick moccasins Ol' Jim threw to me. They were warm and comfortable.

As I was about to go out the door, a thought occurred to me. "Ol' Jim, what do I do if I find an animal that's alive?" He was slumped over on the chair and breathing funny. Quite alarmed, I asked, "Are you okay?"

He shifted in the chair by the stove and grinned. "I'm okay. Just another heartburn. The marten? Why, boy, you just hit it over the head with the axe and it will be dead. But wait, doggone it! I almost forgot. Here, I have to give you this. You leave this to thank the wolves who helped you last night. Once they know you know them, they will always be there to help and guide you. They will know you recognize them. They don't forget, it is the humans who do."

I thought about the black wolf I saw last summer. I picked up the pouch of tobacco Ol' Jim held out to me, and he sat back in his chair and resumed puffing. I could see sweat on his brow. I don't know about this. He's acting weird. But I guess he's okay. I'd better get going and take the axe too, to bonk the animal over the head with.

226

I followed the path down the west shore, and it led me to the traps along a small creek. I hurried. I wanted to make it back before the storm hit. It took me an awfully long time before I came upon the creek he had said was only a short distance away. By this time, the wind was whipping around my face and blowing so much snow in front of me that I could hardly tell where the path was. I checked for the crossbars he said he left on all his traps. Soon I spotted one, and then another, along the river. I went to the first one and put a stick into the trap and heard it snap. Then I pulled it out of its anchor and undid the wire. I threw the trap into the packsack on my back. I did the same to the second and third trap. I walked farther along the river on a trail that sometimes disappeared. I was relieved when I spotted the fourth and last one. But something had happened here. There was a lot of blood around the trap. What do I do? There was no sign of the trap, but the wire to it was twisted, and it disappeared into the snow. I yanked it out. There was just a piece of black fur attached to the jaws of the trap and nothing else. It was covered in blood. Some other animal had recently ripped whatever had been caught in here right out of the trap! I threw it into the packsack on my back. It was getting very heavy. Now came the hardest trek, back to camp. Boy, I could swear I was right in the middle of a thick cottonball. The wind was whipping around my legs, and at times I lost the trail altogether. I found that I couldn't detect the second and third layers of hard, walked-on, packed layers of snow under my feet because I was not heavy enough to sink that deep. I kept wandering off to the left and way off to the right and, finally, by some miracle, I had circled around and stumbled over my own tracks again. The snow was coming down in huge chunks, quickly obscuring the path and the footprints I had left behind.

I could no longer see where I was going! I stopped. I knew I was either at the edge of the shore, in the middle of the lake, or at the edge of the opposite shore. Then I remembered something. I dug into my pocket and pulled out the wad of tobacco. I released it into the wind and yelled, "Here, this is for you!" That was all I could think of to say. I heard a noise, but I couldn't tell where it came from. A wolf? Wait! There it was again! It was not the howl of a wolf, but the sound of an aeroplane! What the heck was an aeroplane doing in a storm like this? I listened, but I didn't hear it again. I turned and tried to get my bearings before I started walking again. Soon I felt something solid under my feet. Then I knew for sure I was on the path, but I didn't know if it was going away from or to the tent.

The snow became thinner and thinner until, at last, I could see the shoreline. I was so relieved and happy when I smelled the woodsmoke and saw the tent in the twilight. I ran the rest of the way to the tent and poked my head in the door, but no one was there. The fire was almost out, and I threw the last log into the stove. Where could he be? He should have been back by now. He had said the path leading to his woodpile was along the east shore. I hung the packsack on one of the branches of a tree beside the tent and took off down the path.

The snow had almost stopped now and before long I found a path that led into the bush. As I stumbled along I saw the woodpile. I looked around and noticed something sticking out through the snowdrift among the piles of logs. Ol' Jim's coat! I screamed and scrambled over the logs and pulled out an arm, then his head. I pushed the clinging snow off the rest of his body.

"Ol' Jim! Ol' Jim!" I screamed, but he did not move.

I saw where he had left the sleigh. I dumped the snow off and pulled it closer to his body and tried to roll him on it, but he kept slipping off. I could feel my tears melting the snow off my cheeks as I struggled to get him on the sleigh, pulling and tugging on sleeves and pantlegs until, finally, I did it. I tied him on so he wouldn't roll off. I tried to pull the sleigh, but it wouldn't move. I pulled some more and, at last, it began to slide. Once I got it going it was all right, but I must not let it stop. I might not be able to get it going again. I ran, stumbling through tears the rest of the way. When I arrived at the camp I pushed the whole sleigh into the tent. It slid halfway in and became lodged in the doorway. I pulled at his arms and tried to drag him through, but he was much too heavy, so I started pushing his legs through with my feet as I braced myself on the doorframe. His body started to roll, and I pushed him some more until he ended up in the middle of the floor. I yanked the sleigh free and shoved it out the door. The fire! I have to get the fire going. I searched for kindling. I couldn't believe the fire would go out that fast. I ran outside and rounded up enough wood and kindling to get the fire going again. I lit the lamp. I rolled Ol' Jim on his side. He was not breathing! That means . . . that means he is dead!

"Ol' Jim! Ol' Jim!" I yelled again at the top of my lungs, but there was no one there. He was like an old log lying there. I put a blanket over him and went and sat by the stove. I looked at the blanket, then at the hand sticking out. The hand was open. What was it Mr. Old Indian had said? He said something about if the hand is open in death, the spirit is gone, the time was up, or something like that. That would mean that Ol' Jim knew he was dying or that he was ready to die. Is anyone ever ready to die? What about Henry? I had not seen Henry's hand . . . I shouldn't think of this! I have to think about something else! I didn't know what else to do. Wood. I need some wood. I have to keep the fire going all night! I have to. I have to. I stood up and went outside. I found a log beside the tent and hauled it onto the sawhorse, then picked up the handsaw off the tree branch and started sawing. When I was finished, I could barely see in the dark as I split all the pieces. Then I slowly gathered one armload at a time and brought them all in. The blanket roll had not moved. I sat down again by the woodstove. All I could hear was the wind blowing. Time passed, and I got up occasionally to put a log into the fire. I knew I would have no wood by morning, but I didn't care.

About three o'clock in the morning, the wind stopped blowing and all was quiet. The full moon came out. I had no more wood to put in the stove. I couldn't just sit there, so I went outside and found the axe. I started chopping away at a small pine tree behind the tent. One last hit and the tree swayed and fell to the ground. I chopped off the branches and proceeded to saw it into sawhorse lengths. These I put on the sawhorse and cut down to foot-and-a-half lengths. Only then did I enter the tent again. The fire barely had any embers left. I threw in some pieces of paper and a few dry dead branches, lit it, and threw some woodchips and whatever else I could find before I threw in a piece of the pine tree. The fire got going and soon it was quite warm inside the tent. I noticed that it was getting daylight.

Ol' Jim had said he was waiting for an aeroplane. Would it come today? I put the teapot on the stove and rummaged around the boxes and cans until I found the package of loose tea. I threw in a handful and waited. For what? Daylight and the aeroplane. I sat still until the tea was ready. I poured myself a cup and waited some more. My solitary breathing seemed loud in the stillness. The clock ticked away the minutes into hours and the greedy stove went through one block of wood after another.

Where did the clock come from? Ol' Jim never owned a clock in his life! Wait, yes, that was the clock Billy bought for Ol' Jim. The package of tobacco I had brought for him still lay wrapped on top of the table. I blinked to clear my eyes and took a sip of tea. I had forgotten about our gifts for Ol' Jim.

I woke up with a stiff neck. The noise that woke me up came again. I had fallen asleep over the table. The cup of tea was now stone-cold in my hands. An engine was roaring over the lake—the aeroplane! I rushed outside and ran down to the lake just as a small Cessna pulled up to a stop by the waterhole. The propellers stopped and a man got out, then the pilot emerged.

I ran down to the lake, yelling, "Help! Help! Ol' Jim is dead! Ol' Jim is dead!" I had not realized that I was sobbing until a pair of arms came and grabbed me, crushing me in an embrace. I looked up into his face. "Dad! Oh, Dad!" I saw the tears roll down his face as he held me tightly. The pilot ran to the tent, then reappeared, shaking his head at my father. A stiff, cold feeling came over me. I heard my voice saying, "I found Ol' Jim by the pile of wood over there yesterday, in the evening. I had a hard time getting him into the tent . . . "

My father cupped my face between his hands for a moment before he said, "Sh, sh. It's okay, you did real good." He turned and walked to the pilot.

It's okay? What does he mean, it's okay? It is not okay! I followed the path along the shoreline and stopped to watch them. They unloaded quite a few supplies from the aeroplane, including a toboggan. I sat down on a stump and watched them pulling the sleigh out of the tent with Ol' Jim on it. They loaded the body into the aeroplane and the pilot got in. The engine started and the propellers became a blur. The roaring of the engine grew louder as the plane turned around and headed out to the middle of the ice. I watched the figure of the big man standing by the waterhole.

When the plane disappeared over the treetops, he turned around and walked toward me. I studied him for the first time since he had arrived. I wasn't sure I knew him any more. Mr. Daniel Lynx came toward me. I was almost embarrassed that I had called him "Dad." As he stood in front of me, I kept my eyes down, examining the moccasins Ol' Jim had given me. His feet came into view. He had moccasins on too.

"Where did you get those?" I asked, pointing.

"They're mine, from way back. I went and picked up my trapping gear from the reserve last week. Here, Tom said to give you this."

Tom? Freckle-faced Tom? I reached for the little silver pocketknife he held out to me. "Thanks," I said, turning it over in my hand, remembering the time I had pushed it into Tom's hand by the railway station, remembering the pain, and the reason why I ran away. Suddenly I whirled around and got busy. I had to do something. I grabbed the sackful of traps and began to hang them up the way Ol' Jim had them, tied together and hanging on the branches of the tree beside the tent.

Without a word, he turned and walked to the lake. I could see him pulling a sheet of canvas over the toboggan. Well, what am I going to do now? Walk back to Collins? When will Billy come? I can stay here until he comes. No. I don't want to stay here. I don't think I can sleep in there. A dead body has been in there all night. I looked at my father, repacking stuff into two boxes. I was scared. I didn't want to walk back to Collins all alone. I didn't want to be by myself right now. He came up the path dragging Ol' Jim's sleigh. I sat down on a stump and waited. He propped the sleigh against the tree and stopped beside me, but said nothing.

When I figured I had finally got my wits together, I kept my head down and asked, "Why did you come here?"

His voice came softly, "Danny, I had to see you. You are my son, you are my life. And, there is something I have to tell you."

I said nothing. I felt nothing. I didn't seem to have any feelings left.

He knelt on the snow beside me and said, "We have a lot to talk about. I have so much I want to say to you. But right now we have to decide what to do."

Still I did not reply. What's to decide?

His voice came again, "There's a cabin at Whitewater Lake. I decided to take over Sam's trapline. That is where I was going from here after I talked to you. You have to make up your mind now if you want to come with me or stay here and wait for Billy to come back and get you."

Anger began to fill me, deep inside my chest. What is he going to do, leave me here all alone for heaven knows how long, waiting for Billy? He is forcing me to follow him. I cannot stay here alone! I bit my lip to keep it from pushing out. I opened the knife blade and ran the tip under my nails, scooping out the dirt. I wonder how so much dirt got under my nails.

My stomach growled and his knees snapped as he stood up. "Come on, let's make something to eat inside." I looked at the tent. The fire had died. There was no smoke coming out.

Suddenly it was very important to me that he not enter and eat at the place where Ol' Jim had been. I didn't want any ugliness in there! I shouted at his retreating back, "No! I . . . I don't feel like eating, and I don't want to go back in there. I feel like Ol' Jim is going to come out of the tent any minute and yell about the fire being out."

Tears were filling my eyes again. I could feel them wetting my cheeks. The pressure in my chest was very heavy. I turned around and faced the path where I had run with the traps yesterday. Billy? Who will tell Billy about Ol' Jim? I whirled around to ask him and saw that he was crying. He just stood there, silently looking up at the sky, chest heaving, the tears pouring down his face.

A tremendous shock went through me, and I turned around again. This is scaring me. I have to get away! I stood up and moved to the tent. "I have to get my sleeping bag out of the tent," I said as I walked by him. The sun was casting an eerie light in there as I stepped in. I spotted my sleeping bag in the corner and I rolled it up into a sausage. Everything was as it was last night. Even the pot of beaver was still beside the stove.

I'm sorry I can't clean up, Ol' Jim. Things will freeze anyway. Maybe Billy will come and put your things away. I looked around one last time at the shirts and jackets hanging on the nails along the half-wooden wall and the stretchboards leaning by the doorframe. He had no skins stretched. Maybe he hadn't gone trapping in a long time. He must have known he was sick.

There was nothing else to take. Ol' Jim's tobacco sat on the table. I went to the stove and pulled up the lid. There were a few embers left at the opening. I scraped some together, then I picked a large pinch of the tobacco and slowly filtered it over the embers. Smoke came up immediately and I whispered, "That is for you, Ol' Jim. Happy journey." I closed the lid and pulled the wooden door shut behind me and tied the latch. I turned to see my father writing a note on a piece of shopping-bag paper. When he was finished he slipped it on the door latch.

"A note for Billy," he said as he turned and looked at me. "Well then, let's get the toboggan loaded and we'll have lunch somewhere along the trail. We may as well start out to Whitewater Lake. Billy will come and get you there when school starts. He probably will come anyway, after all this. What do you say?" He smiled.

I studied the square jaw, the deep black eyes with the dark eyebrows. I saw some white hair sticking out from under his fur cap at the corners of his eyes. The full lips were dark brown.

He spoke again. "You have grown so big."

I immediately drew back when his hand came up and picked a twig off my toque. I remembered the screaming, angry man coming at me, to punish me, the hand that came up to hurt me.

I stood there with my head down. Then something triggered. "Why don't we go to Collins instead?" I asked.

He studied me a moment, then said, "There are people waiting for me at Whitewater Lake. They will be worried if I don't show up. There are no telephones here, so we have to do exactly as we tell people we are going to do."

A shock went through me—the witch! He has the witch waiting there! He kept looking at me with a puzzled expression. I swallowed a lump in my throat, looked him in the eye, and asked, "Is she there?"

I watched him closely, reading him the way Mr. and Mrs. Old Indian had taught me. His eyes blinked, flicked around, and then he said, "No. Sarah moved in with another guy in Nakina. She said the baby wasn't even mine anyway. What a sucker I was!" He looked down and kicked the snow at his feet, sighed, then said, "Well, I like it better out here anyway. That was the second time I tried to live in town. I seem to remember that our reason for moving out of our trapper's shack, your mother and I, was because of you. So that you could go to a school. Well, sometimes things don't work out. Come on, let's get that toboggan loaded up." I didn't trust him!

I followed him to the pile of stuff down by the lake. There were two paper boxes, a big green packsack, an axe, two pairs of snowshoes, the toboggan, and the canvas. I watched his wide shoulders as he picked up the canvas and began wrapping it over the arranged boxes on top of the toboggan. I shoved my sleeping bag into the packsack as he directed. Billy will find me. He will come as soon as he hears about Ol' Jim. He'll know where to find me.

When Daniel had the boxes all tied up inside the canvas cover, he pulled a wad of rope out of the outside pocket of the packsack, tied one end to the toboggan and crisscrossed it over the canvas, tying the load up securely.

My voice sounded strange as I said, "It seems like a long time ago, but just the other night I was laced up in a canvas sheet like that, dragged, and dumped out in the middle of Smoothrock Lake."

He turned his face to me, looking shocked and angry. "What! Billy? The idiot! He should have been more careful!" There was my father—I saw him now—the instant temper.

I shrugged. "It was an accident. As you can see, I'm fine. Besides, I learned a lot about snowmobiles, storms, and wolves . . . "

Daniel stood looking down at me for a moment. "Wolves? Ol' Jim knew a lot about wolves."

Ol' Jim knew all right! That's why he gave me the tobacco. Then I remembered the howl during the storm.

"Did that aeroplane come near here yesterday?" I asked as I tied on my snowshoes. Hey, they fit real good. How did he know they would fit me?

He finished tying his snowshoes on, then he pulled off his fur cap and put it on top of the snow-chisel beside the waterhole. His thick black hair spilled out and he stood there smiling at me. Then he came over to adjust the strap on my left foot before he answered, "Yeah, the pilot thought we could get here and back, but that storm came up too fast. Rather than try to land blindly—I mean we just couldn't see anything—he decided to go back to Armstrong. It was just one big thick cloud. The snow didn't even reach Armstrong or Collins, though. Why?"

"Because at that time, I was walking back from the marten traps when I heard what I thought was the engine. I walked toward the sound and that is where I found the path. I kind of got lost in that snow."

He swung the packsack to his back and slipped the toboggan pullrope over his shoulders and across his chest and said, "Come, let's go. We've got quite a walk ahead of us. If you get tired, just jump on the toboggan. You have a dog, why didn't you bring Snotty? He could have pulled the toboggan for us," he said as he led the way.

"How did you know about Snotty? Billy tell you?" I asked.

He stopped and turned around with a big grin on his face. "Yeah, Billy, Jim, and I have been having some pretty interesting conversations since last summer."

I remembered the times when Jim came home steaming mad. Billy too, for that matter. I wondered what he had said that got them so mad. Daniel turned around again and pulled the toboggan forward. I looked back at the point where the waterhole was, beside the lake.

"Daniel." He turned around. Our eyes met and I tipped my head in the direction of the tent, saying, "You forgot your fur cap on top of the ice-chisel." We could see the black dot on top of the slender pole.

He laughed out loud and threw some snow at me. "Billy will bring it when he comes!"

I watched my father glance at the clear blue sky, then he gave me a wink before he turned around again. He seemed pretty happy about something. I jumped on the toboggan as he pulled, and we climbed steadily, smoothly, and slowly up the hill to the bush road. I looked back and saw two lines on each side of the toboggan track, the back tips of my trailing snowshoes. I was just glad to be going somewhere, doing something. I don't think I could have stood it if I had had to wait there for Billy to show up. He will find me. He will follow our trail. He'll know where we've gone.

Chapter Twenty

ABOUT HALFWAY THROUGH THE PORTAGE, we passed through some deep snowdrifts and I had to jump off the toboggan. My snowshoed feet couldn't fit in the space between the snow and the toboggan. I walked briskly along behind. Soon we were on the other side, and he stopped to wipe the sweat off his forehead.

"Want to stop for lunch?" he asked.

I nodded and started gathering twigs and breaking off branches for the fire, while he untied a box from the toboggan. I came back with birchbark and dried pine branches. He shovelled off an area with his snowshoe and lit my bundle of wood. The bark and twigs sizzled into a ball of black smoke and fire. He had a little pot that he filled with snow and placed on top of the fire. He was already hacking off some more wood from the bushes beside the trail. I sat on the toboggan to rest.

The sun was shining brightly and there was no wind at all. The smell of the fire was wonderful. It reminded me very much of Ol' Jim. I could feel my eyes filling up again. I blinked my tears away and wiped a sleeve across my nose. I watched Daniel pull out a roll of garlic sausage and a loaf of French bread from the box. He hacked off a four-inch piece and passed it to me. He put the bread on top of the box.

"Help yourself. You want to roast your sausage a bit?" he asked as he sharpened a stick with his pocketknife.

I was too hungry, so I shook my head and went about making a big sandwich. Mmmm, that was absolutely delicious. I watched his sausage sizzle while he rummaged around in the box again for the tea and sugar. He said the milk was already at the cabin at Whitewater Lake. That's okay, I don't always use milk anyway. I smiled when I saw him hurry to the fire with a chunk of bread in his hand. His sausage was turning black while he balanced the teapot more securely on top of the wood. Finally he came and sat beside me and started on his sandwich. I was already finished with mine. He grinned at me between each bite. He seemed so happy.

Now it was my turn to watch the teapot. I threw in more snow until the pot was full of water. I stepped off the trail without my snowshoes and sank up to my knees in snow. I could hear him laughing as I pushed my way to the bush to get more wood. When I came back, the teapot was boiling and the tea bags bobbed all around the pot. I put a stick under the handle and brought the pot to a spot beside the toboggan. But the hot pot started to sink because it was melting the snow. It began to tip over so I tried another spot, but the same thing happened. I made four neat circles in the snow before I finally thought to put the smoking pot back near the edge of the fire where the sticks provided a bottom layer for it. Daniel just sat there, chuckling, with his mouth full. I shot some snow at him as I pulled out two plastic cups from the box. I couldn't find a spoon so I used my little pocketknife. Then I sat down beside him again as we sipped our tea.

"Danny, look in the outside pocket of the packsack," he said.

I got up and searched the pocket and pulled out four chocolate bars! I stuck two back into the pocket and gave him one and slowly sank my teeth into mine. I sat back against the boxes and munched on the chocolate bar. I sighed. I was so tired.

Daniel said, "I even bought a box of potato chips for you. They're at the cabin with all the groceries already. I was there a couple of days ago. That's when I called Billy to bring you here."

I glanced at him. "How did you know I was going to come with you? What if I didn't come and you had all those potato chips?"

Daniel laughed. "I would have had to send them to Billy, I guess. He's the one who insisted that I get them for you. 'Make sure you get potato chips for Chips,' he said."

I began wondering just how much he knew about me. "What else do you know?" I challenged.

Daniel grinned and took another sip of his tea before he answered, "I knew where you were all the time. First, you went with Mrs. Grey to Armstrong. Then you stayed with Roger's grandmother and the kids for the day. Then you showed up at Charlie's. By the way, Charlie still hasn't given me that punch he promised me. Then I visited Mr. and Mrs. 'Old Indian.' Wasn't that what you called them? They went to live with her son at Minaki for the winter. Did you know that the old man is her brother? Then you showed up at Jim's cabin. Then you were at Weeby's in Whiteclay—"

"Who? Who's Weeby?"

"Ol' Jim's son at Whiteclay Lake."

I felt a weak smile stretch my lips, and I sounded rather tired as I repeated, "Weeby. I just called him Hog."

Daniel grinned. "Yeah, his name is Wilbert, but Weeby for short. I hope he never heard you call him a hog! Anyway, from there you went back to Armstrong for a few hours and ran into Jim."

"No, only about one hour," I interrupted.

Daniel continued, "By the way, Jim and Norma are expecting a baby in the spring. Did you know that? Come on, we'd better get going or we'll be walking in the dark." My jaw still hung open. I scrambled to help him put all the stuff away, and soon we were on our way again, with me struggling to keep up.

A baby. Jim is going to have a baby. And Henry only being gone . . . Had Henry known? Was that what was bothering Henry this fall? Was that his big secret? I can just picture Jim with a baby. It will be a very lucky baby, like Henry was.

My father's voice came back to me again, boisterous, "I must admit, though, you gave me quite a scare when you disappeared from Armstrong that night and no one knew where you went until Charlie called Tom's father the next day on the CN phone, and then the time Jim called and said you had taken off in the middle of the night and no one saw you the next day. It was a big relief a couple days later when some sectionmen in a motor car remembered seeing you in the canoe with Ol' Jim. So I figured you were heading out for Whiteclay Lake. By the way, do you remember a big red-haired man?

Hang us all again. "Yeah, Angus Solligan."

"He called me at home one day in September. He wanted to give you a birthday present. That's what I was bringing when you disappeared on me again. That, too, is at the cabin."

"What is it?" I asked. I remembered the record player he left for me at Billy's place. It was still there, under the bed.

He laughed. "I won't tell you, it's his surprise."

Suddenly he stopped and turned around. "Exactly where were you on your twelfth birthday?"

I answered in a very monotone voice, "I put on a girl's dress and went to Savant Lake with Charlotte and her mother."

He laughed and turned around, and the toboggan started moving again.

I continued, talking to his back a little louder, "You walked right by me when you got off. I met Jonas that night and that's when he told me the old man was his uncle."

Daniel looked back, saying, "Jonas? Is that the son's name? The one from Minaki?" I found someone he didn't know. That made me feel better.

I added, "Yep. He was on the train the night you got on from Collins and I got off."

It's a weird feeling when you think you have been all alone and find that someone knew where you were all the time, well, most of the time . . . Why does that make me angry? I never asked for his help, that's why! I never asked him to follow me or worry about me! And how did he help me? He let me know he was close behind me, that's all! I watched the puffs of mist from his breath as he turned his head to look up at the sky again.

We crossed a small lake and a short portage. Then we emerged onto another small lake. There was an opening with boulders and brown ice in the middle. A river. We detoured the area and entered the portage trail and emerged well down the river, and again we crossed and followed a channel until we reached a steep hill. Daniel strained to pull the toboggan up the bank. I kept popping snow into my mouth. I was very thirsty. It was well into the afternoon now.

He stood there wiping his forehead with his hand. "Want to stop for another cup of tea? We just have to go over this portage and through the channel and across Whitewater Lake and then we're there." Somehow, I wished he hadn't told me how far we had to go yet. I sat down where I stood. He laughed and said, "Okay, we'll cross the portage first. Then we'll build a good fire and dry off the sweat, have a good meal, and we'll take our time crossing the lake."

I hopped on and rode the whole length of the portage on top of the toboggan. I didn't have much pride left at that point, I was too tired.

Hey, I recognize this place! I stayed on the toboggan when we came to a stop in the clearing, and said, "This is where Ol' Jim and I came through. I remember that tree there. There were lots and lots of mosquitoes here. And when we got to the channel there, Ol' Jim set the fishnet. And a moose swam across the net early the next morning. Ol' Jim disappeared and I couldn't find him. He was busy in the bush, picking up fish all the way up the hill. When he came back he was really mad!" My voice shook and my lip quivered as I bit it between my teeth again.

Daniel laughed at the story as he went about cutting down branches and dry little trees. He has no business being so happy. Ol' Jim is dead! I jumped off the toboggan and pulled the branches to the place he had cleared. Soon we had a good fire going. He put some pine branches on top of the snow. Then he put the teapot over the fire and put the rest of the coiled sausage on a stick over the flames. Next he opened a large can of spaghetti, which he put on a bank of hot ashes.

I leaned back against the boxes on the toboggan and asked, "What are you going to do all by yourself when I go back to school? Will I stay with Billy again?"

Daniel turned around from the fire, saying, "Yeah, Billy has no problem sharing his cabin with you until spring. I'll come to Collins in March or whenever it gets too dangerous on the ice. Well, there's just the two of us now, so we'll figure out something." I thought about that for a moment. Then he breathed a big sigh and sat down beside me. "Why did you keep running away?"

I couldn't think of anything to say. "Because . . . " He sat there waiting. Finally I murmured, "Because you always get mad at me. I was afraid you'd hit me for running away." I saw his hand reach for mine, but I moved away. I wasn't finished yet, so I continued, "That time at Savant Lake, were you going to hit me if you had caught me?"

He drew in his breath and said, "No! I was not going to hurt you. I remember what I said, it just came out all wrong. Everything I did, I thought I was doing for you. I was so busy trying to control things that the more I tried, the more things got out of control. Out here, I am myself. This is my world and I belong here, and I know that as hard as I try, I will never be happy anywhere else. I am strong, I am healthy, and I know I can take care of us now, you and me."

He stood up and looked up at the sky and said, "I did my best to try to tell you, but I just couldn't reach you. I wanted so much to be with you when you found out. I wanted to tell you myself . . . Danny, your mother died in October in Alberta. Her family took her home. She is buried there."

A shock went through me and I almost forgot to breathe. My mind took the information and put it somewhere, well away from my feelings. I shook the snow off my boot. The tears were all gone. No. I was beginning to feel them hot against my cheeks again. No. No more, please. No. Not Mama . . . Not Mama!

I watched him lift the teapot off the fire and place it beside the can of spaghetti, very gently, carefully. An incredible anger began to fill me as I watched his slow careful movements. Suddenly I jumped up, grabbed one snowshoe, and swung it with all my might. The fire and ashes went flying. The teapot clanged against the can and a billow of steam and ashes erupted from the fire as I swung the snowshoe again. I saw him standing by the toboggan, and I hurled the snowshoe at him, then I ran.

I stumbled on blindly in foot-deep snow toward the channel. I heard him yelling behind me and I instinctively ran as fast as I could. Fear flooded through me—I didn't want him to catch me. Mama! Mama! My shrill voice echoed in my ears and my throat started to hurt. Oh, Mama! Help me! Suddenly I tripped and Daniel came down on top of me. I felt like something ripped inside my chest, and I could feel my face stretch as I screamed. I felt his arms come around me and I sobbed, screamed, and hollered until I couldn't cry any longer. All that time, his soothing voice continued beside my ear, "I love you, son, I love you."

Totally exhausted, I lay in his arms for a long time before I could get my brain working again. Daniel got up, pulling me with him. We sat there in the middle of the lake for some time before I could get my mouth working again. My words came out in a whimper. "I was always running to Mama. I knew Mama would be there—if I could only have found her." I swallowed and sucked my lower lip back in. "Now she's gone. I have no one to run to!"

He grabbed my shoulders and shook me. "Danny! There is no need to run! I am your father, I will always be beside you. There is no need to run away from me. I will never hurt you again."

I slumped forward and tried to focus my swollen eyes on his face. I remember I used to try to pull out the hairs inside his nose. I could see them now, as he ran his hand across his nose. My brain wasn't working at the moment. My mind was blank.

"I promise," he murmured, "I promise," and he pulled me forward into a big hug. After a moment, he pulled back and smiled. "We can't sit here in the middle of the ice any longer. Come on, let's go back and get the toboggan."

I followed. I felt as if I was dragging fifty-pound feet as we retraced our steps to the fire. I stopped and surveyed the mess when we got there. The teapot lay upside down in the snow and wisps of smoke rose from the charred wood. The sausage was in the ashes and the spaghetti was tipped over in the snow.

I stood there watching as he went about packing the stuff away. He cracked a weak smile at me as he came and shoved a chocolate bar into my hand, then tied the boxes into the canvas again. Still holding the chocolate bar, I climbed on top of the toboggan. I could see where we had wrestled on the side of the path. The snow that went in my collar was now melted and felt cold and damp next to my skin. The sun had gone down behind the treetops. We seemed to be making a lot of noise in the evening silence.

We crossed the channel, and I looked at the place where Ol' Jim and I had camped. Best Island looked so different in the winter. I felt good knowing there was a sand beach under all that snow.

Daniel stopped and turned. "Are you still awake? Don't fall off if you fall asleep."

I put up a hand and he turned again. I still had the chocolate bar in my hand, so I shoved it into my pocket. The toboggan moved as he pulled again, and I listened to the "swish, swish" of his snowshoes on the hardening snow. I noticed a snowmobile trail coming from the channel on the right. It merged with the one we were following on the shore. The path was harder and well travelled here. It was rapidly growing colder as we entered the path that ran right across the island where the swamp was.

I hopped off the toboggan when Daniel paused a moment. I could see the straight line of the snowmobile trail going right across the lake. Then I remembered the hermit we saw on the island last summer.

"Is that old man still there on the other side of the island?"

He turned his head to me. "No, he's gone for the winter. He'll be back again in the spring."

"Who told you that?" I asked.

Daniel laughed and answered, "Sam told me last fall. Have you noticed that Native people are generally like one big family? Everyone knows everyone, or someone knows of someone who knows the person in question. You'd be amazed how many relatives you could find if you took it into your head to find out."

I cleared my throat and asked, "Then why didn't anyone know where or who Mama was when I was asking everyone I could see last summer?"

He stopped and turned around. "For one thing, you did not remember to use her maiden name, did you? That is the name you should have asked for. And another thing, she wasn't from this area. They would not have known her unless you happened to ask someone who knew me or her family. And something else, I told her you were looking for her. She did not want you to find her. She said it would hurt you too much. She was dying of cancer at a hospital in Alberta. She did not want me to tell you. Her family forbid me to see her. For whatever her reason, those were her wishes. I'm sorry, Danny, I did the best I could."

He turned around and I followed behind the toboggan. We crossed the lake in silence as it became dark. I walked with my head down, one foot in front of the other. Why didn't Mama want to see me? Did she not love me any more? Didn't she know I loved her? I wouldn't have cared what she looked like! I would only have loved her more. Oh, Mama, I love you.

The path was quite hard here so I stopped to kick off my snowshoes. I was light enough to run on the surface crust. I caught up and shoved my snowshoes under the ropes, criss-crossing the load. I felt so light. Like I didn't weigh anything. I bet I could just run across the lake like the blowing snow ghosts. I could reach Collins in no time! The ice under my feet . . . it was like last night all over again. Was it only last night? It seemed so long ago. No, it was two nights ago because I just kept the fire going all last night . . . Ol' Jim. Why had I made a fire? Was it to keep me warm, or to keep Ol' Jim's dead body warm? Was I not supposed to keep it cold? Don't they keep dead bodies cold?

Boy, am I hungry. Henry. I will see Henry again, Billy said so.

I couldn't seem to think straight any more. Why hadn't anyone told me about Mama? They just sat there and watched me, knowing all that time that she had died! Billy. Jim. My eyes found the black shadow of my father and I focused my gaze on his back. If I was big, I would punch him very hard! Why hadn't he told me? He could have found a way to tell me. He could have written a letter. Would I have read it? If Billy or Jim said that it had to do with Mama, I probably would have read it. But then, he said he wanted to be with me when he told me. That could have been forever, if he hadn't just shown up this morning. Had they told Henry? Surely he would have told me, because he had lost his mother too. They must have told Ol' Jim just recently. That's probably why he agreed to let my father come there. I had been tricked, and I didn't like it. The pain was burning deep in my chest.

I lifted my head and looked along the shore. We had come around a point and I saw a light from a window. Where are we? As we got nearer, a door opened and in the light, there stood a woman with red hair! He lied to me! It's the witch! He lied to me!

I whirled around and started running again, as fast as I could. Another trail broke to the left. I tore down that path like the devil was after me, then shot out of the bush very fast and found that I had emerged on the other side of the point. It was very dark out. Then I noticed another cabin on the right. A dog ran out from underneath and started barking. I slowed down and approached.

The light was on inside but there was no sound. The dog came and sniffed at me, wagging its tail. Snotty? No, of course not! I petted it on the head and went up the steps. Still there was no noise. I pushed the door open. No one was in there. The stove was going and I smelled something cooking in the pot. As I stood there, I heard a man coughing behind the cabin and the crunch of boots approaching. Instinctively, I dived for the bunkbed and pushed my way underneath. The door opened, and when I peeked out I could see a bearded man standing by the door. He moved to the stove and all I could see were his boots. I heard him pick up the pot and walk to the table. Soon I heard the scraping of a knife on a plate and then the munching started. I was very hungry and all at once my stomach exploded into a series of high-pitched gurgles.

The man stopped and all was silent for a minute. My stomach set off another gurgle that sounded like a pebble rolling off the roof. Suddenly he got up and went out the door. I listened to the footsteps fade in the distance. He probably guessed it was me! He has gone to tell the witch and my father where I am! They will find me and hurt me, and make sure I never get away again! I lay there under the bed, scratching my face with both hands, scratching, scratching. What am I going to do? Where am I going to go?

Then I heard voices, footsteps coming, then a woman's voice, the witch, planning what she was going to do to me! Here they come, I can hear my father's voice. I'm cornered. No! I must get away! I must get away! I scrambled from under the bed and there it was, a gun. I'll just scare them away. I grabbed it with both hands. Boots crunched on the doorstep. I swung around and pointed the gun as the door swung open. I felt it jump in my hands as a deafening "crack" exploded in the room. I heard the loud clatter as the gun dropped to the floor at my feet, then my father sagged to the ground. I saw a Native woman pull a reddish, fuzzy toque off her head, and long black hair spilled out as she knelt beside my father. She wasn't the witch! Dad? The other man came in slowly and picked up the gun off the floor beside me. I can't move! Dad? Dad, get up! Dad! Mama!

Epilogue

I LIE STRETCHED OUT ON THE MOSS-COV-
ered rock, listening to the crashing waves beside me. I take a
slow deep breath and try to relax as I watch the clouds rolling
by, trailing puffs of white behind them. Suddenly, chipmunks
come scurrying by, racing to the boulders at my feet. I jump
up and swing my arms back and forth as I stride to the large
rock by the shore. I used to dive from this rock when I was a
little boy, straight down to the deep bottom.

Today is July 11th, 1979. It's a special day for me. "Dan!"
Here she comes. She appears on the path between the trees—
Charlotte. Her long black hair blows in the wind, and her eyes
dance as she laughs. I walk slowly toward her. We are to be
married at ten o'clock this morning. She looks lovely in her
new dress. She stops and waits for me. Like a grand lady, she
takes my arm, and then she pinches my side. I chase her back
to the clearing, and she disappears into the open door of our
new cabin. We built our cabin beside Billy's, finishing it just a
few days ago. I never worked alone.

I walk on to Linda's old cabin in the middle of the clearing
and think about all the card games people have played in her
home. We moved in about eight years ago when Linda
married Billy.

There he is. Every morning, snow, rain, or shine, he flings
the door wide open and sits there basking in the morning sun.
I stop in front of him. He refused to move out of there to live
with us. I didn't argue. It's close enough to hear him snore at
night. I will hear him whenever he needs me.

"Are you ready?" I ask. Daniel clasps his hands over his belly and I walk around his wheelchair and push him down the ramp and across the path to the new cabin. Our cabins now form a triangle in the clearing.

"And what are you so dreamy-eyed about this morning?" I ask as I park his wheelchair by the door. His wasted legs lie like sticks below his chest and arms. His greying hair on the sides has spread to the top of his head, but the square jaw is as stubborn as ever.

The bushy eyebrows rise and dark eyes look up at me as he says, "Why, my lady Sarah of course! She said she would come dancing over the grass to deliver me my breakfast this morning." He smiles.

Charlotte giggles from inside where tables stand from wall to wall. I go in and pour myself a cup of coffee.

Soon Jim arrives with Norma, nine-year-old Jason, and seven-year-old Tracy, their arms loaded with food. And there is Sarah. She comes down the path by the lake and slowly makes her way to the door, carrying four dozen eggs. She is thin now, but still in very good health. Her pink cheeks shine as she cracks a big smile at Daniel and threatens to drop the bowl on his head if he tickles her, as he is making out to do.

Charlotte's father passed away five years ago, and her little sister married a young man from Toronto. We haven't seen her since then.

Suddenly Daniel's whistle sounds, sharp and loud from the front door. I know it is for Billy's wife and sure enough, there is Linda, arms loaded with bread. She is one huge lady! She must weigh a good two hundred and fifty pounds. Well, maybe not that much. Billy comes in, one arm on shaky Little Foot. Little Foot lives with Billy and Linda now. They had to add another room, though. They never had any children of their own, but they sure had more than enough kids to take care of. I believe they have about four with them right now.

Amid the bustle of shuffling feet and laughing faces I look at Daniel. I bite my lower lip as I always do when I think of him. Something happened to me that awful night. I have never fully understood what. They reported it as a hunting accident. I couldn't talk. My voice didn't work for the longest time. I keep remembering him, even now, the way he looked when I first saw him again at Ol' Jim's cabin. The tall muscular body . . . and then the doctor's words saying, "Your father will never walk again." Then, always, the memory of my father's words as I followed him down that winter trail. "I am strong. I am healthy. I can take care of us now, you and me," he had said. That is what I have tried to do for him. I will look after him and take care of him for as long as I live.

You can't escape the silent words of your memory. They grow on you, layer after layer, year after year, documenting you from beginning to end, from the core to the surface. I built my cabin with silent words.